Gladys

**"YOU WANT TO BE MY MISTRESS. THERE'S
ARROGANCE FOR YOU! I ONLY HAD ONE
TUMBLE IN MIND. HOW DO I KNOW YOU'D BE
ANY GOOD?" HE TAUNTED AS HE PULLED HER
INTO HIS ARMS.**

"Since I am untouched . . . I'd be only as good as you
made me."

Her words sent a surge of hot lust through his body. He
raised an eyebrow at her. "Untouched? Unused? Unsul-
lied?" He paused, then whispered maddeningly, "Untrue!"

She answered him in kind. "Unwilling! Unyielding!" She
paused, then whispered her challenge: "Untamed!"

"Life is a game," he said softly, caressing her silken skin.
"This is a game between us, Sabre, but if you want to play
you'd better know all the rules. In every game there is risk.
In every game there is a winner and a loser."

"If you think I'm not going to win you are badly mistaken!" She hated him with a passion, her breasts heaving
with her agitation.

"Take off your clothes and let's see how you show," he
dared her.

Also by Virginia Henley:

THE RAVEN AND THE ROSE

THE HAWK
AND
THE DOVE

Virginia Henley

A DELL BOOK

Published by
Dell Publishing
a division of
The Bantam Doubleday Dell
Publishing Group, Inc.
666 Fifth Avenue
New York, New York 10103

ISBN: 0-440-20144-6

Printed in the United States of America
Published simultaneously in Canada

September 1988

10 9 8 7 6 5 4 3 2 1

OPM

Dedicated to two ladies who really know their stuff. My editor, Maggie Lichota—the best in the business, and Kathe Robin, who never abuses her infinite power

THE HAWK
AND
THE DOVE

Chapter 1

Cheltenham, 1586

Spring had not yet arrived. Icicles hung by the river and the horses' breath formed frosty clouds upon the air as the two young riders playfully raced the last hundred yards before reaching the stables.

Inside, the warmth enveloped them and the tang of horse, leather, and hay heightened all their senses in a most disturbing fashion. The young man, so fair, took both hands of the vibrant beauty into his own and drew her toward him. He knew he must taste her or go mad. "Sara." He breathed her name raggedly against her lips, before covering them in the kiss they had both been anticipating for weeks.

Now that they were finally fused, they had no strength to pull apart. Her arms were lovingly entwined about his neck and his hands caressed her back and slowly moved to cup and fondle her breasts. He moaned low in his throat and sank down into the hay, pulling his beautiful tormentor with him.

Sara was tempted, tempted badly. She had never felt like this before. It was as if her bones wanted to melt with the delicious languor that was stealing over her. "Andrew, no, we cannot."

"Please, Sara, please. I'm going to offer for you." And once more he covered her protesting mouth and fumbled with the buttons of her riding dress. He had managed to undo three before she found the strength to tear herself away from him.

It wasn't that she didn't believe him. She knew he was as good as his word and that he would certainly offer for her. But others had offered for her and nothing had ever

come of it. Now she held his hands firmly to keep them in
check. She laughed up at him lovingly. "You haven't
even proposed to me yet!"

"Sara, darling, will you marry me?"

She heard the words echoing in her mind, then the
scene dissolved in a shimmer as she gazed through the
window, unseeing. She forced back unshed, unwanted
tears before anyone ever suspected she was crying. She
would rather die!

Witches! thought Sara Bishop, barely hanging on to
her infamous temper. She set her teeth and faced her four
half sisters in the beautifully appointed family room. The
two older ones from her mother's first marriage were
dark, sleek, almost smug from their secure position in the
family hierarchy. The pair younger than herself, from her
mother's third and present marriage, were pretty and
blond, spoiled and selfish to the core.

They had gathered to organize the details of the upcoming wedding—to make lists of potential guests, to
word the actual invitations, and to choose material for
their gowns. Their gently bred mother, Mary Bishop, had
already retired with a headache; never had she been capable of coping with her daughters en masse.

" 'Tis a conspiracy!" Sara stormed, and her hair, the
color of pale molten copper, flew about her shoulders.
"You know damned well that deep rose pink makes me
look hideous, and 'tis precisely why you always choose
it."

"Sabre Wilde, stop that swearing instantly," hissed
Jane, who at twenty-two was the eldest.

"Don't you dare to call me Sabre Wilde! You lot are

enough to make a saint swear," shouted Sara in exasperation.

"Saint?" They hooted with laughter.

"Saint?" echoed Jane. "Devil's spawn, more likely, Sabre Wilde." She emphasized the name derisively.

"You earned the nickname for yourself," smirked Ann, the youngest. "Jane, is it true that when her father died she trailed his sabre about the house for weeks and even insisted on sleeping with it?"

" 'Tis true, and she was only four years old. She had such a dangerous temper, she ruled the household, terrorized poor Mother, and was so willful she attempted to wound the servants with that sabre."

"I'll go and fetch the bloody thing now if you don't shut up!" Sara threatened.

"If you swear again, I shall report you to father," Jane threatened as she rose from the writing desk now littered with the forgotten lists.

The room seemed stifling to Sara. The spring weather had been unusually sticky and oppressive, and now that her blood was up, her cheeks flushed and she tried to breathe deeply to calm herself. Her beautiful high, round breasts quivered with her great agitation and her older sister Margaret eyed them enviously and said with great malice, "The color of Sabre's hair screams so loudly, she would be a disaster in any shade we chose. We all know 'tis not the color of the bridesmaids' dresses that has angered her, but the fact that sweet little Beth has received an offer of marriage and she has not."

" 'Tis not fair!" cried Sara. "Andrew was supposed to be my husband. After Jane and Margaret were married, I was supposed to be next. I'm almost twenty years old! Beth is only fifteen."

The sisters were greatly amused at this. "You are living in a fantasy, Sabre Wilde. You will never receive an offer of marriage. Your Irish father left you without a dowry and everyone for miles about knows you for an *eccentric,*" Jane pointed out.

Reverend Bishop threw open the door of his study, where he had been trying to compose a biting sermon for next Sunday. The girl was causing trouble again. She had been the only thorn in his side in an otherwise perfect marriage. His tall shadow fell across the doorway just as Sara shouted, "My Irish father, let me point out, was the only one of her husbands my mother married for love! The first she married for money, the last she married for respectability. You are four jealous witches!"

The girls' father issued a one-word command. "Apologize!"

Sara spun about with fear in her eyes. Then, determined to defy him, she drew herself up to her full height and said softly, "I'm sorry. . . . I'm sorry they are jealous witches."

His mouth curved downward cruelly and he issued his orders without hesitation. "Fetch her in here. Put her across the table."

She was livid to be handled so and would have successfully fought off her two older sisters, but their father cruelly clamped a hand to the back of her neck and reached for his cane. They held her down gleefully to receive the beating they had never had to endure. The thin cotton of Sara's gown and petticoat was scant protection against the sting of the cane wielded so heavily by the reverend. She felt the blood rush to her head but she would be damned if she'd give them the satisfaction of seeing her faint.

"Go to your room, mistress," the reverend finally ordered. "She has the devil's mark upon her." The words followed Sara up the stairs and were like a spark to gunpowder as her temper exploded and she swore to be even with them all.

Sara slammed her chamber door and without stopping opened her window, climbed down the huge hawthorn tree, and ran for the stables. She grabbed a bridle, didn't waste time with a saddle but mounted Sabbath and, bending low over her palfrey's neck to protect her sore bottom, rode off toward the beautiful Cotswolds like the wind. She usually took great pleasure in the flowering trees and gamboling spring lambs, but today tears blinded her to the beauties of the countryside.

She rode a direct path through the woods, which were carpeted with bluebells, to the edge of the small secluded lake. Slipping down from its back she tethered her horse where it could reach the sweet green grass and stroked its muzzle lovingly. It had pleased her stepfather when she had called the colt Sabbath. The corners of her mouth went up in a secret smile. How furious he would be if he knew the animal's full name was Black Sabbath.

As she knelt by the edge of the lake and bent down to cup a handful of cooling water to bathe her face, she caught sight of her reflection. "I'm not ugly," she said defiantly, then sighed as she thought of her half sisters' beauty.

In reality she was far more fair of face and figure than they, but years of being disparaged had taken their toll. While her sisters were attractive, by comparison she was exquisite. Her hair was all molten flames and fire, her mouth voluptuously curved, and her green eyes were highlighted by dark brows and long dark lashes. Beside

her left eye, on the very tip of her cheekbone, was a
beauty spot. Tentatively she put her finger on the tiny
black mole her family referred to as the mark of the devil,
then obeying an impulse that was as old as Eve, she undressed quickly and slipped naked into the cool, soothing
water.

She smiled as a pair of ducks paddled madly away to
the safety of the reeds, and as her body and temper
cooled and relaxed, her attention was caught by the iridescent colors of the hovering dragonflies. Mayhap she
was wicked, she mused. Hadn't she forged a letter in her
mother's hand to Lady Katherine Ashford at the queen's
court? Kate was sister to her mother's first husband. She
had made a brilliant marriage with Lord Ashford ten
years ago and now held the lofty title of mistress of the
queen's robes. She moved in heady circles indeed! Sara,
pretending to be her mother, had written reminding Kate
that she was the mother of five lovely daughters and was
begging for a position at court for one of them, no matter
how lowly. She intimated how difficult it was to find suitable husbands for them all and hinted that surely among
Elizabeth's court of sixteen hundred gentlemen a husband might be found for just one of her sweet, pretty-
mannered girls.

It had been over two months since Sara had sent off the
letter and she would have to keep a sharp watch to inter-
cept an answering message from Lady Ashford.

Her imagination soared deliciously as she floated in the
water. She saw herself dressed in a pale green ballgown
fluttering a jeweled fan at a gentleman who would not
quite behave himself. The brilliant room was lit with a
thousand candles as she watched herself go into the
man's arms for the dance.

Suddenly a shot rang out and she cried out in alarm for the poor duck that, having risen up from the lake, had dropped back to the water stone dead. The man heard her and came to the water's edge. It was Margaret's husband, John.

"Sabre! God's bones, you're naked!" He licked his lips and felt himself harden in response to his delicious sister-in-law.

"Bugger off!" she swore.

His retriever swam after the downed waterfowl, but John only had eyes for the nymph before him. He was a handsome young man and he smiled slyly as he realized the compromising situation of his quarry. "There's one way of making sure my lips are sealed, sweetheart."

"Go home to your wife!" she said coldly.

"You should have been my wife, Sabre. I offered for you first."

"Piffle! You soon grabbed Margaret when you found out I was penniless, but she was mistress moneybags."

"Our parents arranged it; I had little choice in the matter. Be kind to me, Sabre, you know you broke my heart."

"I'd like to break your head, you lecher!" she cried.

"I'm coming in." He grinned wickedly and bent to remove his boots.

Though fear gripped her and her heart pounded frantically inside her breast, she would not let him see her fear. "John Thatcher, my lips will not be sealed if you make one more move toward me!"

He hesitated for only a second. "You wouldn't dare let the worthy reverend know you'd been cavorting naked in the woods."

"What could he do to me? Thrash me? I've already had one beating today," she retorted bravely.

He finished disrobing and plunged into the lake. Sabre quickly ducked beneath the surface and swam underwater, not surfacing until she reached the grassy bank some thirty feet away. She flung on her petticoat and dress and was in the saddle almost before he spotted her.

"Sabre, help! My legs are tangled in the weeds," he called, and she could hear the irritation in his voice.

She laughed as she dug her heels into Black Sabbath's haunches. "I hope you never untangle them!"

Sara thought she had gotten away with her escapade when three days had passed and the wrath of God had not descended upon her. She grabbed an opportunity to go into Gloucester so that she could collect the mail for the church and priory. Her mother and Beth, the bride-to-be, were traveling into the city of Gloucester to select bed linen and deliver the wedding invitations to the aunts and uncles and cousins related to them through Mrs. Bishop's three marriages.

The Swan Inn was the posting house where the coaches brought the mail up from London. Sara quickly sorted through the papers that were addressed to the rectory and church and her heart skipped a beat as her fingers closed about the long-awaited reply from Lady Katherine Ashford in London. She stuffed it down the neck of her gown and wriggled it inside her busk, where the long-anticipated message it might hold almost burned her breasts. She then took the rest out to the coach and turned it all over to her mother.

Her heart was singing with such joy that even a dreaded visit with the cousins could not quell her happiness. She closed her ears to the incessant chatter of weddings. Beth was wearing a pale blue silk afternoon dress with a fetching little pelisse in the same shade. Her blue satin slippers also matched and she sat crossing her ankles so that her pale blue silk stockings could be glimpsed by all.

Sara's thoughts were diverted from the letter when one of her cousins said, "That dark wine gown doesn't become your odd coloring, Sabre. It looked much prettier on Margaret before it was handed down to you." Beth and her cousins all giggled.

Sara answered sweetly, "But I fill the bodice out better, don't you think?" Then she pointedly looked at each girl's small breasts.

The name of the game was spite as her cousin asked, "You must be very upset because Beth has had a proposal. Before we know it, Ann, too, will be betrothed, and you will be left a spinster."

God, how she hated them all. Her cheeks flushed and she said loftily, "I'm not in the least upset, for I shall very likely be going to court shortly." She could have bitten her tongue the moment the words were out. She had such a habit of saying the first thing that came into her head, and it usually landed her in hot water.

Beth laughed and said, "Why, Sabre, that's an outright lie."

Her cousin, instantly jealous that there might be a grain of truth in Sabre's remark, said to Beth, "I'm afraid Sabre suffers from delusions of grandeur. There are many locked up in the Gloucester Asylum with such afflictions."

"Is it your habit to visit asylums? Amazing they don't mistake you for an inmate and detain you," replied Sara lightly.

"If you don't watch your tongue, Sabre Wilde, I'll get Daddy to give you another beating," threatened Beth.

"Beating?" asked her cousin breathlessly.

"We held her down across the table while Daddy took his cane to her bottom!"

Somehow Sara's teacup slipped through her fingers and its contents ruined not only Beth's blue silk, but the afternoon visit as well. Everyone watching would have sworn it was an accident, yet they knew better. Beth was in tears, incoherent, then hysterical, and there was nothing Mrs. Bishop could do but gather her two daughters and depart quickly amid a flurry of apologies for the disastrous turn of events.

Mary Bishop leaned her head back onto the velvet squabs of the coach and closed her eyes. Sara felt guilty, for she knew her mother had a delicate constitution. Beth was carrying on ridiculously, so Sara had no alternative but to fix her with a penetrating look. "If you don't shut up instantly, I'll thump you." Beth sat back quietly and sniffled, for without the backing of her cousins or sisters, she was gutless.

When the coach arrived back at Cheltenham priory, Mrs. Bishop ushered Beth into the house to repair the damage to the blue silk and Sara stayed with the coach as it was taken to the stables. She reached into her busk and drew forth the treasured letter.

With eager eyes she scanned the contents, skipping over the flowery salutations and small talk. Ah, here it was. . . . *As mistress of Her Majesty's wardrobe I do indeed have need of many assistants and I would be pleased to take one of your gentle daughters under my wing, should you decide to send her to court. I know that you will appreciate this great opportunity I am offering and*

assure you that a gentlewoman with manners and breed-
ing may receive many offers of marriage which would be
otherwise closed to her. We are at Greenwich until the hot
summer months make London an unhealthy place, at
which time we go on progress, so I urge you to hasten your
daughter's departure and rest assured I shall welcome any
child of yours wholeheartedly. All I ask, dearest Mary, is
that you do not saddle me with the little redhead of the
volatile temper. I need a girl who is both amenable and
biddable, and we both know that the "Wilde" one is nei-
ther.

Sara let the letter fall from her fingers and a single tear
slipped down her cheek; all her fine dreams and schemes
reduced to ashes. It was almost an hour before she gradually became aware of her surroundings. The smell of
leather and horses teased her nostrils and she stirred herself, sighing deeply for what might have been, and walked
slowly to the house. As she passed her stepfather's study,
his cold command reached her ears. "Come in here!"

She pushed open the doors and met his eyes. Suddenly
she knew the reprieve of three days' standing was over.
He knew that she had swum naked. She stood motionless
through the endless sermon, only longing to know her
punishment and to get it over with. She was the scandal
of the neighborhood. Her behavior was wanton, wicked,
eccentric. She was an instrument of the devil. Her Wilde
Irish blood was tainted and she responded neither to
chastisement nor punishment; she neither regretted nor
repented. She heard him list her long catalogue of sins
and waited for his verdict. When it came it was totally
unexpected. It was said quietly without anger, yet it was
more terrible for her than any beating.

"From now on you will be deprived of your privileges,

beginning with your riding. To ensure your obedience, I sold your horse today."

"No," she whispered, stunned. "Who did you sell her to?" Her mind screamed its denial.

"Silence!" he ordered.

Her pale green eyes narrowed. She dipped him an insolent little curtsy and departed with dignity. Cheltenham was a small enough town that she soon discovered where Sabbath had gone. At the moment she was helpless to do anything about losing her, but she resolved to get her horse back come hell or high water when it was possible, and until that time she accepted the fact that she could only visit her occasionally and then only after a two-mile walk in each direction.

The wedding of Beth was imminent. Such loving attention had been given to each detail of the lavish affair that Sara was sick to death of it all and wished the ordeal were over and done with. She dreaded the wedding ceremony itself with her stepfather officiating at the marriage of his own daughter. Jane's husband was to walk Beth down the aisle of the English church, which would be packed with all their relatives from Gloucester and all her father's regular congregation from Cheltenham. The church would echo to the rafters with whispers about why she was not being married. After all, it was her turn, and Beth was almost five years her junior. In Tudor England girls married before the age of sixteen or were considered to be left on the shelf—unsuitable, unmarriageable, unwanted.

Damn, I'd like to give them something to talk about, she thought unhappily. She sat in the orchard, thinking up one scheme after another, rejecting her ideas almost as quickly as she thought of them.

The deep pink bridesmaid gown, which she hated, was finished and hanging in her room. She felt depressed every time she looked at it. Ah, well, in two days' time it would all be over but the shouting, and then she would have the attentions of three brothers-in-law to dodge instead of just two, for the bridegroom had already caught her alone a couple of times and tried to steal kisses from her.

As she walked past the washhouse she saw one of the servants busy over a large washtub. "What are you doing, Mrs. Pringle?"

"Ah, lovey, I'm busy dyeing the choirboys' cassocks. The reverend sets great store by a grand show in the church. These cassocks are to be scarlet, do ye see. With the white lace surplices over the scarlet cassocks it will be like a pageant!"

"Do you need any help, Mrs. Pringle?"

"Well, now, lovey, ye know how sore me old back gets. While I'm taking these cassocks out to the orchard to dry, you can empty the tub with yon bucket. But be careful to let it cool down first so ye don't go scaldin' yerself."

As Sara watched the scarlet dye bubble, her own wicked juices began to stir. Did she dare? Why not? The only color that would make her look worse than deep pink would be scarlet! She wasted no time in smuggling her pink bridesmaid gown down to the washhouse.

The wedding day dawned and none had time to give Sara Bishop a passing thought. She would keep her cloak on until the last possible moment; then she would throw it off as she walked down the aisle and everyone would recognize that Sara's alter ego, Sabre Wilde, had turned up.

Every pew of the church was packed. Her mother was escorted to the front row, while the bridegroom and the Reverend Bishop stood at the altar. Fourteen-year-old Ann was to go first in the procession, scattering rose petals, then the lovely dark-haired Margaret and Jane, so alike, were paired to walk hand in hand. The bride, on her brother-in-law's arm, was to be followed by Sara, who would carry her train.

Beth was far too concerned over her own wedding attire to pay heed to eccentric Sara, who had insisted upon wearing her cloak until the last possible moment. The notes of the virginal rang out and the choirboys' sweet voices rose like the sound of angels. Then the solemn little procession started down the aisle and an expectant hush fell over the congregation.

Suddenly the musician struck a discordant note, the choirboys forgot the words to the hymn, and the assembled congregation gasped in unison. The girl was in bright red! The color screamed aloud its shocking unsuitability for a nuptial ceremony, especially inside a church, a hallowed place of God.

Sara had her revenge, upsetting the smug propriety of her half sister's wedding day, and at the same time reducing the Reverend Bishop's sacrament to the level of farce. The wedding would be talked about for months, and after the first shock waves wore off, people could not hide their laughter. That Sabre was a red-headed virago who had a penchant for scandalous behavior and they would never tame her!

Chapter 2

The magnificent dragon symbol on the sail was sighted from Devonport long before the ship was brought expertly into harbor. A cry went up from the seawall and was carried to every person abroad in the port town this fine May morning. "The Sea God! The Sea God!" The children took up the cry until the cobbled streets rang with it. Shopkeepers left their stores and along with their customers came out to witness the spectacle that always accompanied the arrival of their beloved native son, for the Sea God did not refer to the name of one of his ships, but to the man himself.

The Hawkhurst family, with its vast shipping empire, had ruled the sea town of Devonport near Plymouth for over a century, but it had taken the good sense of the present queen to reward that family with its first title of nobility. Early in Elizabeth's reign Sebastian Hawkhurst had been named Lord Devonport and appointed her lieutenant for the County of Devon. Now his seafaring days were past, but his sons carried on the glorious name of Hawkhurst, rivaling Howard, Raleigh, and even Drake in the eyes of the townfolk of Devonport.

His elder son, Captain Hawkhurst, had been at sea for almost six months and did not know yet that his father was ailing. A crowd had gathered on the seawall and jetty, all jostling for a position that would afford them a look at the magnificent, near-legendary figure. The women almost swooned in anticipation of a glimpse of the handsome, powerfully built man the queen called her Sea God. They were agog over the prize he had in tow. It was obviously a Portuguese or Spanish galleon and they speculated about its cargo of gold or silver, or jewels at the very least. They would have called a liar any man who referred to Hawkhurst as a freebooter or pirate. To them he was a merchant seaman, a privateer, and a defender of England's sea lanes. No wonder Britannia ruled the waves when the queen had the sworn loyalty and strength of men such as the Sea God.

He stood on the forecastle bridge, his deep masculine voice booming forth his orders to his seamen. The steering sails were pulled in by sailors high in the rigging, then the ship lowered anchor, once more safe in harbor. A cheer went up from the crowd and The Sea God's teeth flashed white in his bronzed face as he waved his acknowledgment. He was well over six feet tall, with surely the broadest shoulders in England. He was deeply tanned and his hair, which was naturally black, had highlights where the strong sun had streaked its tips. He wore it long and it reminded one of a lion's mane.

The crowd waited patiently until he came ashore, knowing the show he would provide would be well worth the wait. Seamen carried his trunks and chests up to the big house on the cliff. Then came his matched pair of Irish wolfhounds, which traveled everywhere with him, and his beloved black stallion, Neptune. Sooner or later his personal manservant would emerge from belowdecks —the monklike "baron," who wore a long dark robe and never uttered a word. Lastly would come the small doll-like woman with the slanted almond eyes, dressed in richly embroidered silk pantaloons and slitted tunic. The tales of her strange origins and the Sea God's possession of her would run the gamut from concubine to slave.

At last Hawkhurst stepped ashore to wend his way to the mansion. When men shouted his name, he answered them by their names. He blew kisses to the women who were waving at him wildly and tossed handfuls of coins to the boys who ran after him, imitating his bold gait as he regained his "land legs."

The women sighed after him, but excitement lingered within each bosom, for arrived home with the Sea God were a hundred of his sailors—husbands, lovers, unattached bachelors all starving for the company of a generous woman to warm their beds this night and the nights yet to come. Hawkhurst men were special—all seasoned veterans, utterly without fear, for their commander was a genius at seamanship and a master of deceit. He concentrated on richly laden Spanish treasure ships and stalked them with an unholy fervor. Hawkhurst men received a share of the prizes they took and always had well-lined pockets.

Every servant Devonport House possessed managed to be on hand for Hawkhurst's arrival and assure him of their warmest welcome home. His beautiful mother, Georgiana, had been watching for him from the highest window in the house and rushed down the spiral staircase to be engulfed in his great arms. She was a dark-haired beauty, her eyes the deep, deep blue of a summer's sky. Always very feminine, she was elegantly fashionable in the extreme.

"My darling Shane," she said, "I'm so glad to have you home." She was the only one who called him Shane. He signed his documents only S. Hawkhurst, and since his father's name was Sebastian, most people assumed that they shared their Christian name. Mother and son had such a deep bond, he was instantly aware that she was upset.

"What's amiss?" he asked, keeping a steady, protective arm about her.

"Your father's been gravely ill, Shane." She hastened to reassure him. "He is improved . . . a little . . . but" —she hesitated in order to steady her voice—"he has a paralysis all down one side of his body."

"Will he recover? What does the physician say?" he demanded.

"He holds out little hope. I even sent to London for a physician, but he attributed your father's affliction to a stroke, and said another one such as that will kill him."

"I'll go to him," he said quickly. He was halfway up the stairs when she called softly, "He's not to be excited, but already he's at fever pitch knowing you are returned. You are not to argue with him, and no strong spirits!"

"Hawk, my boy! God's bones, I hate for you to see me so diminished."

Shane Hawkhurst was shocked at his father's appearance. He had always been so strong, only showing softness where Georgiana was concerned. The voice was badly slurred from a mouth drawn down at one side. Only his father's eyes were as bright as they had always been.

"So, you plucked another prize from the Spanish fleet. Ha!"

He sensed that his father did not wish to speak of himself and his illness. He would give him time to grapple with the words and the decisions that would have to be shared between them for the Hawkhurst dynasty to be passed smoothly from the elder to the younger while there was still time.

"What cargo?" asked Sebastian.

Shane grinned. "Silver the Spanish were sending home from Peru and Mexico."

"God's cock!" The old man was astounded. "Elizabeth will knight you for this."

Shane's eyebrow slanted quizzically. "I might let her have a quarter of it . . . *might,*" he emphasized. "Bess is too damned greedy; too tightfisted with her honors. I still don't have official letters of marque to sail for England, but, by God, I'll wring them from her this time, even if I have to bed her!"

The treason joked about in this room would go no farther, but still Sebastian warned him. "Have a care. Her network of spies may have already informed her you have taken a prize."

Young Hawkhurst grinned. He never ignored danger, he simply enjoyed it. "Aye, I have no doubt of it, but I have enough cargo in the caves beneath the cliffs and stored elsewhere to fill the prize with Spanish leather, wine, and artifacts. I may even be generous enough to donate the galleon to our fleet instead of keeping it for myself."

The older man had tired visibly and a deep frown of concern appeared on his brow as he worried how deeply this son of his was involved in dangerous plots of which he knew nothing. He didn't want to know—the shock would likely have killed him long ago, he thought ironically.

Hawk saw his father's agitation. "I'll let you get some rest," he said, rising to leave.

His father raised his hand to stay him a moment. "Tomorrow we will talk at length of more serious matters; tomorrow before young Matthew returns from London."

Now a worried frown marred Hawk's handsome features.

"Ask your mother if she can tear herself from your company to spare an old man a few of her precious smiles." His grin was a grimace. "I worship the woman, what can I do?"

The east wing of Devonport House was Shane's private domain. It had its own outside entrances back and front so that his men and servants need never enter the main house. He repaired there now where a bath awaited him and two fresh sets of garments were laid out. The first were riding clothes, so that he could exercise Neptune over the familiar countryside that they both loved; the second were more formal clothes suited to a drawing room, for this first night at home he would join his mother for dinner.

The baron as usual had seen to all his needs efficiently, smoothly, and silently. Neptune was restive, as if he sensed he would soon be stretching heavily muscled legs across the soft turf of the Devon fields. Hawk patted his neck and soothed him with his deep voice as he saddled him and led him from the stables. "Tomorrow I'll put you to one of the mares," he promised.

His own spirit soared as he let the stallion have his head. Truth to tell, they'd both been confined too long and needed to unleash their pent-up energy and vitality on an unsuspecting countryside. Horse and man seemed to follow a predestined path that took them over seven miles of meadows and rose-dotted hedgerows, finally arriving at a quaint stone inn where they had enjoyed pleasant sojourns for years past.

The pretty barmaid squealed her delight when she saw

him, and the corners of her mouth went up in a smile
that she couldn't have concealed if she'd wanted to.
"Welcome home, m'lord." She curtsied deeply, then hurried to draw him a tankard of strong Devon cider. His
bronzed arm slipped about her in a familiar hug though
her name eluded his usually perfect recollection. Her
Devon burr delighted him. She was a buxom country
wench who had never been pampered a day in her life,
yet she possessed all the feminine instincts of a London
courtesan. She leaned low across the table to display her
luscious titties and rubbed the velvet sleeve of his riding
coat with roughened fingers. "Ye ben't in 'urry to take
yer leave, m'lord?" she asked breathlessly.

He laughed and shook his head and watched her dim-
ple with delight. He was easily the handsomest man she'd
ever laid eyes on and she could never believe her own
good fortune that occasionally he rode over to sport with
her. She caught her breath now as her imagination had
flown ahead of her to when they would be upstairs in the
feather bed and she would experience the deep pleasure
of seeing his magnificent body stretched out in all its
naked perfection. Already she had a deep ache in her
belly. She reached for his empty tankard and said saucily,
"I'll jus' fill ye up again, an' then ye can return the favor
upstairs."

He laughed aloud as her name popped into his mind.
"It will be my pleasure, Polly."

Her eyes were big and serious for a moment as she said
fervently, "Nobody fills me like ye do, m'lord."

He chased her up the stairs, tickling her ankles and
letting his hands go up her skirts as she ran before him.
He knew he was in for an hour's good fun as they would
laugh and tumble about the feather bed. Ah, there was

nothing to match the uncomplicated enthusiasm of a
sweet country wench.

The dining salon at Devonport House never ceased to
amaze him. The ceiling was hung with a gilt-filigreed
chandelier holding a hundred candles. The rosewood table and chairs had delicately curved legs and tapestry
cushions done in apricot and pale lemon. The sideboards
were filled with Venetian crystal and heavy silver; the
walls with tasteful paintings. Georgiana's fine hand was
evident in every detail, and it was as elegant as the London house, even though it was in one of the wildest parts
of the country.

Shane complimented his mother upon the superb
dishes she had had set before him this night.

"I brought the chef back with us from Hawkhurst
Manor. We'd spent the winter there because it was a comfortable forty miles from London." She closed her eyes
momentarily to still her quickened pulses that
Hawkhurst Manor evoked still, after all the years. Shane
saw the emotion wash over her and knew of whom she
thought, but kept silent. She was in control again and
finished her tale. "Your father went twice to the royal
court, then had many business meetings at Hawkhurst. I
don't know what happened in the last weeks there, but
we came home abruptly and no sooner did we arrive than
he was stricken down. My heart aches to see his great
physical deterioration."

"I admit I was shocked by his appearance, and his
strength is all but gone," he said gravely. "Yet his mind is
still keen."

"Thank God for that, at least," she said fervently.

"I have much business in London. If I sail up there at

the end of the week, will you be able to manage him on your own, do you think?"

"Shane, my darling, I always have managed him one way or another." She smiled sadly. "I haven't always been the perfect wife, but I am very, very fond of him, you know." She added wistfully, "Almost twenty-nine years . . . and I'm so afraid we won't make it to thirty."

He got up and poured each of them a brandy. He warmed the bowl of the snifter by cradling it in his palms, then sipped it slowly, savoring the magnificent French brandy pilfered from some ship long ago.

"I'll take some of this to Bess when I go up to court next week. She doesn't drink much herself, but she takes pride in serving the best."

"The queen is ungrateful, I don't know why you bother." She tossed her head.

He nodded. "Shrewd and ungrateful, that's Bess."

"Mayhap that's how all women should be. Mayhap that's the way to have men at your feet."

He smiled. There was never any love lost between Elizabeth and beautiful women. They could never comprehend the allure of an aging, vain woman, and really it was so simple—the greatest aphrodisiac in the world was power.

"Would you like me to stay with him tonight?" he offered, worried about the anxiety he saw written plain in her beautiful face.

"Nay, I'll stay with him until he sleeps, then retire to my own chamber. I've left the door open between our two chambers all our married life. He knows if he needs me I'm there." She smiled at him.

"Well, I hope you know if you need me . . . I'm there too," he offered simply.

* * *

The master bedchamber in the east wing glowed with
sandalwood-scented candles and the fragrant fumes of
incense curled from a jade burner, as Shane Hawkhurst
entered. Immediately, Lak Sung Li came forward to relieve him of his doublet and shirt. The first time he had
heard her name it had sounded similar to "Larksong,"
and so he called her because the name pleased his senses.

She bowed low, her straight black hair flowing forward
like a silken waterfall. "Does my master wish to smoke?"
she asked softly, indicating the hookah water pipe in the
corner of the room.

He shook his head, declining, and said, "Why must
you call me master, Larksong?"

"It is fitting," she insisted in her low musical voice. "I
will get the oil for your massage," she said, and when he
did not decline she bent low to a lacquered red-and-black
cabinet and took from it a flask of perfumed oil and a
thick towel. She removed the cushions from the long
wooden window seat and spread out the towel, a ritual
that had been observed many times before.

He stripped off the remainder of his clothes and
stretched out naked upon the wooden bench. Larksong
knelt beside him, poured the perfumed oil into her small
cupped palm, and began the slow, smooth, rhythmic
massaging she had learned while she was still a child. He
felt the tension begin to leave his taut muscles and as he
gave himself up to the sensual pleasure of her ministrations his mind went over all the people he must meet with
in London. Some of these meetings concerned business.
His solicitor was tracing who owned the land in Ireland
he wanted to purchase. Some of these meetings combined
business and pleasure—the queen along with certain

members of the court. Other meetings would be covert and he hoped he would have enough time to make all the necessary contacts before he had to return here, where he was soon going to be needed.

The pressure of Larksong's small hands urged him to turn over onto his back so that she could attend to the muscles of his wide chest, his belly, and play her magic fingers about the area of his groin. She offered such a varied menu of erotic delights, yet her attitude was always one of meakness and passivity. In sensual matters she was expert, yet he was growing a little disappointed that he could get no great emotional response from her. She was meek, submissive, and polite, everything a woman should be, and yet . . . and yet . . . Gently he pushed her fingers away and stood up. He held out his hand to her and said simply, "Come, Larksong."

Sebastian Hawkhurst looked pitifully frail, yet Hawk sensed that he was gathering all his strength to approach his son on a matter of grave importance.

When he told Hawk what he wanted of him, the younger man was both annoyed and amused, and refused to take his father's request seriously. "Marry? I have no intention of doing any such thing." He laughed heartily.

"Hawk, you are twenty-eight. You should have been settled years ago." He was losing patience now and said angrily, "Marriage would be a steadying influence. God knows you need one! Before you come into the title, I want you to marry."

"I'll not do it," said Hawk lightly. "You can't force me to it." He grinned to soften his words.

"I can and I will if I have to," shouted Sebastian Hawkhurst.

Hawk raised a black eyebrow, questioning his father's meaning.

"On my death the title of Lord Devonport goes to my heir . . . my legitimate heir . . ." He left the significant words hanging in the air and Hawk was momentarily shocked into silence.

"How long have you known?" he asked quietly.

"Known what? That your real father is that Irish spawn of the devil, the O'Neill?"

Hawk was afraid that his father would become so worked up he would take another stroke, but suddenly the old man visibly relaxed. He smiled and his face softened with the deep love he felt for this son. "I've known for almost twenty years." He shook his head, remembering all those years back. "We'd enrolled ye at that fine gentleman's school near London and the summer ye were about nine or ten I was missing ye terrible. I'd sailed up to London on business and went down to the school to visit and that's when I discovered ye never spent the summers there, only the winters. I was baffled, astounded . . . I put men on the case to learn yer whereabouts and they traced ye to Ireland . . . to the O'Neill."

Shane put out his hand and gripped his father's shoulder hard. "I would have spared you such knowledge."

Sebastian shook his head. "The hard part for me wasn't that Georgiana had been unfaithful to me, for she was a rare beauty and what woman could resist such a wild Irishman as the O'Neill? Nay, the hard part for me was knowing such a fine son was not sprung from my loins. She sent ye off to him every summer and I let it continue, for hadn't he the right to a share of ye as ye grew to manhood, and hadn't ye the right to know and consort with your own father, your own flesh and blood?"

Shane was deeply touched by such an attitude. "You were ever the most generous man on the face of the earth. You forgave my mother and you loved me." It was a statement of fact.

"That wasn't generosity. That was selfishness! I wasn't about to cut my nose off to spite my face. Where else could I have found a woman to equal your mother in beauty or passion? Where else find a strong son who made me burst with pride?" He chuckled softly. "And I've always cherished the hope that perhaps, just perhaps, there was the slightest possibility that you could have been my seed."

Shane felt humbled. How could he refuse this man his dying wish? How could he not be generous in the face of such overwhelming generosity?

"So ye see, 'tis all a sham that I'd deny ye my title, but, Hawk, ye'd make me rest happy if ye'd give me your word that ye'll wed soon."

"I'll give you my word, if we can find a woman who'll have me, but what makes you think marriage will keep me out of trouble?" he joked.

Sebastian Hawkhurst grimaced. "That whoreson O'Neill—I know you supply him with money . . . arms . . . and worse, information! I've a terrible fear he'll get ye hanged, all in the bloody name of freeing Ireland!" He labored for breath. "When I was in London I thought Walsingham had a file on you and I had a hell of a job confirming it. To the best of my knowledge he hasn't . . . yet. But I suspect he has a thick file on O'Neill."

Hawk hastened to reassure his father. "They have spies all over the world—the Netherlands, Italy, France, Spain

—who can tell them when the king farts, but Ireland is another matter entirely. They grope about in a heavy fog and their spies can tell them nothing."

Sebastian's face jerked with a spasm, and alarmed, Hawk said, "Leave it, Father, leave it."

Sebastian shook his head and had his say. "A wife would wean ye from him."

"And what if I married an Irish girl?" he jested, winking. Actually he did not feel lighthearted in the least. His conscience was like a lead weight in his chest. How much part had worry for him played in Sebastian's grave illness? He had always congratulated himself on his ability to conceal his dealings with Ireland, yet if his father knew of these things, who else might know? He could see no advantage in sharing their conversation with his mother, for at the moment her own conscience was probably plaguing hell out of her, but it was vital that he tell the baron everything that had been said today. There was many a time that his safety and even his life rested in the hands of the baron and there were no secrets between them, ever.

The promised marriage did not weigh him down overmuch. Marriage was a technicality that could be gotten around somehow. He temporarily dismissed it with the contempt he thought it deserved. "Young Matt should be here tomorrow to cheer you up," he said, but he saw that his father had exhausted himself and fallen into a heavy sleep. He looked down upon him and thanked God that he did not know that he had already secretly met with O'Neill in a hidden bay tucked beneath the Mountains of Mourne and given him half the silver that the Spanish prize had carried.

* * *

While Shane was with his father Georgiana's conscience was indeed plaguing hell out of her. She thought she had exorcised all her guilt years ago, but now it was as painful as a fresh wound in her breast. What made it worse was that it had all begun while she was on her honeymoon. Sebastian had taken her with him to London, where he was to receive the title of Lord Devonport from the queen. They stayed at Hawkhurst Manor, which had been in his family for near a hundred years. On the days her new husband was busy in London or at the seaports along the Straits of Dover from Hastings to Hythe, she had ridden every day into the Weald and Ashdown Forest. She rode wildly, as she had when she was a child in Ireland before her parents moved to Devon. On that fateful day she had collided with a man who rode faster than she had dreamed possible. At first glance she had been terrified of the giant with the wild red hair and rugged features. He cursed her vilely in Gaelic and she blushed to the roots of her hair.

"You are Irish!" she said.

"Not just Irish," he shouted arrogantly, "I am a prince of Ireland!"

"You may be a prince, but you are no gentleman!" she cried angrily.

"If you understood me, you are no lady!" he threw back at her.

They both dismounted, blood up, ready to do battle, and then it happened. He raped her. Nay, thought Georgiana, not rape, for she had wanted him with the same all-consuming passion he felt for her. The truth was they had ravished each other, there on the ground where they had met barely moments before.

* * *

Hugh O'Neill had a bloody history behind him. His father should have been the O'Neill but he was murdered by his own brother Sean, who would share power with no man. Sean then went off to England to charm the queen and claim the vast O'Neill holdings in Ulster. He swore loyalty to her and agreed to make war on all her enemies. He took his murdered brother's two younger sons with him and at the queen's suggestion placed them in noble English households. Elizabeth believed if she got the princes of Ireland young enough, they would become civilized, once weaned from Catholicism to Protestantism. Hugh O'Neill was placed with the aristocratic Sidneys and Sean returned triumphantly to Ireland. It soon became evident that he was thumbing his nose at the young queen. The taxes were not sent to England, but diverted to Sean O'Neill's coffers. Eventually she had had enough and sent an army to Ireland and defeated Sean O'Neill. He took refuge with the MacDonnells, who promptly murdered him. This left Hugh O'Neill, Baron Dungannon, the heir to Ulster, and when he had been in the Sidney household until he was fourteen, the queen decided to return the civilized young man to Ireland to teach the wisdom of English rule to his subjects. He had been converted to Protestantism and was loyal to the crown. He returned and proclaimed his fealty to the crown. However, so civilized was he that the day he returned he murdered his cousin, the late Sean O'Neill's remaining son, and then bought time by professing himself the peacemaker. The queen was so pleased with him that she promised if he could keep the peace and keep the unruly clans from rebelling, she would make him the earl of Tyrone and give him all the O'Neill lands and fortunes in Ulster.

It was when the queen recalled him to England to receive his honors that Georgiana had first met him. The O'Neill had been gifted with more charm than was good for a mere mortal. He would do anything to gain a heart and hold it. Irish princes were famous for carting off other men's wives, but though the lure of him was magnetic, Georgiana resisted throwing away everything and going to him. Instead she gave him their son. The O'Neill had a great and ruthless mind. There was no crime, sacrifice, or sin that he would not commit to gain his own ends. He kissed the queen's fingers while cursing her under his breath. He paid lip service to the crown while robbing it blind. For years he had worked at uniting the clans so that they would be under his control for the day when he would order them to rebel en masse and free Ireland from its English yoke of domination. Now he had his rich bastard son to help him.

Chapter 3

The only thing that saved Sabre Wilde's bacon that fine summer was the arrival of a stranger. Since the wedding, which she had so effectively ruined, she had been confined to her chamber with not one member of the family wishing to speak with her. Her only communication was with Mrs. Smite, an iron-faced servant loyal to Reverend Bishop. She had been examined by a doctor, who shook his head portentously and declared that in his humble opinion the girl was willful, wild-blooded, and even eccentric, but he could not go as far as to declare her insane. He prescribed a diet of bread and water to thin and cool her hot blood and recommended that they leave her to her own company for a month to sweeten her temper and make of her a more amenable young lady.

Sabre, for so she now thought of herself rather than as Sara, welcomed her solitude at first. She was rid of her family's hated company, she was spared attending church thrice a week with the reverend's repetitive sermons predicting hellfire and brimstone, and she was free to spend hours daydreaming about *someday.*

Someday she would own a dress that had been chosen especially for her. It would be pale green or deep cream or perhaps a daring peacock-blue. Her imagination conjured up a myriad of shades from which she was free to choose.

Someday a man, other than a brother-in-law, would try to steal a kiss from her. Her imagination was vivid and the men she pictured were as varied as the dresses she dreamed of owning. She sighed.

Someday she would leave this dreaded place. Once she

had gone she vowed she would never return. Her dream destination was, of course, the royal court. Her favorite fantasy consisted of telling her stepfather and stepsisters that she was going to court and watching their faces turn pea-green with envy.

Her reverie lasted a week, by which time she felt frustrated enough to scream. Without freedom she realized life was intolerable. She had always been so active but now that she was deprived of riding, even of walking, she felt restless and imprisoned and, yes, hungry! She was trapped, and until the key to unlock her misery should be found she was helpless.

When the stranger arrived she saw him from her window; the same window the good reverend had nailed shut with his own spotless white hands. The stranger's horse, his clothes, and his bearing bespoke a man of affluence; a man with business to conduct. She was filled with curiosity and highly annoyed to think she might never discover who he was or the reasons for his coming here.

She watched and waited for his departure, but after two hours he was still within the house. She began to speculate about him, but never in a million years could she have guessed the reason for his visit.

Downstairs in the reverend's study Jacob Goldman painstakingly explained matters one more time. "Mr. Bishop, I appreciate the fact that you are the young lady's stepfather, but in this matter it is impossible for you to act on her behalf. I am a solicitor, sir, and I do know the law. It has taken me months to trace the person who has legal title to these particular lands in Ireland. My principal has authorized me as his agent to acquire these lands from whoever owns clear title to them. Since that title passed from one Rory Wilde, upon his death, to his sole survivor, one Sara Wilde Bishop, I will need Sara Bishop's consent, Sara Bishop's signature, and Sara Bishop's receipt for the monies paid to her." Jacob Goldman gave two quick nods with his head to indicate there should be an end to the argument. Behind hooded lids his shrewd eyes had weighed up and assessed the small-town cleric with the authoritarian's need for control and obedience.

"Very well, Mr. Goldman, I shall allow you to speak with my daughter. But I shall remain, and hope you entertain no objections to her being guided by me in these transactions. Women, you must agree, have no comprehension of business or legal matters. These Irish lands were considered worthless tracts of barren soil piled with rocks and stones. If I had known they had any value I should have had them transferred into my keeping years ago when I married her mother and became Sara's stepfather."

"Mr. Bishop, you are probably right in thinking them barren tracts," Goldman said. "Their only value lies in the access they afford to other more valuable holdings."

The Reverend Bishop stepped from his study and dispatched a servant to summon Sara. His wife overheard the order and approached him with a question in her eyes. He dismissed her with a pat of the shoulder. "Business, my dear, don't worry your little head over it. Run upstairs now and make sure that Sara's appearance is respectable before she presents herself."

Sabre hesitated at the study door. The room held only hurtful associations for her. She could not help thinking the next blow would not be long in arriving.

"Come, come, girl, our time is precious," said her stepfather impatiently. It galled him to have her consulted on any matter, let alone one connected to Rory Wilde, his dead rival for his wife's affections. "Mr. Goldman, this is my daughter Sara."

She curtsied to the short, dark man. "Good day, sir."

Goldman was startled, though he didn't show it outwardly. The girl was breathtaking. The ill-fitting, nondescript gown did little to conceal her glory. Her beautiful face was crowned by a coronet of red-gold braids. Her mouth was set in stubborn lines at the moment, but if it smiled she would be glorious. Her pale green eyes, set off by dark brows, long, dark lashes, and the black beauty mark, were startling, almost mesmerizing, when she leveled them at him.

"Miss Bishop, I am here on business concerning land in Ireland your late father bequeathed you."

Her brows rose in astonishment. The man was here because he had business with *her*!

Reverend Bishop said, "This will be difficult for you to understand, Sara. Mr. Goldman needs you to sign your name to a paper. It's really as simple as that."

She leveled her gaze upon her stepfather, thrust up her chin dangerously, and said, "Please don't address me as if I were a four-year-old." She turned to the other man, but her attitude did not soften. "Mr. Goldman, I assume you are a solicitor and you need my signature on a legal document concerning my land in Ireland. Why?" she asked baldly.

Jacob Goldman concealed a smile. She possessed intelligence as well as beauty. She also had spirit. So much spirit this narrow-minded, small-town, Bible-thumping authoritarian hadn't been able to quell. "Miss Bishop, I am acting agent for a gentleman who wishes to purchase your land."

"It is not for sale, Mr. Goldman. You see, it is the only thing I have left of my father besides his sabre. The Irish land is the only dowry I possess."

Reverend Bishop could not prevent his mouth from hardening into a thin line. "The land is worthless, you stupid girl, so filled with stones and rocks that crops cannot be grown on it."

"If it is worthless, why is this gentleman so avid to purchase it?" Her delicate brows arched their question.

"Mr. Goldman, you can see she is impossible to deal with. I apologize for such impertinence. I am ashamed that a young woman under my roof would offer you such insult!"

"Not at all, Mr. Bishop," Goldman said smoothly. God's feet, if the man didn't shut up he was going to jeopardize the deal he had come to finalize. "Miss Bishop, please feel free to ask any questions at all. The gentleman I act for needs your land for easier access to his own lands. May I ask if you have ever seen your Irish holdings?"

"No, sir, with deep regret I have not, but I hope to remedy that situation one day."

"Your land is in Ulster. It lies between the Mountains of Mourne and the foothills of Slieve Croob. There is a long, narrow waterway that leads almost to Newry. My client owns all the land around Newry, almost up to Armagh, but your few acres separate his land from the waterway that provides access to the sea. I am authorized to offer you two hundred pounds to purchase your acres outright," finished Mr. Goldman.

"I'm sorry, sir, the land is my only dowry," she declined politely.

"Are you mad, girl, or merely possessed of the devil?"

thundered Bishop. "Dowry indeed! Who in their right mind would take you as wife? If you had any sense of duty you would take the money and give it to your mother and me for your keep. The likelihood of your ever receiving an offer of marriage is slim, and we shall be obliged to pay for the privilege of your company for years to come!"

The animosity in the room was almost tangible. Mr. Goldman despaired. He sighed inwardly and suggested on a soothing note, "I am actually authorized to go as high as five hundred pounds, Miss Bishop. The five hundred pounds could be set up legally as your dowry, which in my humble opinion would be more attractive to a suitor than a few acres in a godforsaken country, begging your pardon for the blasphemy, Reverend Bishop."

Sabre almost jumped at it. Surely five hundred pounds would bring her a husband. She looked at her stepfather and read his expression clearly. If she did not agree to this sale he would be enraged. Why did he want it so badly? she asked herself. To be rid of her? If that were so, why hadn't he accepted the offers he'd had for her? At least two of her sisters' husbands had offered for her first. No, he wanted her to accept the money so he could fill his own coffers. He certainly couldn't spend land.

"Your offer is most generous, Mr. Goldman. Please understand, it is not the money that makes me refuse you. My father gave the land into my keeping and there it shall remain." She flashed her stepfather a triumphant glance. "Good afternoon, gentlemen."

"You see?" demanded Bishop after she had left. "As a man of the law surely there is some way you can legalize my signing the papers for her."

Jacob Goldman closed his leather portfolio and

thought scornfully of the churchman's ethics. "I shall report to my principal, sir. If he still wishes to obtain the land, I shall again contact you. Good afternoon." He bowed his way out into the fresh air, glad that he had refused all offer of refreshment. A country inn would be a more congenial atmosphere for dining.

Sabre returned to her room, this time taking care to lock the door from the inside. Reverend Bishop would either be incensed enough to commit violence upon her person, or would use more subtle means to bend her to his will, and until she knew which tack he would take, she decided to lock her door for protection.

Shane Hawkhurst had spent ten summers with the O'Neill from the ages of eight to eighteen and as a result of his strong influence Shane's loyalties were divided. He had tried to serve and please two fathers all his life, no easy task, for they were both strong-willed, demanding men in their own right. Shane had a network of couriers who went back and forth between England and Ireland. One of his ships used solely for this purpose was not even registered to the Hawkhursts. It was registered in the name of its captain, Liam O'Malley, who had been chosen for the job because of his name. If he was ever caught it would be assumed he was connected with the pirate queen, Grace O'Malley. The name of the ship was the *Liverpool Lady,* sailing between the port of Liverpool and Carlingford Lough to Newry. The halfway point between London and Liverpool was Birmingham and the couriers who went back and forth were referred to by these cities' names rather than their own.

The O'Neill ruthlessly traded on his son's loyalty, taking all by way of arms, monies, and information and giv-

ing nothing in return. O'Neill was building an army with
modern weapons right under England's nose.

Shane did what he could to free Irish prisoners either
by paying their fines or ransoms, or by bribing their jailers so they could escape. The baron often acted as go-
between, especially where matters of the greatest secrecy
were involved. He was almost invisible when alone, ap-
pearing to be merely another monk wandering England's
countryside. Sometimes the country roads seemed glutted
with these holy men since the late King Henry VIII had
closed the great monasteries.

The baron took a message from Hawkhurst to Francis
Drake in Plymouth. It was short and to the point:

"Rumors true. Armada being built."

The baron returned with an equally brief answer:

"At court—next week."

Matthew Hawkhurst's ship arrived in port on schedule. He had just returned from Holland, where he had
taken supplies to the English forces fighting there, helping the Dutch in their war against Spain.

Hawk was on the quay by the time Matthew dropped
anchor, and the two brothers embraced heartily.

"Hawk, you old sea dog, glad to see you safely returned." He was a younger, slimmer version of Shane,
much less serious, with an open, laughing countenance.
He was a sweet-tempered youth who set maidens sighing
and brought out the maternal instinct in older women.

"Matt, you young devil! Did you encounter any trouble with your deliveries?"

Matt grinned. "Nay, I've had five runs while you were away and I did what you suggested each time."

"Good lad!" approved his brother. Elizabeth was a miser when it came to supplying her English armies in Holland. The commanders were paying their men out of their own pockets, because the crown would not foot all the bills. Hawk told Matthew to take half the armor, muskets, and ammunition from each cargo and store them in their own warehouses. The space on the ships was then filled with food, uniforms, blankets, and much-needed horses. The horses came from Ireland and Hawk exchanged the stolen weapons for horses through the O'Neill.

"How's Father?" Matt asked anxiously.

Hawk shook his head unhappily. "Worse each day, but he'll be better for your company, I'll wager."

Matthew nodded his head toward the Spanish prize. "Are we keeping that in our fleet?"

Hawk ran his fingers through his mane of hair. "She's a bit toplofty. I'm having the men take off four brass cannons to mount on our ships, then I think England can have her. Tomorrow you can help me select some cargo to take up to London."

Matthew grinned, knowing his brother's tactics. "What did you smuggle?"

Hawk rubbed his nose. "Enough! God's cock, why don't ye shout it from the topdeck? You're getting too big for your breeches!"

"That's what the ladies tell me," Matt said with a suggestive leer. Hawk threw his arm about his younger brother and they went up to the big house.

After supper, when Hawk visited his father, he found him and Matt laughing together. He held his tongue when he saw that Matt had somehow concealed a bottle of brandy from his mother's sharp eyes and joined them in a toast to Sebastian's return to health, although both knew this was unlikely. Their father then proposed a toast.

"We'll drink to the upcoming nuptials."

Matt was so amused, he sprayed a mouthful of brandy across the room as he guffawed at the jest. Hawk scowled darkly, which told Matt there was perhaps a grain of truth in what their father had said. "Who's the bride?" he asked, trying to keep his face straight.

Sebastian said, "Matthew, I'm serious. Your brother has given me his word that he will marry before he comes into the title."

"Poor bitch!" said Hawk mockingly, and the two brothers bent double at the dark humor of it all.

In the morning they gravely doubted the wisdom of their revelry, for Sebastian had slipped into a comalike state from which he could hardly be roused. After a quick consultation with Matt and Georgiana, Hawk decided to leave for London immediately so that he could return before anything worse happened. It was plain that death was inevitable; only the timing remained unknown.

The Hawkhursts loaded jars of powdery red cochineal and chests of indigo balls with which to dye good English cloth. They set jars of olives and bottles of olive oil carefully in the hold. Hawk chose some fine Oriental porcelain and bolts of silk that had probably come all the way from the Philippines and been hauled across Mexico before he had taken it as contraband off the Azores.

Georgiana spoke privately with him before the flood tide once more took him away from her. "I know Sebastian has extracted a promise of marriage from you, but if

you wait until you are Lord Devonport you will probably
do better in the marriage market. There will be dozens of
titled heiresses to chose from at court."

"Mother, you are deluding yourself if you think Elizabeth will let me marry one of her ladies. She flies into a
jealous rage at the merest hint of marriage. When I wed
I'll likely have to keep it secret or spend time in the
Tower."

"Then marry a Devon girl and let her stay here with
me. Every single friend I have has a daughter who has
tried to wangle an invitation to meet you. Shane, darling,
you are a legend!"

He gave her a short, deprecating laugh. "Legends pick
their own women, surely?"

Contrite, she knew she had stepped over the boundary
line by suggesting she choose a wife for him. "Good-bye,
darling, hurry back."

The two galleons sailed through the Straits of Dover,
rounded Margate, headed for Southend and up the River
Thames toward the London Pool. As soon as his ship
was sighted off Margate the news of his arrival would
spread like wildfire until it reached the ears of the queen
herself.

Hawkhurst preferred to announce himself, so keeping
his famous dragon sail hoisted in the stiff river breeze, he
waited until he drew abreast of Greenwich Palace, then
ordered a cannon be fired for one salute. The queen's
private apartments overlooked the river where she could
watch ships from all over the world travel this busiest of
her highways.

Hawkhurst knew the startling uproar the boom of a
ship's cannon would create so close to the palace, but he

loved to be dramatic. He allowed five minutes to elapse to give the queen and her court time to run to the windows, then he swept off his feathered cap and bowed low in homage to Gloriana.

The corridors of Greenwich Palace were abuzz with the news of the Sea God's arrival, accompanied by the whispers and giggles of every female, from the lowest scullery maid to the highest-ranking lady of the bed-chamber. Within the hour he strode through the public gallery resplendent in the latest fashion from France. His soft leather boots reached his thighs and he wore a short fur-edged cape and a narrow Italian rapier in a jewel-encrusted sheath. The white pleated ruff at his neck set off his bronzed face and lion's mane of hair. Today he wore two great thumb rings, one a black diamond, the other a blood-red ruby as big as a pigeon's egg.

He made his way to the presence chamber, where the queen greeted many guests as she sat in her great chair of state. In the ensuing hour she had changed her dress twice and her jewelry thrice, losing her temper with her ladies even to the point of slapping Mary Shelton's face. She had finally decided upon the Tudor colors of green and white. The deep green satin sleeves were slashed to show white undersleeves encrusted with crystal beads. She had selected a stiff lace neck whisk to show off her white breasts and throat and she wore no fewer than ten strands of pearls. A pearl-and-diamond coronet anchored down a vivid red wig, and she wore a different-jeweled ring on every single finger of her long, slim white hands. Her skin was as white as Albion rocks, bleached by a secret lotion she always used. Her nose was too long and her lips too thin, yet she expected her ladies to tell her

how beautiful she was, and her gentlemen to tell her they
would die of the passion they had for her.

In spite of the fevered preparations of the past hour she
sat now in the chair of state and looked past Hawkhurst
as if he were invisible. Shane smiled to himself. She was
punishing him for shooting off the cannon and for being
away for six months. He wondered arrogantly how long
she would be able to resist him. Cynically he gave her
half an hour, but at the end of fifteen minutes in the
crowded room, she arose and ushered everyone from the
room with an imperious "Leave us now. We would be
alone." She paused dramatically, then commanded,
"Captain Hawkhurst, I believe you desire private audience."

She had not dismissed her ladies-in-waiting yet and
they encircled her in the pale insipid gowns she insisted
they wear so she would stand out like a jeweled center-
piece. Every female in the room lusted for him and he
was fully aware of it, yet not by one look or gesture did
he acknowledge or notice them. He knew intimately of
each lady's youth and beauty, but at this moment he had
eyes only for the queen's most precious person. She was
well pleased with him. The black pupils of her eyes glittered. "You may leave us now. The queen would be alone
with her Sea God."

Before the door to the privy chamber had fully closed
behind her ladies, Shane swept Elizabeth into strong
arms and strode with her down the room to the chair of
state. "Bess, I'm starved for the sight of you!" Hawkhurst
knew she loved a man to be independent and daring. She
could not stomach weakness in a man.

"Put me down! God's blood, you are a bold fellow!"

"Who intends to be bolder," he said, pressing his lips

to her neck just beneath her ear, then sat himself in her chair of state and held her in his lap. He grinned down at her. "I brought you a present."

"I heard about the Spanish galleon. Your daring transcends ordinary sanity!"

"I mean a present for you, Bess, not England."

Her black eyes glittered with excitement at being held captive against his broad chest.

"Where is it?" she commanded.

"Find it!" he challenged.

Her long, slim hands made short work of frisking his body until she detected a box tucked inside his doublet. Her fingers slipped between his doublet and his silk shirt, but still could not close over the treasure, for it was beneath even the shirt. Her nimble fingers undid a button and slipped teasingly between the silk and his naked flesh, and he pretended to groan with the passion she aroused in him.

Exultantly she drew forth the box and opened it greedily. There lay a magnificent pair of dangling ear ornaments of jade and emeralds. She was inordinately fond of jewels and allowed him to fasten them onto her ears. Then he looked deep into her eyes and said suggestively, "What hidden treasure do you have for me, Bess?"

She slapped his bold hand from the hem of her gown. "You forget yourself because I call you a god."

"Nay, I'm all man!"

"Knave is more like it," she scolded archly. "If I invite you to return tomorrow will you bring me another jewel?"

He grinned. "Aye, but if you invite me to return tonight, I'll give you that which I treasure most." Then he bent and kissed her full upon the mouth.

She melted into his arms; then, like quicksilver, she jumped from his lap and assumed her queenship again. "Sirrah, I command you to come for the dancing tonight. More you dare not hope for."

"I dare anything, Bess."

"You have been away overlong, my Adonis—six months, was it not? I demand equal time."

"Your Majesty, my father lies near death. If aught happens to him I shall have to beg your permission to leave court."

Her eyes narrowed. "A few days only. I want you to join our summer progress in July."

Although it was the farthest thing from his heart he said, "I shall be honored, Your Majesty." He bowed low and she offered him her hand to kiss, but before he could depart she threw out the question he had been expecting. "What is my share of the profits?"

He hid a grin and said, straight-faced, "Forty thousand pounds, Your Grace." She half smiled, and he added, "And I'll throw in the galleon for good measure." Then she smiled fully and the effect was dazzling.

Back on board he changed out of his peacock garments and got on with his other business. By nightfall he had unloaded all the cargo into his own warehouses, which were guarded twenty-four hours of the day. Tomorrow he would tally up forty thousand pounds' worth of silver and other rare goods and have them transferred to the treasury.

He then sought out Jacob Goldman at Gray's Inn, the preserve of all London's lawyers. "Good evening, Goldman."

"Not so good, Captain Hawkhurst. Though I traced

the owner of the land you wanted, I was not able to procure it for you."

Hawk uttered an oath, then advised, "Try again—raise our offer."

Goldman nodded his understanding and Hawkhurst waved it aside. "We've more pressing business. Draw up marriage contracts."

Jacob Goldman's eyebrows rose in surprise. "Who is the lucky bride, m'lord?"

"Ah, that's the tricky part, Jacob. You must find one for me."

Jacob Goldman thought his dealings with the Hawkhurst empire had inured him to surprises, but as he listened to his client he could hardly believe what was being asked of him.

Hawk finished, "So you see, I gave my word to my father. God knows, he's asked little enough of me."

"So, what are your requirements for this wife?" Silently he wondered, *Where in hellfire do I even begin?*

Hawkhurst helped himself to a mug of ale from a jug on the sideboard and paced the room. "My requirements are few. First, she must not be from London. A young lady from a small country place would be best, I think. Within reason she should be of marriageable age. Someone too long in the tooth would be set in her ways; I've always found girls more amenable than mature women. She need have neither beauty, wealth, nor title, so long as she is from an impeccable background."

Jacob Goldman looked at him blankly. "Is that all? Surely, m'lord, you will be more selective than that?"

"Jacob, I have no time to be selective. Good God, man, I'm not picking a mistress. I need a girl who is willing to marry in less than a month's time, say June fifteenth, and in view of the unseemly haste I'll settle five hundred pounds on her and another five hundred on her family." He put down the empty tankard with a thud and demanded, "Do you think you can help me?"

Silence hung on the air, so that in the far distance a dog could be heard barking. Then Jacob Goldman began to laugh. For a moment he couldn't talk and tears of laughter rolled down his cheeks.

Hawkhurst glowered at the solicitor and demanded, "What is it, man?"

"You won't believe this, m'lord," he said, taking out a linen handkerchief to wipe his eyes, "but I've got a wife for you!"

Shane felt relief and dismay in the same instant.

"The land in Ireland you need for sea access to your own lands belongs to a young woman in Cheltenham. She would not sell the land because it is her only dowry, bequeathed to her from her Irish father. Her stepfather is a reverend of the English church in Cheltenham—impeccable family background. So you see, if you offer for her . . ."

"I get a wife and I get my land," finished Hawkhurst.

"Exactly! When can you arrange to travel up to Cheltenham to see the young lady?"

"I can't," he said flatly.

"But surely you wish to see her, speak with her?" insisted Goldman.

"I trust your judgment implicitly, Jacob. Draw up the contracts."

"You wish the marriage arranged for June fifteenth, then?" he asked, pushing all his doubts aside. Would the girl agree? Would the stepfather? He thought he'd have little problem with the latter because of the settlement involved, but what of the girl? His only hope was that the animosity between her and her stepfather was so great that she would accept the marriage as a means of escape. He must succeed in this mission, for if he failed Hawkhurst in this he knew he could say good-bye to any future business dealings.

By nine of the clock that same night Shane Hawkhurst, resplendent in pale blue, was lifting the queen high in the gavotte in the music gallery at Greenwich, and stayed dancing attendance on Her Majesty and her ladies until past midnight, as he had been commanded to do.

By one o'clock his clothes had been exchanged one more time for the serious business of his first night in London. He and the baron, garbed head to foot in black and heavily cloaked and daggered, made their way from the docks down Gracechurch Street toward the corner of Threadneedle, where they slipped unseen in the back door of a brothel. From the street it was shabbily nondescript, for the London night house operated behind a blank face. It was to his credit, or discredit, whichever your view, that he did not go there to whore.

Chapter 4

Sabre had reached such a low point that if she could have reversed her decision about selling her land, she would have done so. She realized the money would have enabled her to escape even if she had forfeited it to Reverend Bishop in return for her freedom.

Reverend Bishop also wished he had acted differently when the solicitor had interviewed his stepdaughter. Perhaps if he had treated her with kid gloves and showed her some fatherly affection, he could have altered the little hellcat's decision. So when Jacob Goldman once more arrived at the large rectory house in Cheltenham, he was ushered in with the greatest deference, introduced to Mrs. Bishop, and served refreshments.

"Reverend and Mrs. Bishop, the man I represent is Captain Hawkhurst, heir to the great Hawkhurst shipping enterprise. His father, Lord Devonport, is gravely ill and in the event of his death his title will be passed on to Captain Hawkhurst."

Reverend Bishop was suitably impressed to be dealing with the nobility. Therefore, when Goldman broached the subject of marriage, the reverend's mouth fell open.

"I bring an offer of marriage from Lord Devonport's heir to your daughter Sara, providing the wedding can take place June fifteenth."

His youngest daughter, his precious Ann, jumped into the reverend's mind, but as soon as he proposed her name for the brilliant match, he realized that of course the girl who owned the coveted land would get the noble husband.

"Captain Hawkhurst sends his apologies for the unseemly haste, but I have drawn up the marriage contracts and he has most generously agreed to a settlement for Sara's family as well as herself."

Mrs. Bishop was effusive in her praise for her child. "I always knew Sara would marry well. She's special, you know."

"Then you don't forsee any objection on her part to this proposed union?" asked Jacob Goldman, feeling most uneasy about broaching the matter to the beautiful young woman they were discussing.

"Objection?" demanded her stepfather irritably. "I shall overrule her objections, sir. It is my place to accept or decline offers of marriage for my daughter—she has nothing to say in the matter!"

"Ah, Reverend Bishop, that of course is true," agreed Goldman tactfully, but don't you think perhaps if Sara thought it was her decision to make, we would stand a better chance of a speedy and mutually beneficial conclusion to this matter?"

"Yes, George, you do have a tendency to make Sara do exactly the opposite of what you wish, although I have no idea why that is so." Mary Bishop sent him a look that beseeched him not to spoil their chance of being connected with the nobility.

"Very well. Just to please you, my dear, we will have her down and *ask* her, rather than tell her."

When Sabre had heard the whole story, she couldn't quite believe that this was happening to her. She looked from one to the other, hoping that she wasn't dreaming the whole thing. She realized she had received the offer because of the land, but that was what it was intended for —her dowry. To marry a stranger was frightening, but it was also exciting, and the prospect of going to court was like a dream come true. She realized that if she didn't grab this chance, she might never have another. When offered two alternatives she had always chosen the bolder course. When she smiled at Jacob Goldman, his heart lurched. "May I sign the contract now?"

Her mother was making a great fuss over her and even her stepfather looked fatuously pleased. Mr. Goldman directed her to read everything carefully and showed her where to affix her signature, and she signed *Sara Bishop* in triplicate, but all she was aware of was the bold, dark name already on the bottom of the contracts—*S. Hawkhurst.*

As if a magic wand had been waved over her, her life changed dramatically. Suddenly she had become the center of attention. As well as being the pivotal figure of the family's fevered activity, she was the focus of great curiosity and envy from all the aunts and cousins, and word was spreading throughout the congregation and beyond to all the townspeople of Cheltenham and Gloucester.

Sabre basked in her moment of sunshine. At every opportunity she emphasized, "My husband-to-be is a great favorite at court, you know; I will be spending much time there." Her excitement grew daily until she could not sleep at night, and she could not resist sending smug little smiles in her half sisters' direction when she was being fitted for her wedding gown.

Finally she was having her choice honored and she had chosen a cream-colored satin embroidered all over with pearllike beads. She would have a cream lace half-ruff, so she could wear her glorious hair down in display for her bridegroom, and when she tried it on and preened in front of the looking glass, the copper curls sat on the ruff as pretty as a wedding cake!

Sabre could not help rubbing raw the nerves of her sisters and cousins when she saw their mouths tighten with envy. She laughed when their whispers reached her ears; it would take more than their venom to ruin her wedding day; in fact, she believed nothing on earth could spoil it for her.

She walked about in a dreamlike trance thinking of the bridegroom who would come to claim her. Her thoughts were obsessed with him as she envisioned his height, his hair, his eyes, his mouth, his hands, and then she would shiver with excitement. His manners would be courtly, for he was used to the company of the glorious queen of England, another magnificent being her imagination gifted with all the graces. Someday in the not-too-distant future he would become Lord Devonport and he would transform her into Lady Devonport. She was breathless at the thought of it, though it saddened her that his dear father must depart this earth before it became a reality.

She displayed her small trousseau of busks, petticoats, night rails, slippers, and one traveling outfit to her cousins, and when they pointed out how meager it seemed, she waved her hand airily and explained her husband would provide her with a whole new wardrobe in London, for the fashions of the court were far ahead of anything that Gloucester could provide. The styles were so daring at court, she told them, that worn elsewhere they would create a scandal. Each and every female was consumed with envy, for they knew Sabre Wilde was quite capable of creating a scandal, daring fashions or no.

Hawkhurst and Drake sat on the balcony of the Grapes in Narrow Street. It jutted out over the Thames, affording them a clear view of the river and its traffic.

"I can confirm the rumors of Philip's Great Armada.
It is being built at Cádiz," said Hawkhurst in low tones.

"Of course! Cádiz is so well hidden," said Drake, his
eyes flashing with the intensity of his feelings for the subject. "I scouted the Bay of Biscay from San Sebastian to
La Coruña, then all down the coast of Portugal to Lisbon, and found nothing!"

"Philip is raping Mexico and Peru of silver and gold
and is pouring it into ships to conquer England."

"Have you told the queen?" asked Drake.

Hawkhurst shook his head. "Pointless, Francis. You
know she has a woman's fear of war and accuses us of
inciting Philip's hatred for our own glorification. Essex
gets the full force of her wrath each time he brings up the
subject of war. She disassociates herself from our pirating
Spanish treasure, pretending ignorance of our actions,
though she is quick enough to hold out her hand for the
profits."

Drake nodded his agreement. How many times had he
argued with Elizabeth until he was blue in the face? All
to little or no avail. "We'd do better to furnish the information to Walsingham and Cecil," he said decisively.

Hawkhurst inwardly blanched at the mention of the
queen's secretary, Walsingham, then replied, "You see
Walsingham and I'll talk with Cecil."

The two men operated quite differently. Hawkhurst believed you should always cloak your real desires, think
twice before you spoke a word, and never ask directly for
what you wanted, while Drake, the son of a country par-
son, was respectably married and honest and open to a
fault. On the other hand, he was a genius at sea and
Hawkhurst would choose his company over any other

when a Spanish man-of-war was firing cannonballs up your arse!

A Hawkhurst merchant ship arrived in London bringing messages from Georgiana and his brother Matthew, urging him to return to Devonport with all possible speed. He had accomplished so much in the quick trip to London that he felt he could afford to quit the court for a short time, and dusk that day saw him and the baron saddled up for the long ride to Devonport, almost two hundred miles across country.

They rested a few hours only after the first hundred miles was behind them and reached Devonport House in the middle of the night. He had arrived barely in time to see his father breathe his last labored breaths, and by the time the red fingers of dawn reached up from the sea toward the sky, he was the new Lord Devonport.

With his usual energy he saw to the details of the burial and the comforting of his mother, and made the myriad decisions concerning their shipping empire. Along with the title, he had inherited the queen's lieutenantship for Devon, which meant he was responsible for supplying foodstuffs to the navy and overseeing musters of all able-bodied men between sixteen and sixty in case war broke out.

Shane knew the first thing he must do was appoint a deputy lieutenant in his stead and toyed with the idea of bestowing the honor upon Matthew, but finally he appointed a younger brother of his father's, another Hawkhurst and one of his best captains. He had other tasks for Matthew at the moment, and the sooner he laid the plan before his brother the better, for the days were galloping toward June fifteenth.

He invited Matthew to dine with him in Devonport's

east wing, and his younger brother was sorely disappointed that Larksong was nowhere in evidence. The two men had large appetites and Shane let Matthew enjoy the hearty food before broaching his subject. Then he settled his brother with a large brandy and deemed him to be in a pliant mood.

"I'm transferring ownership of the *Devon Rose* to you, Matt. You've had command of her for over a year, so now she's yours."

Matt's eyebrows rose in surprise. His father would never have taken a ship from the family company and given outright ownership of it to a family member, son or no. Shane had had to purchase his ships (or steal them), for none had been given to him.

"It's time you started making money for yourself as well as for the family."

"How can I thank you?" asked Matt, delighted with his good fortune.

"Well, there is something I need you to do for me, Matt."

"Name it!" offered Matt wholeheartedly.

"I'm to be married June fifteenth to a young woman from Cheltenham. I want you to go up there and take care of all the details for me."

Matt let out a whoop. "God's teeth, you're a dark horse! When did you meet her? How long has this been going on? I'm honored to be your groomsman. When do we leave?"

"We don't," said Shane shortly. "I'm commanded back to court in a few days time. I want you to go up there and marry her by proxy." He observed his brother's reaction through half-closed eyes.

"You're jesting!" said Matt with disbelief.

"Not for a moment," said Shane smoothly. "The young woman I am to marry is Sara Bishop; her stepfather is a reverend of the English church. The legal marriage contracts have been drawn up by Jacob Goldman and signed by all parties. You will simply marry her in my name. All quite legal and binding, I assure you."

Matt whistled through his teeth. "Christ Almighty, you're being cool about this. Do you mean to say you've never even seen her?"

"Nor do I intend to. After the ceremony you will convey her to Blackmoor Hall, where she will reside, and I will have fulfilled my promise to Sebastian. It is a simple legal arrangement."

"Blackmoor?" Matt gasped. "You'd send a young girl from the pretty Cotswolds to that bleak, lonely pile of stone near Exmoor Forest?"

"God's teeth, boy, you don't expect me to have her dangling round my bloody neck at Bess's court, do you?" demanded Shane.

"Well, no—a bride is a secret you'll have to guard well. But Blackmoor?" Matt protested. "That's cruel, even for you," he said bluntly.

"Damn it all, Matt, this marriage brings her wealth and a title. What more could she want? She's a simple country girl who will be amenable to my wishes. Blackmoor needs a chatelaine; its been run solely by servants for too long. She'll have a free hand to practice her housewifery and there will be enough to do managing the estate to keep her from mischief. I can't bring her down here and palm her off onto Mother, for two women under one roof would be hell for both. I think it is a perfect solution."

"But what will Sara think?" asked Matt with daring.

"I'm not in the habit of consulting a woman concerning my decisions," said Shane curtly. "Matthew, the easiest for you will be to sail from Devonport into the Bristol Channel and anchor somewhere up the River Severn, then sail back, take Sara to Blackmoor Hall and see that she's settled, then sail the *Devon Rose* up to London. I've a profitable cargo you can take from my warehouses across the pond to Calais."

Matt shrugged. It was blackmail pure and simple, but when had his brother ever caviled at something so tame as blackmail? The scent of sandalwood incense emanated from the adjoining room, along with the whisper of silken garments. Matt licked his lips and began hesitantly, "I don't suppose . . . you'd consider—"

"Don't even ask," said Shane, cutting short his young brother's fantasy.

Sabre's three brothers-in-law had each cornered her separately to test her reactions to what was happening. Each man had a corner of his heart reserved for Sabre. Each was convinced she had been his first love, and equally convinced she held a soft spot for him in her affections. Each knew the other two men had offered for her before settling for the wives they got, but there was no jealousy among them because each man was convinced Sabre preferred him in her heart of hearts.

Now everything would change. A stranger would have her, a wealthy, titled man from the queen's court, and their jealousy ran very deep and very hot. David caught her in the vestry of the church where she had gone alone to give thanks for her deliverance and to pray to St. Jude for a husband who would love her. He pressed her against the thick oaken door. "Sabre, you'll never know how I always wanted you." The moment he touched her, he almost lost control. Though it was impossible for anything to penetrate the velvet of his doublet, he could have sworn he felt the heat of her lovely breasts pressed against him.

"Take your hands from me, David. I am now private property," she warned haughtily.

"Sabre, let me have you just once . . . let me initiate you." He was panting heavily now that he was fully aroused, and his arms turned into bands of iron with his heightened passion. She could feel him full and hard against her and experience had taught her if she cried the alarm and someone came, she would receive the blame for being a teasing wanton. She had learned to rely upon her own devices, so quite deliberately she brought her knee up sharply between his legs. He doubled over and uttered a filthy obscenity.

"Initiation can be painful, David," she whispered with relish.

"By Christ, I hope yours is, you wild little bitch. I hope Hawkhurst rapes you!"

The second encounter was in her very own chamber, where she had assumed no man would ever dare, but she had not reckoned on John's daring. She was just leaving her room one morning as he happened to be passing her door. Without hesitation he pushed her back into the room and closed the door behind him. He knew she wouldn't want to be found compromised a few days before her wedding and gambled that she would keep her mouth shut.

"Sweetheart, we have some unfinished business. You eluded me at the lake, but I've snared you well this time."

"John, you're a good-looking bastard, but you have a

yellow streak up your back a mile wide. I could have forgiven you for trying to swim nude with me—after all, you can't help it if you're ruled by your lust—but I'll never forgive you for telling my stepfather. He punished me by taking Sabbath away."

"I'll let you ride me," he said with a leer, and before she knew it he had her laid out flat upon the bed, her skirts lifted to expose her thighs. He undid his breeches quickly and was about to push them down. With a thankful prayer upon her lips Sabre felt beneath the bed and withdrew her father's weapon; the one she had been named for. The long, curved blade touched his belly.

John was whispering frantically, "Sabre, for God's sake, be careful. I'm sorry, I didn't mean anything by it. Let me leave now unscathed and I promise I'll not bother you again." He was almost babbling, so great was his fear. She carefully pressed the tip into his belly so as to draw a drop of blood without really hurting him, before he fled.

Her third encounter was more subtle. Andrew found himself alone with her in the stables. It brought back to them both the earlier time when he had asked her to marry him and they had almost made love. Though he drew close, he made no effort to touch her. In fact, he knew if he did touch her, he would be undone. "Sara," he said hoarsely, not teasing her by using her nickname. There was an awkward silence between them. "Please forgive me, Sara, I made a terrible mistake."

She caught her bottom lip between her teeth. "Do you know how much you hurt me, Andrew?"

"I've been punished a thousand times over. Beth is selfish, shallow, unbelievably spoiled . . . and useless in bed, like a little girl."

"Damn it all, Andrew, she is a little girl. She's only fifteen!"

"I cannot bear the thought of Hawkhurst having you. I love you, Sara . . . I still love you!" he said miserably. "My parents and Reverend Bishop were the authors of my marriage to Beth instead of to you."

The scent of the stables—leather, hay, horses—made her nostrils flare as she remembered the sweet tenderness between them that other time. "I thought I loved you, too, Andrew, but I was wrong. You are hardly more than a boy . . . I need a man." She saw Andrew's weakness now and was glad she hadn't married him, but still she felt the need to gloat a little. "By all accounts I'm marrying a man of strength. When he arrives, take a good look, Andrew. Take a good look at a real man!"

Actually, she had neither patience nor time to think of the previous men who had been in her life. The center of her being, of her very existence, was Hawkhurst. She daydreamed of the first words he would say to her and she practiced offering her hand for him to kiss. At night, when she did manage to fall asleep, she dreamed of a bridegroom who was beautiful, gallant, and who cherished her with every look and word.

The days ran together with such speed that suddenly it was the day before the wedding and she found herself with her nose glued to her chamber window for the first glimpse of his arrival. She prayed fervently, "Please, please, St. Jude, don't let me be disappointed. This is to be the most important moment of my whole life. Please, please!"

One brief glimpse was enough to set her pulses racing. He was so tall! If her eyes weren't playing tricks, he was handsome too! *Oh, thank you, thank you,* she kept whis-

pering under her breath. Suddenly she really felt like a
bride, all fluttery and shy, and because she was letting her
guard down a little to allow her feelings to show, she felt
helplessly vulnerable. She flew to her mirror for the hun-
dredth time. This time she wasn't admiring the lovely
pale green day dress, the first such flattering color she
had ever owned, this time she was searching for a flaw in
her dress or her face which might mar the first impression her bridegroom would have of her.

She was exultant that all four of her half sisters and
two of her hateful female cousins were below to witness
his arrival. She tried to be patient while she awaited her
summons, but patience wasn't in Sabre's nature. She was
breathless to race downstairs and come face-to-face with
her future, her fate.

Matthew Hawkhurst found the situation disconcerting,
to say the least. He managed his introductions well
enough, but realized almost immediately that Jacob
Goldman had not prepared them for a proxy wedding.
The damned coward, thought Matthew with disgust, but
he understood Goldman's reluctance when he'd had a
chance to size up Reverend Bishop.

As well as Mrs. Bishop there were six young women
present and Matthew could not discern which one was
the bride, for they all seemed avid for details of the unusual proxy arrangement. He explained firmly that circumstances made it impossible for his brother to be there
in person to exchange vows, and he was acting as proxy.
He glanced about the room, uncomfortable to be making
excuses and explanations in front of the whole family, but
to his surprise each girl looked suspiciously happy.

"Under the circumstances it will be inappropriate for
the lavish church wedding and reception we had planned.

I will dispatch messages immediately, canceling the affair," said the reverend with deference to the wealthy Hawkhurst, yet still needing to control the situation. "Since it will require only a legal, civil ceremony it can be done in the privacy of my study."

Relieved, Matthew nodded his agreement and glanced again at the young women to see if he could identify the bride. He was shocked to see them exchanging gleeful glances and laughing behind their hands. Only Mrs. Bishop looked unhappy and confused.

"I think we had better have Sara down and explain matters to her," the reverend said calmly.

Mrs. Smite, who had hovered behind the door long enough to hear most of what was transpiring, was dispatched for Sara. The iron-faced woman gave her a sly smile and muttered something about "comeuppance," but Sabre was in such a rosy glow, she almost apologized to the woman for calling her "Mrs. Spite."

She ran lightly down the stairs and along the center hallway, her steps only slowing with sudden shyness when she reached the archway to the elegant drawing room.

Matthew was stunned. His first thought was that his brother had gulled him, pretending not to know her. This bride had been chosen with more care than he had taken in selecting an entire crew for one of his beloved ships. She was so breathtakingly, heartstoppingly lovely. From across the room she lifted her heart-shaped face to him and their eyes met before she swept her lashes to her cheeks. They were pale green pools in which a man might drown . . . willingly. She approached him and sank into a graceful curtsy, and barely above a whisper she breathed, "Mr. Hawkhurst."

He cleared his throat and replied, *"Matthew* Hawkhurst, your betrothed's brother, Mistress Bishop."

Her face fell and he could have kicked himself for wiping the beautiful, expectant smile from it. Clearly she was disappointed that he was not to be the groom, and in that moment, so was he. However, it told him that without a doubt she had never met his brother.

He clasped her hand and raised her from her curtsy. "Mistress Bishop, I am here as proxy for my brother. I am to give his responses in the marriage service. It was impossible for him to leave court at the moment."

Her body went stiff and her eyes widened in shock and disbelief. This couldn't be happening to her! The bridegroom she had flaunted and bragged about couldn't even be bothered to show up for the wedding! She was aware of eight pairs of gloating female eyes at her back and a shameful blush crept up her throat and suffused her cheeks. She was utterly devastated.

Matthew strove to fill the awful silence. "My ship is anchored in the Severn. It will be my honor to give you safe escort, mistress."

"To court?" she managed to whisper.

It was Matthew's turn to flush. He looked away from the accusing eyes and said quietly, "No. I am to escort you to Blackmoor Hall near Exmoor Forest. It is one of my brother's estates which is in need of a chatelaine. He has sent you letters of instruction about the estate," he finished lamely.

Her eyes burned with green fire. Anger and hatred consumed her to such a degree, it made it impossible for her to hear and think clearly. The whoreson Hawkhurst had slapped her in the face with the greatest insult she had ever received. It was the final, ultimate humiliation.

She tried to speak, but the words choked her. Her hand went to her throat, then groped the air as her body swayed toward him. Matthew saw she was about to faint and swept the delicate burden into his arms. He looked down at her with a deep tenderness he had never felt before. Her eyelids fluttered like the wings of a dying butterfly and came to rest upon her cheeks. Her sweet mouth looked so young and so vulnerable. His brother was a swine to have done this to an innocent girl.

Chapter 5

Mrs. Bishop was at Matthew's elbow. "Oh, dear. Could you carry her up to her chamber, Mr. Hawkhurst?"

Matthew followed her upstairs, glad to escape from the roomful of women. He quickly averted his eyes from the bed, and instead laid his burden upon a small sofa under the window. Mrs. Bishop fluttered about ineffectually, and he found himself now calming the mother. "Do you have any brandy, ma'am?"

"Oh, no!" she said, shocked. "The reverend wouldn't allow such a thing in the house. Whatever am I to do? Burn feathers, do you think, or slap her sharply in the face?"

"No, no, ma'am. She will be fine. She will come to in a moment. It is just shock. Mrs. Bishop, do you think I might have a private word with Sara? I'm sure I can explain the situation to her in such a way that she will accept and understand."

Mrs. Bishop cast him a doubtful look, but she turned matters over to him without demur. She wasn't feeling at all well herself and sought her own bed before collapse should overtake her.

When the door closed, Matthew drew forth a small silver flask and gently tipped a small amount of brandy to Sara's lips. She choked and bolted up from the sofa, almost knocking him to the floor.

"That bastard!" she panted. "He's made me the laughingstock of Cheltenham!" She put her hands to her temples and gave vent to a piercing scream. Matthew eyed the door nervously, thinking an outraged father would fly through the door to avenge his daughter.

Sabre laughed hysterically. "None will dare come through the door while the 'Wilde' woman is throwing a tantrum." She reached under the bed, drew forth the sabre, and waved it in the air. "That rotten sod, if I had him here I'd run him through."

"Sara—" he began, very worried now.

"I'm not Sara. They wouldn't allow me to be Sara Bishop. I'm Sabre . . . Sabre Wilde . . . named for my father and his weapon."

He looked at her with awed admiration. "Sabre is a magnificent name. It suits you perfectly."

"Your brother has ruined my life!" she cried dramatically. "I'll ruin his if it's the last thing I do!"

"Sabre . . . in all honesty, he couldn't be here. The queen commanded him to remain at court."

"The queen?" She scowled, finding another outlet for her hatred. An unreasoning jealousy flamed through her heart. Her bridegroom had ignored her to dance attendance upon the bloody queen! "By God, I'll show Hawkhurst! Him and the queen, on my oath! I'll make them pay . . . I'll make them pay forever!"

She threw down the sabre with a flourish and her breasts rose and fell as she took great breaths to calm herself.

Suddenly Matthew began to laugh.

Green sparks shot from her eyes. "Gaping jackanapes . . . what's so funny?" she demanded hotly.

"Nay, lass, I'm on your side. I agree 'twas a damned shabby trick even for a Hawkhurst, but, God's blood, the joke is on him. He hasn't the faintest idea of what he's depriving himself. When I first saw you I thought you lovely enough to thicken a man's blood in his veins, but now that I've seen you in a rage, I realize you are magnificent. If he got one look at what was his, he'd kill any man who dared glance twice at you."

"I'm not his yet! We haven't exchanged vows."

"Will you cry off?" he asked. If she did he would propose to her himself.

A frown marred her lovely brow as she thought over her alternatives. She couldn't stay here. In fact, she didn't quite know how she was going to face everyone tomorrow.

"In all fairness I should tell you that if you do go through with it, you will be Lady Devonport."

She brightened instantly. "Then I shall do it!"

"You'd marry him just for the title?" he demanded.

She flared. "He's marrying me for my land—a fair exchange, don't you think?" Then it dawned on her. "Oh, I'm so sorry, Matthew—that means you have just lost your father." She knelt beside him, instantly contrite and filled with tender concern. Matthew squeezed her hand. "His strength was so diminished, it was a blessing, really. He wouldn't have wanted to live like that."

"I'm sorry for your loss. My father died when I was four. People thought I was too young to understand, but I wasn't. I mourned and grieved for him so very long. He was the only person who ever loved me. He was my friend."

"I'd like to be your friend, Sabre," he said softly.

"Matt . . . how lovely. I do feel comfortable with you. When I curse, you don't mind; when I rage, you laugh. I shock everyone, it's my stock-in-trade, but you are wonderfully shockproof."

"I'll be the perfect foil for your wickedest thoughts," he teased.

"Oh, you won't just listen to me, you'il aid and abet

me," she promised as she picked up the silver flask. "May I have some more?"

"Slowly, Sabre," he cautioned, "you sip it slowly so you don't gag. It's brandy. Don't breathe in before you take a sip or the fumes will make you choke. If you take a large swallow, it will feel like it's burning a hole in your gut."

She was pleased with her first lessons in learning to drink. Matt was going to prove an invaluable ally. "Oh, God's blood, Matt, how will I face them all tomorrow? They'll be falling down laughing; they'll be kicking their legs in the air laughing at me."

"Sabre, your stepfather has sent messages canceling the church ceremony and reception. We will exchange the vows privately in his study. Then we'll leave if your trunks are packed. You will be Lady Devonport. The title gives you much authority."

"Authority? Mmm, authority . . . oh, how I love the feel of that word on my tongue," she said with a smile. "Did you bring money?" she asked suddenly.

"Of course. I have five hundred pounds for you and five hundred pounds for your father. Of course, on top of that there are funds you can draw on for any expenses at Blackmoor. Hawk explains it in his letter."

Her eyes lit up. "Come on, let's go and give Reverend Bishop his blood money!" She took his hand and propelled him to the door. Her hair flew about her shoulders like pale molten copper, and his heart turned over in his breast at her handclasp. Holding her head erect, Sabre swept into the drawing room with Matthew at her back.

Everyone stopped talking instantly and stared in amazement. Only when she had everyone's undivided attention did she announce, "Lord Devonport's brother has a settlement for you, Reverend Bishop. Matthew, pray give him five hundred pounds, and be sure to get a receipt for my account book." She turned to her eldest sister. "Jane, have the servants pack my trousseau in my trunks and take special care with my wedding gown. I'm sure Lord Devonport will insist upon a second wedding so he may say his vows to me personally. Matthew and I are going out on business. I've decided to buy back Black Sabbath. I shall take my own horse aboard with me. Did you know that Lord Devonport's brother captains his own vessel? Oh, I'm sure you did. The Hawkhursts are legendary, are they not?"

She swept out with Matthew in her wake. He waited until he was outside before he bent double with laughter. This young woman was a delight, but better than that, he knew she was a match for anything his brother could dish out.

Early in the morning Sabre sought out her mother and said her good-byes privately. She knew her mother's life would run much smoother with her out of the way. She almost felt as if their roles were reversed as she kissed her mother's brow and whispered farewell. She was startled when her mother pressed her hand and whispered, "I loved your father to distraction. I don't think any woman can withstand a wild Irishman once he has marked you for his own."

Later in the day she stood in the reverend's study and exchanged the vows. How strange that Matthew spoke the vows as if he were his brother. "I, Shane, take thee Sara . . ." *So that's what S. Hawkhurst stands for,* she thought. *Why does he have an Irish name?* She would find out. Yes, she would find out everything there was to know about Shane Hawkhurst, Lord Devonport.

The heavy gold ring was slipped onto her finger and the short ceremony was completed. She had heard her sisters' spiteful giggling throughout. She and Matthew stayed only long enough for fruit cordial and wedding cake, then the trunks were loaded into the carriage that would convey them to the ship and then be returned. Matthew's horse and Sabbath were tied to the back of the carriage, as he would sit inside with the new bride for the eighteen-mile drive to the ship.

She wore a lovely apricot traveling dress and matching cloak. She knew she had never looked lovelier. Matthew was about to hand her into the carriage when she begged him to wait there for her while she went back into the priory to say good-bye properly to her family.

They were all there except her mother, who was having a quiet weep upstairs. She swept her eyes over Beth and Andrew, Margaret and John, then Jane and David. She flicked her gaze to Reverend Bishop, and the corners of her mouth went up wickedly. "Well, it's been a slice of heaven being a part of this family. Since I won't be seeing any of you again, I have some sisterly advice for you. Beth, your new husband thinks you a little girl in bed . . . after knowing me." Into the shocked silence she plunged again. "Margaret, I really did swim naked in the lake, but John forgot to mention that he swam with me." Her eyes swept across the room. "Jane, darling, when you go to bed tonight, ask David to show you the little brand I put on his belly."

"Sabre Wilde, you are a disgusting trollop," said Margaret, using the worst word she'd ever uttered.

Reverend Bishop was outraged. "You are a shameless, wanton strumpet."

Sabre's eyes glittered dangerously. "Yes, and my name is Lady Devonport."

Jane said coldly, "Devonport, perhaps . . . Lady, never!"

She swept regally from the house, but once inside the carriage her eyes welled up with tears and spilled over as she sobbed out her unhappiness.

Matthew's arms closed about her. He held her tightly against his chest and murmured soothing words to comfort her. Finally, when she couldn't cry more, she raised her eyes to his and the tears glistened upon her lashes like diamonds. He bent his head and kissed her gently. He could not help himself. Suddenly her laughter bubbled up and spilled over deliciously. With great chagrin he asked, "May I know why my kisses amuse you?"

"Oh, Matthew, up until today I'd only been kissed by a brother-in-law, and now I've *still* only been kissed by a brother-in-law!"

Sabre watched Matthew gentle and calm the horses to get them aboard. She was amazed when he showed her the section of the hold that contained heavily timbered stalls. "We transport horses quite frequently," he told her. "Most come from Ireland, then we ship them to Holland, France, even as far as Morocco, then once in a while we'll bring back Arabians from that part of the world. All Hawkhurst ships sail with special grooms who do nothing but look after the animals."

The ship fascinated her. She had had no idea how many crew it took to sail a seagoing vessel. She took an avid interest in everything and the seventy-man crew returned the compliment.

Matthew insisted she take his cabin for the overnight run to Blackmoor, and he moved into the quarters of his first mate. It was small but very comfortably furnished, with sleeping berth, desk, leather-upholstered chairs, built-in cabinets, and a fine wool carpet to keep the chill of the sea from seeping into one's bones.

Sabre begged him to let her come up on deck with him so she could watch the *Devon Rose* catch the flood tide down the Severn and into the Bristol Channel. Matthew led her up to the bridge, bade her hang tight to the railings, then, bracing himself against the roll and sway of the ship, he raised his voice and shouted his first order. The tackle creaked overhead and it caused Sabre's gaze to wander aloft. She gasped as she saw small figures moving about in the rigging, readying the mainsail for unfurling from its yard. They hung like monkeys with only an arm crooked over a spar, waiting for just the right moment to catch the breeze as they moved out into the open water of the Bristol Channel.

Her eyes sought Matthew's and he grinned down at her, taking pleasure in watching her excitement.

"Port the helm," he ordered, and his voice was carried by the wind the whole length of the vessel. "The land to starboard is Wales—a wild place."

She nodded vigorously.

"Sky's coloring up, we should have a showy sunset— just for you," he said, grinning.

The salty tang of sea wrack filled her nostrils. The stiff sea breeze had taken the hood of her cloak from her head, and her hair flew about in wild disarray. Seabirds screamed and dipped around the tall masts, and the sound of the ship's bow cutting through the waves set up a rhythm she could feel in her blood. She had never experienced such an exultant feeling of freedom in her life. In that moment she experienced a rebirth. This was her be-

ginning. She was going to meet her future head on. Never
again would she let anyone make a victim out of her. She
knew she was strong-willed. From this moment forward,
she vowed, she would take the cup of life into both hands
and quaff deeply. She would do exactly as she pleased.
She would live well; she would take her sweet revenge,
and it would taste like nectar. She filled her lungs with
the intoxicating tang of the sea air and swore an oath that
now she had begun really living, nothing would ever stop
her again. She mapped out her course as she stood at the
railing. It was all so very simple. Of course Matthew
would object strenuously, but she laughed aloud, for she
knew she had already conquered one Hawkhurst and
now she just had one more to go. She licked her lips over
the poor bastard!

Blackmoor Hall was craggy and windswept. Its atmosphere of mystery and isolation gave the impression that
it was located at the end of the world. Matthew was embarrassed to be taking her to so wild and lonely a place
and offered an apology every few minutes, starting when
a ferocious pack of Irish wolfhounds almost attacked
them before they were through the gates and their keeper
had to whip them off.

Sabre fell in love with the place on sight, but she kept
her true feelings from Matthew. He introduced her to the
entire household as Lady Devonport and the head housekeeper, a handsome woman with cheeks like Devon apples, presented her with the enormous ring of chatelaine
keys.

Matthew gave personal orders to the cooks to prepare
enough food for his crew and told two of his sailors to
take aboard fifty casks of cider from Blackmoor's wine

cellars. Sabre and Matthew took supper alone in the parlor, where a cozy fire had been built. For though the day had been filled with sunshine, it hadn't penetrated the thick stone walls of Blackmoor and they welcomed the warmth as they sat before it.

Wisely Sabre had waited until Matt was replete with good food and wine before she told him her plans.

"Absolutely not! My brother would have my—brains!"

"Matt, you did exactly as he asked. You stood in for him at the wedding ceremony and you delivered me safely to Blackmoor. Your duty is finished, ended. I don't intend to go to court as Lady Devonport. My aunt is Kate Ashford, mistress of the queen's robes. She wrote to tell me she needs assistance." Sabre wasn't exactly lying, and anyway, she was prepared to do more than lie to get what she wanted.

"When my brother finds out, our lives will not be worth a penn'orth of parrot shit!"

"There's no way he could possibly find out unless you tell him, Matt! He married Sara Bishop . . . I'm Sabre Wilde."

"You're mad! It would be playing with fire! Dammit, Sabre, why do you look pleased as hell when I say that?" he demanded.

"Well, you might be afraid of him, but I'm not!" She threw out the challenge.

" 'Tis impossible. Though court is bulging at the seams, you couldn't be an anonymous face in the crowd . . . you'd stand out anywhere. Believe me when I tell you my brother would notice you."

"In other words Shane Hawkhurst is a womanizer?" she asked.

"Where women are concerned, Hawkhurst is a bloody predator, as his name suggests," said Matt bluntly.

"Good! I intend to become his mistress," she announced with green fire flashing from her eyes. "I will call the tune and I will lead the measure."

Matthew stared at her as if she had gone mad. "You'll pay the bloody piper too. The answer is no!" he shouted.

The corners of her mouth went up. Matt was her friend, he wouldn't leave her here to rot! She'd see to that!

Chapter 6

Matthew Hawkhurst sailed slowly down the coast of Devon. He dropped anchor at Tintagel to show Sabre the legendary castle that was said to have been King Arthur's. They rounded Land's End and again he anchored at the quaint seaport of Mousehole for Sabre's amusement. He used every delaying tactic he could think of. He knew Shane had been commanded to go on progress with the queen, and he didn't intend to deliver Sabre to Greenwich until the second day of July.

Shane Hawkhurst, knowing the queen would depart on her progress July first, also dallied on his return trip to court. The last thing he wanted was to leave London; he had too many contacts to meet. He delayed his departure from Devonport another week to assure himself that Georgiana would be all right and to avoid Elizabeth's departure.

Both Hawkhurst brothers miscalculated by one day. Her Majesty's progress had been planned for the county of Norfolk, ending at Norwich in East Anglia. Her first stop was to be at Theobalds, Cecil's country house just outside London. Her usher of the Black Rod was sent ahead to make all the necessary preparations for the queen and her court. Her ladies had been to Theobalds before and had been appalled at the accommodations available. Though the queen's apartments were lavishly luxurious, her ladies of the privy chamber were crammed into one room with the lesser servants, and her male courtiers were crammed into another.

Dismayed to find Bess was only just leaving for Theobalds, Lord Devonport seized upon the appallingly inadequate accommodations as his excuse to join the progress when it moved to the castle at Bishop's Stortford. Hawkhurst seldom occupied his permanent rooms on the fourth floor at Greenwich because he had a London residence of his own along the Thames, but he and the baron intended to stay there the next few days, as there were apartments he wished to search, once their occupants had left on the progress.

Sabre couldn't believe the crush of people at Greenwich, not only in the palace, but in the park and the courtyard and stables. It reminded her of a fair she had attended once where jugglers and players put on a fine show for the townspeople. The clothes were so colorful and exaggerated, they seemed like costumes. Everyone had a purpose and went about it noisily with little or no thought for the next man.

Matthew promised to look after the stabling of Sabbath and keep her two trunks until she returned from Lady Ashford's. There would be room aplenty for them in the palace when everyone accompanying Her Majesty had departed. Sabre missed seeing the queen by half an hour, as she had already departed for Theobalds; however, there was a backup of her baggage train and attendants, and in turn their luggage and servants. She despaired of finding Lady Kate Ashford in the throng, for it seemed people were too busy to give her more than vague directions at best.

The halls and corridors of the palace were most confusing to Sabre. She went right, then left, then right again, ascending at least three flights of stairs in her search for her aunt. Finally a young page, curious about the new face, ushered her to the rooms where the queen's wardrobe was housed, and she came face-to-face with a woman who looked considerably older than she remembered. The two women stared at each other rudely for the space of about two minutes, then Sabre took a deep breath and ventured, "Lady Ashford? . . . Aunt Kate?"

The tall woman, who at one time must have been quite handsome, ruefully pursed her lips and said bluntly, "So, they stuck me with the redhead after all!"

"I'm afraid so," said Sabre, mirroring her aunt's rueful expression.

Suddenly Kate's eyes gleamed with a hint of humor. "In chapel this morning I asked both God and the devil to send me an extra pair of hands . . . it looks like one of them has complied!"

Sabre smiled and dropped her a curtsy; she knew they would be able to get along tolerably well together.

Kate Ashford talked incessantly. She never shut up. She was a well of information, advice, instruction, and gossip, and she set about Sabre's education with a vengeance. "Actually, you couldn't have arrived at a better time. The queen has gone on progress and left me behind to clean and refurbish all the wardrobe she didn't take with her. A vast undertaking," she said, shaking her head. "Her Majesty has at least two hundred gowns— and that's just at Greenwich . . . same thing at Windsor and Hampton Court." Her sentences ran into one another, allowing Sabre only space enough to nod her understanding.

"Faugh! The palace stenches. Let's get these windows open. These progresses are ostensibly so her people can see her at every little country burgh along the way, but in reality the progress was designed to empty this place, which has housed fifteen hundred bodies all winter—fifteen hundred unwashed bodies, by the reek of it," she

said, wrinkling her nose. "By God's feet, they had better
get the privies emptied before the weather gets any hot-
ter, or we will all be down with the plague!" She scarcely
reached for a breath before going back to the subject of
her own responsibilities. "It's not only the dresses, it's the
underpinnings, the shoes, the jewelry to be cleaned and
repaired, to say nothing of the *wigs*!" She said the last
word in a loud stage whisper and rolled her eyes. "I've
two assistants who between them haven't the brains of a
louse. At least you look as if you might have initiative. I
shall have to pay you out of my own household purse. Of
course, the palace will provide your room and board, so
eat until you positively groan, 'tis the only thing you'll
ever get out of her. She's so tightfisted she'd cut a raisin
in half! That's another advantage of a progress, d'ye see?
The poor bloody gentry she visits get stuck scouring their
countryside and neighbors to feed and entertain over a
thousand people, and all so she'll dance in their bloody
manor houses. Well, enough of this chatter. I'll give you
one of our chambers, it will only be a tiny space, but at
least it will have a bed and a window, which is a luxury in
itself. Would you believe there are rooms without windows at Greenwich? Now you'll be on the third floor, so
get your bearings . . . Sara, is it?"

"No, ma'am. I am called Sabre . . . Sabre Wilde."

Kate gave her a penetrating look. "Ah, yes, I remember now." Kate took her to the small room on the third
floor and instructed, "As soon as you get settled, come
back down to the wardrobe and I'll put you to work. The
dresses need sponging—under the arms—sweat stains
you won't believe! And that damned white paste she
daubs all over her face; 'tis made of egg white, alum, and

borax. Borax is hell to clean off ruffs and . . . *wigs.*"
Again she whispered the dreaded word.

Now that she was alone for a few minutes, Sabre adjusted herself to the smallness of the room. There was at least a comfortable bed with decent covers. There was a cupboard built into the corner to hold her dresses, and a small washstand with bowl and pitcher, and the cupboard beneath the bowl held a chamber pot. By far what made the room habitable were the tall windows that reached from floor to ceiling. She grasped the window handle, pushed it open, and stepped out onto a tiny stone balcony. She pulled back the heavy drapes as far as they would go and left the window open to air the room; this high up from the ground she needn't worry about intruders.

Again she needed the services of a page to direct her back to the stables, where it took her another half hour to find Matthew. He took her trunks up to the tiny chamber, then they faced each other and said in unison, "I don't think we'd better be seen together." They laughed, reading each other's thoughts, and Sabre said, "When we meet we must pretend it is for the first time. If anyone asks about me, all you know is that I am Lady Kate Ashford's niece. Now, I suppose you must have business with the high-and-mighty Lord Devonport, and if the knave is curious as to what his wife looks like, tell him I am toothless, cross-eyed, and positively avid to have him dash up to Blackmoor to bed me!"

"Oh, I won't have to worry about Hawk for a while," he said airily. "He's gone on progress with the queen."

Sabre's face fell. Damn the man, dancing attendance upon a woman whenever she crooked her finger at him, merely because she was a queen. Well, before she was

finished with him, he'd dance for her, dance as pretty as a
corpse on the end of a hangman's rope!

Sabre didn't bother to unpack her trunks, as she felt
she had neglected her aunt as long as she dared. These
first few days she would work hard to gain Kate's respect
and secure her position. She would absorb everything like
a sponge, and what better teacher than the talkative mistress of the queen's robes?

"There you are, child," welcomed Kate in her deep
voice. "I've already sorted out the busks and petticoats
and ruffs for the laundry maids. I have to keep an accu-
rate tally, you know. The blasted wenches would steal me
blind otherwise. You see, every article of the queen's underclothing is embroidered with her monogram, *Elizabeth Regina,* and a crown, see? They'd be flogging them
in the back streets—ten pounds for the queen's drawers
—can't you picture it? So one of our responsibilities is
output and input; it must tally exactly. Now you start
sponging these gowns. Some of the more elaborate sleeves
are detachable. In a few days we will go over them all
again to sew on the jewels and beads that are ready to fall
off. Now, I've just to check on the girls I set to cleaning
Her Majesty's wardrobe of shoes, slippers, and boots. She
has over five hundred pairs, you know."

Sabre's mouth fell slightly open at such extravagance.
She herself owned a pair of small riding boots for outdoors and a pair of soft black leather slippers for indoors.
Sabre sat herself upon a stool and took a soft soapy cloth
and began to clean the queen's gowns. The bodices were
stained with food, wine, sweat, and cosmetics, while the
skirts were soiled with mud, dust, and even stable drop-
pings.

When Kate returned she took up a stool next to Sabre and worked on the gowns diligently.

"I've never seen such rich, ornate garments in my life," said Sabre, stroking the jewel-encrusted velvet.

"The court must encapsulate the majesty and mystique of the monarchy. A great queen must have a setting worthy of her. Its visual impact must be stunning. Her ladies are supposed to act as mere foils so that the queen stands out in sharp relief. Let me warn you . . . the merest hint that their attractions exceed her own sets Her Majesty aflame, and our sovereign in full temper is an awesome sight to behold and terrible to suffer. She is moody, demanding, and her temper is alarmingly erratic. Occasionally she beats her ladies, but usually her assaults are purely verbal. She has a sarcastic tongue and a withering wit, which makes her an object of terror. Her ladies are required to wear white or other insipid hues so that these bejeweled ensembles appear to best effect. None must eclipse her. All must sublimate their individuality in order to glorify the cult of Gloriana!"

"You hate her?" It was more a statement than a question.

Kate looked up and blinked rapidly. "Nay, that would be treason. We love her."

"But if she reduces everyone to tears and makes life unbearable, why do ladies vie for positions at court?" asked Sabre.

"Ah, but she is multifaceted, do you not see? She is often kind and gracious. She can be affable, familiar, and friendly; beguiling, even. Her smiles and endearments can warm your heart. She never bores you. She casts a golden spell over all. Women cannot resist the siren song of her

court. Besides, where else are the pickings so good to find
a rich man?"

Sabre laughed at her aunt's wicked humor. She spoke
the bloody unvarnished truth!

The palace population had thinned down to a few hundred servants and a handful of courtiers by the time Kate
took Sabre along to the dining hall. There was no lack of
dishes even though the queen wasn't in residence. If anything, the wine flowed more freely and the trestle tables
groaned under their burden of food.

"Usually after supper there are masques and balls on
special feast days, and dancing and cards until midnight
on ordinary days, but of course there will be nothing
going on tonight. I, for one, am grateful. I shall be happy
to lay my weary bones in my bed this night."

"It has been a long day for me too. Aunt Kate, I appreciate what you have done for me," Sabre said quietly.

"Pshaw, child, 'tis a pleasure to have a new pair of ears
to bend. Rumor has it I like the sound of my own voice."
She laughed and patted Sabre on the shoulder. "Shall we
go upstairs now?"

Sabre was glad to have Kate accompany her, because
for the life of her she could not tell one corridor from
another. In her small chamber she was relieved to be
alone. She was also relieved that she had her first day
behind her; she had made a good start. Now she saw it
was an advantage to have the queen away, for it would
give her time to become familiar with the palace and its
workings before Elizabeth and her court returned.

She lit the candles in the sconce and, stripping off her
dress, hung it in the cupboard. Then she splashed water
from the jug into the bowl and washed her face and neck.
She then stripped off her little busk and washed her

breasts and beneath her arms. She took off her shoes, stockings, petticoat, and drawers and washed her long, slim legs and feet.

Dressed in black from head to foot, Shane Hawkhurst drew his black cloak about him and stepped through the window of his apartment on the fourth floor of Greenwich Palace. He remained motionless until his eyes became accustomed to the darkness, then smoothly, with fluid motions, climbed across two balconies and, with great stealth, dropped to a stone balcony on the third floor. His eyes searched the darkness for any movement in the grounds below; then a blurred motion inside the room caught his attention. He saw a young woman squeeze the water from a pair of stockings and reach her arms up high to hang them over the wall mirror to dry. She was as naked as the day she was born! He caught his breath as she knelt before a trunk and searched inside for something she apparently could not locate.

Sabre knew she had packed two lawn smocks for sleeping, but realized they must be in the other trunk. *"Peste!"* she swore in French, then looked up toward the windows. With the drapes undrawn she suddenly felt very exposed. Reason told her she was up too high to be observed, yet she needed to draw the curtains for her own modesty, since it would take her a while to locate her night rail. She stood up and advanced to the window.

Hawkhurst's physical response to the naked young woman was immediate and pronounced. As he stood motionless, hot blood surged into his loins, wiping out all thoughts except one. He stared unblinking lest he miss one moment of the lovely vision displayed before him. Her breasts thrust upward, deliciously round and tempt-

ing above a waist that was only a man's hand span, but
the most exquisite thing about her was her hair. It fell to
her hips in a coppery cloud. He licked his lips, which had
suddenly gone dry, for now she was so close he could
have reached out a hand to touch her. As she reached up
to pull the drapes across the window he was startled to
see that her face was also beautiful.

Robbed of his vision, he felt cheated, angry as a dog
separated from its meat. He was just about to push open
the casement and step inside to take what he desired
when he suddenly remembered that the baron was waiting for him, and worse, he had left him too long where he
would be exposed to danger. How could he have forgotten what he was about? The pulsing insistence between
his legs did nothing to improve his temper, and he cursed
the wench who had aroused his lust so easily.

The next day the cleaning of the palace began in earnest. Every casement and window was thrown wide to
allow the stale air to escape and fresh air to rush in. Men
and women cleaners were sweeping out old rushes, removing cobwebs and dust from gilt picture frames, wall
sconces, and ceiling cornices, scrubbing floors, and rubbing each piece of furniture with beeswax and turpentine.

Sabre worked on the queen's gowns once more with
Kate at her elbow, absorbing every word of advice and
gossip that dropped from her aunt's lips. At lunch she
was introduced to a group of ladies who had not, for one
reason or another, accompanied Her Majesty. Katherine
and Philadelphia Carey, two sisters who had not the
means to travel in the style expected on progress, sat at a
table with Lady Leighton, Lady Holby, and Lady Barow.
All were very friendly and relaxed, for usually meals

were served with a maximum of formality. Usually a lady-in-waiting rubbed each plate with bread and salt, then bowed three times. Each dish was tasted for poison and then the meat was presented to the queen for her to carve off the portions she desired. All such formalities were abandoned today.

Sabre, observing the gowns of the other women, decided hers were old-fashioned, almost prim. She must procure scissors and thread and tonight restyle the necklines of her three gowns. Today she wore the pale green, and although she knew the color did wonderful things for her, she glanced down at the modest bodice, making note of just how she could cut it to expose her breasts, lest she be laughed at as a country bumpkin.

The Carey sisters wore only simple pearls and one ring apiece, but the jewels of the other ladies caught Sabre's admiration. She had seen portraits of Elizabeth that showed her wearing rings on every finger, and her ladies obviously copied the style. Sabre did not possess one piece of jewelry, but her mind now set to work on how she could acquire some.

"We are so dull here now that the queen has left, we are positively moped to death," complained Lady Holby.

"There's absolutely no excuse for it! I've decided to throw a small party tomorrow evening," said Lady Leighton, "and I've talked Lady Barow into helping me. Would you care to join us, Lady Ashford?" They used each other's titles with deference.

"I'm glad of the time to myself to just rest, thank you, ladies, but perhaps my niece Sabre would enjoy your generous hospitality. She is new to court from the country and needs to cultivate as many friendships as she can while the vultures are away."

"Aye, she is pretty," conceded Philadelphia Carey, "she'll have no trouble making enemies with that face."

Sabre smiled. "Your name is unusual."

"Yours, too, is an odd name and will serve to draw attention," said Philadelphia.

Lady Anne Leighton lowered her voice. "Spread the word to as many men as you can. You'd be surprised at the number of gentlemen who haven't accompanied the queen, and every last one of them will be looking for diversion."

Katherine Carey's eyes shone as she warmed to the subject. "Last night I saw the Fox and the Gypsy, and 'tis rumored the Sea God hasn't left yet."

Sabre was momentarily puzzled, until Kate laughed and said, "Most of the men at court have code names personally selected by Her Majesty."

Anne Leighton winked saucily. "All the ones worth bedding, at any rate!"

Sabre was shocked, for she was almost certain that Lady Leighton was married.

"God's blood, I'm perished with all these windows open," her aunt said. "I hate to admit it, but my bones feel every draft these days. Sabre, be a good girl and fetch me a shawl from my chamber."

Sabre left the long dining hall and hesitated a moment over the direction she should take. She decided the wardrobe rooms were to the right, but then she turned left to the staircase that led to the corridor, which in turn opened to the central staircase leading to the third-floor apartments. One more turn found her in a part of the palace she had not seen before. She was at a crossover point for two wide hallways; one contained many doors, while the other was a long, mirrored gallery.

She spun about and tried to retrace her steps, but nothing looked remotely familiar and she realized that she was lost. She sighed with relief when she saw a gentleman advancing toward her from the mirrored gallery. As the distance closed between them she realized he must be a noble of some rank, for his clothes were richly flamboyant. He wore scarlet, slashed with black. His thigh-high boots were of supple black leather with startling scarlet linings where they were folded down from their tops. He wore a short, rakish cape in the latest fashion, which emphasized the unbelievable breadth of his shoulders.

Sabre's knees turned to water as she saw the white teeth flash against the deep tan of his face. He was such a handsome rogue that her blood seemed to thicken and slow in her veins. They were so close, she imagined she felt the heat of his tall, muscular body. "Sir," she breathed, startled at the sudden huskiness of her voice, "I'm hopelessly lost."

He gazed down at her in mock solemnity. "So am I, mistress." His hand covered his heart.

Her lashes swept to her cheeks, then her green eyes flashed up at him. "Pray, m'lord, do not mock me."

He took her small hand in his strong brown one. "This way, sweeting."

"But—but I haven't told you where I wish to go," she protested weakly.

They were in a secluded alcove, and as he looked down at her she realized his grin and his intent were wicked!

Hawk was delighted to discover that the temptress's eyes were like pale green pools. He'd lain awake hours picturing their color. His own, a shade of deep indigo, raked her now as he pictured again the nubile curves she offered beneath the gown. His eyes were playing with her

body, and she realized that in another moment it would
be more than his eyes. He lifted her high against him and
took her mouth in a teasing kiss. Power and forcefulness
emanated from him. He had enough muscle to make her
feel completely dominated. She opened her lips to deny
him, but his mouth came down hard on hers, silencing
her objections with a fierce, devouring kiss. Hot waves of
sensation were sweeping through her body. Quickly she
pulled her mouth from his, and as she did so she noticed
the tip of his tongue. My God, she thought wildly, would
he put his wicked tongue in her mouth?

Her hand swept back and the stinging slap startled him
momentarily. It was the last thing he was expecting. He
lowered her feet to the ground and with narrowed eyes
demanded, "What game is this you play, mistress?"

"You lecher. . . ." Her breasts heaved with her outrage. "You—you . . . ravisher of virgins!"

He laughed, genuinely amused at the quaint phrase.
"Virgin? I think not, sweeting. You invite me to take you
to an alcove by pretending to be lost, then tease me with
slaps and deny me what you were just begging for."

"Pretending . . . oh, you damned rake . . . to take
advantage of my innocence," she stammered.

"Innocence?" He laughed. "Any woman who has been
at this court longer than twenty-four hours has lost her
innocence."

Her eyes blazed their outrage. "I have been here exactly twenty-three hours—you have one hour left in
which to debauch me!" she challenged, and suddenly he
felt he was in the wrong. Her nearness had had the same
throbbing physical effect upon him as the previous night.
Usually he had an iron control over his body, and it irritated him that this little wench, with her flaming hair,

could so easily make him lose that control. He bowed formally. "May I escort you, mistress?"

"Go to hell!" she snapped, and turning upon her heel, she marched off as if she knew exactly where she was going.

"Little bitch!" He swore under his breath. "Rebuffs me when I play the man, rebuffs me when I play the gentleman." He stood staring after her. Was she an innocent or a practiced courtesan? Either way she needed a good bedding!

Kate found Sabre lost in a trance, staring from the window of her chamber. "Wake up, sleeping beauty. I thought you'd been kidnapped."

"Aunt Kate, quickly, who is that man riding off on that black stallion?" She pointed her finger through the glass.

"Ah, no wonder your senses have been addled. That's the Sea God! All the women are hot as bitches in heat for him."

I wouldn't spit on him if he was on fire, thought Sabre vulgarly, but she knew she was lying through her teeth.

"Come, dear, if we can get a few dozen gowns finished this afternoon, we can start cleaning her jewelry tomorrow. You'll take such delight in the jewels, Sabre. Any woman would sell her soul for them. Wait until I unlock some of her coffers. You did very well to get an invitation from Anne Leighton for tomorrow night. I hope you know how to play cards. She'll have gambling to lure the men, don't you see?"

Sabre didn't know how to play cards very well and thought about consulting Matthew. "Isn't Lady Leighton married?"

"Of course, both she and Mary Barow. Their husbands are off fighting in Holland with Leicester. But of course it wouldn't make a scrap of difference if they were present tomorrow night. All husbands and wives at court learn to turn a blind eye where advantageous liaisons are concerned." Kate gave her a sharp look. "You must keep a shrewd head on your shoulders and quickly sort out the strong protectors from the weak, else you'll be like a lamb to slaughter. Keep your legs crossed until you settle on a victim, and for God's sake have the wit not to be undone by a handsome face."

Before she retired for the night, Sabre made her way by stealth to Matthew's chamber. A low knock brought his dear familiar voice to her before he even opened the door. "Come in, sweetheart, you're early . . . oh, Sabre, it's you."

"I'm in trouble!" she said urgently.

He drawled, "That's what all the ladies tell me."

"Oh, Matt!" She laughed. "You shouldn't say such things to me . . . 'tis indecent."

He winked at her. "You shouldn't understand the innuendo. Come in before anyone sees you." He had just finished shaving. He rinsed his ivory-handled razor, then poured them each a glass of wine. She sat beside a small table and took a sip of the blood-red wine. "Not so powerful as brandy," she commented.

"Ah, but perhaps more subtle. You expect brandy to pack a punch, but often by the time you realize you have imbibed too much wine, your inhibitions have fled and it is too late."

"Thank you for the warning. I've been invited by Lady Anne Leighton to a party she is giving tomorrow night, and I must learn all about playing cards."

"Sabre, I've been gambling a lifetime and Hawk can beat me nine hands out of ten. You can't learn to play cards in one lesson."

"Well, teach me something . . . how to fake . . . or how to cheat!"

He looked at her with raised brows. "Are you serious? Would you really cheat?"

"My own grandmother," she said, wrinkling her nose at him.

"Let's see. I could teach you how to play sant, perhaps." He handed her a deck of playing cards. "Take out all the cards lower than seven. We play with only thirty-two." He laughed as she dropped more than she held, but soon she was handling them with dexterity and began to shuffle and riffle them as she had seen others do. "There are four suits and the ace is high," he explained patiently. "Now deal each of us twelve cards."

She listened carefully, intent upon learning the game.

"They'll play for stakes; money usually," he warned her.

She lost badly and he said, "You now owe me one gold piece."

"Oh, Matt, it's too hard!" she wailed.

He leered. "That's what all the—"

"—ladies tell you," she finished for him, and slapped him for his naughtiness. It took her over an hour, but she managed to start winning.

"You play very well," he complimented.

She flashed her green eyes at him and teased, "That's what all the gentlemen tell me."

He found her delicious company and regretted that he had invited another female to spend the evening with him.

"Well, I'd better leave before your guest arrives." She sighed and stood up.

"Sabre, if you'll stay, I could get rid of her," he offered.

"Matt, please don't spoil our lovely friendship with all that other rubbish." She gave him a quick kiss on the cheek and was gone.

Damn, thought Matt, *I didn't even warn her that Hawk is still in the palace.* After giving it some thought he scribbled a note, found her room, and pushed it beneath her door.

She didn't see it until she was about to blow out her candles. It read, *Sabre: I must warn you that Hawk is still in residence. I will try to learn when he leaves on progress. Matt.*

She caught her breath as she read the words. Hatred for the man rose up in her like a fever. Her Irish blood targeted him as the enemy. She would learn every intimate thing about him there was to know. She would discover his likes and dislikes, his haunts, his habits, his strengths and his weaknesses. She clenched her fists as she lay in her bed. Silently she vowed that when she had discovered his weaknesses, she would destroy him.

Chapter 7

Sabre awoke early with heightened anticipation that to-day might be the day she would meet *him*. She only knew that they were both here at Greenwich, that she could see him, and that when she did she must look beautiful. She took her cream gown from the cupboard and cut a heart-shaped neckline into the bodice. The knowledge that it had been intended for her wedding gown fanned the flames of her anger toward the man who had made a mockery of that occasion.

She missed breakfast so that she could finish altering the gown, then she went off to find Kate without taking time to try it on. Today Kate took Sabre into the queen's privy chamber and on through to her bedchamber.

"Her Majesty took a great deal of jewelry with her, and of course the lord chancellor has the keys to her jewels for state occasions, but that still leaves me with a heavy burden of responsibility for the rest of her jewels." She unlocked a large cabinet that contained dozens of drawers. Each one held a jeweled caul or neck whisk sewn all over with every gem under the sun. As well as diamonds, rubies, emeralds, and pearls, there were milky opals, purple garnets, green peridots, and incredible blue-green Ceylon sapphires.

The top drawer held a tray of loose jewels that had fallen from the queen's priceless gowns and cauls, and Kate set about affixing the missing gems into the intricate patterns on the stiffened cloth.

Sabre, using vinegar, a tiny brush, and a chamois cloth, cleaned the cauls and neck whisks and bejeweled ruffs and laid them out to dry. In the late afternoon Kate unlocked a large casket containing necklaces and brooches of semiprecious jewels. Their variety and color took Sabre's breath away. She ran her finger over coral, jade, topaz, jet, and crystal, and coveted every one of them.

"Give them all a quick once-over," her aunt instructed. "She seldom wears them anyway, and I'll be back to lock the casket when you're done. After that I think you deserve a little rest before tonight's festivities. My feet feel like two plates of meat the dogs have been gnawing. I'll have trays sent up to us instead of going to the dining hall."

As soon as Kate turned her back, Sabre lifted the necklaces from the casket and held them to her own neck in front of the mirror. Her eyes were as iridescent as the jewels she admired. How could one woman own so much? It wasn't fair!

She lifted a jade necklace studded with turquoise. One great pear-shaped turquoise as big as a pigeon's egg dangled from its center. She held it to her neck with reverence, her fingers caressing the large turquoise drop possessively. Why not? she asked herself as her pulses quickened with the danger. The colors looked so right on her, as if they had been especially designed to contrast with her flaming tresses and deepen the shade of her eyes. She'd return it tomorrow before anyone noticed it was gone.

Quickly, before her courage deserted her, she stuffed the necklace far down into her busk, wriggled about until it seated itself there with a minimum of discomfort, and set about cleaning the contents of the jewel casket with a vengeance.

Kate did a cursory inspection and nodded with satisfaction at the sparkling richness her niece's efforts had uncovered. Sabre refused to think about the specifics of how she would return the necklace on the morrow, for she felt confident that a way would be found.

Tonight she drew her drapes before she bathed. She shivered with excitement as she took the lovely cream gown from her cupboard. Her blood sang with the delicious anticipation of her first party at the palace. Kate had warned her about the men's advances and she had tasted a sample of such behavior firsthand. Tasted . . . the word brought a blush to her cheeks. The blush deepened as she saw how the rounded globes of her breasts thrust from the much-lowered neckline. The heart shape seemed to cup and push her breasts forward in a positively wanton show.

Her heartbeat quickened as her fingers fastened the jade necklace, and she gasped as the heavy turquoise dropped into the valley between the swells of her breasts. It was designed to draw every male eye. She took her brush and swept up her hair in the very latest fashion. It exposed her neck at the sides and back to show off the necklace to its full advantage.

She carefully counted out ten gold pieces to wager on cards and slipped them into the tiny change purse that dangled from her wrist. She picked up her fan and hurried down to the second-floor music gallery. Already the gathering numbered sixty or seventy, and it was yet early. Lady Mary Barow greeted her warmly with a kiss and whispered, "There are at least two males to every female, so I think we can claim success."

Sabre felt alarmingly self-conscious. The eyes of the men seemed to be fastened upon her breasts as if they were waiting for the moment when they would pop from the restraint of the low bodice. She kept glancing down with alarm, until she sternly chided herself for being a coward. After all, were not the tempting female fashions designed specifically to lure men's eyes?

She sat upon a low stool near a group of ladies who were showing off their skills with lutes, harps, and virginals. She loved the music and gave it her rapt attention. Anne Vasavour was singing a love song, her large expressive eyes giving added subtle meaning to the words. Sabre felt her cheeks warm and raised her fan to cool herself. As she did so she glanced about and saw at least a dozen men watching her with speculative eyes. A sigh of relief escaped her lips as she saw Matthew come toward her. She arose and gave him her cheek to kiss, as was obviously the fashion.

"Oh, Matt, thank you for coming."

"Did you get my note?" he asked.

"Yes. Have you spoken with him yet?"

"Ah, yes. I've had my audience with His Lordship and managed to convey the impression that I had delivered his dutiful bride to Blackmoor."

"He didn't seem suspicious?" she asked.

"The thought didn't occur to him that anyone, least of all a woman, would disobey his orders." He frowned and said, "I'm off to Calais in the morning for a load of expensive French silks. Sabre, promise me you won't do anything foolish while I'm gone." His eyes kept lowering to her breasts; he didn't seem to even notice the magnificent necklace.

"Matt, would you be a darling and get me some wine?"

The moment he left her, half a dozen admirers joined him and asked for introductions to the voluptuous new quarry. At the same moment Philadelphia Carey joined

Sabre. "Are you going to be selfish with that devastatingly handsome rogue or will you be generous enough to introduce me, Sabre?"

Matt brought her wine and the men formed a semicircle about her. "Sabre, I'd like you to meet a few people." He said the names one after another without stopping. "Lord Oxford, James Clinton, Sir John Heneage, Anthony Bacon, de Villiers the French ambassador, and William Herbert, who I believe is the earl of Pembroke's son. Gentlemen, may I present Mistress Sabre Wilde, niece of Lady Kate Ashford and newly arrived at court."

Each took his turn to press a lingering kiss upon her hand while she murmured, "M'lord," to each face she could not pin a name to. A little push from behind reminded her of Philadelphia. "Matt, I would like you to meet my friend Philadelphia Carey—this is Matthew Hawkhurst."

The girl's eyes widened in appreciation. "Are you brother to Lord Devonport?"

"No," said Matthew, teasing her, "he is brother to me! Would you ladies care for some cards?" asked Matthew, trying to draw them away from the other men; but as they moved off toward the card tables, the men tagged along to stand about and watch. He seated Sabre to his right and Philadelphia to his left. James Clinton quickly filled the fourth seat. Matt said smoothly, "Shall we play sant? I think it's a game the ladies particularly enjoy."

Sabre puzzled over how four could play when there wouldn't be enough cards, but of course Matt put into play two packs of thirty-two cards and her frown disappeared. Sabre lost every hand and her small supply of gold coins was soon gone. Finally she won money from James Clinton and suspected that he had let her win. She didn't mind if she won or lost because she was enjoying the challenge, the witty repartee, the laughter, and the admiring glances.

The wine flowed freely; she felt reckless and as a consequence lost the rest of her money. Philadelphia flirted openly with Matthew, accidentally touching his hands and his knees beneath the table. A look of alarm clouded Matthew's face as he gazed across the room.

"What is it?" asked Sabre softly, following his gaze.

"Trouble," said Matt. "Here comes—"

Sabre stiffened. "I know perfectly well who it is," she said coldly, "Her Majesty's darling Sea God."

Hawk jerked his head slightly and Matthew obeyed the silent order instantly, relinquishing his chair at the table.

Philadelphia stood when Matt stood, unwilling to be parted from him yet. When the lady stood, James Clinton politely got to his feet and Hawkhurst's bark of laughter mocked them. "That leaves just the lady to play with me," he said suggestively.

Sabre flashed him a glance as cold as green ice. "I'm afraid not; thankfully I've lost all my money," she said with relish, and started to rise.

A strong brown hand unceremoniously fell to her shoulder to prevent her from rising. "No matter, we'll play for this little bauble."

She gasped as she felt the jade-and-turquoise necklace lifted from her with deft fingers and placed on the table between them. Her mouth was dry; quickly she glanced about for Matt, but the young coward had abandoned her to the Sea God.

His face was stamped with strength and humor and male arrogance. He was dominating and unpredictable and dangerous. The last words she had said to him hovered between them. *Go to hell!* She wanted to shout it now but made an attempt to stifle the deep physical antagonism she felt at his nearness.

"I cannot play for such high stakes, my lord. You take advantage . . . I am only learning to play."

His eyes were cold, his mouth unsmiling. "Whenever we meet, you whine. First I'm taking advantage of your innocence, now I'm taking advantage of your ignorance."

She swallowed the bait instantly, anger flaming through her veins at the insulting words.

"For God's sake, 'tis only a game," he scoffed. But she knew it was a deadly game. She knew the outcome and so did he. It was as if he knew the necklace was not hers and he would deliberately and effectively relieve her of it.

"What stakes do you put up, m'lord?"

"What do you suggest?" he asked.

She looked deep into his eyes, although it was an effort for her to pretend calm. "You have nothing I want," she said slowly, emphasizing each word.

His predator's grin flashed her a promise that before he was finished with her, she would want something from him, beg something from him.

"Five hundred crowns, then; all women want money." The sum he named was outrageous, his manner boldly insolent.

She felt a need to be as bold as he. The odds were heavily against her, so she evened them to fifty-fifty. "Let's just cut for high card. I refuse to sit and play out this farce."

With a flourish he offered her the deck. She drew a ten; he drew a knave. "How apt," she snapped. Sabre snatched up her fan and almost overturned her chair in an effort to escape him, but he caught hold of her wrist and said low, "I have apartments on the fourth floor. If you play your cards right"—he dangled the necklace before her eyes—"I can be a very generous man."

Anger and hatred almost robbed her of speech. She pierced him with an icy green look of contempt. "Go to hell!" Her legs trembled as she swept across the room, putting as much distance as she could between them, and yet she knew she must not let that necklace out of her sight. She refused to think of the nightmare that awaited her if she could not get it back. She had no choice but to follow him. She would find out which were his apartments and somehow steal back the necklace. She surreptitiously watched him from the tail of her eye. Damn, every woman in the room approached him, laughed up at him with open invitation in her eyes. He attracted women as if he had a bloody magnet in his chest, she thought angrily.

At last he managed to extract himself and left the gallery. She didn't even murmur a polite excuse to the poor gallant who had wasted half an hour's compliments on her. She followed him at a discreet distance to the fourth floor of the palace and was surprised to see how close his apartment was to Matthew's room. She waited until he had been inside for a good five minutes, then crept along to Matt's door; but it was locked and no light came from beneath it. Suddenly she heard a door opening and barely had time to slip around a corner and press herself to the wall. She heard footsteps going the other way and let out a sigh of relief. She gathered enough courage to peep around the corner and was just in time to see a tall figure in a black cloak descend the stairs.

He had had just enough time to put the necklace away safely and leave again. She knew she must not hesitate.

She must act now, for a chance like this was not likely to present itself again. She moved quickly down the corridor and slipped quietly into the room.

Her eyes widened. She was in a spacious, richly appointed bedroom, nothing like the small cell she occupied. Beyond this chamber, through an archway, was another, which she supposed was a sitting room where he could entertain.

The great bed, curtained in red velvet, dominated the room, and the pile of the thick carpet was so deep, the toes of her slippers disappeared. The room boasted a fireplace topped by a marble mantel and a mirror that ran up to the ceiling. She caught her reflection and tucked up an errant copper curl that had fallen to her shoulder. Her mind was going over places where the necklace was most likely to be. She stiffened as deep within the mirror's depth she caught his reflection watching her.

He leaned casually against the archway. Gone was the doublet and his white shirt was unlaced all the way to the tight waistband of his black breeches. Their eyes were locked in the mirror and she found she could not break their gaze. The mocking look was gone, replaced by one that was as tender as a caress. "I knew you'd come," he said softly.

She saw him move toward her and still she was rooted to the spot, so hypnotic was his effect upon her. As his hands closed over her shoulders to turn her to him, a great shiver ran through her. He was too close, too big, too male, too damnably, overpoweringly handsome.

"I came for the necklace," she confessed.

"Did you?" he asked honestly, forcing her to acknowledge that it was not only the necklace that had drawn her. As she looked up into the tanned face, his dark unruly mane of hair tempted her fingers. It was as if there were some strange bond between them, as if she had known him from the beginning of time. He bent his head and she knew he was going to kiss her. The moment he molded his mouth to hers everything was swept away—her anger, her fear, her resistance.

His fingers took the pins from her hair, then buried themselves in the coppery cascade. His hands left her hair and cupped her face tenderly, drawing her mouth up to his again. He whispered against her lips, "I'm half in love with you and I don't even know your name."

"Sabre," she whispered, "Sabre Wilde."

He buried his lips in hers again. His kiss was lingering and so compelling, she felt it all the way down to her knees. She melted against him, her breasts crushed against his hard, muscular chest. He whispered against her mouth, "Shane Hawkhurst."

Her heart stopped, then began to hammer wildly as a million sparks exploded inside her brain. Guided by pure instinct, her hands went to his waistband and sought the handle of the knife she had vaguely noticed earlier. She drew it forth and stepped back panting. "Bastard!"

He threw back his head and laughed wholeheartedly, for she had named him correctly. "Little wildcat, the dagger suits you. Look at its handle."

She was disconcerted that he wasn't afraid or even the slightest bit alarmed that she had his knife. She glanced down at the dagger and saw its handle was fashioned in the shape of a wildcat. From somewhere he had produced its mate. "Now we each have one . . . a matched pair . . . keep it."

As she faced him the full realization that he was her husband hit her. England's law, aye, and God's law, too,

gave him the power of life and death over her. As she
faced him she realized she was wearing what should have
been her wedding gown and she was almost undone.
Tears sprang to her eyes for what might have been, then a
raging anger dried them instantly. This, then, was the
enemy. This was the one man she would know intimately, the one she would enslave, the one she would
destroy. How to begin? Instinctively she fell back on
parry and thrust. She curled her lip. "I came only for the
necklace. It is mine!"

The mockery was back in his eyes. "It is the queen's."

"Ha! Whatever gives you such a ridiculous notion?"

"I gave it to her. You must get it back from me and
replace it before you are discovered." His words told her
plainly her only alternative.

"In return for the necklace you actually expect me to
become your mistress?" she demanded hotly.

"Mistress? By God's blood, there's arrogance for you.
I had only one tumble in mind."

She was so stung by his words, she lunged at his gut
with the knife. He set his teeth and almost crushed the
bones in her wrist. The dagger slipped to the carpet and
he swept her into his arms. His tongue flicked over her
lips. "How do I know you'd be any good?" he teased. His
lips traced a path up to the tempting little beauty mark
and he tongued it sensually.

"Since I'm untouched . . . I'd be only as good as you
made me."

Her words sent a surge of hot lust through his body.
His hands held her captive against his hardness. He
slanted an eyebrow at her. "Untouched? Unused? Unsul-
lied?" He paused, then whispered maddeningly, "Untrue!"

She answered him in kind. "Unwilling! Unyielding!" She paused, then whispered her challenge: "Untamed!" She bit him.

He held her eyes with his. "Life is a game. This is a game between us, Sabre, but if you want to play, you'd better know all the rules. In every game there is risk. In every game there is a winner and a loser."

"If you think I'm not going to win this game between us you are mistaken; badly mistaken. I have resolved to win!" She hated him with a passion. Her breasts heaved with her agitation and the pink nipples became more visible with each deep breath she took.

"Take off your clothes and let's see how you show," he taunted.

She pulled from his embrace, angry enough to kill him if she'd had her sabre in her hand. "Take off your clothes, my Lord Devonport, and let's see if *you* measure up!"

Very deliberately he took off the shirt and slowly turned before her so she could inspect him. The impact of his body stunned her. The taut muscles rippled across his chest and back, and across one incredibly wide shoulder blade was a dragon tattoo. Desire rose up in her like a hot tide sweeping through her body. She knew a raging need to be pressed against his naked length in the great bed. Incredibly, she wanted to touch him, taste him. Slay the dragon . . . or be slain. Her legs would not support her; she slipped to the rug, burried her face in her hands, and sobbed out her misery.

He did not lift her up, but lay on the floor with her and gathered her to him. "Hush, sweeting, don't cry. I enjoy being a cruel bastard. Mayhap you spoke the truth. But your innocence will be fleeting at court, my little wild-cat."

He smoothed the tumbled coppery tresses and shuddered at the feel of her hair beneath his fingers. He buried his face in it and groaned. "Let me be your protector, Sabre."

An easy conquest would bore him quickly. That she didn't want, couldn't afford. She knew he wished to seduce her that he might be the master; she wished to keep him desiring to seduce her, so she denied him. "I'll be no man's mistress! Only my husband will take my virginity," she vowed.

"We'll see about that," he taunted as he stood up. "I warn you, my efforts to change your mind will be relentless." Grinning wickedly, he offered his hands to her. She arose gracefully without his help, but not before he had been treated to a display of her exquisite breasts. Without a word he offered her the necklace and the dagger. She took both.

Alone in her room, she was exultant! She had won the first round and couldn't keep the smile from her face as she held the turquoise and jade to her neck and looked at her reflection in the mirror. " 'Fore God, I almost had him begging!"

Next morning she awoke with a heightened anticipation that the day or the night would bring them face-to-face again. It was child's play to replace the necklace when Kate unlocked the jewel caskets. She hadn't felt this alive in her life.

When she learned that Hawkhurst had actually gone to join the queen's progress she was stunned like a bird flown into a wall. She voiced every curse and invocation she'd ever heard and hurled them at the queen. How could she be jealous of an aging virago? But she was!

She resigned herself to an uneventful summer. She furthered her female friendships, learned to love the fascinating city of London, and with cool disdain kept the men of the court at arm's length.

When Matt returned from Calais he let her pick a length of expensive French silk from his cargo, and she chose a watered silk of pale lemon shot through with silver. He took her to dine at Gunter's in London, very fashionable; but it was a most daring thing to dine alone with a man. Matthew told her he was going home to visit his mother. She had been alone since Sebastian had died, and since Hawk could not undertake the filial responsibility, he must.

By August the queen's wardrobe had been refurbished. Kate was pleased with Sabre and insisted she wouldn't have managed alone one tenth of what they had accomplished together.

Sabre had had a busy day. Kate asked for her assistance while she went into the city. They had, with the help of an armed guard, taken the queen's broken jewelry to the goldsmith's in Lombard Street and the broken fans to the fanmaker's in Eastcheap. Elizabeth seldom threw anything away, so everything had to be tallied on long descriptive lists and copies given to the craftsmen making the repairs.

She had still made time to exercise Sabbath, for she had begun to really enjoy her rides along the river. She didn't discourage gentlemen from joining her, but always made sure she accepted more than one escort.

Her small chamber felt airless, so before she climbed into bed, she opened the casement just a crack. Tomorrow she promised herself she would begin cutting the pattern for the new silk gown.

* * *

The farther from London the queen's progress traveled, the more Shane Hawkhurst's thoughts lingered on Greenwich. He cursed the time he must waste in useless social activities that had taken them all over East Anglia, ending up in Norwich. Bess kept him at her side, along with Robin Devereux, the young earl of Essex. He and Essex were not friends, yet they were not enemies either. Rather they were rivals for the queen's affection and patronage, and between them managed to manipulate her rather well. For if she gave a favor to one, then in fairness she would reward the other. Bess had made Essex her master of horse, since his stepfather, her beloved Dudley, the Earl of Leicester, was off commanding her troops in Holland. To prevent jealousy she had made Lord Devonport a gentleman pensioner, a member of the Queen's Own Guard.

Hawkhurst lay with his arms crossed behind his head, his body sated for the moment but his mind in turmoil. His companion was piqued at the fact that five minutes after he had made love to her, he was again a distant stranger. He hadn't even bothered to remove his shirt or breeches.

"You never kissed me, Lord Devonport," the queen's lady-in-waiting said, pouting prettily.

He turned absently toward her and was shocked to see how shopworn she looked. *No wonder,* he thought with disgust. *Essex, Southampton, and I pass the queen's ladies around as casually as a shared bottle of wine.* All to alleviate the boredom of cooling our heels, dancing attendance while Bess ignored impending threats from every direction. She had no foreign policy, but shifted with the wind and somehow survived, even flourished. She was assailed from the north by Scotland. France was going to dishonor its treaty with her to make a separate peace with Spain. That country's king, Philip, was at this moment building his great Invincible Armada, so it was no wonder the Irish intended to seize this time for rebellion to free themselves from the English yoke. Yet here they dallied night after night, filling their hours with fireworks and fornication!

Lady Mary Howard slipped from the bed and brought back two silken cords, which she held out to him. "Would you like to play a game, Lord Devonport?"

He cynically realized it was a new diversion Essex must have taught her. He noticed how brilliantly her eyes shone at the thought of being tied so he could have his way with her. Hell's fire, the wench was so willing, where was the thrill? After the erotic practices he had learned on his voyages to exotic lands, this was tame fare indeed. He stifled a yawn and prepared to enter the game. She regretted it later when he forgot to untie her before rolling over in a sound sleep.

The next day began badly for Hawkhurst when the earl of Southampton, having lost a vast sum to him dicing, kept drawling sarcastic barbs directed at his integrity. His irritating lisp exacerbated Hawk's temper. Southampton was the type of youth who could be vicious as a dog when the mood was upon him, or appealing as a playful puppy when everything was going his way.

Hawkhurst, always on a short fuse, had laid the youth out flat, all sprawling six feet of him. Then, to make matters worse, Bess had had petulant words with him and Essex about the stallions they rode. Essex had acquiesced and chosen a gelding, but Hawkhurst was damned if he would.

Before the sun began its afternoon descent into the western sky, he found himself booted and spurred and riding the hundred miles that separated him from Greenwich. Sabre Wilde . . . the punishing ride would be worth it when he sought release between her thighs. After Bess's close company for a month he needed his freedom, he needed to feel the powerful stallion beneath him, and the wind in his hair.

As he climbed to the third-floor balcony and swung his legs across the stone balustrade, he mocked himself for a fool. What if another warmed her bed? He had ridden most of the night hell-bent for leather, only to hesitate at the last moment. He slipped quietly into the room and crossed to the bed. The moonlight spilled across her, showing that she had twisted free from the coverlet and lay in a pristine lawn smock. He was aroused by the sight of her, but it was her innocence that sent desire flooding through his veins.

He searched the room for evidence of a lover. The cupboard held only three gowns, and her other possessions were quickly and thoroughly tallied—no gifts, no jewels, only a small store of coins. He knew a need to wake her, to see her green eyes widen at his presence. He ached to touch her, taste her, fill her with his great heat, but he crushed the raw cravings he felt rather than disturb one moment of her peaceful slumber.

He reached out thumb and forefinger and touched a tress of the sable fire, exulting in its silky texture. What an impulsive fool he had been to ride a hundred miles for just a glimpse. He sighed and, taking a small object from inside his doublet, placed it on her pillow.

As he left he pulled the casement tight to keep her safe. He promised himself there would be endless nights when he would come to her and enjoy the green eyes widening at his boldness. Always when he closed his eyes to conjure her image, the same picture rose up. It was the first moment his eyes had devoured the coppery, hip-length curls mingled with those between her legs.

He would not waste what was left of this night. Now that he was in London and all thought him at Norwich, it was a heaven-sent opportunity to execute a fine piece of business. He knew he must be back in Norwich before the evening's festivities, and by the time dawn found him riding north, six Irish political prisoners had escaped from the Devlin Tower, through the water gate, and by now were safely hidden aboard a Hawkhurst vessel crossing the Irish Sea.

When the governor of the Tower, and later Walsingham, questioned the guards, only one admitted seeing anything at all. He stuck to his story of seeing a "black shadow," and before the week was out London was rife with rumor and the Black Shadow was on the lips of every gossip.

When Sabre opened her eyes she snatched up the jewel lying on her pillow. The brooch was a wildcat fashioned from diamonds with large green emeralds for its eyes. There was no doubt whatsoever in her mind who had given her the priceless gift, but considering when and how he had done so sent shivers up her spine. The knave had been here under cover of night, watching her sleep, yet he was a hundred miles away, wasn't he?

She smiled a secret smile, the corners of her mouth turning up saucily. This was just the first of a vast array of jewels she intended to collect. Her days at court had already taught her that riches meant power. The Golden Rule had new meaning—those with the gold ruled.

Chapter 8

Suddenly it was September and the queen and her court were returned to London to start the brilliant winter season of entertaining and great festivities. London took on new life; its excitement could be felt in the very air. Entertainments, masques, parties, and feasts were planned. Every theater in London presented a new play, and the playbills were handed out on every street corner.

Kate gave Sabre a final lesson in the hierarchy of the court. The highest-ranking ladies were the grand ladies of the bedchamber, then came the ladies of the privy chamber, then the substream ladies of the presence chamber who had no specific duties, but simply attended the queen when she received foreign ambassadors or parliamentary delegations. On formal occasions six unmarried maids of honor formed the queen's train.

Her ladies were expected to accompany Her Majesty on her morning walks, attend her at church, dance nightly in the council chamber, ride to the hunt with her, and never step over the boundaries of obedience and chastity, which of course they sometimes did, and then they were expected to stand meekly before her while she vented her spleen of all its venom.

Kate was one of the chief gentlewomen of the privy chamber who must always be present at the robing, the most important ceremony of the morning. There were so many gowns to choose from, so many jewels to be tried on then discarded. A caul chosen to match a gown; a hat spangled with gold to match a bodice spangled with gold. The ruff alone could take half an hour; a half-ruff or a shoulder-wide starched ruff to set off huge padded leg-o'-mutton sleeves.

It was the express duty of her ladies to shower her with compliments, and it would be Sabre's express duty to restore order from chaos by putting away whatever Bess had discarded.

Sabre couldn't wait to get a firsthand view of the queen she had heard so many contradictory things about and to form her own opinion. Kate advised her to attend church the first morning Elizabeth returned, so that she could observe without herself being observed.

Sabre sat well back in the queen's chapel and received one surprise after another from the moment Elizabeth arrived. Her entrance into the chapel was noisy, rather than hushed, as a holy place required. She walked very quickly, as if a ghost were upon her heels, and all her ladies had to hurry to keep up with her. The gaudy spectacle she presented reminded Sabre acutely of her own red dress episode. The queen was outfitted in bright orange with rows and rows of gold spangled braid. She wore two or three rings on every finger of her exceptionally long, white hands. She was so vain of their beauty she continually gestured with them in an exaggerated fashion. She wore a wig which without doubt was the brightest, most unbelievable color of hair Sabre had ever witnessed. Her eyes were brilliant black and missed absolutely nothing. And she was as flat chested as a boy.

Everything went smoothly until her chaplain began his sermon. Unfortunately he chose to speak of a woman's duty to marry and beget heirs. The queen stood up in a high rage. "Leave that! Leave that!" she shouted. "The matter is now threadbare!" Then she spat upon the floor.

Sabre was astounded. If she hadn't witnessed it with

her own eyes, she would never have believed it. Elizabeth wielded supreme power. She made it crystal clear to all that she would say and do exactly as she pleased and woe betide any who stood in her path.

Greenwich Palace overflowed with courtiers. Meals were suddenly lavish, formal affairs with the dining hall so crowded, Sabre had to squeeze in wherever the tiniest space on a bench could be found, and all the talk was of plans for the masque to be held to celebrate the queen's birthday on September twenty-seventh. It was rumored the court would remove to Windsor, where there was more room and where the queen could indulge her love of hunting.

Bess had a robust constitution, and the second night she was back in Greenwich the dancing was expected to last until midnight. Sabre wore the new gown of lemon silk shot through with silver. She had fashioned the neckline in a deep V that lured the eye to the breathtaking breasts swelling out of the bodice, and she pinned the wildcat with the emerald eyes at the bottom of the V. She wore a half-ruff to allow her hair to be worn in careful dishevelment around her shoulders and down her back. It was all the rage to wear the hair up in the latest style, so of course Sabre would be different.

The absolute latest fashion was for a woman to affect a "bodkin" or small dagger, so she had designed a sheath into the sash of her gown and tucked in the blade Hawkhurst had given her. Of course the knife was no lady's ornament, but a very real and lethal dagger. However, she could not resist wearing both the wildcats with which he had gifted her.

Anne Vasavour was flirting with Lord Oxford, but the moment he saw Sabre he asked to lead her out in the

dance. Anthony Bacon also danced with her and later in
the evening introduced her to his brother Francis, reported to be the most brilliant mind at court. He had an
unfortunate stutter and seldom indulged in social chatter
with the ladies, for they were always trying to help him
by putting words in his mouth or finishing his sentences
for him. It never occurred to Sabre to do such a thing and
Francis Bacon took an immediate liking to her.

Essex had escorted the queen, and never wavered from
her side for the first hour, but as the evening wore on and
Gloriana became surrounded by the admiring Walter Raleigh, the lisping Southampton, the fawning ambassadors
from both France and Scotland, and the flattering Lord
Devonport, he allowed his assessing gaze to wander
about the hall and settle upon the delectable newcomer
who was laughing with Lady Leighton. He had eyes for
all the women, of course, and they for him, but his eyes
were drawn again and again to the girl with the magnificent hair.

Matthew arrived and walked directly toward Sabre. It
was deeply satisfying to say hello to her, for she always
bestowed the most dazzling smiles upon him and tonight
she greeted him with a kiss.

"Oh, Matthew, how can I thank you for this material?
'Tis the prettiest gown I've ever owned!"

His eyebrows went up when he saw the weapon she
was wearing. He knew there was only one person she
could have gotten it from. "That's rather formidable
. . . for a woman."

"Surely my sex should make no difference. You have a
large dagger."

He gave her a teasing smile. "That's what all the ladies
tell me." She slapped him smartly with her fan, and both

Essex and Devonport, who were watching the byplay, knew that the young man had said something suggestively spicy to her.

"Matt, be serious, there is something I want you to do for me."

He placed his hand upon his heart and promised solemnly, "Anything, fair damsel."

She kept her voice low so they could not be overheard. "September is begun and I'm no farther ahead with your brother than I was two months past."

"If you are impatient for lovemaking, may I offer my services, sweet?"

"Matt, will you help me or not?" she demanded impatiently.

"Would you have me bind and gag him and deliver him trussed to your bed?"

She turned her back upon him to show her displeasure and he immediately relented. She laughed to show him she was not really angry. "In truth, some men do need bludgeoning into offering for a woman. I want you to make a wager with him that he cannot make me his mistress."

He looked at her with something akin to awe. "You know a lot about men, don't you, Sabre?"

"I'd better, if I intend to tangle with *that* one, don't you think?"

One piece of music ended, and Sir John Heneage, who had just partnered Philadelphia Carey, asked Sabre to dance before the music began again.

Hawk slapped Matthew on the shoulder. "Did you manage to turn a fine profit on the run to Calais?"

Matt nodded and thanked him.

Hawk shook his head. "I may need you for a run across the Irish Sea some moonless night."

Matt's spine tingled with the implied danger.

"Did you manage to get down to see Mother this summer?" asked Hawk, changing the subject.

"Yes. As a matter of fact, I brought her up to Hawkhurst last week. The change will do her good."

Hawk nodded. "Don't encourage her to come up to the London house."

"She wouldn't intrude on you. She knows the London house is yours now."

Hawk looked his brother in the eye to make his meaning clear. "Georgiana will always be welcome at Thames View, as well she knows. I simply don't want her at court; it's too corrupt."

Matt's eyes had never left Sabre while she danced with Heneage, and Hawk asked idly, "Have you bedded her yet?"

Matthew flushed darkly at the suggestion, revealing clearly to his brother that he would like to. "No, I haven't bedded her," he said loudly.

Essex overheard him and said to the two brothers, "No? Then, by God, I intend to before the week's out."

Hawk stood rigid, the urge toward violence pulsing through his veins like liquid fire. The muscle of his jaw jerked as he tried to relax his clenched teeth and he forced himself to show only a mild interest.

"You fancy a new mistress?"

"God's blood, man, are you trying to get me clapped in the Tower? She's far too beautiful to escape Bess's eagle eye. She'd stand out in any crowd. Her tits alone are enough to earn Bess's venom. I thought perhaps a very short, very secret affair might ease some of the lust I feel." And he adjusted the material more comfortably over the bulge between his legs. "I hadn't thought of making her my mistress."

"That's most fortunate," said Matt, seeing an opportunity to perhaps make his wager with Hawk, "for the lady swears she will be no man's mistress."

Hawk drawled, "They all protest; 'tis the fashion."

"Aye. According to my stepfather Leicester, from the beginning Bess and her court pretended to demureness to quell scandals."

Matt pressed on. "Nay, I believe Sabre Wilde to be a lady of virtue." He turned to Hawk. "I'll wager you can't make her your mistress in a month!"

"Sabre . . . outrageous name," mused Essex, "I'll bet she's amusing in bed." He turned to Matthew. "I wager you I'll do it in a week."

Hawk ground out, "And I in a night!" Matt was forgotten as the two rivals faced each other.

Essex said, "I bet you I bed her before you do. I'll put up my Arabian against your Neptune. Matt, you are witness to the wager."

He strolled off in the direction of Sabre, and Hawk could not keep the murderous look from his eyes as he spoke to his brother. "You wouldn't have enough brains to pour piss out of your boots if you picked them up by the heels!"

Matt realized he'd made a tactical error by saying anything at all in front of Essex. The thing that worried him most was what Sabre would say to him when she learned what happened. He looked on the bright side. If he didn't tell her of the wager, Hawk and Essex weren't likely to. For once he would try to be discreet and say nothing.

Essex presented himself to Sabre and she sank into a

deep curtsy. He raised her immediately. "Your beauty almost blinds me, Mistress Wilde. Though I long to dance with you, I dare not for fear of bringing the queen's wrath upon your head. I would see you away from court, though. Would you attend the play with me tomorrow afternoon at the Rose?"

She knew him for a young lecher; gossip was he had gotten one of the queen's ladies with child. She almost refused him, but Hawkhurst advanced toward her possessively and she found herself saying, "It would be my pleasure, my Lord Essex."

His eyes were on the jeweled wildcat between her breasts. "You like unusual jewels, Mistress Wilde. I shall have to gift you with one."

She flashed her green eyes at Hawkhurst before she smiled at Essex. "Ah, sir, I could never accept jewels from a gentleman. This I had from my grandmother"— and her lashes swept down to her cheeks to hide her triumph at Hawkhurst's frustration.

"Will you dance with me, Sabre?" asked Hawk, his voice caressing her name.

"You are a bold man indeed to risk the queen's wrath," she said vainly.

"If Bess wants to behead you, I'll go down on my knees to get her to spare you," he teased.

As Essex watched Hawk lead her off to the dance, he murmured to himself, "God's cock, I'll go on my knees for you, or better yet have you go down on your knees for me." The wicked pictures he conjured kept him randy until he was once again beside Bess. She glanced coquettishly up at him and beckoned him with a long white hand. He sighed and felt his rigid state soften and diminish.

It was an ironclad rule that none must leave before the queen, but there was such a crush of people it would have been impossible to keep track of everyone. Hawk danced only as far as the first exit, then guided Sabre with a firm hand at the small of her back through two archways and into a dark, secluded withdrawing chamber. His finger traced the outline of the diamond wildcat. "Your grandmother has expensive taste," he whispered.

"How dared you enter my chamber while I slept?" she demanded.

"I dare anything," he said low, proving the point by letting his finger move upward to trace the swell of her breast. Sabre knew he was going to kiss her, but instead of drawing away she lifted her face to his. He buried his hands in her hair and kissed her with long, slow, lingering, melting kisses. The tip of his tongue traced her lips to tease her, then insisted that she part them. The moment she did he made his first penetration of her. His tongue entered her intimately to explore her mouth, while his hands moved down her back to do their own exploring. He lifted her body to fit it tighter to his. His mouth hardened its demands with fierce, devouring kisses that sent jolts of wild sensations that reached from her lips to her very toes. His tongue teased and plunged savagely, leaving her in a fever of longing.

Trembling, she touched her own tongue to him and he immediately drew it into his mouth and caressed it with his own. He refused to let her withdraw it until he was ready. Then his lips traced kisses across her cheek until his mouth found the tiny beauty spot. He worshiped it with his tongue, then moved down her throat, leaving a trail of heat where his lips had traveled. His hands came up to cup her breasts, and as they swelled from the bodice of the low-cut gown, his mouth sought the sensitive pink nipples as he first licked, then kissed, and finally sucked them hard.

Wild desire swept through her as his mouth on her breasts evoked tingling, throbbing sensations between her legs, and she would have given her soul in that moment to have him naked beneath her hands so she could lick his muscular back where the dragon rampaged.

"Will you come and see my house, Thames View?" he asked.

She gazed up at him. "I swore I wouldn't dance with you. I promised myself I would never be alone with you . . . and I've just done both," she said breathlessly. "If I did consider visiting Thames View, would you give me your word that I would be safe, that I could trust you?"

"No, Sabre, never be foolish enough to trust me." His mouth crushed down upon hers and she felt the violence in him. It excited her. She knew him for a dangerous but worthy adversary. She felt reckless enough to play the game with him, knowing it would be no easy victory to vanquish such strength and wit and cunning. She would use guile and the subtle seductive arts of womanliness. If she lost she would be totally devastated, but if she won she knew it would be rapture akin to ecstasy.

"I'll come, m'lord," she murmured huskily. Then she shivered with excitement. "One day soon."

Shane Hawkhurst cursed himself for a fool. His life did not need complications, the damned thing was convoluted enough as it was. He sighed, and determined to handle one complication at a time if he was to create any sort of order from the chaos.

He made very gentle love to Larksong that night, then

drew her into the curve of his arm to ease the way to cutting the knot that had secured her to him. Over the summer months he had pondered long and hard on what course to take. The sheer sorcery of Sabre Wilde had worked its magic in his blood, and he knew she would soon become the most important woman in his life. He knew full well she was too much woman to put up with another female in the shadows, and he had to find an honorable way of ending his present liaison. Larksong had been a gift from the dey of Algiers as a token of thanks for opening up the trading vessels of the Hawkhurst empire, and Shane had accepted her knowing that if he did not she was destined for the premier brothel of Algiers, the Garden of Bliss. Many men had offered him fortunes for her, and though in his time he had bought many a woman, he could not quite bring himself to sell one. He had toyed with the idea of gifting the queen with her, but his suspicion that she would be looked upon as an oddity like the queen's dwarf gave him pause for thought, and in the end he had done nothing.

"Larksong, do you ever long for your home?" he asked softly.

She remained silent for long minutes. She had known before him that she was a responsibility which would grow into a burden. She had only allowed herself to hope that when he tired of her, he would pass her on to a kind master.

"I try not to dream of the impossible," she murmured.

"If you came from China, I, too, would say it was impossible. But you told me your mother was brought out of the Orient by your father, who is a Turk. You spoke of a very beautiful city on the shores of a great sea."

Larksong nodded her head. "Byzantium, the center of the universe, where the continents come together."

"Where Asia and Europe join is the great shining city of Constantinople."

"Yes, yes!" She nodded with excitement.

"My sweet Larksong, have you the courage to sail to Constantinople and seek your home?"

Her cheeks were wet. He would not dishonor her by passing her on to another man.

"Baron," he called sharply, swinging his powerful legs to the carpet and swiftly donning breeches and thigh boots. The baron appeared at the chamber door. "We have to contact Grace O'Malley. I want safe passage for Larksong to Constantinople."

Lord Essex escorted his two sisters, Dorothy Devereux and Penelope Rich, to the Rose Theater along with Sabre. She wished the play could have gone on forever, so much did she enjoy it. The party had all gathered at Essex House along the Strand, where Robin introduced Sabre to his sisters. Six different wines were offered from sack to alicante, and Sabre wisely took hers with rosewater. She realized it would be incautious to become flown with wine so early in the afternoon.

Before leaving Essex House they all donned masks to conceal their identities. They were cleverly fashioned in the guise of animals and decorated with fur, feathers, and sequins. Dorothy chose a cat's mask, while Penelope selected a colorful butterfly. Robin picked out two matching ones for himself and Sabre. "A fox and his vixen," he said with teasing eyes, "since we are both redheads."

Sabre struck up an immediate friendship with Penelope Rich. She was a beautiful girl with golden hair and a voluptuous figure, but it was her quick tongue and easy wit that captured Sabre. She had made a wealthy marriage but was resigned to the fact that it could never be a happy union, for her real love was her brother's friend, Charles Blount. They had been having an affair for years, but at the moment he was commanding a thousand horse in Holland. She begged Essex for news of him, but he told her little to alleviate her apprehension for her lover. She knew the Dutch were fighting a bloody war against Spain and there were as many battles lost as won.

Sabre learned that the queen would not accept Robin's sisters at court.

" 'Tis not us she hates," Penelope explained to Sabre. " 'Tis our mother, Lettice. She will never, ever forgive her for marrying Leicester. They are cousins, you know, mother and Bess. Bess got the throne and Lettice got the beauty and the queen's surrogate husband. A fair division, to my way of thinking." She winked at Sabre.

Sabre knew she had a strong ally against the queen and could speak freely in her company. "Perhaps that is why she has made m'lord Essex her favorite. If Lettice stole the most important man in the queen's affections, then to pay her back Bess will try to steal the most important man in Lettice's affections."

" 'Od's blood, I think you've got something there," agreed Penelope, then she lowered her voice. "For the life of me I cannot see what my mother saw in Dudley. He was ever an insatiable lecher who offered any woman of the court three hundred pounds to lie with him. I declare his greatest attraction was that the queen considered him her own property. My mother only married him to spite her."

Essex joined them. "She married him for wealth and power. Love certainly had nothing to do with it."

Sabre and Penelope enjoyed their afternoon together so much they decided to go again the following week, and in the meantime they agreed that a trip to the fortune-teller's one evening would be fun.

Penelope had her own luxurious coach and horses and offered to drop off Dorothy. This left Sabre to ride in Essex's coach. They wore their masks still on their ride through London, but Sabre thought it an affectation, since the earl's device was emblazoned on the doors of the coach, and its drivers and attendant footmen were so sumptuously uniformed that none could mistake its occupant.

When Robin told the driver to take them to Essex House, Sabre protested. "M'lord, 'tis impossible. I've been gone most of the day. Lady Ashford will be sorely in need of me."

"But, sweet, I'm sorely in need of you." He took Sabre's hand and placed it on his swollen member. She was so angry, she trembled. She removed her mask and looked him directly in the eye. "M'lord Essex, if you are in need of a whore, I suggest you stop the coach and pick one up from a street corner, but pray do not insult me."

"Sweet, I don't insult you by showing how you arouse me . . . I compliment you." He removed his mask and moved across the seat to sit beside her. He slipped an arm about her and she was a little afraid when she felt it tighten with the strength of an iron band. He dipped his head to taste her lips and her brain whirled with a hundred thoughts. Why did she feel nothing for him? His kiss left her totally unaffected. Why? she asked herself. He was the premier bachelor of England; women almost swooned at his feet. He was physically attractive, well muscled, and decidedly amorous, yet her reaction to him was one of indifference. She was deeply shocked to feel his hand go up her skirt and inch its way toward her thigh. She clamped her legs together tightly and gave his face a stinging slap. Green fire blazed from her eyes. "Stop this coach instantly. I shall find my own way back to Greenwich, sir."

Reluctantly he removed his hand, but he pulled off one of her garters as he did so. He laughed and tried to make amends. "Sweet, it was only a jest. I did it on a dare, that's all. Stealing a lady's garter is all the rage."

"A dare? A dare from whom?" she demanded.

He shrugged helplessly. "Devonport . . . am I forgiven?" he begged.

She was seething and her tongue had a cutting edge to it. "Men have two lusts that drive them continually: power and loins!"

He did not take offense at her insult, and she forced her temper to calm. She was lucky that he had only stolen her garter, for 'twas certain if she'd been the slightest bit amenable he would have taken her there in the coach.

Chapter 9

Finally Drake and Hawkhurst were granted an audience by Cecil, Lord Burghley. Drake had already seen Walsingham and told him of the ships that Philip of Spain was building. The report tallied with what Walsingham's spies had reported and he told Drake that he would advise the queen. Drake and Hawkhurst both knew that if Elizabeth listened to any man's advice it was Cecil's. While she was the princess Elizabeth he had shown his loyalty to her. Her sickly brother Edward was on the throne and the wily duke of Northumberland had sent a message to Princess Elizabeth at Hatfield House. *Your Grace should come with all speed, for the king is very ill.* The courier, however, had another message concealed upon his person. It was from William Cecil, and Elizabeth would never forget it as long as she lived. *The king is already dead. It is the wish of Northumberland to place Jane Grey and his son Guildford on the throne, and to seize the persons of yourself and your sister. To obey the summons would be to place yourself in Northumberland's hands.*

Elizabeth, who had learned guile at an early age, took refuge in her bed and illness. She knew she could count on Cecil when everyone else failed her.

Now Hawkhurst took the initiative. "I saw the ships being built with my own eyes, m'lord Burghley, at the port of Cádiz."

Drake jumped in. "I propose to take a small fleet of ships and destroy this armada before it ever leaves Cádiz."

"Her Majesty will listen to you, my lord," Hawkhurst urged.

Cecil held up his hand and laughed. "It is true the queen trusts my loyalty implicitly, but, gentlemen, you labor under a misapprehension if you think she takes my advice. She listens respectfully, then does exactly as she chooses. I must urge, plead, cajole, coax, wheedle, and flatter to budge her one inch down the road to retaliation against Spain."

"But, m'Lord Burghley, the threat to England is very real; it is no figment of an overactive imagination."

Cecil held up his hand again. "Gentlemen, when the queen took the throne, her coffers were empty. Her father Henry VIII gathered a fortune from the church following his dissolution of the English monasteries. Then he turned around and squandered it on soldiers and war equipment to invade France. Her Majesty has built up prosperity for England and herself from peace, not war. She resents every penny piece spent on the military; witness our paltry efforts to aid Holland."

"Are we to just wait until Philip sails into English ports and steals her crown?" demanded Drake.

"Or take matters into our own hands and destroy the enemy while the queen pretends to turn a blind eye?" asked Hawkhurst.

"Gentlemen, the time is coming when England will need heroes such as you. Each of us in his own way must urge her to move, I at the council table, you at the masques and pageants, until inch by inch we prod her down the road to action."

Essex lost no time in waving Sabre's garter beneath Hawkhurst's nose. "Say good-bye to your trusty steed; it's as good as in my stables already."

Shane didn't believe for one moment that he actually

had Sabre's garter, yet the next time he saw her he took hold of her wrist and against her will guided her into the gardens.

The sky was like black velvet with millions of diamonds scattered upon it. A silver crescent of moon sent unusual shadows across the lawns that sloped down to the Thames. As they neared the river they disturbed the swans, which glided out upon the water majestically.

"How did Essex get your garter?" he asked, his voice curiously husky.

Damn men! Why must they brag about their petty conquests? "I went for a swim in the Thames; he must have filched it from my clothes on the riverbank," she improvised lightly.

He took hold of her shoulders none too gently and turned her to face him. "That is a damned lie, for I'll wager you cannot swim."

"I assure you, sir, I can," she asserted.

In a flash he lifted her in his arms and threatened to throw her in. "I'll make you prove it," he said through clenched teeth.

She screamed and their privacy was invaded by three other couples who had come to stroll in the moonlight. He let her feet touch the grass, but clung to her in a close embrace. His lips touched her ear. "If I guarantee you a private place to swim, will you let me watch?"

She felt very seductive. "If you promise only to watch, then my answer is yes, but if you try to play wicked water games I will drown you!"

"I could drown in your eyes every time you look at me," he whispered against her cheek, then he bent her over his arm and captured her lips. He kissed and caressed her into insensibility. She was all awakening passion. Soon she would be ready to be taken, and he received deep pleasure from making her dizzy with desire. She was a contradiction, so headstrong, fiery-tempered, and saucy-tongued, yet he sensed her innocence and inexperience and vulnerability. At one and the same time she managed to be an alluring woman and a bewitching child.

Hawkhurst gave a piercing whistle and a wherryman pulled his barge over to the water steps.

She hung back. "Where are you taking me?"

"You promised to come to Thames View with me. After you've seen it, there is something I want to ask you." He removed his short cape and placed it about her shoulders. The night was warm, but out on the river the breeze could be chilling, and he was consumed with the need to protect her. He sat with a strong, possessive arm about her, which anchored her to his side while he murmured love words against her gloriously disheveled hair. Shane felt a rising excitement that sent the blood beating in his throat. If she said yes tonight, she would be his until dawn.

Thames View was close by Kew Gardens, so it was a short ride. They ascended the river steps and walked up the lush green lawns that led up to the house. All the servants were abed at this hour, save one man. "Sabre, my sweet, this is the baron. On board ship he is both doctor and priest. On land he is closer to me than my shadow."

She held out her hand and the man in the monklike robe took it and held it reverently between his own. "The baron doesn't speak," Hawk explained.

She smiled. "He speaks with his eyes."

He showed off his house to her, wanting her to love it

as he did. The entrance hall was vast, high and wide and very formal. Behind it was a receiving room to entertain visitors. They went through the kitchens and dipped their fingers into a bowl of clotted cream, then he showed her the elegant dining salon, the library, and the luxurious withdrawing rooms. The colors were muted in the dimness of the few lights burning, but she could see the classic good taste in every room of the house.

Upstairs he showed her a bathing room, indicated the servants' wing with a negligent wave of his hand, and guided her into the master bedroom. It was definitely a man's room. The walls were paneled in dark red Moroccan leather. The carpet was Persian, cream in color, with a curiously designed border. Before the marble fireplace were scattered animal skins; wildcat and wolf. The windows ran the whole width of the room to overlook the river, and a built-in, carved window seat ran beneath the leaded panes, piled high with furs and velvet cushions. The bed was massive and curtained against the drafts.

He pulled her into his arms and gazed down at her. "Sabre, could you be happy here?"

I'm mad in love with him, she thought wildly.

He could hear the rustle of her petticoats and inhale the scent of her flesh and every inch of him responded. "Sabre, my love, I want you to come here to me whenever you can steal away from court."

"You are asking me to become your mistress?"

He groaned. "I mean you no dishonor. Circumstances prevent me from offering you more."

"You mean the queen?" she probed lightly.

"No, damn it, I mean I am married, though that is a secret I would ask you not to divulge. 'Tis a marriage in name only and means naught to me," he vowed.

His words brought her to her senses. She, better than any other, knew his marriage meant naught to him, but to actually hear it from his own lips, while at the same time he was proposing an adulterous relationship, cured her instantly of the love she'd been feeling for him.

"Sabre, darling, I'll let you have carte blanche. Do you know what that means?" he asked tenderly.

"It means anything I want," she supplied. "Could I have a hundred gowns?" she tested him.

"Of course," he assured her.

"The keys to one of your warehouses?"

"They will be on your pillow in the morning."

"The deed to this fine house or one of equal value?" she tested.

"Yes," he promised, "I have many estates; you shall be allowed to chose."

"In Ireland?" she questioned.

He hesitated for the first time. "I have land in Ireland, but it's wild, godforsaken land. You wouldn't care for it."

"So, there is a limit to what I can have."

"Darling, I swear there is not," he vowed. He was entranced with her. He was a connoisseur of fine female flesh and could feel the current of their mutual attraction. Damn, she had him so hot, he was prepared to give her his soul. His arms tightened and his head dipped to taste the tempting honeyed mouth so teasingly close. While she was lost in the first sensations of the kiss, his hands deftly swept beneath her skirt to caress the bare flesh of her thighs at the intimate place where her silk stockings ended.

A shock ran through her body as she felt his fingers inch closer to his desired goal. His boldness took her breath away. Sabre knew if she said yes, he would have

her in that bed this very minute! She looked at his mouth,
imagining it covering her body with kisses, and grew
faint at the thought. She knew he would cherish nothing
that was not hard won. Let him wait and wonder! She
was not going to let this wealthy, arrogant lord think she
was easy.

"Please, darling?" he begged.

With a gasp that let him know how shocked she was at
what his fingers did, she firmly removed his hands. She
tossed her hair over her shoulders and said, "You go too
fast, m'lord. I will think on your offer, but that is all I can
promise."

She retreated a step in the face of his imperious black
look, but the fingers of his hand tightened on her shoulder in a cruel, punishing grip. "Look at that bruise when
you go to bed tonight."

She smiled her secret smile. She had hurt him, or he
wouldn't have found it necessary to hurt her back.

When they met at court they paid scant attention to
each other. Each knew that their relationship would
eventually become very intimate and it was in their own
best interests to keep the liaison from the queen's ears.
But each time their eyes met there was a burning intense
question in his. Nonetheless, she ignored his looks. She
would tell him when she wanted to tell him.

On the morrow was the visit with Penelope to the
fortune-teller's. What she did not know was that Essex
had talked his sister into an elaborate scheme for a ren-
dezvous. He had arranged for Penelope to take Sabre to
one of his own houses, where he would be in costume as
an Eastern astrologer who would foretell her affair with
the great, redheaded earl. It would be great fun and he

would throw off his costume and make love to her. Essex felt very confident of winning the wager with Hawkhurst and couldn't help taunting him about Sabre each time they met.

Shane sought out Sabre in the queen's wardrobe. As soon as Kate saw who her niece had attracted, she left the two discreetly alone and went into an adjoining wardrobe room.

Sabre wore the yellow silk with silver ribbons. "You look very fetching today," he said, his eyes licking over her like a candle flame. "You promised to show me how you could swim, remember?"

"I remember I said *if* you found me somewhere private."

"I've rented the Roman bath for the whole day. No one will be allowed in but us."

He expected her to refuse and she knew if she did he would force her to keep her promise. "What is it like? Was it really built by the Romans?" She was really very curious about such a place.

He leered at her. "It's opulent—decadent, really. It's made from beautiful white and azure marble. The bathing pool is a hundred yards long and six feet deep. 'Tis reported some of the more daring ladies swam naked. There is a gallery above the pool for spectators, but of course that will remain closed today."

"I will come with you on one condition, my lord," she said, smiling.

"Name it," he said, expecting her to worm her way out of it by one trick or another.

"If you observe me from the gallery above, I shall swim for you."

"Meet me by the water stairs as soon as Kate will let you."

She kept him waiting two hours on purpose. He'd been pacing the water stairs angrily for the last hour, and when she finally arrived he didn't know if he wanted to shake her or embrace her. He looked down into the pale green eyes. "How you madden a man, little wildcat."

She looked inordinately pleased at his admission.

He never took his eyes from her as the wherryman maneuvered the barge into the current of the river and expertly flew beneath London Bridge and then Blackfriars Bridge. Shane pondered on his fatal attraction to her. Granted she was one of the loveliest, most vivid females he'd ever laid eyes on, in any country he'd ever visited. Her body was slim and exquisitely curved and would give rise to a dead man. But he tried to identify the elusive quintessence that drove him to possess her. He shook his head as it once again eluded him.

They alighted at magnificent Somerset House and walked the short distance to the Strand and the Roman bath. The streets were packed with vendors hawking their wares, from milkmaids to rat catchers. He bought her an armful of golden roses. They were full blown and would not last until the morrow, but now, at the peak of their beauty, their perfume was intoxicating. Sabre buried her face in them and inhaled deeply. Desire flared in him, for she never did anything by half measure. He believed she had lain with no man yet, but he would never describe her as innocent, for she had the age-old allure of Eve and he knew that once he had awakened her, she would take him to the Garden of Eden.

Sabre drew in her breath at the splendor of the huge marble bath. The water shimmered a pale azure, inviting, tempting, luring. As she watched Shane climb to the gallery, she knew exactly what she would do. She used one of the small cubicles to undress, but instead of wearing the short petticoat as she first intended, she stripped off every stitch. She would swim nude for him.

She shook out her hair so that it cloaked her to the hips, gathered the roses to her breasts, and stepped out to the edge of the pool. She slipped gracefully into the water and let the golden roses glide about the surface of the pale azure water. Slowly, and very gracefully, she kicked out and floated through the water, her beautiful pale copper tresses drifting out behind her. She swam to the far end of the bath, then swam slowly back again. Once more among the roses she turned upon her back and looked up at him.

He leaned upon the gallery rail, entranced by her performance. She was like a mermaid from some mythic tale, and her beauty pierced his heart and soul. She swam for him for over an hour and he could have watched her forever. Finally she smiled up at him and blew him kisses. By God, he had his answer. She had given it to him in her own spectacular way. Only a mistress would gift a man with such an intimate, luxuriant display. Suddenly he knew exactly what attracted him. It was her courage. She would dare anything. She saw his intention to come down to her, and in a flash she was out of the water in an attempt to clothe herself before he swooped down on her. He was so fast, she had donned only her flimsy shift, and the pretty yellow silk gown with silver ribbons lay just out of her reach.

He lifted her high against his heart and shouted with joy. "You were like a mermaid! A fitting mate for a sea god. Your answer is a resounding yes, isn't it, my love?"

"Of course; was there ever any doubt?" she teased unmercifully. "Dress me," she whispered against his mouth.

"No!" he refused. "I want you . . . here . . . now!" he insisted. His hands on her body showed clearly that he thought he owned her.

She panicked for a moment. Had she inflamed him beyond the point of control? She admitted to herself that she had indeed been wanton in her behavior and could expect no less from a man as virile as Shane Hawkhurst.

His hands had already half lifted the shift from her body, and his lips were doing forbidden things to her. She pulled from him with a transparent excuse. "My hair is too wet . . . please . . . don't."

He undid the buttons at his neck. "Take my shirt to dry it," he pressed her.

She suddenly went weak at the knees and had to cling to him momentarily. "Oh, please, don't bare the dragon to me or else I'm undone." She was not teasing him now, but had gasped out her true feelings without thinking.

Now he slipped the shift from her shoulders, and as her breasts swelled upward, free of their gauzy restraint, his restraint vanished also. He threw his black cloak onto the beautiful white marble floor and knelt before her. His hot mouth trailed fiery kisses from her navel to the triangle of coppery curls which was the core of all his fantasies.

"Shane . . . please . . . not here, not like this. . . ."

"Yes! Here . . . just like this," he insisted.

"Shane, I'm cold . . . please, not in this public building . . . I want you to make love to me in your bed."

He groaned. "Of course you do. I'm sorry, darling." He helped her into her gown, uttering mild oaths under his breath as his fingers dealt with its buttons and fastenings. When she was fully clothed, he enfolded her in his cloak and held her fast. "When will you come to me, Sabre? Tonight?"

"No," she said softly.

"When?" he demanded hoarsely.

"I shall come . . . when I come," she answered elusively.

He hovered on the brink of violence. She exulted that she could play him like a trout on a line.

"You mean when the whim takes you?"

She smiled irresistibly. "Precisely!"

She spent the morning carefully putting away the queen's discarded clothes and jewels as she did every morning after the important robing ceremony. Her own dresses, though pretty in color, were woefully lacking in rich ornamentation, and so few in number as to cause comment. *Well, as of today all that is at an end,* she thought as she aired the sumptuous gowns before putting them away in the wardrobe.

She rushed off to meet Penelope Rich and arrived at Essex House early in time to watch Penelope at her elegant toilette. Sabre's color was high and her eyes sparkled like emeralds.

"Sabre, you look as if you are in love," declared Penelope. "Are those stars in your eyes for my brother Robin?"

"No," answered Sabre honestly. "I told Hawkhurst I'd become his mistress. I want you to take me to your dressmaker, Penelope; you have the most glorious clothes in London. I declare I'm dressed like a beggar maid. I need so many things, I don't know where to begin. The season is begun and I don't intend to be seen in the same thing twice. I have a fantastic idea for my costume for the queen's birthday masquerade, and oh, I need riding dresses, everything!"

"Will he pay?" asked Penelope.

Sabre looked at her and smiled. "There are many things about Lord Devonport that I don't yet know, Penelope, but of one thing I'm very certain—he will pay and pay and pay!"

"Oh, dear," said Penelope, realizing this put an end to her brother's plans regarding the fortune-telling.

"What is it?" asked Sabre.

"Robin had concocted a plan for me to deliver you to his arms this afternoon. He was to be the fortune-teller."

They laughed unabashedly at Essex's plight. "Let's go to the dressmaker's instead. If Robin looks into his crystal ball he should be able to divine all," said Sabre, laughing.

Sabre didn't know it, but Essex's day was already spoiled. Hawk confronted him in the courtyard at Greenwich. "The lady is mine," he said with satisfaction. "I'll send a groom for your Arabian tomorrow."

"In a pig's arse! The lady and I have an assignation this very afternoon. Tomorrow you may have my leavings," he sneered.

Hawk's eyes narrowed dangerously. "Take that back, m'lord Essex, or be prepared to defend yourself," he growled.

"I'll meet you anywhere you suggest," he answered, his eyes cold and deadly.

"Like hell, we'll settle this now," snarled Hawkhurst, throwing off his doublet and drawing his narrow sword.

The clash of steel rang out and the air seemed to hang in stillness, then a crowd gathered in the courtyard. Both were excellent swordsmen, their styles of offense rather than defense identical. Hawk sprang into the attack, forcing Essex to give ground to avoid his whirling, darting blade. Essex parried and thrust quickly, yet very surely. Sweat beaded their faces and stuck their shirts to their backs. Then, only a moment apart, each man nicked his opponent, blood showing crimson on their white shirts. Just at that moment Elizabeth arrived on the scene, returning from her morning walk.

"God's death, stop that this instant!" She was enraged. She loathed quarrels and forbade dueling. "I am sick unto death of young men's tantrums! Devereux, Hawkhurst," she said, deliberately denying them their titles, "I shall deal with this in private. Get you to the throne room."

The two men waited stiffly inside the throne room as the queen decided to let them cool their heels. After half an hour their eyes met; then, as the long minutes ticked by, the earl of Essex, more used to the queen's wrath, said, "We'd do well to concoct a tale that will hold water."

"Meaning?" demanded Hawk.

"If she suspects our quarrel was over a woman, God help us. Her fury knows no bounds."

"Then we must say the quarrel was over her," decided Hawkhurst.

The inner door opened and the queen swept in. She sat upon the throne and the two men had no choice but to kneel before her. Suddenly there was a tap upon the door and a lady of the privy chamber entered and said, "Your Majesty—" The queen instantly took off her shoe and threw it across the room toward the unfortunate woman's head. "Get out!" she screamed. The two men were left in no doubt about their sovereign's mood. She glared at them. "Men of blood live out only half their lives!"

"Your Majesty, I beg you forgive me for drawing my sword near your most precious person," said Essex.

"I humbly apologize, Your Grace," murmured Hawkhurst.

"A fig on your apologies! I will have the cause for this insolent brawl."

The earl of Essex had a facile tongue. "We both picked the same jewel for Your Majesty's birthday."

Her eyebrows went up and her look of displeasure almost disappeared. Hawkhurst, damned if he would let Essex best him, said, "A large black pearl on a diamond chain. But I withdraw from the competition and concede victory to m'lord Essex. He may gift you with the pearl."

She eyed both men, wondering if they had conspired, but knew it was to her advantage to forgive them. "Never quarrel again in my presence or you will find yourselves forbidden court. You may leave."

Outside the throne room Essex, his good humor restored, said, "Where the hell am I to get a black pearl on a diamond chain?"

"It just so happens I have one for sale," said Hawk, laughing.

"I thought you might have, you bastard," Essex replied, enjoying the jest.

Lord Devonport faithfully attended the dancing each night in the council with its adjacent music gallery. This did not interfere with his other nocturnal activities. He planned them for well past midnight after the queen and her court retired to their beds. Of late, he suspected that he was being followed. By so-called friend or foe he knew not, but he determined that next time he would find out. He needed no more rumors that the Black Shadow had been seen again.

On the second night of dancing he thought he'd been patient long enough with Sabre. She let him find a secluded alcove for them, where she allowed him all the kisses he hungered for. He fondled her shamelessly until she was limp with desire and his own nerve endings screamed for the release his body demanded, yet still she eluded him. She gave vague and elusive answers when pressed to come to Thames View.

The third night was a repeat of the second. He was like a man starving and kissed her so passionately that she eventually fainted in his arms.

The fourth night saw an end to his patience. He had had enough dalliance in corners. He led Sabre out in the first dance. He said only one word to her. "Tonight!" It was not a question, it was an order. She tossed her head and went off merrily with a new partner. After a few more dances he led her out again. "Midnight sharp! In the courtyard."

She knew her time for eluding him was finished. He would not allow her to neglect him further. As their dance ended he said lustfully, "You can be thinking of something unique for us to do in bed." He retired from the dancing and took himself off to play gleek, never glancing her way again.

A few minutes past midnight Sabre walked through the courtyard in the warm September night. A dark cat slunk across her path and the warm air carried sounds from an occasional vessel still upon the river. Suddenly she saw a dark horse and rider. She was afraid as it headed straight toward her, but as he came alongside and

swept out a strong arm to lift her to the saddle, she saw
his face. He took her inside his cloak and she was
stunned to feel his warm bare flesh. "You have no doublet
or shirt," she breathed.

"No. I once saw with my own eyes the effect my naked
chest had upon you. I needed to see it again."

Her arms slid up his hard torso and slipped about his
neck. "You are mad!" she whispered.

"Aye, and you are the cause of my madness."

She could hardly contain the excitement she felt. It
was a special kind of thrill to steal away from the palace
at such a late hour when it was expected that all decent
people had retired for the night. The risk and danger
involved made her heart race and her pulses quicken. If
the queen learned of such behavior they would be punished and banned from court.

He held her against him, then took her mouth in a
savagely demanding kiss. He spurred his horse and the
three of them sprang forward down the moonlit river
road to his own estate. He dismounted and, lifting her
from the saddle, carried her into the house and up to the
master bedchamber.

He threw off his cloak to reveal the wide expanse of
hard, rippling muscle. His dark mane of hair fell wildly
to his shoulders, and his white teeth flashed their wolfish
gleam against his deeply tanned face. His black breeches
fit his muscular thighs as if they were molded to him. Her
pale green eyes played seductively with his body until she
saw it harden and swell with his need for her. She was
wearing her cream wedding gown with the deeply cut-out
décolleté. With one teasing finger he traced the high swell
of her breast, then dipped his head to place the tribute of
a kiss upon each swell. His lips traveled a fiery path up

her throat to her ear, which he touched with the tip of his tongue, then whispered, "Did you think of something novel we could do in bed?"

"Yes . . . let's eat in bed. I'm hungry, aren't you?"

"Starving, but not for food."

"Please?" she begged prettily.

"Since I'm going to be living here a good deal of the time, let me send for a servant and give the order?"

"At this time of the night?" he asked incredulously.

"You said you wanted to do something different . . . unique."

"Are you really that innocent?" He shook his head in wonderment. "God's truth, you're not much good to a man yet."

"Don't you dare laugh at me." She thrust out her lower lip and he immediately kissed her pouting mouth.

He waved his hand expansively. "You are mistress here. Do whatever pleases you."

She rang the bellpull and Shane came up behind her to undo the back of her gown.

"Whatever are you doing?" she cried as he put his hands on her breasts. "The servant will see!"

"Well, he'd better get used to it, don't you think?" He took the pins from her hair and the heavy silken mass fell over his hands, making him shudder with anticipation.

There was a discreet knock upon the chamber door and she called, "Enter!"

A middle-aged man opened the door and with a studied impassive air asked, "Yes, my lord?"

Shane's eyes glittered shamelessly. "This is Mistress Sabre Wilde, Mason. She will be spending a great deal of time with us. I believe she wants to practice on you."

Not by even a raised eyebrow did Mason show any

surprise. The master's antics had ceased to surprise him long ago.

Sabre gave Shane a scathing look, went over to Mason, held out her hand, and asked, "What's your first name?"

Now he was surprised. "Why, it's Charles, my lady." She knew he was just being polite, but it was the first time anyone had used her correct title and it secretly thrilled her. "Well, Charles, I have a craving for something delicious. What does a Sea God keep in his larder . . . ambrosia?"

His lips twitched. "No, my lady, but may I suggest blackberries and cream?"

"Oh, yes, please. Two bowls. We're going to eat them in bed." She winked at him and he knew at last young Hawkhurst was going to have his hands full with this one.

"By God, you're a brazen hussy," Shane teased, finishing the job of removing her gown.

"A moment ago I was an innocent lamb."

"Mayhap you're both." He undid the tapes that held her petticoats and she stepped out of them clad in busk, drawers, and stockings. "My undergarments are very prim for a mistress, my lord, but you will be delighted to learn that I have already ordered dozens of the most scandalous underpinnings you can imagine. My suggestions for their design even shocked Penelope Rich's modiste."

"Your prim drawers are adorable." He kissed her nose, then poured them both a glass of sack, a dry sherry mixed with Barbados sugar and spices. There was another discreet knock upon the door and she looked pleadingly at Shane. He shook his head wickedly. "Ah, no, *you* must face him and get your just desserts."

She was bold enough to march to the door in her drawers and take the silver tray from Mason. She closed the door with her bottom but Shane took the tray from her in a flash. "First we undress, then we get into bed, then we eat!" He felt a bolt of desire tear into him. "Sweetheart, your mouth was made for kisses, not blackberries and cream." He pressed his mouth against hers, then let his lips travel the length of her throat. His fingers trailed across the top of her busk, then dipped into the valley between her upthrusting breasts. "Your body holds sweeter fruit I long to devour," he murmured. "Your breasts are like melons, ripe for the tasting, with hard little fruits at their tip." He slowly removed the busk, and her breasts spilled out into his strong hands, which caressed and lifted them worshipfully to his mouth for its anointing. "Sabre, you are so beautiful, it's sinful!" he whispered between kisses.

He slowly pushed her backward into the bed to draw off her stockings. Every inch of silken flesh he exposed received his kiss. He made her feel totally beautiful— from her ankles to her earlobes. Each and every part of her body received his praise, until at last he finally removed her drawers and showered her with love words. He was determined to draw out their hours of intimacy so that each of them would receive the fullest and richest pleasure possible.

He stripped off his breeches and stood before her. With their eyes they began to make love to each other. As his eyes caressed and worshiped her, he was conscious of the blood flowing hot and thick in his veins and of the heavy, sweet ache that had flooded his loins.

In turn she adored him with her eyes. Her glance traveling the full hard length of him, lingering on his mouth, his shoulders, his hands, his belly, and finally coming to rest on the huge tapered lance that thrust boldly up past his navel.

At this moment she thought him the most magnificent man ever created. No wonder the queen called him her sea god. She could not get over her incredible luck that this devastatingly handsome male was actually her husband. He was a rake, a rogue, and a ravisher, but by heaven and hell, he was all man! She had never felt like this before, never even dreamed that she could feel like this. She couldn't wait for him to do bad, wicked things to her, and she knew if she glimpsed the dragon, she would fall upon his body and begin to kiss and bite it.

She held out her hands for the tray, and when he handed it to her she placed it between them as a barrier to her lust. She sat cross-legged upon the bed. Her copper tresses fell all about her in disarray and mingled with the copper curls between her legs. He found her wildly beautiful. He lay on his side, head propped on his hand, and watched her, entranced. He groaned as her pink tongue darted out to lick the cream from each blackberry. When she was finished, she began to feed him, and he sucked her fingers erotically each time she brought the fruit to his lips.

He put the tray on the floor. "Come to me, love." He knelt over her, his face hard with passion, and reached out to caress her aching breasts. At his touch she turned to fire, to molten lava, her bones melted to wax. He buried his face in the hollow between her breasts. Her hands roamed his body, feeling his great strength, the heavy shoulders, the powerful thighs. Her hands could not get enough of him. Her fingers spread through the thick mat of hair covering the solid muscle of his chest. Her fingertips explored his nipples, then stole upward to encircle his neck.

He crushed her mouth with his and she opened readily, as he had taught her, to receive his kisses and his tongue. She protested as he tore his mouth from hers to travel a downward path to her belly and below. She felt the power in his hands as they tightened around her, his mouth fastened hungrily to her flesh, feasting on her unmatched beauty. His aggressive mouth moved ever lower until his lips journeyed to tease the triangle of copper ringlets. She shocked herself, because she did not want him to stop.

His hands slid up the backs of her thighs, forcing her forward into his kisses. She felt his tongue flit across the swollen bud of her desire, then explore the soft places of her secret part. His fingers spread her open and she thrilled as his tongue thrust into her and plundered unmercifully. She began to thrash and moan as waves of unbelievable pleasure swept through her body, fulfilling her darkest fantasies. She cried out for more and more and more and he gave her all she begged him for. Her fingers dug into his shoulders, then entwined in his dark mane of hair, holding him to the center of her volcanic pleasure that felt as if it were going to erupt with molten fire. She sprawled, writhing wantonly beneath his expert mouth, then his hands smoothed up her body to her breasts to play with and squeeze hard the thrusting pink nipples. She came up from the bed with a jolt, and a scream was torn from her throat as she reached her highest peak and spilled over into a million splintered lights. He licked her once more before removing his tongue, then held her cradled against him to feel every last shudder of her magnificently generous response to him.

She ran her fingers over the scratches her nails had made on his bronzed shoulders. "My little wildcat," he said hoarsely. She was avidly curious about his body. She could actually see his hardened shaft throbbing with his heartbeat. She reached out her fingers to touch him and was amazed that it felt as solid as marble. Her eyes lifted to his, uncertain for the first time. "You are so enormous," she breathed, realizing that very soon he would mount and enter her.

He embraced her and promised, "If I hurt too much, I'll stop, my darling. The first time can be painful, that's why I loved you the other way first. I'm sure you're ready for me, my love. Try and relax and take me into you. There's no hurry, my lovely one," he said against her lips, and she felt she would surely die from his kisses.

A sharp, imperative rapping came upon the door. Shane knew the urgent summons could not be ignored. He uttered an oath and slipped from the bed to the chamber door. The baron handed him a note which Shane quickly held before the candles to scan its contents. This time the oath he uttered was obscene. He ran his fingers through his dark mane of hair, nodded quietly to the baron, then closed the heavy door. He came back to the bed and took her into his arms. "Sabre, my love, forgive me for what I must do. I wouldn't leave you at this moment for any reason on earth, except this one. I know I can't expect you to understand; there are so many things I cannot tell you. Someone's life is in grave danger."

"Is it a summons from the queen?" she asked jealously.

"My darling, I swear to you I will never leave our bed to go to that bitch. Try to get some sleep." He pulled the covers up and tucked her in safely. "I may be gone for days."

"I have to return to court tomorrow, but I would like to bring some of my things here, if it's all right."

"Sabre, darling, this is *our* house now. Come and go as you please." He bent to kiss her one last time. "I'm a swine to leave you like this, but I swear I'll make it up to you," he promised.

She watched him dress all in black. She watched in silence as he armed himself with sword, daggers, and pistols, then covered all with a long black cloak. Already he was totally withdrawn from her. He had a secret life that absorbed and occupied most of his thoughts, and she knew instinctively that when she learned about it, it would give her all the ammunition she would ever need to destroy him. She gave no thought to the danger that lay in wait for him; rather she envied the adventure that he and the baron would ride through the night to enjoy.

Chapter 10

Shane Hawkhurst had received a message that the O'Neill was about to be arrested and taken to Dublin Castle for questioning. Both Shane and the baron knew the conditions in Dublin's Bermingham Tower and they knew of the unauthorized, hideous tortures that went on in its dungeons. Walsingham's rack and rope were insignificant when compared to the Spanish chair, the scavenger's daughter, and the iron boots made to hold boiling oil.

Bagenol, the queen's Irish marshal, would be quite capable of assassinating the O'Neill once he had him behind bars, for he believed if every Irish lord lost his head, Ireland would be tame as a lamb.

Shane believed his father's only chance was to get to England. If he answered any charges laid against him directly to the queen, he would be able to vindicate himself. O'Neill had such charisma and powers of persuasion, he could charm the ducks off the water. Women were like putty in his hands and the queen was all woman.

Making sure they were not followed this night, they rode north to Liverpool, stopping only at Birmingham to change their horses for fresh ones that Hawk kept posted there for such emergencies. The *Liverpool Lady* took them across the Irish Sea and dropped anchor in the secluded Carlingford Lough near Newry. Shane planted his feet firmly and faced the baron. "I want you to remain aboard. It is too dangerous for you to set foot on Irish soil. The murder warrant on you is still in effect and we both know none of the clans can be trusted. Some would betray you for the sheer pleasure of the act; most would betray you for profit."

The baron's eyes were filled with pain, but after a few minutes he nodded his agreement. He had been steeling himself for the ordeal of returning to the land where the massacre of his whole family had taken place. He had been a chieftain and a rebel, and when they laid down their arms in unconditional surrender to the English, they had been butchered down to the last man, woman, and child, and every building and crop of the villages he ruled had been burned black. He was the only survivor and a murder warrant had been issued because in retaliation he had gutted the English officer who had killed his wife and children.

Accompanied by two stalwart crewmen of the *Liverpool Lady,* Shane rode like the wind for Dungannon Castle. Because he had acted immediately, Shane had arrived in Ireland before Bagenol had received his signed warrant from the crown. The O'Neill needed no prodding to come to London. He was all for storming the queen's private apartments the moment he arrived there, but Shane's cooler head finally prevailed on the voyage back across the Irish Sea. It would be prudent for O'Neill to lie low with none knowing of his whereabouts until Shane could sound out the queen to see which way the wind blew.

When Sabre returned to court at dawn the next morning, Kate told her it was official that one week hence they would all be removing to Windsor for the queen's birthday so she could enjoy some good hunting.

Kate sighed. "There our work shall begin all over again."

"How many dresses do you suppose the queen owns?" asked Sabre.

"Oh, they number over a thousand. Let's see, there must be close to three hundred here and three hundred at Windsor. Whitehall, I'd say, houses about two hundred very formal state costumes for the parliaments and such, and then there's over two hundred at Hampton Court."

On the spot Sabre decided to double the number of gowns she had ordered from the dressmaker's. She went into London and bought everything from fans to shoe buckles, from lace neck whisks to wired farthingales. She purchased an abundance of fancy soaps and bath oils, each scented with almonds, or cloves, or attar of roses. She bought cosmetics such as rice powder, rouge, and purpurice to redden her lips.

Sabre, Anne Vasavour, Philadelphia Carey, and Essex's two sisters, Dorothy Devereux and Penelope Rich, began to go about together. All five were vividly lovely; their different colorings complemented one another. Sabre, Anne, and Philadelphia stole more and more time away from court and enjoyed the "fast" company of Essex's sisters.

They went shopping, had their tea leaves and cards read, attended all the plays, watched a bear-baiting at the pit behind the Rose Theater, and finally, after much giggling, hesitating, and vacillating, they agreed to Penelope's suggestion that they spend the evening at a brothel where they could watch one or two *acts of sex*. Penelope had been there before with Essex and she assured them it was a hilarious experience they would not soon forget. Sabre had no hesitation. She had a great curiosity for the mystery of sex and knew she needed educating in the things that went on between a man and a

woman. Her intimate experience with Shane the other
night had been like drawing a veil from her eyes. She was
awakening to the demands of the body and he had done
things that thrilled her, drove her wild, but she wanted to
know more, so much more. If she hoped to become the
consummate mistress, she would have to learn what
pleased a man, what thrilled him and drove him to madness. She wanted to learn all the tricks that would bind
him to her, body and soul.

At the last minute Philadelphia Carey and Anne
Vasavour backed out of the evening's adventure, but Sabre decided she would go along with the other two
women, whose reputations were so notorious, the queen
would not have them at court despite her favorite's pleas
on his sisters' behalf.

In the afternoon Sabre went into the stables at Greenwich, slipped a stable boy a few pence to saddle her beloved Sabbath, and rode her to Thames View. She decided that from now on Thames View would be Black
Sabbath's new home as well as her own. She was delighted when Mason told her there were four great boxes
awaiting her, delivered only this morning from the most
expensive dressmaker in London. He had discreetly put
the bills that were delivered with the boxes in Lord
Devonport's library on his desk, for in his wisdom he
knew that Sabre would not wish to be bothered with tri-
fles.

"Would you assemble the female staff for me, Charles
—and," she added with a plea in her voice, "stand
staunchly beside me while I make myself known to
them?"

He coughed politely and with only a slight twinkle in
his eye said, "I've already had a word with them, Mis-

tress Wilde, and I don't think you need concern yourself with any problems from that quarter."

"Oh, you are a marvel, Charles. I am most ignorant about the mores of London society—and many other things, for that matter," she added candidly, "so please don't hesitate in setting me straight when I am about to make a faux pas."

Mason introduced her to the ample-bodied cook and the efficient, no-nonsense housekeeper. Three young housemaids goggled almost openmouthed at her. She spoke to the prettiest. "What is your name?"

"Meg, ma'am." The girl curtsied and blushed.

"Meg, would you like to be my maid?"

"Oh, yes, please, ma'am," breathed the girl, bending her knee again.

"Good. Stop that bowing and scraping. Go and run me a bath; you'll find lots of bath soaps and things in my saddlebags here. Then we'll hang up some of my new dresses and you can help me to dress for the evening."

Meg cast glances at the other two housemaids, clearly flashing them the message that the new mistress liked her best. Then, clutching the saddlebags, she hurried upstairs to prepare the bath.

Sabre had taken over the master bedroom completely. Her new clothes lay everywhere, on the bed, the window seat, and on the chairs and the desk. The gowns were magnificent and took up a lot of space with their wide sleeves and balloon skirts. She couldn't decide which she liked best, but it was a deliciously decadent feeling being able to have so many that it didn't matter which she liked best.

One of her very favorites was the new riding dress, probably because it was so impractical. It was white velvet edged with black braid. The low-cut doublet met in a deep V at the waist, showing the tiniest black silk waistcoat. The matching hat was a tiny white velvet tricorn with an immense black ostrich feather that curved deliciously beneath her chin. Then there was a copper brocade gown heavily embroidered with gold thread and edged in sable fur. It had cost the earth. Another outfit was coordinated green velvet-and-gold brocade. The fitted jacket was green velvet banded at the low bosom with gold, its sleeves slashed with the same gold. The skirt was just the reverse. It was gold brocade banded with green velvet. There were green velvet shoes with golden rosettes and a gold-filigree fan threaded with green velvet ribbons.

She decided on a dark color for the night's adventure. After all, she wished to see, but not be seen, while at the same time she wished to appear sophisticated enough for the racy atmosphere of a brothel. She wore a black lace gown embroidered with silver beads. She shivered with excitement as she smoothed the black silk stockings up her long, slender legs and put on the black, rustling petticoats. Decidedly she had never felt so wicked in her life. She wore a fitted black velvet jacket over the lace gown rather than a cloak, and a black lace face mask completed the outfit.

She took a sedan chair to meet Penelope at Essex House. To Sabre's surprise Essex had decided to join them, but he had Frances Howard in tow, fast becoming known as the biggest little whore at court. Penelope was using an unmarked coach, which blazoned no coat-of-arms this night, and for that Sabre breathed a sigh of relief. They were off down the cobbled stones of the Strand, through Ludgate Circus, and up the hill toward Cheapside and Threadneedle Street.

The occupants of the crowded coach spilled out onto the dark street amid ribald offerings from the Earl of Essex, who was in a particularly witty mood tonight.

"You are in a clever mood, brother," said Penelope, laughing. "Do you perhaps know who is visiting the house tonight and hope to spy on him?"

"God's blood, that would be a lark. What if we uncover Southampton enjoying one of his bum-boys!"

The ladies giggled, but Sabre didn't understand the slang. There were many entrances and exits to the tall dark building, but Essex led them without hesitation through a doorway into a plush reception room. The large man at the door opened it wide as he apparently recognized the head of the party, although he was masked. It was only moments before a tall, striking woman with hair powdered white welcomed them effusively with what seemed to Sabre a French accent. Madame Va Te Faire Foutre, as she was waggishly called, sized up the situation immediately. Essex had escorted four women, so she knew they were there as voyeurs.

"We've come to see a show," ventured Penelope, handing the procuress a small bag of gold.

"Ah, my two principals were to perform the Dance of Love tonight. We will give you a private performance in the *petit théâtre.*" She led the way to a small darkened room with comfortable chairs where they were served wine spiced with myrrh. Their chairs faced a small elevated stage. Before their glasses were drained, the curtain was drawn and two dancers appeared. Both were physically beautiful. The man was tall and heavily muscled, while the girl was small and delicately curved. At first glance in the greenish light they were naked, but as the eyes grew accustomed to the colored light of the stage, two tassles could be seen dangling from the tips of the female's breasts and another tassled fringe covered her mound of Venus. The male's sex was covered by a sheath that lengthened it unnaturally to ten or twelve inches. Both bodies had been painted all over with a silvery-green substance lending an ethereal, otherworldly atmosphere.

Although the movements of the dance were graceful and controlled, it was obvious that the male wished to mate the female. He began to manhandle her brutally, while she tried frantically to escape him. When she managed to elude him, he caught her and dragged her back across the stage. The first time it was by winding her hair about a strong arm and pulling her kicking body back to him. The second time he gripped her delicate ankles cruelly and dragged her across the stage and up onto his thighs. When her legs were crossed behind his neck he stood and swung her until she was limp.

Then began his domination and mastery over her. He stroked her from head to toe with his long shaft and the female first became submissive, then aroused, then frenzied with desire. She slithered her body over and around his torso with sensual, writhing movements. The dance was designed to arouse its audience, and of course it succeeded.

Sabre was both fascinated and repelled by the exotic performance, but she felt her body respond as if it had a will of its own. She could feel the fabric of her underclothing against her nipples and between her thighs. Suddenly a small platform like a table arose in the center of the stage. The male laid the female upon it, then fell upon her and impaled her over and over with his unnaturally long member until she screamed and fell dead. The triumphant male withdrew his weapon and by some magic trick of fireworks the end flew off and showered the female's body with a cascade of sparks. The curtain fell and all except Sabre applauded wildly. The curtain opened again and to her great relief she saw the dancers taking a bow. Sabre had thought the girl had actually died of the abuse. She gasped for air and knew she must get out of that room. She regretted having come; she felt soiled.

The madam returned and led them all laughing up a staircase and along a narrow hallway where peepholes were incorporated into the walls of certain bedrooms. The madam bid them be more quiet and they stifled their laughter as they watched the sex acts that were taking place. Sabre felt nauseated and asked to use the jakes. At first she thought she was going to be sick, but once she was alone, she took a few deep breaths and her stomach righted itself.

She mentally scolded herself for being a baby. Men and women could be gross and there would always be places like this that pandered to the prurient, but somehow she felt the men who availed themselves of the flesh offered by Madame Va Te Faire Foutre were not nearly so wicked as they who had paid to watch.

All the way back to Essex House she was regaled with the bawdy goings-on they had seen and heard in the bedrooms.

"By the rood, the Bible says all men are created equal, but a visit to a brothel soon proves otherwise," said Penelope, laughing.

Sabre blushed furiously, while Frances Howard giggled and moved over onto Essex's knee. The coach pulled up in the courtyard of Essex House and they descended and headed for the front door. Sabre let them go. She needed a few minutes alone to collect herself, and besides, she had no intention of rejoining the group. She would ask Penelope's driver to call a chair and linkboys for her. She got out of the coach wondering if she should spend the night at Greenwich or Thames View when she saw the door of another unmarked coach open and Hawkhurst stepped out.

He had taken the O'Neill to the brothel in Threadneedle Street, where the madam was not French at all, but a loyal Irishwoman. She had become extremely wealthy from her English clientele and kept her top floor reserved as a safe haven where Irishmen true to the cause could hold their secret meetings and escaped prisoners could be concealed until it was possible to secure them safe passage out of England.

Shane had looked from the top-floor windows and seen Sabre enter the front door. At first he told himself he had mistaken her identity—after all, the copper-haired woman had been masked—but when the gay party had departed, he recognized Essex and instructed his driver to go straight to Essex House.

Sabre gasped. Hawkhurst was dressed from head to foot in black like a devil sprung from a dark underworld. His face was closed and forbidding. "Get in!" he ordered.

She was not certain why he was angry. Had he been waiting at Essex House to see if she had been out with Robin? As she stepped forward to offer an explanation, his hand closed over her wrist as if he would crush the bones there; his other hand came up to grab her about the waist and shove her into the coach. Her shoulder jammed painfully into the velvet squabs. He flung himself in after her and slammed the door. Instantly the coach lurched forward and she again fell against the seat.

"How dare you handle me so?" she flared. The words almost stopped in her throat when she saw the savage fury that contorted his features. He did not trust himself to speak until he had his hatred and fury under iron control. The silence inside the carriage increased until it became a tangible thing. His black anger was so terrifying to behold, she was frightened enough to scream.

The small carriage caged him, imprisoning her with him until she could fully sense his strength, his male recklessness, his cruelty. It was like being trapped with a black panther. His eyes burned into her with loathing. He knew if he touched her in that moment he would kill her. His hands would take her slender throat and snap it. "You trollop!" he told her through set teeth.

Suddenly she knew he had seen her leave the brothel. He had been stalking her and she felt like his prey.

"Let me explain!" she cried.

"Be silent!" His voice was so quiet and menacing she felt her blood run cold. Fear of him sprang up full-blown inside her as she saw the aristocratic face so arrogantly tilted, his hawk-visaged features made more predatory by the shadows. He laughed bitterly. "Did you enjoy making a fool of me? I had actually begun to believe you were a virgin."

"I *am* a virgin!" she cried. "Can't you see that's why I went to such a place. I felt so utterly ignorant, I thought I might learn—"

He grabbed her chin. "Silence, I said!" He glowered at her, silencing her quite effectively, then pulled his hand back.

His blood was high and surging; he always rode when he was this angry. He needed to feel the stallion under him between his legs. Well, she would do; he would ride out his anger on her this night. "You may be a whore, but you are *my* whore, bought and paid for."

The carriage jolted to a stop outside Thames View. They were home! Sabre caught her lower lip between her teeth. He was going to take her upstairs and beat her— she could already feel the violence in him. Her eyes closed. Could this possibly be the same man who had worshiped her flesh with his mouth less than a week before? Her legs were so weak that if he hadn't dragged her from the carriage into the house, she wouldn't have made it.

In the front hall she took off the black lace mask and appealed to him with her eyes. Anger flared in him again. Those pale green pools of innocence in which he'd wanted to drown himself would work their magic on him again if he let down his guard for one moment.

"Upstairs!" he commanded.

Meg appeared on the landing, surprised that the master was home and in one of his black Irish moods. "Get to bed," he ordered, and she fled, grateful to God that his anger was not to be vented upon her.

Sabre's legs buckled twice as she mounted the spiral staircase. She heard herself sobbing, "Please . . . Shane . . . listen to me . . . I swear I only watched. . . ."

He was totally indifferent to her pleas and ignored her words, which fanned her anger. She would have this out with him. She would not allow him to beat her. She jumped as he crashed the oaken door closed behind them and locked it.

His gaze swept the room, seeing the expensive gowns tumbled in disordered splendor. When he advanced toward her she stood her ground with chin high, back straight, and breasts thrust forward. He put two strong brown hands into the neck of her gown and tore it viciously to the hem. "I believe I bought this whore's outfit you strut in?" Clad in her daring black undergarments, she would have tempted a saint. Suddenly he couldn't bear the thought that any rutting male with coin in his pocket had coupled with her. She was a lying, deceiving bitch with a luscious, ripe body. He wanted to make love to her till she died of it!

Savagely he tore off her black petticoat and busk, and her heavy breasts sprang free. Her copper hair fell down her body to meet and mingle with the curls between her legs and she stood trembling before him clad only in black lace stockings. She saw his anger mix with uncontrollable lust, a deadly combination, and suddenly she knew he was going to commit the ultimate male punishment. He was going to rape her!

Quickly he removed his cloak and his full array of weapons, carefully locking away his sword, his daggers, and the wicked-looking blade from his boot. He stripped off his doublet, shirt, and breeches. "Get into bed," he growled.

She turned to flee, but he caught hold of her magnificent hair and yanked her back to him. His hands were brutal, and she felt such panic she again broke free. He lunged after her and caught her by her black lace ankle. She realized they were going through the same gyrations as the couple she had witnessed in the Dance of Love. "Shane . . . please . . . no!" she begged.

Fury raged within him. How often he had longed to hear her call him Shane! How he had wanted to taste his name upon her lips.

He threw her powerfully to the bed and positioned her

facedown across his knees. He lifted his hand in uncontrolled rage and slapped her bottom hard.

"You bloody bastard!" she spat.

"I'll teach you a lesson you'll never forget. . . .I'll show you who is master here," he ground out. He continued to spank her curvaceous bottom, but her spirited protests and the sight of her luscious body wiggling before him only served to inflame his desire further into a maelstrom of passion he could not control.

Quickly he flipped her onto her back and pressed her into the feather mattress. Despite her struggles and her exclamations of outrage, he managed to mount her and then plunged into her virginal passage until his shaft was seated to the hilt. As Sabre screamed, he felt the barrier, felt it tear, but it was too late. He withdrew immediately, shocked beyond belief at what he had just done. It was not that he had deflowered her, but that he had done it brutally, defiling them both, and he felt hot shame. With aching tenderness he gathered her to him and cradled her against his heart. Very gently he wiped the blood from her thighs, and she could hear him murmuring against her hair, "God forgive me, God forgive me."

It tore at her heart that things had turned out so badly. She could not stop the tears that filled her eyes slowly and spilled over her cheeks like tiny silver rivers of pain.

He felt her pain like a dagger in his heart. When the racking sobs began, he gently rocked her and allowed her to cry until she was empty. Then with great feminine dignity she pulled away from him and said softly, "Please don't touch me."

"Sabre, my love, I must touch you. . . . I must make it better."

"You'll never be able to do that. Please . . . take me back to Greenwich," she begged.

"No! I cannot let you go like this. I brutalized you," he said with anguish and self-loathing. "I don't want you to think that's the way it is between a man and a woman."

She tried to leave the bed, but her movements were slow, as if he had rendered her so delicate she could be broken with a touch. Unable to bear it, he picked her up and cradled her against his heart, all the while murmuring soft love words against her ear. Sabre felt limp with the exhaustion of her ordeal and managed only a weak resistance against his towering strength.

He laid her gently facedown upon the bed and whispered, "I will kiss away all the hurt, my darling." His kisses trailed all the way up her legs and across her buttocks, then his sensuous lips traced her backbone. A warmth was spreading through her body that washed away the violence and hurt of the previous hour. He pushed her silken mass of hair aside and nuzzled the back of her neck. When she was limp with longing, he gently turned her over and his mouth began its slow, tantalizing journey down her body. Incredibly, he was taking away her hurts in a way she hadn't dreamed would be possible. His tongue bathed her breasts and belly and wound its inexorable way to her core.

"You loved this last time," he murmured as he spread her legs and gently ran his tongue down the rose-pink flesh, then flicked the sensitive jewel of her womanhood. He was flooded with tender relief when he heard her moans of rapture. He spent the next two hours making her feel safe and loved and cherished. "My darling Sabre, I'll never hurt you again," he pledged. "Now that I have made you mine, I will do as you ask and take you back to Greenwich."

Chapter 11

Luckily, Sabre was given no time to dwell upon her hurts or to allow her hatred of Shane to fester deep, for before the light of dawn crept up the sky, Kate Ashford entered her small chamber to announce the move to Windsor.

"The queen simply leaves her apartment in Greenwich, walks into her apartment at Windsor, and finds all in readiness. She hasn't the faintest notion of the over-whelming effort it all takes. You must pack your things instantly and then you'll have to finish my packing for me. Thank God I stored all her clothes with lavender and camphor to keep the moths and must at bay, but they'll still need a good airing before they touch her precious person. She gave me a list two yards long of things she couldn't possibly exist without, and I've been up all night packing them." She paused for a short breath and added pointedly, "While you've been off enjoying yourself."

Sabre gasped at her choice of words, hovered on the brink of tears, then inexplicably she began to laugh. "Oh, Kate, you have a way of turning tragedy into farce." She could see the bedroom at Thames View strewn with her extravagant gowns. She saw herself standing defiantly, clad only in black lace stockings, before Shane, and she realized for the first time his terrible black anger masked the deep pain and hurt he was feeling. Just the suspicion that she had lain with another had wounded him to the point of madness. He had clearly revealed the depth of his feelings for her. It would be a simple matter to make him love her. Once she had accomplished that, she would bind him to her until she became a craving in his blood.

The corners of her mouth went up as she anticipated their next encounter.

When Shane had taken Sabre back to Greenwich in the predawn, he was in a savage mood. Because of the urgent mission to Ireland he hadn't slept in days. At that moment he was disgusted with the world in general and himself in particular. A sixth sense alerted him to the fact that he was being followed. Too bad for the poor bastard who had picked this night when his temper made him so dangerous. The reflexes of years of training never leave a man. He sauntered toward the water steps, then flattened himself against the wall's wet, dripping stones to await his prey. He had him by the throat in an instant, pressing his thumb into the man's windpipe to separate him from his breath. He bent the other arm up his back and held him immobile without even the help of a weapon. His voice was deadly calm as he murmured, "You are making a habit of this. I'm afraid I shall have to give you a short, sharp lesson. To whom do you report?"

The man remained silent, but when Shane jabbed his thumb in farther he could smell the fear upon him. He repeated, "To whom do you report?" then eased out his thumb to allow the man to speak.

"W-Walsingham," he croaked.

Shane bent back the fingers on the hand he had twisted up the man's back until the bones snapped and the man screamed in pain and fled up the water stairs into the blackness.

So, thought Shane, he was under suspicion. His teeth gleamed in the darkness, for he was well aware if they had just one piece of evidence against him, he would now be in the Tower.

* * *

Sabre directed the two footmen who were loading the
baggage cart for Lady Ashford, then hurried to her own
chamber to gather things. She saw the exquisitely
wrought jewel casket upon her pillow immediately and
snatched up the letter sealed with wax and stamped with
the device of a hawk. Her eyes lit up as she opened the
casket to reveal a jade nacklace, studded with turquoise,
almost the twin to the one she had borrowed from the
queen.

My darling Sabre, you are more beautiful than any
queen, and I will give you jewels befitting that beauty.
Shane

She folded the almost treasonous note and tucked it
safely into the casket.

She was allotted a similar chamber at Windsor close by
Lady Ashford's apartment, and inexplicably there was
another message awaiting her arrival. She broke the wax
seal with her thumbnail and scanned his letter eagerly.

My darling Sabre, there is a gift awaiting you in the
stables with my own groom, known as Alex. I would
not have the queen better mounted than you, my love.
Shane

She had to work for several hours beside Kate in the
wardrobe before she could slip down to the vast Windsor
stables. When she found Hawkhurst's groom, he showed
her the small, milk-white Arabian mare and displayed for
her the specially designed silver-and-black saddle and
harness. With Sabbath safely stabled at Thames View she

had forgotten that she would need a mount for the hunting in which the queen indulged almost daily in Windsor's sixty vast wooded parklands.

She stroked the animal's soft muzzle with awe as she realized the price of an Arabian was beyond most people's means. "You are so beautiful," she crooned. "I will call you Jasmine." Incredibly, one of the riding habits she'd had made matched the black and white exactly. How had he known? It seemed Lord Devonport knew more about her than she knew about him. She must remedy the situation immediately. Where did he and the mysterious baron go on their midnight excursions? Already she suspected him of criminal activities such as piracy and smuggling, and now that she thought about it, perhaps there was a great deal more he was involved in. The sooner she moved to Thames View, the sooner she would be able to gather a few facts together.

She must steal some time away from Kate to work on her costumes for the queen's birthday masquerade. She needed one costume for early in the evening when everyone would recognize her, and one shocking costume for later on which none must recognize. The next morning she arrived early at the wardrobe and found there had been a delay in Elizabeth's robing. Her legs almost turned to water at the queen's tirade.

Lady Catherine Grey had fainted after holding up five different gowns from which Her Majesty might choose. Elizabeth's black, beady eyes narrowed dangerously as her mind jumped to the most likely conclusion.

"You sly, malapert strumpet! Dare you stand before me swollen with the fruit of your lust?" the queen shouted.

Lady Blanche Parry, the oldest and most loyal of her

ladies, tried to calm her. "Dearest Majesty, you know how easy it is for these things to happen."

"Easy?" cried the queen, her hair standing on end from her great agitation. "Easy for harlots! This is supposed to be a lady of virtue!" Elizabeth strode toward the hapless Catherine Grey and began to disrobe her. The girl's sobbing pleas were ignored. "What do you have to fear if your conduct has been above reproach?"

It was evident to all present that the girl was heavy with child now that her stays had been loosened. Catherine Grey sank to her knees and whispered, "Your Majesty, I am married."

"You harlot! You dare tell me that? Married? So your crime is even greater. What right did you have to marry without my consent? 'Tis done on purpose to spoil my birthday tomorrow!" The queen's face was livid with anger and jealousy. "His name, mistress," demanded the queen in a voice that brooked no evasions.

"Lord Hertford," whispered Lady Grey, terrified as a trapped doe with the pack at its throat.

Elizabeth stared about the room. "So, you have all conspired to keep this secret from me. Guard! Guard! Escort Lady Catherine Grey to the Tower and arrest Lord Hertford this day!"

The sobbing young woman had to be carried out and the robing ceremony was finished in icy silence. When Kate and Sabre were at last left to restore order from chaos in the wardrobe, Sabre whispered, "Is she demented?"

Kate pursed her lips and said very low, "On the subject of marriage, yes. I fear her mother's death gave her a neurosis of marriage."

Sabre's hand went to her throat. If the queen ever

learned that she was wed to her precious Sea God, what would she not do to her? She vowed to have no contact with him here at court under the queen's very nose.

Blanche Parry came back into the wardrobe room for a furred cloak. She looked at Kate knowingly and said, "You know what's brought this on, don't you? She's about to turn fifty-three and knows she's too old to bear a child."

"Will the birthday celebrations be canceled?" asked Sabre.

"Good heavens no, child. Her moods swing with every change of the breeze. A morning kiss from Essex will have her purring."

Hawkhurst, making doubly sure he wasn't followed this night, made his way to Threadneedle Street. He found O'Neill pacing like a caged lion. He had known it would be difficult to keep him indoors and unobserved with the tempting city of London on his doorstep. The older man pierced Shane with burning eyes. "Ye did not tell me ye are now Lord Devonport."

"I see you've wasted little time catching up on the latest news," remarked Shane, inwardly dreading the next question.

"How is Georgiana?" asked O'Neill.

"In mourning," Shane answered curtly, hoping fervently he didn't find out she was only forty miles distant at Hawkhurst.

O'Neill changed the subject abruptly. "I'll wait no longer to see yer queen," he said bluntly.

Amazed he'd been able to keep his father penned this long, Shane nodded. "You won't have to. Tomorrow night there's a masquerade ball to honor the queen's

birthday. You can attend disguised and reveal yourself to
Bess when you think the moment's right. I have every
confidence you will charm yourself out of a perilous situation. You'll need a gift for the queen," said Shane, thinking aloud.

"I have a gift—one no woman can refuse," he said
with arrogance. Shane's eyes narrowed as the O'Neill
brought home to him the fact that his mother hadn't
refused. This time Shane changed the subject. "We feel
that if you are seen to be on intimate terms with the
queen, the council won't even bother presenting Bagenol's arrest warrant for her signature."

"Don't be seen with me tomorrow night," advised
O'Neill.

Shane slanted a black brow quizzically. It was unlike
his father to show concern for his safety, so perhaps he
had another motive. Shane grinned. "Don't worry, I have
other fish to fry. You're on your own until you wish safe
passage back to Ireland."

September twenty-seventh dawned a glorious day.
Elizabeth thought it her God-given right, yet she was
delighted that the weather cooperated to assure an enjoy-
able hunt for queen and court.

At the morning robing ceremony Sabre was astonished
to see the queen choose an elaborate red brocade gown
and enough jewels to weigh down an elephant. When the
queen departed to her breakfast, Kate laughed at Sabre's
ignorance. "She always hunts in full regalia, as if she
were attending a ball. Never chooses a riding habit. You
notice I pulled three red gowns for her to chose from.
There's method in my madness . . . the blood from the
slaughter won't make her look like a butcher, and if we

don't get all the bloodstains out afterward, it won't be too noticeable."

Sabre shuddered. "She doesn't do the actual killing, does she?"

"Ha! Right in the thick of it. The moment the quarry's brought down, she's there with her knife to slit its throat and cut off its ears to bestow on her favorites!"

Then I shall distance myself from the front ranks, thought Sabre, as she hurried to her chamber to don the lovely white velvet riding dress with its delicious black silk waistcoat, for no one was excused from the royal hunt on the queen's birthday.

The Hawkhurst groom already had her horse saddled and waiting when she arrived late at the stables. The main party of Elizabeth and her courtiers had set off a half hour since, and they set a hard, fast pace for the hunt deep into Windsor's forests. The creamy Arabian was dancing nervously, so she crooned softly to her and firmly stroked her flank before mounting. The horse's flesh quivered beneath her hand for a few moments and then seemed to calm under her touch.

Hawkhurst had been searching for her, riding back and forth along the wooded trails until at last he spotted her. She was the most vivid sight he'd ever seen atop the white mare, in her all-white velvet habit, with her breasts outlined in black silk. Crowning her glorious copper hair was the sauciest feather curving along her cheek, then dipping beneath her chin. If only he could have her to himself, riding on one of his own estates instead of here among this royal rabble.

His eyes sought hers, looking for a sign of forgiveness, but her chin went up at the sight of him and she looked most displeased.

"Sabre, you take my breath away," he complimented.

"If you don't keep away from me, you will take my breath away . . . my life's breath if the queen claps me in the Tower."

At that moment Essex, resplendent in white satin, thundered into the clearing where they sat mounted, and the Arabian mare screamed her fright at the advancing stallion and began to rear. Both men dismounted in a flash and took her bridle to quiet the young horse. Sabre kept her seat, but she was angry at the men for singling her out. "Can you not keep that damned stallion under control?" she demanded of Essex.

He spoke suggestively as always. "He knows a fine piece when he sees one. We are always ready to serve."

A royal page came riding up, his horse badly lathered. "My lord Essex, my lord Devonport, the queen would know your whereabouts and commands you both for her escort."

Both were loath to let go of Sabre's bridle and tried to stare each other down. Finally Hawkhurst ground out, "You're her bloody master of horse, you go!"

"Please, both of you go, I beg you. Did you not know that Lord Hertford and Lady Catherine Grey are in the Tower for having unlawful carnal knowlege of each other? Do not draw the queen's eye to me, I beg you!"

Essex and Devonport looked at each other and bent double with laughter. Essex said, "Mistress Wilde, you sit upon a white Arabian in white velvet and accuse us of drawing attention to you."

Shane's eyes narrowed appreciatively. "You little baggage, if you couldn't be the center of attention, you wouldn't play! Come on, Robin, I'll race you to the queen."

Sabre's mouth curved into a pretty smile. How well he knew her! And tonight at the masquerade ball she would be the center of attention and the talk of the whole court as she stole the queen's thunder. She could hardly wait!

Sabre had never changed clothes so often in her life. She hurriedly exchanged the white velvet habit for a pale blue day-gown and literally ran to the queen's wardrobe. It would take them the best part of two hours to disrobe and disencumber her of her hunting attire and array her in fresh wig, makeup, and the costly gold tissue, encrusted with jewels and sequins. Her costume represented the sun, and as such it was a magnificent creation, with narrowed waist, the skirts flaring out over a wide farthingale. The sleeves were slashed and embroidered with topaz jewels in sunbursts.

The air was filled with the excitement of the special occasion, and the din of her ladies' voices rose high with the fulsome compliments they showered upon Elizabeth, both sincere and insincere. Sabre kept well in the background, wrinkling her nose at the crush of female bodies in the small wardrobe rooms, secretly appalled that the queen did not intend to bathe after the rigorous hunting. When the countess of Warwick brought forth rose-scented bathing water, Bess simply washed the blood from her hands then held up her arms so they could slip on the gold-tissue underdress. As Kate handed the soiled red gown to Sabre, she surreptitiously pointed out the stain of stag entrails that covered the skirt, and Sabre felt the hatred rise in her gorge. This was her rival for her husband's affection; well, even the sun could be eclipsed!

The banqueting chamber at Windsor was able to accommodate twice the number of people as Greenwich. Servingmen staggered beneath platters holding whole kids stuffed with pudding, swans, venison, pike, capons, and wild duck. There were rich sauces of musk, saffron, and ambergris to complement every dish of fish or fowl. The birthday confectionaries were cleverly shaped from spun sugar and marzipan, and every wine known in England was available, including alicante, Rhenish, muscadine, and charneco.

The queen quaffed ale like a man, but kept her head better than most of her courtiers. The music and dancing were to take place in the queen's gallery, which she had had especially built for her in the first years of her reign.

Most of the ladies and gentlemen of the court had spent lavishly on their costumes and jewelry for this birthday celebration. The men dressed as pirates, admirals of the fleet, Arabians, princes, kings, minstrels, jesters, historical figures, highwaymen, and there were at least three dressed as the infamous "Black Shadow." The ranks of the ladies abounded with milkmaids, shepherdesses, angels, fairies, and princesses, though none were foolish enough to masquerade as queens.

Sabre's costume represented spring. It was delicate pale green tissue edged with violets. Her breasts were cupped in flower petals and her mask was in the shape of a swallow-tailed, pale butterfly. Her pulses were hammering madly as she watched the crowds carefully through her mask, seeking Hawkhurst. They recognized each other in the same instant. He had chosen not to wear a costume, though his clothes were a flamboyant midnight-blue, slashed with silver and fastened with diamond buttons. He had conceded to wear a concealing mask, his eyes glittering wickedly through its slits.

Sabre instantly turned her back upon him, and it had exactly the result she had hoped for. His hands grasped her shoulders from behind and he turned her to face him. "Sabre, you are the prettiest thing I've ever seen. I approve of your costume with all my heart."

"I am striving for demureness, m'lord. Your approval is everything to me," she said with heavy sarcasm. "I'm sorry if you wished to dance, but I'm promised to another." She turned and melted into the crush of people behind her.

He was stung, for he was carrying a present he'd had specially engraved for her. He ground his teeth at the rebuff and bided his time by looking for the O'Neill.

At eleven o'clock the queen would take her seat on a raised dais at the end of the room, and those who wished to honor her with their special gifts would bring them forward one at a time. Until eleven Elizabeth would dance every single measure, and young men fought for the honor. As usual the earl of Essex did not dance, but, dressed to compliment her in cloth of gold, he never took his eyes from her. When each courtier had partnered her in the gavotte or the pavane, he returned her to m'lord Essex. Finally he broke his own no-dancing rule and led the queen out onto the floor to broach the subject that was eating at his pride.

"I have heard a rumor which I cannot credit, queen of my heart."

She arched a brow at him, knowing by the sulky look of his mouth that he was displeased about something.

"Rumor has it you intend to make the old lord admiral the earl of Nottingham."

" 'Tis no rumor, but fact. He has given me faithful service for years, his health is not what it used to be, and I intend to honor him before he departs this earth."

"Madame, do you realize when Parliament opens next month, he will then take precedence over me?" he questioned arrogantly.

Her eyes narrowed, yet her feet never missed a step of the dance. "I would have you know that I who made you can unmake you!"

His eyes smoldered at her insult. "Plums for others; threats for me," he hissed.

"I will have you know this court has one mistress and no master!" she shouted, uncaring who overheard.

He cajoled softly, "If I were earl marshal of England, I would take precedence."

She set her mouth in a grim line and said, "I would remind you that your queen will not be badgered into yielding to a brash youth's every whim!"

He bowed stiffly and deserted her in the middle of the dance floor. A deep, soothing voice floated down to her. "Lass, ye are as lovely as ever . . . like a young girl."

Elizabeth turned startled but grateful eyes to the man who towered above her. He removed his mask and looked deep into the black eyes.

"Tyrone!" She used the title she had bestowed upon him, then added her affectionate term she reserved for him alone. "My monster of the north!"

She had always leaned on Leicester, but with him far away in Holland and with Essex's growing petulance, she was sorely in need of a strong male to lean on, if only for a short time. Who better than an older man who thought her still a young girl? "Would you care to dance?"

"Nay, lass, I'm an old man compared to ye. Come sit with me awhile."

"Lying Irish!" she admonished, yet she took him by

the hand to the dais at the head of the room and dispatched a page for ale and marzipan cakes. "What have you brought me for my birthday?" she asked, flirting archly.

He bent his lips to her ear and whispered, "Information, lass. News of yer enemies more precious than bejeweled geegaws. But it will wait until morning. I'll not spoil this night for ye, Bessie." His soft Irish voice lulled and caressed her and he took possession of one of her beautiful slim hands beneath the cover of her full skirts.

Shane was momentarily amazed to see the O'Neill sitting cozy with the queen, then he smiled cynically to himself. *We Irish have a low tolerance for bullshit and yet a remarkable facility with it.* For gain the O'Neill would convince an old queen she was young and strong, while discovering her vulnerabilities to use to his own ruthless advantage.

The music struck up for the saraband, to which a man and woman danced in each other's arms. The queen was forgotten as he sought out Sabre once more.

"M'lord Devonport, I dare not. This dance is meant to inflame lust," she said with an air of practiced innocence.

He held her pale green gaze with his. "Sabre, you'd dare anything. You'd tell me to go to hell, you'd thumb your nose at the queen, and you'd tell the devil himself to kiss your bottom." He took a velvet box from his doublet and pressed it into her hands. It held a gold bracelet studded with diamonds. On the inside was inscribed, *Can you forgive me?* She slipped it onto her wrist and lifted a matching diamond ring from the box. When she held it to the light to read its tiny inscription, she was startled to read, *Can you love me?* She searched his face long minutes, uncertain whether she should accept or reject his token, while her heartbeat hammered in her breast.

Unable to bear the uncertainty longer, Shane grasped her hand strongly and forced the beautiful ring upon her finger.

Damn him, she thought wildly, he has the capacity to make a woman throw everything to the winds in order to spend her days and nights in his strong arms!

Even the tips of his fingers tingled with the desire to touch her breasts and other secret places, and before she had a chance to refuse he swept her into his arms to the seductive strains of the saraband. He held her so close to his body, she could feel his heat, his strength, and even his violence held barely in check. Her eyes went involuntarily to his lips, and she could not stop her imagination from tasting him and feeling his hot mouth covering hers. She closed her eyes and shuddered. There was no distance in the dance between their yearning bodies. They were both weak with desire as the beat of the music set up a rhythm in their blood. Suddenly his hands tightened on her and she knew he would be denied no longer. The muscle in his jaw jerked as he demanded, "My chasing after you is finished. . . .I will not kiss the hem of your gown, begging your favors with flowery phrases. . . .I am a man! I want you, Sabre, and I want you tonight! Is it yes or no?"

"My answer is yes, of course, for 'tis a man I would have for my lover," she said huskily.

He took his hands from her tempting body and forced them to his sides, for they had yet over an hour to get through until midnight. "Meet me at the upper ward by the Norman Gate, where there are many trees to shelter you from prying eyes."

Lord Hatton came to claim the dance she had promised him, but she had to disappoint him, for it was time
for her to go up to her small chamber and change her
costume!

Chapter 12

Sabre's blood sang with excitement as she stripped off the demure green gown representing spring and took from the cupboard the wisp of cloth that would transform her into a figure from Greek mythology. The white silk toga came only to her hips, leaving her long, slim legs completely bared. The white silk toga not only left one shoulder bare, it also exposed one beautiful breast with its pouting, gilded nipple.

She slipped on the small sandals and bound their golden thongs about her bare legs. Then, paying close attention to cover all her copper tresses, she put on a blond wig fashioned from a portrait of a Greek goddess with golden tendrils falling to her shoulders. She was the huntress Diana with real bow and a quiver of arrows, and as she fastened the winged mask across her eyes, she smiled her secret smile at the impact her unclad form would have on the assembly below. She tossed her head in defiance, her eyes shone brilliantly with their dare-me challenge, and she strode boldly down the staircase, confident that she would be the female most talked about and longest remembered when the queen's birthday celebrations were discussed.

She had gauged the time correctly and only had to wait a short time as the last few gifts were presented to the queen. Then she slipped off her long cloak, tucked it into an alcove, and pushed through the doorway of the long gallery. Her courage almost failed her; but she braced her knees, licked her lips, and stepped forward with the confidence of a true goddess.

There was a hush, then the crowds separated to let her

pass through. She heard gasps as her long bare legs were seen and her bared breast with its golden nipple were ogled.

The members of the court stared, gaped, and gawked as she strode purposefully to the end of the room. The whispers began then became louder and louder until the entire room was abuzz with speculation. Some suggested it was a tableau that had been planned, since it was timed so perfectly to climax the celebrations. Everyone wanted to know the identity of the mystery goddess who had sprung among them in a wisp of white silk that revealed her divine form to perfection.

She knelt at the foot of the dais and placed there her gift of a golden arrow, the high cost of which would be borne by Hawkhurst. The queen stared bemused at the spectacle. Elizabeth concealed her shock and would not become jealous until days later when she realized the magnitude of the attention the mysterious goddess was receiving.

Sabre felt the impact of the burning eyes of the arrogant red-haired man who sat next to the queen. She'd never seen him before and didn't know who he was, but she was impaled by his look of malevolence. In that fleeting moment she knew he hated all women and considered himself superior to every mortal in the room. She tore her eyes from him and bowed low to the queen. Then her long legs sprinted back down the length of the gallery like those of a true Diana, goddess of the hunt. Quickly she slipped into the alcove, wrapped herself in her cloak, and removed the mask and the wig. Within ten minutes she was safely in her chamber, locking away the bow and quiver. She bathed her flaming cheeks with rosewater, then slowly brushed out the tangles from her hair until it billowed about her like a copper cloud. She would go to Shane dressed as she was! Her pulses raced at the thought of what his reaction would be. Would he want to kill her for exposing herself to other men's eyes, or would the need to possess her blot out everything save his hunger? She shivered with anticipation at the thought of his anger and lust; a devastating combination.

Shane Hawkhurst pulled the diamond buttons from his doublet and secured them in an inside pocket before he began his ascent of the thick stone walls of the north terrace. Her Majesty's state apartments were in the upper ward of the castle and he was familiar with the queen's private bedroom and its antechambers, which overlooked the gardens of the north terrace through its elegant arched windows. Although the draperies were drawn at most of the windows, he could easily see into the rooms of the queen's private apartment. He waited patiently while her ladies divested her of her golden gown and she selected a negligee that revealed more than it concealed. He smiled knowingly to himself. Bess loved to show off her body to men. Leicester, when he was at court, handed her her shift in bed each morning and often she could be seen in dishabille waving from her windows to a favorite in the garden below.

His mind kept running ahead to the hours he would spend abed with Sabre, and he almost left when he pictured her waiting for him at the Norman Gate; but he forced himself to patience and finally he was rewarded when Bess's ladies left her for the night and he saw her hurry across her chamber to an inner door. She opened it and the unmistakable figure of his father stepped into the room to dominate the small female who had left her queenship outside her bedchamber this night so she could play the woman.

Satisfied that the earl of Tyrone was home safe, now that she had allowed him this much intimacy, he descended the stone walls with a feeling of relief. Because of his quick action in bringing him out of Ireland, he had probably saved his life.

He stood quietly in the shadow of a beech, afraid that Sabre had tired of waiting for him. Then he saw a movement along the garden path and his heart lifted in triumph.

"Darling," he whispered, and gathered her close in a protective embrace. He was impatient to bring her home, so he tucked her beneath one arm. "Come, we'll take the river."

She smiled. He was too impatient to dally with kisses here in the labyrinths of the garden, for Windsor was much farther from Thames View than Greenwich. His shrill whistle pierced the night air and carried onto the water to a wherryman, who brought his barge over to the water steps. "Kew," he said curtly, tossing him a small gold coin, then he drew Sabre to the cushions in the shadows at the back of the boat and took her into his strong arms. His mouth found hers and he whispered against her lips, "Tomorrow I'll order you a barge of your own. 'Twill give us privacy from prying eyes, and I want you to come to me whenever you can, my love."

He tried to be gentle as his mouth covered hers, but his seeking hands went beneath her cloak and came in contact with bare flesh.

"God's blood, you're almost naked," he whispered hoarsely as he let his hands play and slide up her silken thighs. He did not connect her with the female in the short silk toga who had scandalized the court but imagined her to be clad in only an undergarment to tantalize him. "Ah, my beloved Sabre, you are incomparable; one of a kind." He laid her back upon the cushions and pressed her to the hard length of him. "You've led me such a dance; think of all the time we've wasted," he said against her throat.

She teased, " 'Tis only a game we play, m'lord. You told me so yourself. You have enjoyed the chase and I have enjoyed the wooing. I think so far it is a draw between us."

"No game this, I am in deadly earnest, my darling." He groaned. "I've wanted you from the moment I set eyes upon you."

"When I was lost and you took advantage of me!" she accused.

"Ah, no, my beautiful Sabre, you stole my heart from me long before that."

Wildly curious, she pretended indifference. He would tell her in bed, she promised herself. In bed was where he was going to tell her everything she wished to know.

He fondled her shamelessly until she was hot with desire for him. He pushed aside the scant silk undergarment and stroked her unmercifully with his long, hard fingers, never taking his mouth from hers. When he wanted to bring her to a little climax he plundered her mouth with his thrusting tongue and thrilled as she arched into his hand.

The wherryman called out "Kew water steps" in a loud voice, as he knew the couple in the shadows were on the verge of coupling. Sabre felt the tension and desire rise in him. "I cannot let you from my arms," he said. When the barge stopped, he wrapped her cloak tight around her and carried her up the water steps, across the lawns, and into the big house. He swept her up the grand staircase without pause and set her gently on her feet while he locked the door of the master bedchamber and lit the candles.

She stood quietly beside the massive curtained bed until he turned to her from lighting the candles. Very deliberately she unfastened her cloak and let it slip in a dark pool to the carpet, revealing herself to him as the goddess Diana.

His eyes widened in surprise. "It was you!" he said in amazement. She saw his dark blue eyes smolder with anger as he closed the space between them swiftly and, taking hold of her shoulders, jerked her to him. "Why? Why must you play the wanton?" he demanded, shaking her angrily.

She tilted her head back provocatively to take in his great height. "Because I'm jealous of the queen and I intend to steal you from her totally and absolutely."

"Little witch! I'm the one who's mad with jealousy, and well you know it!"

She placed her hands over his on her shoulders to draw the strap of the toga from her covered breast. It slipped down her arm and slithered to the floor. His eyes fastened on her gilded nipples thrusting up impudently, and he was lost. His passion engulfed her and she cried out at a particularly brutal caress, but her cry was smothered as his mouth crushed down upon hers. He forced her head back, arching her until her ripe breasts were pressed full against his hard, muscular chest. He kissed her eyelids and her ears, murmuring passionate, unintelligible words. He licked the little beauty spot high on her cheekbone as he pressed himself boldly against her until every inch of their bodies touched.

She knew he was a passionate man, yet she was amazed and a little afraid at the raging ardor she had awakened in him. Her arms entwined about his neck and he hungrily lifted her against his heart. She let the small core of remaining resistance melt away as she clung to him hungrily, inviting his frankly sensual exploration of her mouth. He lifted her to the bed and stripped off his clothes with sure, deft fingers. His hands were caressing her bare limbs now as he unwrapped the thongs of her sandals and tore away the silk undergarment.

The bed dipped as he knelt above her and his whipcord arms came slowly around her. She knew his great strength, yet she marveled at his ease in lifting her, turning her, and taking her down with him. His hardness was a hot, burning brand against her thighs. He began to explore the secrets of her body with the sureness of a knowledgeable lover. He moved his fingers and his mouth over her with deliberate slowness, savoring what he found, until she trembled beneath his slightest touch. She gasped, wanting more, and he gave it. He buried his face against her throat. "I have waited an eternity for this," he murmured thickly.

Then his mouth began to taste and tease her breasts until her nipples throbbed and she was tight and aching inside with her need for him. She moaned with pleasure and frustration as her nails dug deeply into the shoulder blade where the dragon rampaged. He gasped and thrust into her deeply. His shaft was long and thick, and she felt a quicksilver stab of pain, instantly replaced by a hot, burning, throbbing fullness that went deeper and deeper until she thought she must die of it. She clasped her legs about him and yielded completely to his flaming kisses.

Dimly she heard him shout with exultation at his possession of her. She lay pinioned beneath his strong body; his now at last, totally *his*! He set up a rhythm in the silken depths of her tight sheath and matched it with his tongue. He was making her fly with the wind. She could feel him pulsing and quivering within her soft body, and she felt him growing bigger with his insatiable hunger for her. Instinctively she knew this was greater than what most lovers experienced. Feelings and sensations that ran deep into the soul would bind them together through eternity. He was in her blood no matter how she had tried to deny it, and she would not rest until he was plagued by her night and day; obsessed by her to the point where he would perish without her. She cared not what she had to do to enslave him. She would be witch and angel; she would be everything to this man, slave, concubine, mistress, whore. She would be his wife and she would be his enemy!

Her thoughts spun away from her as she was rendered mindless. She could only feel and taste the pleasure of him now as her blood pulsed through her veins, spiraling her higher and higher, to a point where it was totally, physically impossible to endure more exquisite pleasure. Yet still his plunging thrusts went deeper and faster until every nerve trembled with the fury of his assault. He was savagely demanding in his lovemaking, his body's strength urging her to meet and match his towering passion.

A volcano erupted inside her. She felt her own explosion and then she felt his scalding burst of fire flood into her with the force of a thunderbolt. It tore a low scream from her throat and a great shuddering sob from his. They lay entwined, still as death, and she wondered if she would ever be able to breathe again. After a very long time she stirred against him, but his arms tightened, one leg moved across her to pin her to the bed, and she felt him still within her, unwilling to separate his body from hers now that he had finally claimed and taken possession of it.

Finally, drugged with love, they slept for two hours. They clung together in sleep, as they had when awake, as if bound to each other body and soul. Sabre awoke drowsily to find his warm body molded against her. He kissed her closed eyelids and she submitted to his questing hands, which aroused tingles of delight in every nerve.

"Brute," she whispered. "I cannot move a finger."

He laughed deep in his throat. "Your dragon of the night, m'lady, has need of you again." His lips brushed her throat, and as his possessive hand slid down over her belly, she knew she would surrender herself to his masterful embrace. She cried out in protest as he left her.

With pantherlike grace he stepped from the bed to relight the candles, then he pulled the cover from her and spread her hair across the pillows like flowing, molten copper. She had the face and body of a beautiful temptress, and for one suspended moment his Irish imagination took control of his mind and he wondered if she were a mortal or some magic fairy woman from the otherworld.

Her pale green glance made him melt and grow hard in the same instant. She was becoming conscious of the sensual attraction his hard body had for her. His fierce onslaught of desire shook his body as once more he hungered to feel her supple, silken body beneath his and to taste the sweet mouth that haunted him. His eyes traveled the length of her, making her feel that he was devouring her. He felt a need that he had denied for weeks but could deny no longer. He needed her to love him. He reached out a finger to trace the swelling curve of her breast and up to its golden peak, all the while studying her eyes to watch them grow dark with desire, watching her soft mouth open with yearning. He leaned down to kiss her waiting lips, then murmured low against her mouth, "Love me, Sabre, love me."

She had no will of her own. Was it possible to love and hate at the same time? Nay, she'd never admit she loved the man, but she was honest enough to admit that she loved his body. The feel and smell and taste of his skin aroused her so much she had to bite her lips to keep from screaming with excitement. As the sensual male-female mysteries unfurled for her, her senses heightened, widened, and expanded. Nothing remained the same. Physically, mentally, and emotionally she was altered forevermore. It was truly an awakening that was almost spiritual.

This time he made love to her slowly, leisurely, until it became exquisite torture for both of them. He paid homage to every inch of her body, savoring, worshiping with gentle hands and lips as if she were made of the most fragile porcelain. He took her tenderly, drawing out their hour of love until it peaked into a starburst totally different from the time before. It was as if they were making love for the first time, and the last.

When they awoke again, the eastern horizon had begun to lighten. She lay nestled close, cradled in his arms, and the slow, powerful beat of his heart lulled her with a deep, safe sense of security. Wistfully she sighed. "Dawn comes so quickly." She tried to arise, but his arms shot about her like bands of steel.

"Nay, love, I'll not let you leave me today."

"But . . . the queen," she protested.

He shook his head. "She has her hands full, I'll warrant. Kate will manage without you, but I will not. It's taken me too long to capture you to release you so quickly." Half afraid she would flee, he loosed his hold upon her, but she sat back upon her heels and smiled down at him. Her hair cascaded wildly over her naked body. His hands lifted the silken tresses from her breasts so his gaze could roam unhindered. "Lord, are you angel or witch, for I am surely spellbound." He lifted her to straddle one of his hard thighs, and she rode it in playful abandon.

"Ah, I remember now," he said, feeling the scratched furrows across his back, "you make love like a wildcat when receiving your pleasure."

Suddenly she dipped her head and darted her tongue into his navel. He gasped at the thrill that ran through his body like wildfire.

"You are a bold wench, Sabre Wilde. Are you bold enough to tame the dragon?"

"I'll slay the dragon," she whispered wickedly.

He lifted her onto his great manroot so she could finish her ride. She thrust her hips forward and arched her back so that her hair cascaded down upon his thighs, and he thrust up deeply in rhythm with each of her downward plunges. He refused to release her until she had twice let down her love juices to anoint his manhood.

She sat between his legs, her back against his broad chest, his knees slightly drawn up for her to rest her arms upon. It was to become a favorite position for them whenever they wanted to talk in bed. They shared the breakfast tray Mason had brought them, grinning guiltily because their vocal, tempestuous lovemaking had alerted the entire staff of Thames View to her presence in their master's bedchamber.

"Shane, who was that man with the queen last night?" she asked idly.

She felt him stiffen at the question and was immediately alerted that he sensed danger. He told her some of the truth. "Though the queen has forbidden the name, it was the O'Neill, known in England as the earl of Tyrone."

She looked startled. "The uncrowned king of Ireland?" She shuddered involuntarily. "The man is trouble," she murmured.

He lifted her hair, and his lips brushed the nape of her neck. "A wolf among wolves. That's what I meant when I said Bess had her hands full at the moment," he said lightly.

"He has the same kind of arrogance as you . . . except . . . except he is cold, pitiless, brimful of hatred." She hesitated. "Keep away from him."

Shane laughed mirthlessly. He'd been trying to do that for years, but never succeeded. His father had him on an invisible thread; all he needed to do was tug on it.

His arms tightened about Sabre as if she were his salvation. "When he and the queen have played their little game of domination and submission, he'll return in triumph to Ireland."

She stretched and made a face at him. "You have made every muscle in my body ache. I'm going to have a long, hot bath, then I'm going to exercise Sabbath."

"I know what you need," he said, smiling.

"Oh, no you don't, Hawkhurst. You are insatiable!"

He chuckled. "No, really, I'll give you a massage." He flexed his hands and slanted a brow at her. "Secrets learned in the Far East," he promised, as he took a flacon of perfumed oil from a cabinet and stretched her out upon her stomach. *So, rumor was true,* she thought jealously, *he did have an Oriental mistress before me.*

He straddled her hips, holding her captive between his muscular thighs, then, pouring the scented oil into his cupped palm, he rubbed her shoulders and back with long, firm, sensual strokes.

"Tell me of these secrets of the East," she cajoled, stretching luxuriously beneath his ministrations.

"I was only teasing," he said lightly as his hands slipped beneath her to fondle her soft, round breasts.

"Shane, tell me, I'm wildly curious."

"Your curiosity is most titillating and exciting, my little wildcat, but, you see, Oriental culture is always geared toward the man's pleasure. An Oriental woman takes a totally passive role in sex, with all focus on pleasure for the male. She is eternally submissive, a role which doesn't suit you at all, thank God," he said, dropping little kisses on her satin-smooth skin. He moved farther down, to straddle her legs, and let his strong hands massage her delicious buttocks.

"Tell me more," she begged, writhing beneath his fingers.

"In the Orient nothing is more tempting than the forbidden. They do things that break through Western taboos." He hesitated, then decided to describe a practice that was sure to shock her. "Would you like to know of the Seven Knots to Heaven?

"Yes," she said, giggling.

"The female puts seven knots into a silken cord, then very gently inserts them into her partner . . . here." He placed his finger on the intimate spot between her buttocks, and she was shocked speechless.

"Then, when the man reaches his climax, she pulls the silken cord out slowly and with each knot he experiences another orgasm . . . seven in one!"

She gasped in disbelief, and he laughed and said, "Your innocence is truly a delight to me."

Though they quickly became aroused, she would not permit him to make love to her again and she firmly locked the door of the bathing room. She would save these things for another time lest he become sated with her.

They spent the day together intimately, excluding the world. Both knew their time alone together would be sporadic at best, so they made the most of their day. They rode together, dined, talked, laughed, dreamed, and all the while they were handclasped like a young boy and girl. Shane looked at her as if she were the first female he'd ever laid eyes on, and acted as if he'd just discovered his manhood.

After supper the baron delivered a note to him and fear struck her heart.

"Darling, 'tis nothing. I must go out for a short time, but I promise I'll be back in time to carry you to bed."

"And if I ask where you're going, you will fob me off with a lie. And if I asked you why you were at that brothel last week, you would tell me none of my damned business. But mark my words, Shane Hawkhurst, I'll have the tale from you."

"I can't be cajoled," he replied lightly.

"Ha! Can't be cajoled," she said, laughing, as her eyes played about his loins until she saw him rise up.

"What colors for your barge, sweetheart?"

See, she said to herself, he was doing it now, fobbing her off with an expensive present.

"Let's see . . . white and purple . . . royal purple!" she ordered.

Chapter 13

Shane went into the city alone to answer the summons from O'Neill. He climbed to the top floor of the brothel on Threadneedle Street, removed his black cloak, and shook off the raindrops that had just started to fall.

O'Neill's eyes, those dark orbs that saw everything and said nothing, sought those of his son. Shane knew he'd never grow used to them. The two men extended their right arms until with a dull thud their hands fell on each other's shoulders. Such a blow would have almost felled a horse, but neither man flinched. Finally O'Neill's voice broke the silence. "I played her like an Irish harp. The moment she became pliant, I seduced her with my golden tongue. I told her plantationing Ireland was wrong, yet her men in Dublin went blindly ahead with it. I told her graft was rampant in Dublin's government. English lords are voracious for Irish land, and for coins placed in the right palm they are handed five thousand acres apiece. But to a man they are absentee landlords with overseers who make slaves of the Irish! I told her the English of Dublin rob her government in England as viciously as they do Ireland. I demanded an honest governor and in exchange I would keep all the clans neutral."

Shane nodded, waiting for the rest. O'Neill's neck was safe, but whom had he betrayed in safeguarding his position?

"I told her there was a Catholic underground with directives coming in daily from France and Spain. I told her plainly her English Catholic lords had plans to restore Catholicism to England and put Mary of Scots on her throne. She demanded names and I supplied them—

Henry Garnet, Robert Southwell, Throckmorton at Mile End, and Babington. I told her the Ship Tavern at Lincoln's Inn Fields in Holborn was a Catholic gathering place."

Shane would have to warn the Irish Catholics who gathered there, for he knew O'Neill would let them all be sacrificed.

"She bade me inform Walsingham this night, so if there is any business you must take care of before he gets this information, you'd better be about it."

Shane thought O'Neill must have balls of brass to face Walsingham with the dossier he must have on him. The O'Neill gathered up his cloak and bent to slip a blade into his boot, then he snuffed the candles with bare fingers. They did not wish to risk being seen together, so O'Neill started toward Cheapside to the Strand and Walsingham House and Shane turned toward Gracechurch Street and the river, but after a long pause he turned and followed his father at a discreet distance. Suddenly he stiffened, for out of the shadows stole a dark, menacing figure which was clearly following the O'Neill. He instantly dismissed thoughts of a footpad or cutpurse; this was a spy Shane had unwittingly led to O'Neill. Now the two of them would be connected, and the cover of the brothel blown to hell for Irish spies. Shane cursed beneath his breath; he had no choice but to eliminate the man.

His progress was impeded by Cheapside whores who sidled up to him from doorways asking, "Want yer door-knob polished, luv?" One glance from his deadly cold eyes and they quickly dissolved back into the shadows. As O'Neill rounded St. Paul's Churchyard his assailant quickened his pace to close the gap, and with horror

Shane saw the glint of steel in the man's hand. He bellowed a warning, "Tyrone!"

The O'Neill whirled about, slipped on a rain-slimed cobblestone, and his giant frame went down heavily. Shane was afraid his assailant would cut and run now that he knew he was against two, but the dark figure flew at him like a devil out of hell. Shane raised his arm to stab him and to his complete amazement felt his assailant's knife plunge into his armpit to the hilt. Yet Shane's arm carried through with his own knife, which went true and steady into the heart. The man's scream was cut off as his mouth frothed with his life's blood.

Suddenly they heard the running bootsteps of the watch and knew they would be arrested for murder. Half a dozen uniformed men armed with lanterns and muskets advanced in the name of the queen. O'Neill was on his feet in a flash. He lifted the dead man and held him erect with a long arm thrown about him. Shane swayed on his feet, pulling his black cloak to conceal his bloody wound. The O'Neill straightened to his full six and a half feet and towered over the men of the watch. "We are coming from a late meeting with the lord chancellor. I'm afraid my friend here has had too much to drink." Then he spoke in Gaelic to the watch, who was burly and dark-haired, and Shane saw with relief that the man understood. The watch lowered their lanterns and allowed the three to go on their way toward the river. They half carried, half dragged the deadweight toward the Mermaid Inn, then let the body slip from the pilings into the fast-flowing Thames. Only then did Shane fall against the wall of the inn, weakened from his great loss of blood.

O'Neill placed an arm about him and helped him to the water stairs by Blackfriars Bridge.

"Go on," Shane gasped, "I'll go home."

O'Neill considered for long minutes, then said grudgingly, "I'll take you to the baron."

Shane, hearing the reluctance in his voice, laughed aloud, then promptly passed out in his father's arms.

Sabre amused herself by trying on all her new gowns, preening before the oval cheval mirror. The pretty clothes lifted her heart, and as she hummed a tune and hung up a whole row of new and expensive finery it came to her that she hadn't been this happy in a very long time. She wondered idly what was keeping Shane, then decided to take his pair of wolfhounds for a walk while she investigated the grounds of Thames View.

The dogs shot off into the shadowed twilight, and for one disastrous moment she thought they had run away; but to her relief she saw them circle back and streak past her, following the scent of some trail. Thank God he has them well trained, she thought. She rather expected to meet him returning up the river, but after lingering by the water's edge for half an hour, she strolled back to the house, a slight frown marring her pretty features.

She went into his library and browsed through a shelf of fine books. Finally selecting one, she took it upstairs with her. As the time ticked past, she found herself unable to concentrate on the book. She arose and went to the window, but night had fallen and she stared out into blackness. Uneasy, she began to pace the chamber.

Sabre wasn't the only one pacing at Thames View. The baron cursed himself for not having accompanied Shane. He knew he was able to handle himself in any situation, yet in all his dealings with the O'Neill, the baron's unease persisted. It is a joy and curse to bear the blood of Erin,

he thought. Sometimes there is a dark morbidity that is
the private hell of an Irish mind. He tried to shake off his
fears, but his sixth sense persisted.

Sabre was becoming annoyed that so new a lover could
neglect her so shamefully, and yet she admitted her annoyance masked her apprehension. Finally she faced it
squarely. What did she fear? The answer came back that
her fear was for him. Why should she care? Didn't she
want her revenge? Wasn't she going to hurt him? The
answer came back, yes, she wanted to hurt him, but inexplicably she didn't want anyone else to hurt him!

She decided to seek out the baron. If Shane had gone
on one of his secret adventures, perhaps he would be
gone for days and she would have to return to Windsor
tonight, late as it was. She heard raised voices from the
east wing of the house and hurried in their direction.

"Wounds taken under the arm are fatal, man, and well
ye know it!" shouted the red-haired giant Shane had told
her was the earl of Tyrone. "I'm off . . . more time I
cannot waste."

The baron fixed him with a dark stare. "Waste? He's
your son!"

Sabre stood transfixed at the entrance to the baron's
chamber. The baron could speak after all, and the words
he spoke were unbelievable, yet it was the other's words
that had constricted her heart. Her eyes flew to the still
figure stretched across the table between the two men.
"He's dead!" she cried in anguish, rushing forward. She
turned upon O'Neill wildly. "This is your doing—
whether by your hand or another, you are to blame!"

The look he gave her was terrible to behold, but she
stood her ground as the candles cast shadows across the
ceiling's beams.

He sneered, "The queen sets the pace for independence in Englishwomen. In Ireland we make good women by beating and bedding them regularly."

The baron was rapidly divesting Shane of his clothes, oblivious to the others in the room. The unconscious man groaned and Sabre cried, "He lives! Let me help you."

O'Neill picked up his cloak and said with scorn, "Now that his whore has arrived, ye won't need my assistance."

She watched the baron arrange knives, scissors, and strange surgeon's instruments on the bedside table. He had a cabinet filled with bandages, potions, and unguents of every hue in strange bottles and boxes. She saw him sprinkle crystals into a silver bowl of hot water and it turned dark purple. Then he sponged the gaping wound, which still spewed blood.

"Will he live?" she breathed. Silence filled the room. "Speak, damn you. He lied to me—told me you couldn't speak, yet I heard you."

The baron's voice was a thing of beauty when he finally spoke. Modulated, cultured, and kind, yet strong and reassuring. "He did not lie. He said, 'The baron *does not* speak,' not 'The baron *cannot* speak.'" He paused. "O'Neill was right. Wounds taken deep in the armpit are nearly always mortal wounds, and yet he is the strongest man I have ever known."

"Then you think there is a chance he can survive this?"

"It is up to you and me to see that he does," he said with calm conviction. He packed the wound and bound him so tight, the pressure prevented him from expanding his lungs.

"He cannot breathe," she protested.

Patiently he explained, "This is just while I carry him up to bed—else the last of his lifeblood would flow from

him." When Shane was laid out in his own bed, the baron
once again with sure, gentle hands repacked the wound
and bound him tightly, only this time allowing the unconscious man to take shallow breaths.

"What can I do?" she asked humbly.

"Keep him in this bed," he said simply. "I will go and
brew up some herbs to strengthen him. Call me the moment he regains consciousness."

Sabre gazed down at the man in the bed. He wore a
death mask, so pale and still did he lie. Now she knew the
real reason he was called Shane. He was Irish. He was a
prince of Ireland. It all seemed so inevitable, as if she had
known . . . their destinies bound together for good or ill
since the dawn of time.

Suddenly he threw off the covers and thrashed about.
He did not open his eyes, so she did not know if he had
regained consciousness. She covered him and tried to
hold him still but he would not. She began to croon to
him, in a calming, loving voice, willing him to obey her
soft commanding incantation, and he did begin to respond: calming when she crooned, thrashing when she
stopped. The paleness had begun to leave him, but it was
replaced by a flush, and when she laid her hands upon his
body, she felt him burning.

The baron came in with a large goblet. He handed it to
Sabre, then gently lifted Shane's head from the pillows.
She put it to his lips and they patiently waited until he
had swallowed half the contents. She brought a ewer of
cooled rosewater from the bathing room and gently
sponged his face, neck, and chest. Then the baron lifted
his head again and they tenderly coaxed the rest of the
elixir into him. The baron stayed for two hours while the
potion did its work to break the fever, and they held him

still, one on either side. When the crisis came and the dry
fever broke, moisture poured from him until the bed
sheets were saturated. Sabre took fresh linen and, with
the baron's help, remade the bed.

Shane opened his eyes, sighed her name, and closed his
eyes again as if in sleep. "He needs rest and he needs you.
I suggest you lie with him. I will come back every hour,"
he promised.

Sabre undressed quietly, laid out a velvet bed robe for
the times she would have to arise and see to his needs,
and then, naked, slipped into the wide bed and lay with
her arms about him. She quietly and steadily willed him
to live. She did not know if it was possible to transfer her
strength into his body, but she tried. She was alarmed,
for his heartbeat, always so strong and steady when they
had lain together before, was now erratic. She could not
dispel the metallic scent of blood from her nostrils, and it
filled her with dark dread. It seemed to her that in these
long, still hours of the night she shared him with death.
She feared if she closed her eyes in sleep for one unguarded moment, the Shadowy Lord of the Gates would
snatch him to the other side.

Once she rose up with a scream in her throat, throwing
her arms out to shield him, but it was only the cowled
figure of the baron bending low to see if he still drew
breath. She lay against him and examined her feelings for
this man who for better or for worse was her husband.
Her heart and her mind were opposed. Her innermost
thoughts and emotions tangled hopelessly together and
were a mystery to her, as deep as the mystery that surrounded this man beside her. She only knew that she was
irrevocably, fervently involved and that there was no

turning back. At the end of the path lay a destiny . . .
good or evil . . . win or lose . . . life or death!

Shane began to talk. Her heart lifted with joy that he
was improved enough to speak, then plummeted as she
realized he was out of his mind and thought them aboard
ship. "Don't be afraid, love, she's made of solid English
oak from Devon. She's high-riding and I've struck the
topmasts to ease the roll. Though we run with the wind
we'll not lose our rigging." His good arm slipped about
her and his lips brushed her temple. "We'll be snug and
dry down here as a dog's buried bone all the while the
black storm rages. Don't be afraid, love."

"I won't be afraid if you won't leave me. Stay close and
be safe," she implored.

"I promise never to leave you, Macushla. I must get
the arms and ammunition to O'Neill. . . .I must swear
you to secrecy." His hold on her tightened and he threatened to rise up, so she soothed him with lies.

"I swear, love, you may trust me with your life.
. . .I'll keep your secrets forever."

"It's so good to have someone to share my thoughts
with . . . someone I can trust. . . .I never had anyone
before. I place my life in your hands without a second
thought. . . .It is the others you must swear not to betray . . . O'Neill . . . Fitzgerald . . ."

She'd swear no such thing; she hated the O'Neill with
a passion. "Who is Fitzgerald?"

His voice altered to a ragged whisper. "The baron is
Fitzgerald, son of the great earl of Desmond. . . .I'm a
bastard, but he's the legitimate son of an earl. No one
knows he lives . . . none must ever know. Sentence was
passed on him . . . I read it. . . .*Drawn upon a hurdle,
through the open streets, to the place of execution, there to*

*be cut down alive, and your body shall be opened, your
heart and bowels plucked out, and your privy members cut
off and thrown into the fire before your eyes, then your
head to be struck off from your body, which shall be divided into four quarters, to be disposed of at the* queen's
pleasure!' "

"Hush, hush, my lord, I beg you." She was being
wicked to question him so in his delirium. She was learning of the horrors that awaited him if he were discovered
a traitor to the crown, aye, and mayhap herself also, wed-
ded to a traitor. All sacrificed for the queen's pleasure,
she thought wildly. "Hush, hush, my lord," she soothed.

"I need to talk, my darling."

"Then talk of gentler things. Tell me of your boy-
hood."

He laughed hollowly, without mirth. "My mother sent
me to O'Neill the summer I was ten. He took me on raids
. . . not considered a man until I'd bloodied my sword
and taken an English life. The atrocities I saw will stay
with me forever. The English butchered half Munster
. . . babies, children . . . women. When I was fourteen
we came across three whole villages where every living
soul had been slaughtered and burned. That night in retaliation we raided the Dublin garrison. Murdered all the
officers."

"Shane, stop!" she ordered with as much command as
she could muster, and with relief she heard his words
revert back to sailing.

"I love the sea . . . so clean . . . so free . . . it was
my escape."

"Your escape from O'Neill? Then why do you still help
him? You'll never be free of him!"

"Because I love him and I hate him. Can you understand such a thing?" he murmured.

She understood only too well. That exactly summed up
her feelings for Shane Hawkhurst O'Neill. She loved him
and she hated him.

She was grateful when the baron returned with another
brimming goblet. She slipped on her bed robe and lit
more fresh candles. "He's been raving, and look, the bandages are soaked through. I fear he's worse!"

"No," he said quietly, "the poison must come out.
Then he will heal." Sabre knew he was referring to more
than the wound. How many times they dressed his
wound afresh and changed his linen and fed him the potion, she never counted, but at dawn of the third day he
fell into a deep, dreamless slumber, never moving for
fourteen hours.

The baron reassured her, "He will survive, there is no
question of it now. No vital organs were touched, only
the wound needs healing. Thank God he has so large a
chest. On a smaller man such a thrust would have
pierced the heart or lung."

Sabre bathed and changed her clothing, and Mason
brought her a delicious supper on a tray. She gave a fleeting thought to Kate Ashford and the court, then
shrugged her shoulders. Some plausible excuse would
spring to her mind when she returned, but for now she
had enough to occupy her. She would keep him abed for
a week one way or another.

On the fourth day he opened his eyes and smiled at
them. He was weak as a kitten and forced to do their
bidding for the first two hours. He suffered through broth
and coddled eggs, but when it came to watered wine he

revolted and threw back the covers. "God's death, clear the room, I'll feed myself!"

"No, no. You will stay in bed if I have to tie you to the bedposts!" she vowed. "The baron and I have worked over you like two galley slaves. You'll not start the bleeding again by your reckless male bravado!"

"The only way I'll stay in this bed is with your warm body pressed to me beneath the covers."

"Issue me no ultimatums, m'lord, I could lay you low with one hand."

He leered. "I could lay you low with one finger."

She blushed. "There is no need to be lewd. Faith, you must be improving if that's all you can think of."

He apologized with his eyes and pleaded softly, "Come lie with me, love."

She relented. So great was her relief at his recovery that against the safe, solid heat of his body she drifted into slumber, and through half-closed, drowsy eyelids he watched her, content for the moment.

A magnificent barge was delivered to Thames View the following morning. Sabre viewed it from the upstairs windows of the house in all its luxurious splendor and could not resist rushing down to the river to inspect it firsthand. It was not overly large, but so well appointed, with brass rails and lamps, polished oaken deck, and even a dragon masthead upon its prow. It was fashioned with gold, white, and purple canopy and heavy curtains to draw against inclement weather. Piles of cushions were provided for comfort in either sitting or reclining, each embroidered with two *S*'s intertwined, for Shane and Sabre.

When she ran back upstairs to thank him, her joy turned to dismay.

"Shane, please get back into bed, you're not yet strong enough—"

He cut her off midsentence. "That statement was designed to goad me to prove otherwise, madam."

"The baron said—"

He did it again. "The baron does not speak." He warned her with his eyes that he would brook no contradiction. Then when he saw her resolve to keep him abed waver, his face softened. "Sabre, darling, October is upon us. Any day now a nor'wester will sweep in from the Atlantic and autumn's beauty will be snuffed out for another year. Today the sun is having one last excessive fling and so are we. Smell the air! The breeze from the river is carrying on a flirtation with the house, wafting up the scent of the last roses. Tomorrow could bring icy fog or pouring rain. Therefore we shall seize the moment and abandon ourselves upon the river."

At his urging she wore only a light lawn smock with nothing beneath and he donned only an open-necked shirt to cover his bandages. They had food and drink aplenty and lay back in the sunshine sharing ripe pears and a loving cup of sharp Devon cider. She watched him crack walnuts with the hilt of his dagger, and she picked up the shells and sailed them like little boats upon the rippling water.

He pointed out the history of the river to her. As they passed the Palace of Richmond he said, "It houses one of England's most magnificent libraries, crammed with books and manuscripts. Some are forbidden, but I have read them."

"Why forbidden?" she said, puzzled.

"They deal with magic and the black arts, collected by the queen's grandfather. I'll show them to you one day . . . you will delight in the cunning secret passages he had built into Richmond."

They sailed past Hampton Court and he pointed out its cockpits, bowling alleys, tennis courts, and tiltyards. "The grounds are filled with mazes and meanders . . . it is a dream garden for secret lovers." He tried to draw her into his arms to kiss her, but she was reluctant with the two liveried oarsmen aboard. He laughed at her and contented himself for the moment with lying beside her. They lay with fingers intertwined upon the cushions as they drifted past the villages of Walton, Chertsey, and Staines. He pointed a long brown finger to the island of Runnymede. "That is where King John changed the chronicles of England forever."

She sat up as the barge neared Windsor Castle, built on its hill of chalk. "You are very daring to boldly sail past where the court is in residence. What if we are seen?" She anxiously scanned the great open-timbered gallery built for timid ladies to watch the hunting.

He put his lips to her ear. "If you will lie back with me, we can draw the curtains and enjoy our privacy." His hands began to seek her silken flesh beneath the lawn smock, and she was thankful for the curtains. Her reluctance and shyness only served to spice his passion. He whispered, "You enthrall me like an enchantress, Sabre Wilde." He stroked her body, kissing her breasts, and tantalizing her almost beyond endurance. She knew where this would lead and was only fearful for his wound. "No, no, you must not!"

His teeth gleamed. "If you forbid a man wine, you plant in him an unquenchable thirst. . . ."

The barge wandered slowly past half-timbered houses and the farms of the Chiltern Hills and on past Wallingford.

He lifted off her gauzy gown over her head. "I want to see you all over, head to toe. Your skin is the color of fresh cream." He murmured, "Irish beauty has something different and pleasing beyond all others. There is something wild as a witch about you." His lips traveled all the way from her throat down to her belly. "You have sparks of hell in your green eyes, as if you'd let me tumble you in a featherbed or behind a hedge for the pure joy of it!" His mouth found the rosebud of her center. "So lovely, so exciting, so womanly."

She moaned with pleasure. "Your wound . . . you must not exert yourself further."

He leered up at her. "No . . . be kind and help me to undress." She obeyed him and he immediately rolled on top of her. His weight was delicious as it crushed her breasts, and he used all his strength to plunge into her. Then he lay still, filling her without moving. She could feel the pounding of his blood, the throbbing of his shaft, and he in turn felt the heart of her inner trembling. His tongue plundered the sweet depths of her mouth until she lay in a wanton sprawl, in a rosy haze of pleasure. Finally she reached such a peak of wanting, she cried out, "Shane! Shane!"

With his strong arm he rolled with her until she was on top of him, then lifted his mouth from hers and said huskily, "You make love to me, Sabre."

Suddenly she was kissing him, using her thighs and fingers like the mistress she was. She aroused them both to such a pitch, she felt she could never absorb enough of him and he felt her sheath contract over him as if to seal him there forever. They both ached to postpone what they knew must end, but in these long minutes her body thrilled to this man she had found to ravish and love her and fill her.

They died or slept, she knew not which, then he drew back the curtains and they rejoined the world. He drew her to the side of the watercraft. "I want you to see where the River Isis joins the River Thame to become one. You are Isis and I am Thame. Joined we become invincible like the River Thames."

She marveled at his strength. She leaned against his strong, tall frame, spent from their lovemaking. Yet he looked all-powerful, he who had stood at death's door a few short days ago.

Chapter 14

In the middle of the night she awoke to find him gone from the bed. He leaned against the long window frame, staring into the blackness.

"Are you ill?" she cried, rising.

"Nay, only troubled." He came to the bed and sat upon its edge. "Sabre, when I lay ill, did I tell you anything?"

There was a long, protracted silence while she weighed her words. Then she said softly, "You told me everything."

He blanched. "Everything?"

She nodded slowly. "Two fathers . . . two countries . . . two loyalties. Your friend Fitz—" He put his fingers to her lips to silence her, then caressed her neck with his long, strong fingers. "If I followed the dictates of my brain, I would have to kill you now," he breathed.

She looked at him steadily, unafraid.

"But I will follow the dictates of my heart and love you." His hands left her throat and cupped her face in a caress. "I wonder, Sabre, will you betray me?" It was musing rather than a direct question, but she gave him a direct answer and wondered wildly if she spoke the truth or if she spoke lies. "Any revenge I seek from you for ills you do me, either real or imagined, will be a personal revenge. I would never betray you to the crown or the queen, for it would not be the crown's revenge or the queen's revenge that would give me satisfaction. It would be Sabre's revenge," she warned him plainly.

He kissed the little black beauty spot high on her cheekbone, his mind reeling with the nearness of her.

"You have all my heart. Thank God I am not torn between two women, at least."

"Are you not, Shane Hawkhurst O'Neill," she accused. "What about your wife?"

"She means nothing to me," he swore. As he vowed his love for her, denouncing his wife in the process, she became so angered at his words that a fine, rare row erupted, and all, incredibly, because she was jealous of her own self!

Before dawn they had been clinging to each other in a frenzy. He had a deep need to assert his mastery over her, and she had a deep need to fill up the emptiness inside her that their row had caused. They were driven to fuse their bodies into one to make up for all the days and nights they'd lived without each other. Their lovemaking always felt as if it were the first time.

He slept so soundly, he didn't even feel her rise from the bed. She donned a chamber robe and went to get them the last breakfast they would share for a while. She knew she must leave for court now that he was recovered. Any day the queen and court would be moving to Whitehall for the opening of parliament and for the whole glittering, festive winter season.

She was taking a tray from Mason when they heard a carriage arrive. He went to the front hall and Sabre hovered behind him, wondering who could have arrived at such an early hour. An elegant woman swept into the hall. "Mason, how are you? Do get a couple of servants to help with my baggage, I'm afraid I have a scandalous amount as usual." Suddenly the beautiful face registered surprise as she spied Sabre standing in her dishabille. Her face lit up. "Darling, you must be Shane's new bride. Let me think . . . ah, yes, it's Sara, isn't it? He's so secretive, that's all I know about you." She inspected her from head to foot with one sweeping glance that took in the thoroughly disheveled hair and her state of undress. "Matthew told me how lovely you were. Let me say that you make a ravishing Lady Devonport," she said generously. "I'm Georgiana, Shane's mother."

Sabre stammered, "No, no, I'm not—that is I am, but —I'm not—oh, damn!"

"I know how you feel . . . your wretched mother-in-law turning up to spoil your honeymoon! If I'd known he'd brought you to Thames View I would have kept my distance, but I swear, *chérie*, I'm here to shop in London for one day and then I'll be gone."

Sabre was in a dilemma. Taken completely by surprise and thrown further off guard by her mother-in-law's warm charm, she somehow could not let the woman think her a whore. "Georgiana," she said, "I have a secret I wish to share with you. Come and have breakfast with me and hear my confession."

Intrigued, Georgiana took off her gloves and hat and followed Sabre into an intimate morning room where a cheery fire had been lit to offset the sharp chill of the October morning. Georgiana helped herself to an enormous slice of ham seasoned with juniper berries as Sabre began her tale. "Your son married me for a piece of land I own in Ireland. He didn't even bother to show up for the wedding. He sent Matthew to Cheltenham to marry me by proxy."

Georgiana's face registered her dismay.

"He ordered me to Blackmoor and went off without a second thought on progress with the queen."

"That man-eating harridan!" cried Georgiana.

Sabre laughed. "I see we share an enemy."

"You have been treated outrageously!" protested Georgiana.

"Oh, I was outraged, but I'm taking a sweet revenge. I came to my aunt at court, Lady Kate Ashford, so that I could become Shane's mistress. He has no idea that he is married to me."

"Oh 'tis like a play by Will Shakespeare! How very daring you are, Sara, to deceive a dangerous man like Shane."

"Please don't call me Sara. I go by the name Sabre Wilde. You and Matthew are the only two people who know."

"Of course, you're Irish. We will dare anything! You remind me too much of myself, darling. Oh, it is a rare jest on him, but one he truly deserves. I shan't spoil it for you. You will tell him in your own sweet time."

"Sabre," a deep voice called, "what the devil are all these boxes of clothes? When the hell did you find time to go shopping? I've kept you abed for five days." Shane's tall figure loomed in the doorway of the morning room in time to see his mother flush at his words. "Georgiana, you are looking well recovered," he said calmly.

"Shane, darling, the last thing on earth I intended was to intrude."

"You don't intrude." He placed a protective arm about Sabre and smiled down at her. "My love, I know you will find it difficult to believe so elegant a lady could produce such a reprobate, but this really is Georgiana, my mother." His deep blue eyes sought those of his mother. "This is Sabre Wilde, mistress of this house."

Sabre blushed and slipped from his arm. "I must dress," she murmured, and fled the room.

Alone with his mother he said, "I realize it's bad man-

ners to have my mother and my mistress under the same
roof, but I make no apologies, Georgiana."

"Good heavens, Shane, I hope I'm not so gauche as to
be shocked." She laughed. "I'm delighted you have such
exquisite taste."

Back upstairs he said, "I'm sorry, sweetheart." He
frowned. "For God's sake, don't let on I was wounded."
He swore under his breath, and she saw clearly that he
was worried.

"I'm going back to court today, so you can stop looking so displeased."

"God's blood, Sabre, I hope you don't think I'm such a
hypocrite." He waved aside her words. "It's O'Neill I
wanted to keep away from Georgiana."

"There's not much chance he'll come," she assured
him.

"He'll come," he said grimly. "Tonight I take him
back to Ireland."

"Damn you, Hawkhurst! I never know when you're
about to leave the country. You never think to tell me
your plans. When will I see you again?" she demanded.

"I'm not in the habit of consulting a woman about my
plans. Don't begin to think I need your permission to
come and go, mistress," he said in a deadly voice.

"Go to hell . . . and take the bloody O'Neill with
you!" she spat.

Inside she was afraid because she knew that O'Neill
could well be the death of Shane.

He advanced menacingly toward her, but the moment
his cruel hands grabbed her, he groaned and pulled her
into his arms. "O'Neill is deadly for Georgiana. I must
get him away tonight."

She wanted to scream no, yet she knew she could not

forbid him. She pulled away from him and said, "Why don't you fight fire with fire. If you don't wish her to fall into his arms, find her another."

"Who?" he asked flatly. "Who in God's name could compete with that fatal Irish charm?" He swore and booted a stool across the room.

"Another Irishman," she said softly. "There is one under this roof who is twice the man O'Neill is, has three times the charm, and he is a friend."

"The baron?" he asked incredulously.

She nodded. "Dress him up and invite him to dine; just the four of us."

"He wouldn't," said Shane.

"He would do anything for you. Ask him."

The crystal chandelier in the dining salon at Thames View held a hundred candles. The table, set for four, gleamed with heavy silver and Venetian crystal upon the starched white linen. A mass of late white roses stood at its center, and the formally attired gentlemen drew back the tall chairs for their ladies.

"It's such a surprise to see you back in England, Fitz. I thought your permanent home was France," improvised Shane.

"I'm so delighted to meet a friend of Shane's. He keeps his life so private," purred Georgiana. She could not hide the admiration shining from her eyes as she took in the measure of the man who was dining with them. His dress and manner were perfection, his beautiful cultured voice so pleasing to the ear, but above all he was warm and so at ease, you would have thought he had known her for years. "Surely you must have a last name, sir. I cannot call you Fitz," Georgiana probed lightly.

" 'Tis Fitzclare," Shane lied.

The baron smiled affectionately at Georgiana. "Please call me Fitz. It pleases me to hear it from your lips."

She lowered her lashes, then raised them again. "Fitzclare is Irish, sir, yet I detect no brogue in your speech."

"Fitz was educated in Europe. He spent his youth traveling about . . . Paris, Brussels, Venice," offered Shane. He was not lying this time. The earl of Desmond had sent his son to be educated in Europe, perhaps fearing contamination from Ireland's thickheaded, bogtrotting savages.

Sabre sat bemused, trying not to stare at the transformation of the baron. Without his cowl his hair was an attractive silver and his eyes, though dark, flashed silver once in a while. His monk's robe had hidden a hard, well-made body, and Sabre could imagine the muscles he would reveal when he stripped. She blushed at the picture and Shane, catching sight of her pretty coloring, raised an amused eyebrow at her. Splendor of God, he thought, how like his mother she was. Though their coloring was different, their spirits were kindred. Their eyes flashed a challenge to every man they met, and what mere mortal male could resist? He would have to be very careful that she did not gain too much power over him.

The baron entertained Georgiana with tales of his travels in Europe. He was amusing and could converse easily about fashions, food, native customs, politics, or sailing the seven seas. She could not help but be attracted to this warm man who gave her his complete, undivided attention. It was the most flattering thing a gentleman had ever done for her.

When Shane saw they were totally absorbed in each other, he turned his attention to Sabre. They were saying good-bye for a few days, each fearful for the other's safety. He could tell by the quality of her silence that she was angry at him for leaving. She had erected a barrier between them which he thought to penetrate with loving words. "The barge is waiting to take you back to Windsor tonight," he said in a low voice as he covered her hand with his. "Be careful, my darling, and remember if you ever need help and cannot reach me, I always have men posted in the stables."

She pulled her hand from his and said, "I'll take care of myself! Since I'm never to know where you are off to, I have no choice. I think I'll go upstairs before that wretched man arrives. I don't want to see him."

"Did he offend you, sweet?"

"He said the queen set the pace for independence in Englishwomen. That in Ireland they make good women by beating and bedding them regularly." Her eyes flashed. "I said, 'I assure you I am bedded regularly and Shane applies his great weapon to my nether regions whenever I am in need of it!'"

"Lying Irish!" Shane whispered, and lifted her hand to his lips.

Her fingers were stiff and cold, and she snatched her hand from him deliberately.

When Sabre rose from the table, the others followed suit, and as Fitz assisted Georgiana to rise, she said over her shoulder, "I have decided to stay at Hawkhurst for the winter season. 'Tis only a forty-mile ride. . . . I would welcome your company if the country wouldn't bore you to death."

He said gallantly, "I could never be bored in your company, my lady. Don't be surprised if I take you literally and actually visit." She cast him a sidewise glance that took his breath away. "Please," she murmured.

The baron pretended that he must take his leave, but actually he intended to be cloaked and spurred in time to accompany Shane to Ireland. If he had been at Shane's back the night he had gone to meet O'Neill, he would never have received the near-mortal blow.

Sabre went upstairs the moment she heard the booted step in the courtyard, leaving father, mother, and son to their own volatile company.

"Hugh!" Georgiana gasped as she recognized the harsh, rugged features of O'Neill.

He looked with disapproval at the low-cut, elegant gown, the diamonds blazing at her throat, the lace fan waved so artfully, but he approved of the full-blooded woman beneath the frippery.

Somehow Shane was no longer afraid of these two coming face-to-face. It was their lives, and they must choose. "I will change my clothes. I'll be ready to ride in half an hour," said Shane, allowing them a little time together.

Sabre was surprised to find that Shane had followed her upstairs. She was also pleased. It showed she had some power over him at least. She raised an eyebrow and said in a cool voice, "I thought we had said good-bye."

"By God, how you madden a man. Are you erecting a barrier between us to see me smash it down?" he demanded.

" 'Tis you who erects barriers! I never know when you will suddenly decide to take off. Then when you return and have need of me to warm your bed, you crook your little finger and I'm supposed to come running!"

"You sound like a nagging wife. The last thing I need is a wife; I have one of those, remember?" he sneered.

" 'Tis you who needs to remember. The woman could be dead for all you care!"

He threw up his hands in exasperation. "Now I've heard everything! My mistress takes my wife's part in this. I can't win for losing with you, Sabre."

She pressed her hand to her mouth so she would not blurt out that she was his wife. By all that was holy she would save that ace up her sleeve until the perfect moment when the revelation would be most advantageous to her.

He closed the distance between them in two strides. She had pushed him to his limit. He grabbed her roughly and gave her a savage kiss that left no doubt who was master. When he felt her resistance begin to melt, he growled arrogantly, "When I return I'll send a servant to summon you."

Sabre was left with her mouth open. Damn you to hell, Hawkhurst, she cried silently.

At the top of the staircase Shane encountered the baron. They could clearly overhear the conversation that was taking place below, and they listened without hesitation.

"Ye are more English than Irish, woman! Like yer queen ye spend too much time riding to the hunt, playing at cards, gossiping with yer friends, and wasting money buying geegaws." He strode toward her and gripped her shoulders harshly. "Yet still I want ye, lass. Come back to Ireland wi' me!"

Georgiana could not keep herself from comparing this man to the other with whom she had spent the evening. Oh, the feral male-animal attraction was still there, filling the room, but outweighing that was the arrogant, vicious need to rule. The need for power was like a madness in him. He thought he should be the Irish king on the Irish throne and would settle for nothing less, no matter who or what was sacrificed. She saw now that she had done her own share of sacrificing others. She had given him Shane, thinking he would cherish such a son, but it was otherwise. He'd used him ruthlessly and would go on using him. Death would put a stop to it, one day, but she prayed fervently it would never come to that.

"No, Hugh," she said calmly, "I like my geegaws. I am too old to throw my comfort to the wind and exist in that barren pile of rock you call Dungannon. You have little love to spare a woman. You have your clans to unite— your Maguires, O'Haras, O'Donnells, O'Sullivans, and O'Rourkes."

His face was vicious as he looked at her revealing neckline and her diamonds. "Whore of Babylon!" he hissed.

"We are ready," said a deep voice from the doorway.

Relief swept over Georgiana as she raised her eyes and saw Shane and the baron cloaked in black for their clandestine journey.

Chapter 15

Sabre was pleasantly surprised Kate Ashford didn't scold her overmuch for her absence. Though Kate had no idea where Sabre had been, she had a damned good idea whose company she kept. In actuality Kate was simply relieved to have her back in time for the move to Whitehall. The whole court was abuzz with the latest on the Essex-Elizabeth contretemps. Kate told her they were actually laying bets on the outcome. Most of the gentlemen had put their money on the queen, but the more astute ladies had bet on Essex. She always gave in to him.

The queen had instructed Kate Ashford to transport ten new gowns she had had designed especially for the winter season. Sabre was on hands and knees in the drafty Windsor wardrobe, stuffing the sleeves of the gowns with tissue. The sleeves were slashed and heavily jeweled and could be crushed so easily. Sabre had devised a cushioning way to pack a gown in its own box and take it out later virtually uncrushed and unwrinkled.

A voice behind her startled her. "So you are Mistress Wilde. You have been conspicuous by your absence since the great hunt on the occasion of my birthday."

Sabre's mouth fell open as she found herself in the unenviable position of being singled out by the queen. "Your Majesty." She sat back upon her heels and bowed her head. "I—I was indisposed, Your Majesty," Sabre blurted.

"Not the fever?" asked the queen, greatly alarmed.

"Ah, no, Your Majesty. I fell from my horse during the hunt and found it difficult to walk for a week," she lied.

"It has come to my attention that you ride an Arabian," said Elizabeth with a great deal of disbelief mingled with disapproval. The queen made statements in such a bald manner, she compelled you to explain yourself.

"Ah, yes, Your Majesty. I won it playing cards and was not used to such a high-strung animal."

"Which gentleman wagers for such high stakes as Arabian horses, pray tell me?" demanded the queen.

Sabre skirted the truth once more. "Matthew Hawkhurst, if it pleases Your Majesty," she replied primly.

The queen switched subjects with the speed of lightning. Through narrowed eyes she said, "The color of your hair . . . is it natural?"

Sabre's hand went to her copper tresses apprehensively. "Why, yes, Your Majesty."

"I will tell you a secret," said Elizabeth confidentially. "I am wearing a wig!"

Since nothing could have been more obvious and since Sabre had spent hours cleaning her vast collection of wigs, it was difficult to look surprised.

"Just that shade of copper is what I desire. I have a royal wigmaker, Master Hooker, who has been searching for just such hair as yours," the Queen said pointedly.

Sabre swallowed with difficulty. She knew without a shadow of a doubt what the queen was asking, nay, commanding of her. Resentment and anger flared up inside her. How demeaning to be down on her knees wrapping this woman's gowns in layers of protective tissue so she could strut about in her finery. Now the old witch actually wanted the hair from her head to attract young men like Essex and Devonport. Sabre tried to stave off what her heart feared was inevitable. "Your Majesty, the wig

you are wearing couldn't be lovelier. I don't think my
dull shade would flatter you at all."

"I say otherwise, Mistress Wilde, and I am unused to
being contradicted. Kate Ashford told me what a generous girl you were. I sincerely hope she did not lie to me."

Sabre had no choice but to acquiesce. She strove to do
it with graciousness, but inside she seethed with resentment and added it to the score against this aging, all-
powerful creature.

"Your Majesty, I would be honored to provide Master
Hooker with a length of my hair to fashion a new wig."

Now she had exactly what she wanted, the queen re-
verted to their previous topic. "I warn you, Mistress
Wilde, not to play with the elder Hawkhurst, Lord
Devonport, lest you get your comeuppance!"

The warning was so pointed, she was afraid the queen
had heard a rumor linking her with Shane. Sabre saw red.
She wanted to spit upon the floor at the queen's feet to
show her contempt. Jealousy flooded her heart and her
brain. Bessie Tudor was speaking of the man who was
Sabre's husband, Sabre's lover, and she was doing so with
such a smug air of ownership, Sabre had to fight the
impulse to fly at her and scratch out her eyes. For one
dreadful moment when first confronted by the queen, Sabre thought she had been discovered for her masquerade
as the goddess Diana. The reality was so much worse!
The queen would get her beautiful hair and had warned
her to keep her hands off the queen's Sea God. As Gloriana departed, Sabre smiled a secret, terrible smile. Shane
was hers, totally. He was her absolute private property
until the time came when she was ready to toss him aside.
Then and only then could Bessie Tudor have him! Her

mind was already plotting an outrageous costume for her next escapade, one that would embarrass the queen.

Hawkhurst and the Baron decided that the quickest route to Ireland for O'Neill was the port of Bristol. It was the closest port to London on the west coast, and would entail a hard ride of only a hundred miles. Any assassination attempt on the earl of Tyrone's life would come on land before he left England. Once he had embarked on a Hawkhurst vessel, he would be safe.

Shane had intended to go all the way to Ireland, but he received terrible news from a captain in Bristol and knew he must get to the queen immediately. Sir Philip Sidney had taken a wound in Holland at the Battle of Zutphen and it appeared he would not recover. Sir Philip was Leicester's nephew and one of the most beloved of Elizabeth's peers. He was married to Secretary Walsingham's daughter, Frances, who had never been invited to join the court, because of her dark beauty.

After placing O'Neill on one of his ships Hawkhurst rode back to London with all possible speed and directed the baron to ready one of their smaller, faster vessels to depart for Holland on a moment's notice.

During his audience with Bess he kept a tight rein on his temper. That they were suffering defeat after defeat in Holland against the Spanish could be laid directly at the queen's feet. She kept her purse strings closed tightly, sent only a few thousand men, and equipped them so badly, the officers went deep into debt to pay for supplies. When Shane told her that Sir Philip had been wounded at Zutphen she was visibly shaken.

"They shall all come home! Why should we fight Holland's battles for them?" she raved.

He answered stiffly, "Your Majesty, they are England's battles. It is a dishonor not to sail against Spain!"

A courier with dispatches had arrived from Robert Dudley, earl of Leicester, and she called for his messages while Hawkhurst was there to give her his strength—for she feared the worst. With dry eyes she read the missive that announced Philip Sidney's death. All her emotion was reserved for her dearest Lord Robert. She knew he would be devastated by the loss of his favorite nephew. She railed inwardly that the sea separated them and she would be unable to comfort him. She clenched impotent fists in frustration and shouted, "Damn the young fool for getting himself killed . . . 'twas most inconsiderate of the fellow. M'lord Devonport, fetch his body home for burial. I will send instructions to Leicester if you will wait while I compose them."

"Bess, I am sorry for your loss. I have a vessel standing ready to sail today."

The whole court was plunged into mourning, and gaudy clothing was forbidden. Shane sought out Kate Ashford and told her that he was stealing Sabre from her for a couple of days. Since Sabre had done most of the packing for Whitehall, she made no protest. She directed him to the water stairs where Sabre was in charge of the stowing of boxes and trunks onto the queen's barge for the short journey downriver. He took her out of earshot of the servants and said low, "I'm sailing across to Holland and I'm taking you, darling. Pack warm clothes and have your own barge take you to Thames View. I'll meet you there in two hours."

Sabre tossed her glorious copper hair over her shoulder. "Ah, 'tis Lord Devonport, I believe," she said as if they were only slightly acquainted.

A black look of warning flashed from him, which she chose to ignore.

"You, my dearest lord, are laboring under a misapprehension if you think I am solely at your beck and call."

"Hellcat! You are the one laboring under a misapprehension. Let me remind you the duties of a mistress are exactly that . . . to be solely at my beck and call."

She flew at him, fully intending to push him into the river, but he grabbed her, laughing in exultation at how beautiful she was when she angered her. He bit her earlobe and whispered, "I love you, Sabre . . . come with me?"

She relented. At least this time he had asked her to go along with him.

They had ridden side by side to Harwich, where the baron had the vessel readied to sail. The wind snatched away their words, so they had little opportunity for speech, but he was aware of her every moment. One of the things he found so exciting about her was that she was ready and eager for adventure on a moment's notice.

She stood on deck and marveled at the easy way he took command, shouting his orders from the forecastle. Now she understood why his voice was deep and commanding, even rough at times. It was from a lifelong habit of shouting loud and clear to be heard above the slapping waves, flapping sails, whining winds, and creaking timbers. For a terrible moment she thought she might turn green faced while still riding to anchor in the harbor. Then, as she filled her lungs with the tang of sea air, pitch, and tar, her stomach righted itself and she laughed aloud as she pulled her pale gray, fox-trimmed cloak about her and watched him direct his men to heave-to and hoist the sails.

They cleared harbor, and the sails bellied out like pregnant women. As she looked about there must have been over three hundred lines and ropes, each with a name and a proper place and a special knot all of its own. Shane left his command post to give a hand with the hauling and hoisting, and she shuddered at the pain she knew the recent wound would give him. Then she thought of his strong, callus-palmed hands on her body and shivered again. Finally he joined her, bracing a protective arm across the small of her back and grinning down at her.

"How did you learn all the different ropes?" she asked.

"Not by my quick brain," he said, laughing. "When I was a boy on my first voyage out, the boatswain instructed me with a knotted rope to my bare arse!" He hugged her to him. "Come below while I settle you in my cabin."

As soon as they were enclosed in the small cabin he took her in his arms and kissed her deeply. "Splendor of God, how I missed you," he said, looking down at her with wonder in his eyes. "Thank you for coming, love. It's not a happy voyage. Sir Philip Sidney died of a wound he took in the Battle of Zutphen. I'm going to Holland so that his widow Frances can bring his body home."

She put her hand on his arm gently. "Was Sir Philip a friend?"

He nodded. "O'Neill was placed in the Sidney household and lived there many years until he returned to Ireland. Philip never questioned our association. His widow Frances has a young child. That's why I asked you to come with me, Sabre. Frances will need a woman's gentle company in her time of sorrow."

Sabre let the fur hood fall from her hair. "Is she one of

your conquests, m'lord?" she asked, feeling a stab of jealousy.

"Nay, yet she is certainly fair enough to spark jealousy in the queen. Frances Walsingham is daughter to the queen's secretary. You know enough about my affairs, Sabre, to realize he is my enemy and a constant threat. If I can be of any service to Frances, it will be to my advantage. If we support and comfort her in her time of need, she may one day be able to render me a great service." He stroked her cheek with his roughened hand. "If I leave you belowdecks alone, you won't be afraid?"

"I'm afraid of neither man nor beast," she boasted.

He leered down at her. "We'll put that to the test when I return, little wildcat."

He was gone an hour, which seemed like two at least to Sabre, crossing the treacherous North Sea for the first time. She had unpacked her warm clothing and explored the well-appointed cabin. It was snugly paneled in warm satinwood and furnished with a tabletop desk and swivel chairs. The berth was fastened sturdily to the wall and was just wide enough to hold two if they were on very intimate terms. A thick Turkish carpet patterned in red and blue added to the warmth, and brass lanterns swung on rings attached to the walls. Charts and instruments filled the desk drawers, and she noticed a large iron safe had been built into one corner. A great cedarwood chest held thick, warm blankets and fur bed coverings, and a satinwood wardrobe held many changes of dry clothing for the captain.

When Shane came into the cabin he was soaked to the skin. It was second nature to him to strip immediately without drenching the cabin. Sabre watched him rub his body vigorously with a towel, and unable to resist, she took up another and rubbed his wide back. He was freezing cold at first, yet with amazing speed the vigorous rubbing soon had him restored. He tried to take her in his arms, but she resisted.

"Let me see your wound first," she said softly.

He raised his arm obediently, heard her small gasp, and dropped his arm quickly.

"Let me see," she insisted.

"Nay, 'tis too ugly for a delicate female. It will disgust you."

"Your body is a joy to me and a wonder," she said, running gentle fingers along his collarbone, across the bulging muscle, and down to the shoulder blade where the dragon rampaged. He shuddered at her touch, longing to make love to her. She raised his arm, and this time he did not object. The scar was angry red and puckered. "You'll always bear the scar. We should have stitched it," she said with regret.

He shook his head. "The baron is a competent doctor. He left it open to drain any poison." He was shocked, then thrilled, as, incredibly, she put her mouth to the scar and covered it with kisses.

"You do the damnedest things," he groaned as a wave of passion swept from his armpit to his loins.

She smiled at him and whispered, "Why, m'lord, 'twas you who taught me to make love with my tongue."

"Splendor of God, it had better have been me!" he said, his voice rough with desire as his eager fingers unhooked and removed her gown. When she was naked he lifted her high, then let her slide slowly down his body until he sheathed his upthrusting shaft inside her tight, hot center. His hands slipped beneath her round buttocks to support her; then, joined, he walked with her to the high bed. Her arms were twined lovingly about his neck and she thrilled with each step he took as he penetrated deeper and deeper. He did not lie down, but lowered himself and her until he was sitting on the edge of the berth.

"Wrap your legs around me, darling," he urged, and she gasped with the exquisite pleasure-pain as he thrust his long, thick shaft to the hilt, and pulled her onto him another inch and held her there with strong brown hands that gripped her like a vise.

With their mouths fused, he began to flex and relax the great throbbing head of his phallus, and amazingly she felt her own body grip and relax in a compelling, throbbing, sensual rhythm that went on and on and on, bringing waves of pleasure which built and receded, built and receded, until she was sobbing her need for release. He was so attuned to her body, he knew the exact moment to start his seed and plunge her over the precipice. They went down into the vortex together, tasting their names on each other's lips. They lay entwined, still as death, the roll and pitch of the ship lulling them to slumber. Within two hours he was awake so he could go back on deck.

"Where are you going?" she murmured.

"I didn't mean to disturb you, love. I'm the captain of this vessel, remember? I never leave the deck of my ship for more than three hours."

"But in my case you'll make an exception," she said, holding out her arms to him.

"Five minutes," he rationed, and lifted her between his legs with her back resting against his chest. "Ah, Sabre, you fill my senses," he said, breathing in the exciting fragrance of her hair and her sleep-warmed body. "You fill my thoughts." He paused, then admitted, in a voice that was only a murmur, "You fill my heart." He lifted her hair from the back of her neck and kissed the nape. "I adore your hair," he breathed.

"Then you had better get your fill of it. The queen wants me to cut it to make her a wig."

He dumped her unceremoniously onto the berth and was on his feet in a flash. "I forbid it!" he shouted angrily.

"Shane, I have no choice—it was tantamount to a command."

"Tantamount to bare-faced blackmail! Sabre, it is out of the question. I will procure hair for her bloody wig. There are many women willing to sell their hair or any other part of their body. Just leave it to me," he said with finality.

The thought of the queen strutting about in the hair of a prostitute from a brothel had an amusing quality about it. Then she wondered wryly just how many brothels Shane would have to frequent before he found just the right shade!

Hawkhurst sailed his vessel into the English-held port of Flushing. Sir Philip Sidney had been appointed governor of this town, which provided a home base for all the English in Holland. Leaving Sabre aboard, he presented himself to Frances and told her he had come to fetch her home. She was exhausted from the visits of Philip's fellow officers and longed for home. Hawkhurst's strength was exactly what she had needed. He took over and directed the servants to pack everything in readiness for his seamen to take aboard. The coffin was to go in the hold, her little girl and the child's nurse were to get one cabin, and Frances was to have another small cabin to herself.

Philip's horses and leash hounds were made comfortable,
then Hawkhurst was off to take the queen's messages to
Leicester.

Frances came aboard in her widow's weeds an hour
before the tide changed to carry them from Flushing at
the mouth of the vast Westerschelde into the North Sea.
Sabre felt a sharp stab of compassion at the sight of the
tiny, black-draped female clinging to the hand of a sweet
little girl. Shane beckoned Sabre to go below with them,
and when they were in the small cabin he introduced her
to the daughter of the hated and feared Walsingham.

When Frances raised her black veil, Sabre could not
believe her eyes. The small, pretty girl could not be a day
older than eighteen, and looked much younger. When the
child and her nurse were settled into their cabin, Shane
was needed on deck to weigh anchor, clear harbor, and
set the course for England.

Alone with Frances, Sabre felt a rush of affection and
wanted to help in some way. "Would you like to be alone,
Lady Sidney?"

"No, don't leave me, Sabre, and please call me Frances. I'm not a good sailor and I haven't eaten much in the
last days," she said wearily.

Sabre poured her a goblet of wine and mixed it with
sugar water. "This will settle your stomach. Why don't
you get into bed and I'll sit awhile and we can talk."

Frances gave her a grateful look and sipped the wine as
she took off her mourning garments. The wine loosened
her tongue and she started to confide in Sabre. " 'Fore
God, I don't know what I will do. Philip is—was—so far
in debt and everything mortgaged to the hilt."

Sabre was shocked; the Sidneys were one of England's
premier families.

"He—we—owe over eight thousand pounds, and I haven't even the means to bury him."

Sabre drew her chair up close to the bed. "Your father will help you."

Frances laughed bitterly. "My father's health is deteriorating because of worry over money. He has been in debt for years. He pays his spies from his own pocket . . . the queen pays him a mere stipend. Walsingham House is mortgaged to the rafters while the queen dines on gold plate and wears a different fortune in jewels every day of the week."

Sabre said thoughtfully, "There is a lesson there if we heed it. The golden rule, I call it—those with the gold rule!"

"How very true. Faith, I've learned my lesson; I shall marry for money next time," Frances vowed.

Sabre probed, "Were you in love with your husband, Frances?"

The dark young woman hesitated, then admitted, "Nay, it was not a love match. It was arranged by our parents, and I think the queen had a hand in it. Philip was a poet, a dreamer, so unsuited to war."

"Mayhap the queen will see to the expense of the funeral. He will be buried at St. Paul's, won't he?"

"The queen!" hooted Frances, gulping her wine and holding out her glass for more. "Philip died for her, but she is the most ungrateful creature on the face of the earth. Did you know that in her younger days she came down with the smallpox and selflessly Philip's mother, Lady Mary Sidney, alone of all her women, stayed with her and nursed her day and night until she was recovered? The queen was very lucky, her only pockmarks are on her neck below her ruff. My poor, dear mother-in-law

was not so lucky. She caught the pox from Elizabeth and
was left so badly scarred she wears a veil and does not go
out in public. Lady Sidney was given one cramped attic
room at Hampton Court and made to keep from the
queen's company, for Bess cannot bear ugliness or sickness or the scars left from sickness. Believe me, Sabre, the
queen never *gives,* she only *takes*!"

Sabre said confidentially, "I've stolen one of her prize
possessions." Her eyes rolled upward, indicating the Sea
God up on deck. "Why don't you do the same?"

"I shall be in mourning, buried in the country at my
father's farm in Surrey. 'Tis the only roof my child and I
will have over our heads." Suddenly she looked at Sabre
with speculation in her eyes. "Who's the best catch in
England?"

Sabre thought for a moment, "Probably Essex," she
said, laughing.

"Forgive me, Sabre. 'Tis the wine. I am wicked to talk
so with my poor husband's body not yet in his grave, yet
it would be sweet to be free of financial burden," she said,
sighing.

Walsingham, acting upon the information provided by
O'Neill and other sources, had caught Mary, Queen of
Scots, in the web of the Babington conspiracy, though
she was supposed to be safely imprisoned. He had
worked day and night to collect enough evidence to bring
her to trial. The queen was incensed and his triumph was
turned to dross. The death of his son-in-law, whose crip-
pling debts he subsequently inherited, was enough to
break his health.

Walsingham was unable to meet his daughter at
Harwich, where Hawkhurst weighed anchor, and Sabre

had to take her home to Surrey in the barge Shane had bought her. So Frances had come home, but instead of finding a strong family to offer her succor, she instead had to be the strong one in the face of her father's failing health and the daunting debts that were piling up day by day.

Chapter 16

Sabre learned that the court had already gone to White-hall for what was supposed to have been the glittering winter season, but it was fast becoming a nightmare. A pall hung over everything. People went about with long faces, wearing somber clothing, treading on eggs so as not to exacerbate further the queen's temper.

She had more or less ordered home Leicester and her other high-ranking nobles, Fulke-Greville and Blount, and told them to reduce their armies in Holland. Leicester had bluntly refused, telling her it would take at least another six months. Hawkhurst delivered these un-welcome tidings as well as missives from the Dutch en-voys begging for more support.

The queen of England was in an unreasonable rage against Walsingham because of the way he had brought Mary, Queen of Scots, to a trial which resulted in her being condemned to death. She was to have her head severed on the block. Elizabeth had wanted Mary re-moved quietly, not by public execution! Her son James would be the new king of Scots and Walsingham had advised that they liberally bribe him with gold because he feared an invasion from the north.

All the news was bad. King Philip of Spain's Invincible Armada was being finished over this winter and would sail to conquer England in the spring with the greatest number of ships that had ever been assembled.

In an effort to restore pomp and tradition to the open-ing of Parliament, Elizabeth made Sir Christopher Hat-ton her new lord chancellor and caved in to Essex to restore the sweet smile to his lips, making him earl marshal of England so that he would take precedence over the old lord admiral, newly honored as the earl of Nottingham.

Parliament was opened with the queen arrayed in all her magnificence. First came the barons, earls, and knights of the Garter, then the aging Cecil, followed by his son Robert. Next came the new lord chancellor bearing the seals of England, flanked by two squires, one for the royal scepter, the other carrying the sword of state in a red scabbard studded with golden fleur-de-lis. The pages then trumpeted the arrival of the queen. She had an aura of supreme power and all assembled went down on one knee.

Since the court had become so dull, Sabre and the other ladies amused themselves away from it. At Whitehall at least they were in the center of London and could attend the plays, shop in the exchange and at the stalls in Candlewick Street, visit the goldsmiths in Lombard Street, and attend the horse-trading sessions at Smithfield Square.

The whim took Sabre to ride down to Thames View to spend the night. It had begun to snow, and as she looked down from the panoramic windows of the master bedchamber, she was beginning to think he would not come.

It infuriated her that they never really knew when they could be together, since they always had to snatch time from their other duties. It was a continuous bone of contention between them that he was here one moment and gone the next, so that when they did meet they wasted precious time fighting.

Sometimes she slept alone at Thames View and other times he would arrive in the middle of the night, heavily armed, cloaked in black, looking for all the world like a thief. He would steal into bed, slip his arms about her, and they would make love savagely, as if it were for the last time.

Sabre sighed and had almost turned from the window when she saw a rider. She ran down the stairs to greet him and was surprised to discover the tall figure was Matthew. Her loveliness took his breath away, and he wished with all his heart that she had been waiting to welcome him this cold winter's night.

"Sabre, Lord, it's good to see you!" he said, laughing and hugging her and at the same time transferring cold, wet snow from his clothes to hers. "Have you told him you are Lady Devonport yet?"

"No, which is precisely why he still carries me to bed and treats me like a queen. However, I did tell your mother."

"Georgiana came up to London?" he asked, surprised.

"Yes. She walked in on me while I was in a state of undress and naturally assumed I was Shane's bride. I admitted the truth to her and she pledged me that she wouldn't tell Shane."

"Did you like each other?" Matthew asked frankly.

"Yes, thank God. Can you imagine what it must be like to have your mother-in-law for an enemy?"

They sat in front of a warm fire and Sabre poured them goblets of warm, mulled cider. "This will remind you of home. What have you been up to?"

"Curious, really. I've just brought two shiploads of marble from the Isle of Purbeck. It must be for a customer who's doing some fancy rebuilding, and yet Hawk told me to keep my cargo hush-hush. I just want to know where and when he wants me to unload it. I can think of

pleasanter things to do in this freezing weather than jug-
gling slabs of cold pink marble."

The front door was thrown open and Shane ushered in
a small, dark figure along with a swirl of snowflakes.

"Frances!" exclaimed Sabre, "come by the fire and un-
thaw."

"Hello, Sabre. I'm afraid Lord Devonport has rescued
me again."

Matthew was on his feet immediately. "Lady Sidney,
permit me to offer my condolences for your great loss."

Shane said, "As you can plainly see, this is my brother,
Matthew Hawkhurst."

"What's wrong, Frances?" asked Sabre, seeing a look
of defeat about the slender, drooping shoulders.

"We thought we had found a way out of our financial
difficulties. I came up to see Philip's solicitors to sell
some of the Sidney lands, but the will was faulty and
Philip's brother Robert is claiming everything."

"I've instructed my man of law, Jacob Goldman, to see
Robert Sidney on Frances's behalf," said Shane.

"I've sold all my wedding gifts and my silver plate and
only got a thousand pounds for the lot," said Frances
hopelessly. "My father petitioned the queen to settle
Philip's debts, but she refused because she is furious over
Mary of Scotland and this is his punishment."

"You must be exhausted. You cannot go back to Surrey
tonight; I'll put you in the lovely pink bedchamber. She
looked appealingly at Shane. "Darling, have the cook
prepare some food and I'll take Frances upstairs."

"Come on, Matt, we'll raid the kitchen ourselves; I'm
starving." Alone in the kitchen Shane told Matthew to
unload the pink marble from his ships and put them on
Shane's vessels.

"Wouldn't it be simpler for me to just deliver it to the customer?" asked Matt. Shane did not want Matthew involved in his covert operations, so he tried to pass off the subject on a light note. "It's for a lady, Matt, if you must know, and I'm the one who wishes to be the recipient of her gratitude."

Matthew was instantly angered. How could his brother be such a bloody philanderer while he enjoyed the favors of the loveliest woman in London? Abruptly he said, "I must go. Where are your ships anchored?"

Shane gave him a long, speculative look and said evenly, "The *Defiant* and the *Gloriana* are at Southend. The captains have instructions to take on the marble night or day, whenever it is convenient for you, Matthew."

After his brother departed, Shane took a trayful of tempting food up to Frances. He smiled warmly at her and said, "I have two thousand pounds for you, Frances. I want to help you in a practical way, and as I see it, that way is providing you with a little gold."

Frances wrung her hands. "Oh, m'lord, I cannot!" She was clearly at odds with herself. After a moment's hesitation she confided, "I—I have been helping my father while he has been ill and I have discovered that he has a file on you, Lord Devonport."

"I know," said Shane softly, "and I sincerely hope that if the time comes when your father must pass along his files to another authority, you will find it in your heart to warn me. But, Frances, this money has no strings attached to it. I insist that you take it."

Sabre saw her sigh and visibly relax. "Eat up, Frances, it smells delicious. I'll get you a warm bed gown, and you are to put your troubles aside and get a few hours rest."

Frances flashed her a warm look of gratitude. Shane and Sabre closed the door to the pink chamber. "I'd better get a maid to ready a room for Matthew."

"No need," said Shane. Picking her up in his arms, he carried her to their chamber. "He's gone."

"Gone?" exclaimed Sabre in surprise. "Why?"

"I made an innocent remark and his anger flared as if I had set a flame to gunpowder." He set her down in their room and turned to lock the door. "I think he fancies himself in love with you."

Sabre blushed. She knew there was some truth in his words, but after all, Matthew had stood beside her and exchanged wedding vows. She understood perfectly that Matthew thought he had some claim on her. She wanted to shout at Shane, "It is your fault!" but she held her tongue and turned her back to him as she gazed through the tall windows watching the gardens turn white with snow.

He slipped his arms about her beneath her breasts and bent to place a tender kiss on the top of her head. "Darling, I never want you to be left in a mess such as Frances is now in. I've deposited ten thousand pounds in your name with Herriot's, the goldsmith's." She stiffened in his arms, surprised at the large sum. " 'Fore God, men are generous with their mistresses."

He spun her round to face him. "Sabre, I don't think of you as my mistress!" She saw the hurt in his eyes. "You are my beloved. What we have is so special and rare. I took your virginity and I never want you to know another man." He shook her. "Don't you feel bonded to me?" he demanded.

"Yes," she cried, "I want us to be man and wife!"

"Oh, my darling," he said, sweeping her up and carry-

ing her to their bed, "so do I, but it cannot be." He
undressed her gently, murmuring, "My little love, I'll
make it up to you." He kissed her eyelids and smoothed
the tiny curls from her temples. "Marriage isn't everything, sweetheart. Look at poor Frances."

She swirled her fingers in the thick matt of black hair
upon his chest. "You wanted her to be indebted to you,
didn't you?"

"Of course," he admitted as he bit her ear and let his
lips play along her throat. She slipped her arms about his
neck and lost her thread of thought. His fingers began to
work their magic and it was with difficulty that she remembered the question that had plagued her. "What's so
secret about pink marble?"

He groaned. "The marble is for Bess, the countess of
Hardwick. She has a mania for rebuilding her castles. She
happens to own lead and tin mines, so without drawing
any kind of suspicion, I'm able to trade her marble for
lead."

"For O'Neill?"

He sighed. "Do you want to talk or do you want to
play?"

She pressed her legs together tightly, evading his attempt to slip his finger inside her. "You always want to
play . . . you never want to talk."

He groaned. "What is there to talk about?"

"Can't we ever have a serious conversation? I have a
hundred questions I'd like you to answer."

He pulled her against his hardness and whispered,
"Such as how many times we can do it in one night?"

"Shane, stop it . . . be serious with me!"

"Sorry," he teased, "you mean you want to know more
about me."

"Yes . . . I want to know everything."

He said with mock solemnity, "My shaft lengthens to ten inches when fully aroused."

She beat his chest with tight little fists. "You're impossible. . . .I hate you!"

He grinned and whispered, "You love me when I fuck you."

Little by little he managed to coax her from her questions into a loving mood, then overwhelmed her with sheer animal magnetism. He wanted to bury himself within her, to make her beg, to make her cry out at a dozen moments of passion. He knew that he could soon invade her veins with pure bliss which would blot out all questions.

There were seven hundred mourners in Sir Philip Sidney's funeral procession, and Frances was reduced to selling her family's coach and horses to help defray the expenses. Queen Elizabeth was the chief mourner of the beautiful young man taken in the fullness of his youth. She wore a magnificent outfit of black satin brocade, embroidered overall with jet beads and banded with ebony fur. The only relief to the black outfit was a pretty white ruff at her throat.

Sabre attended the funeral with Kate Ashford and her uncle Lord Ashford, who was returned from the fighting in Holland. Sabre could never bear to follow the fashion and be exactly like everyone around her, so she wore pristine white with a low, square-cut neckline and set it off with an unusual black ruff. The effect was startling, especially with her red hair, which she wore upswept so that its length could not be discerned. Once again Sabre's choice of the unique black ruff caught the queen's attention. Sabre cringed as she heard the beautiful voice single her out in the wardrobe room in front of all the queen's ladies.

"Mistress Wilde, you have a knack for that which catches the eye. If I may be so bold as to ask, where did you acquire that fetching little ruff?"

Sabre curtsied to the floor. "If it please Your Majesty, I simply dyed one of my white ruffs."

"It would please me more if you *simply* dyed some of my white ruffs!" As Sabre raised her eyes, she saw the queen inspecting her copper curls with narrowed eyes. "Your last gift pleased me somewhat, so keep your sovereign in mind, mistress, when you come up with these innovative fashions."

The next day at court every lady wore a black ruff. Every lady that is, except Sabre. She had chosen pale mauve, a perfectly acceptable alternative color for mourning.

Each year the festive holiday season began with the feast of All Hallows on October thirty-first when the queen appointed a lord of misrule to be in charge of the fun and games, forfeits and penalties, that carried on through St. Martin's Day and the feasts of St. Catherine, St. Nicholas, St. Lucy, and St. Thomas. Then came Christmas, St. Stephen's, the feast of the Holy Innocents, New Year's, and Twelfth Night. The season ended at Candlemas on February second. This year, however, there were no festivities at court, no masques or mummeries, where kisses and tickling led to whispered assignations or blatant licentiousness.

The queen was entertained in private homes because the court was in mourning and anyone with ambitions vied for invitations to these private affairs. Bribes were used liberally and her ladies-in-waiting were forever passing to the queen letters and petitions along with costly gifts. The queen read the petitions, grimaced, and said, "Pugh!" accepted the costly gifts, then said a flat "No!" Essex's two sisters, Dorothy Devereux and Penelope Rich, were constantly trying to bribe the queen with expensive jewels. The queen would agree to attend a ball they were giving, then of course she would never show up.

Sabre was happy that the court was quiet and that Shane was less occupied with his intrigues, for they were able to spend lots of days and nights at Thames View. Shane was in seventh heaven when they were able to spend Christmas together, alone and uninterrupted. The baron, fashionably attired as Fitzclare, had taken it into his head to visit Georgiana and most of the servants had gone home for the Christmas holiday.

Shane hitched up a horse and sleigh, tucked Sabre up warmly in a fur rug, and off they went into the countryside of Kent. He took her to see Hever, where Anne Boleyn had lived. It was a beautiful little moated castle which totally enchanted Sabre. When Shane saw that her face was pinched with the cold, he pulled up the sleigh at an inn called the Fighting Cocks, where they enjoyed Christmas dinner in a private dining parlor. After they had eaten he sat down before the blazing fire and pulled her into his lap. His hand caressed her stomach. "Your belly's full of claret and plum pudding. I believe you are a little tipsy, my darling."

"I'm drunk with love," she said, smiling drowsily into the fire.

He nuzzled her neck. "Lying little wench, if that were true I'd be the happiest man on earth."

"After the cold air, the hot fire has made me sleepy," she said, leaning her head against his big, comfortable shoulder.

He kissed her ear. "Let's go home," he whispered, "and I'll put you to bed."

The brisk cold air soon revived her, and when they reached Thames View she hid behind the tall hedges until he had seen to the horses. Then she pelted him with snowballs and shrieked wildly as he took after her to bring her down and wash her face in a deep snowdrift.

They waited until they had retired to their bedchamber for the night before they exchanged gifts. Sabre gave him a narrow sword in a gold-chased sheath and a wicked, heavy dagger to match. The handles were decorated with golden, ruby-eyed dragons and Shane was delighted at the obvious time and care she had taken to choose such a thoughtful, personalized gift for him. He was also deeply gratified at her gasp of pure pleasure as he wrapped her in the present he had had especially designed for her. It was a reversible cloak with furs imported from Muscovy. One side was made from rich, black sable, the incomparable skins deep-piled with a glossy sheen. The other side was fashioned from white ermine, and it could be worn with either fur against her skin. She caressed the fur lovingly and blew on it to see how luxuriously deep the sable was.

Clearly, she was enchanted with his gift. Her eyes were lit with green fire as she looked at him and beckoned, "Make love to me on it." She tossed the fur onto the carpet before the fire, slipped off her silken nightgown, and sank down upon the sable invitingly. How could any man resist the lure, the siren song, of her enticement? They both felt wickedly decadent as they rolled about on the black Russian sable, wrapped in the splendor of fur and flesh.

She was thrilled to discover Shane had had a small sabre tattooed on his left breast over his heart. "That's a coincidence—I am getting a tattoo next week," she teased. "At first I thought I would get a tiny version of the dragon on my shoulder blade, then I thought, ah no, that would show when I wore a low gown. I decided upon my bottom cheek so that none but you will see it."

"Sabre, please, I beg you are only playing with me."

She laughed and kissed him. "Do you forbid me?"

He crushed her mouth beneath his to show his mastery over her and whispered hoarsely, "I know better. If I forbid you I know with certainty the next time I pull down your drawers there will be a dragon or a wildcat staring me in the face!"

"Perhaps a phrase would be better than a picture," she teased unmercifully.

He groaned. "What phrase have you in mind, witch?"

She hesitated, wondering if she dared, then said, *"Mistress to the Black Shadow."*

He stiffened and stopped his lovemaking. The silence was deadly. Finally he broke the silence with a crisp demand. "How did you know?"

"I didn't. It was a wild guess, but now I know."

He shot up from the bed, looming menacingly above her. "You will tell me this moment exactly how you found out!" He was deadly serious, and she could see the violence surging in him, barely under control. She shrank back, half afraid, then said boldly, "You have so many secrets, I'm bound to learn some of them."

"Did you have me followed . . . who else knows of this?" he demanded.

She laughed her challenge. "Only I know. Do you fear me?" she taunted. "Does the queen's mighty sea god, the infamous Black Shadow, fear a woman?"

His hard body slammed her back onto the furs.

He plunged into her savagely as if he would impale her with his weapon and silence her forever. She saw his challenge and vowed to match it. She would not allow him to bring her to climax; she was determined that he would reach orgasm before her. She tightened her walls upon him and he redoubled his deep thrusts. It was as if her body were made to receive him. She received wave after wave of sensual pleasure that brought low moans and cries to her lips. She made no effort to stifle them, for she knew how her cries of enjoyment affected him, and brought him to fulfillment. Three times he almost lost control as she whispered erotic love words and tightened upon him to draw his love juice. His teeth closed over her probing tongue so that she retreated a little and withdrew it, then with his own thrusting tongue he raped her mouth as savagely as he ravished her body. Never had he felt a desire like this. It overpowered him until his breathing became harsh and shallow as he was now moving hard, driving hard. She thrashed her head from side to side into the soft sable, but the floor beneath them was so firm a bed, he was able to go deeper than he had ever gone before. He caressed her with his hands, bruising her soft mouth, but she welcomed the pleasure-pain, reaching peaks of desire she had never known existed. She arched against him, crying, "Shane, Shane," as each brutal plunge brought her to the edge of ecstasy. She held on, forcing back the inevitable submission to his magnificent hard body's domination, then her mind and body experienced a cataclysmic explosion that burst inside her, leaving her clinging to him, shuddering and crying and finally fainting. He revived her by raining kisses upon her lips and eyelids. He rolled her from the sable cloak, flipped it over, and said, "Now I will take you upon the white ermine."

Chapter 17

Walsingham worked feverishly to obtain a pact with France and another with Scotland's new king to ensure peace with England on these two fronts because he knew without doubt that war with Spain was inevitable and imminent. He finally convinced the queen that Philip of Spain's Invincible Armada was ready to attack England. She ordered that all coastal fortifications be strengthened and her ships readied. Lord Howard of Effingham was her lord high admiral of the Navy, and he begged her for more ships and supplies. Elizabeth refused money to victual the ships and refused pay for the seamen.

Spain now had the finest ships in the world, with the best ammunition and equipment. The names of these magnificent vessels were on everyone's lips. There was the *Andalucian,* the *Biscayan,* the *San Felipe,* and the *San Juan.*

Essex, Drake, and Devonport pressed the queen continually on a day-to-day basis for war. It became almost impossible for Shane and Sabre to spend time together. The Hawkhurst ships were bringing cargoes to London from Morocco and Algiers, he was gunrunning to Ireland, and making secret plans with Drake to sail for Spain. At the same time Sabre was kept close with the other ladies of the court, for Leicester and the other nobles were returned from Holland and a frantic pace of entertainments had set in as if London and the queen's court would have one last, extravagant fling before war broke out.

The spur to Elizabeth was the return of her archrival, Lettice. In Holland, as Leicester's wife, she had set up her own royal court. Even here in London she openly exulted in her status. She had a love of display that did not sit well with the queen. She always traveled in great style with a horde of outriders and attendants. When Lady Chandos planned a dinner and entertainment for the queen, she backed out at the last minute because Lettice would be there. The robing ceremonies these mornings were particularly harrowing, with the queen changing her mind a dozen times and then throughout the day exchanging her clothes, each time for a more opulent effect.

Now that his stepfather, Leicester, and his mother, Lettice, were at court, Essex doubled his efforts to get the queen to accept his sisters, Dorothy Devereux and Penelope Rich. She listened sweetly to his entreaties, accepted their costly gifts, and behind their backs said, "Pugh! The mother is an impudent, prostituted strumpet and the daughters are worse. I shall never let them so much as set their pretty feet even inside the courtyard of Whitehall."

Charles Blount was returned from Holland with Leicester, and Penelope picked up their affair immediately, which had been going on for eight years. It would have made things much simpler for her if she were only allowed to come to court. Sabre invited them to Thames View for their liaison and Essex opened the doors of Essex House for his friend Blount and his sister Penelope.

Finally, after many secret sessions with Her Majesty the queen, Drake and Devonport extracted her reluctant permission to take thirty ships to Spain to try to hinder the assembling of the Spanish fleet. After much discussion in high places it was decided the vice-admiral of the

Navy, William Borough, sailing the *Golden Lion,* would accompany Drake and Devonport.

Drake and Devonport, however, had their own ideas about successful, covert raids. They were both born leaders, unused to the restraints of the government and the navy, and they agreed that when the time came they would do whatever they had to do to get the job done, and to hell with officialdom!

Sabre was at Herriot's, the goldsmith's, withdrawing a generous amount. She had decided to turn two rooms adjacent to the master bedchamber at Thames View into her own private sitting room and dressing room. Her clothes were spilling from the closets and she clearly needed the extra space. Of course she could have had the bills sent to Lord Devonport, but somehow she enjoyed actually handing the gold to the various tradesmen. An inner door opened from an office into the shop and she was surprised to encounter Walsingham's daughter. "Frances! How lovely to see you. But I suspect you're here to sell your jewelry," Sabre guessed sadly.

"Oh, Sabre, my jewelry went long ago," she said candidly. "I'm here to sell the last of my mother's."

Sabre was outraged. She marched Frances back into the office and demanded the jewelry. "I shall pay her twice whatever you have allowed her." The goldsmith acceded to her wishes instantly. This was the mistress of the queen's wealthy Sea God and her wish was his command. It was late afternoon and Sabre insisted they return to Thames View for a warm meal, since she could not take her back to court.

Over the meal Sabre drew her out about how things were with her. Frances looked down ruefully at the ink stains on her fingers. "I'm acting as my father's full-time secretary now. He is so ill, he cannot bear anyone else near him. I've been going over my father's account books, and the queen owes us thousands of pounds. I've written to Her Majesty and to Lord Burghley enclosing the figures, but, alas, my letters go unanswered." She sighed.

Sabre soothed, "With England on the brink of war and all the preparation and expense of staving off the Spanish Armada, your letters are probably set aside because of more pressing matters."

"The queen has appointed a new secretary to the crown, a Mr. William Davison, but my father has refused to turn over any of his files or papers to the man. He says bluntly that Davison cannot touch anything until after he is dead!"

"Is he dying?" asked Sabre softly.

Frances nodded sadly. "He has made me promise a private funeral. He wants no public display such as Philip had, and yet sometimes I think he asks for a private funeral because it will be cheaper for us."

"He would still be entitled to be buried at St. Paul's, wouldn't he?" asked Sabre.

Frances nodded again. "But, oh, Sabre I am so fearful his creditors will claim his body. 'Tis such a common practice these days, but I could not bear the shame of it."

"Enough of this talk of death!" cried Sabre. "I shall take you to the theater tonight. There is a new play at the Rose that is causing a sensation. 'Tis a love story."

"Sabre, I cannot, I'm in mourning," Frances said regretfully.

"Nonsense, of course you can. You will put off those widow's weeds and wear one of my dresses, and of course a mask. None will ever know. You need a little diversion, Frances. I insist!"

She chose a gown of peacock-blue, which nipped in tightly to show off her exquisitely tiny waist. The matching mask was fashioned from peacock feathers with their brilliant circles of turquoise, purple, and black. Sabre wore peachflower with slashed sleeves of tawny russet, and a magnificent ivory cameo hung between her breasts. Her mask was fashioned of ivory and gold.

They sat enraptured throughout the play, hanging on to every word the star-crossed lovers uttered. They were so wrapped up in the action onstage, they had no idea Essex's attention had been riveted upon them for the last hour. When the final curtain fell on the tragic heroine, they were both crying. The familiar voice startled Sabre.

"And would you die for love, my beautiful Sabre?"

"I should hope I have more good sense than that, m'lord Essex."

"Well, will you not introduce me to this exquisite lady?"

Frances gasped and Sabre said most firmly, "That is impossible, m'lord, her identity is an absolute secret, of necessity."

"So that her husband will not learn of her night on the town, no doubt," he teased.

"My lord, I am a widow," said Frances primly.

"Surely you jest, sweeting, you are scarcely more than a child."

" 'Tis true," said Sabre, "and because of her mourning 'twould cause a scandal, Robin, if we revealed her identity to you."

He was intrigued. He was also smitten. He would learn

who she was, make no mistake. He bowed graciously to
let them pass.

"Thank heavens he didn't learn my identity," breathed
Frances, weak with relief.

"It would be no bad thing to have Essex your friend.
He is the one man on earth who could get your money
from the queen, mayhap."

Frances shook her head regretfully. "My father would
never allow it."

Within a month Sir Francis Walsingham was dead. His
body was brought to London in the middle of the night
with the aid of Sabre's barge. The stones were opened up
from the floor of St. Paul's Cathedral and he was laid to
rest beside his son-in-law, Sir Philip Sidney. Frances,
with deep gratitude for Sabre's friendship, brought her all
the secret files on Lord Devonport, and in return for the
generous gesture Sabre gave her five thousand pounds to
pay off mortgages on Walsingham House so that Frances
could reopen it and live in London.

With Frances's full consent Sabre spoke to Essex when
next she saw him at court. She told him that a certain
friend of hers wished to reveal her identity to him if he
would care to come to Thames View for supper some
night.

The two young women set the scene artfully, with
Frances's costume chosen for its subtle feminine allure.
They had put their heads together and decided she must
not yield to him without marriage. Once the trap was set
and baited, Sabre withdrew discreetly.

"My lord Essex, you are the only one who can help
me. The queen owes us thousands of pounds for my father's services but I have no influence with her. Would
you speak for me, m'lord?" she implored.

"Frances, sweetheart, you ask of me the one thing I cannot do. Bess would be incensed with jealousy if I pleaded the cause of one so young and exquisitely beautiful."

Frances's lips trembled, her lashes fluttered to her cheeks, and she turned from him.

"Money is no problem, sweeting, I have lots." He knew he wanted her, yet it would have to be a most secret affair. This was no maid-in-waiting who would lift her skirts in a darkened court corridor for him. This was the young widow of the noble Sir Philip Sidney, which only made his desire for her all the more piquant.

Shane came home from Plymouth, where they were readying the ships for Spain, as soon as he had word of Walsingham's death. He had ridden hard through the night to Surrey only to find that Frances was in London. He rode on to Thames View for a bath, a change of clothes, and a fresh horse, but when he found Sabre ensconced snugly in his bed, he joined her there.

"My dragon of the night," she murmured sleepily as his whipcord arms went about her and drew her to the hard length of him. She had stayed at Thames View this night because she had known the death of Walsingham would bring him riding hell-for-leather after the incriminating files.

"Is Frances here?" he asked carefully.

"Is that who you came to see?" she teased.

"Sabre, you know how important it is to me," he said, gripping her shoulders tightly.

"Of course I know," she said softly. "That's why I gave Frances five thousand pounds to pay off mortgages on Walsingham House."

"She gave you the files?" he asked intently.

"Yes, without a moment's hesitation." She slipped from the bed to light sandalwood-scented candles, and their exotic fragrance drifted over the bed. She sat cross-legged before him, allowing her long copper tresses to fall about her nakedness, the ends mingling with the triangle of curls between her legs. His pupils dilated with the intoxicating vision she presented, and she watched with satisfaction as the rest of his body responded to the lure she was casting.

With difficulty he concentrated. "I hope you have the files safe."

"Shane, I burned them the instant I had them in my hands," she lied prettily.

"Damn!" he swore, yet there was relief in his voice. "Did you read them?" he demanded, wanting desperately to know what was in them.

"No," she lied, and swayed toward him, her eyes upon his mouth. He gave himself up to the compelling, irresistible magnetism this woman alone exerted over him.

"When do you sail for Spain?" she asked between kisses.

"You know I cannot tell you, other than to say it will be soon." But she could tell by the intensity of his lovemaking that he would go straight from her to the dangerous mission he and Drake had plotted. He could not get enough of her and loved her as if it would be their last time together. As dawn pinkened the sky and still they had not slept he said, "If anything happens to me go to Jacob Goldman, you are well provided for in my will."

"And what of your wife?" she demanded.

He hesitated, knowing that in the past the subject of his wife had caused heated quarrels between them. His mouth tightened as he said, "She also is well provided for, Sabre. It is my duty, after all."

Somehow the words had a strange comforting effect upon her. She pulled his mane of dark hair until his head rested upon her breast; then they slept.

When Sabre awoke, she was alone. The pale spring sun was high in the sky and she knew he would be halfway to Plymouth by now. She pulled up her knees and hugged them tight. Oh, how she longed to go adventuring! Though she did not wish she were a man, she envied men their freedom and strength to sail ships and wage war and return covered in glory and wealth.

In her mind's eye she saw herself dashing down to Plymouth to wave him off and wish him bon voyage and to kiss him for luck. She smiled. Why stop there? Why not smuggle herself aboard the *Defiant* and sail to Spain with him? She frowned. How very angry he would be to discover her on board his ship. A beating was the least she could hope to get away with. She sighed and pushed the covers from her, along with the fantasy. Now that Whitsuntide was over, the court would be busy with plans to move back to Greenwich for the spring and summer, so she decided to put off going back to Kate Ashford and her wardrobe for a couple of days. She'd promised Frances she'd dine at Walsingham House, but of course she was only a sort of token chaperone, because Frances was again entertaining Essex.

She had just stepped from the bath when she heard Matthew's familiar voice shouting up the stairs as he took them two at a time. "Hawk, where the hell are you? Do you do nothing day and night but bed that woman?"

Sabre stepped from the bathing room wrapped in a large towel. She didn't know if she should be amused or offended at Matthew's words. He whistled at her state of undress, then said quickly, "Where is he? I have orders here from the queen."

"He's gone, Matthew, back to Plymouth."

"God, no," groaned Matthew. "She'll have my head for this. I gave her my word he was at Thames View and that I would give him these new orders."

Sabre looked at him speculatively. "We'll just have to go after him."

"What do you mean, 'we'?"

"Oh, Matthew, please, you wouldn't deny me the opportunity to say good-bye to him before he sails for Spain. God's blood, Matthew, if anything happens to him I may never see him again!"

A tear slipped down her cheek and he begged, "Don't cry, sweetheart. I'll take you to him, if it means that much to you."

"I'll dress and be right with you."

"Better dress for riding and pack some warm clothes. The *Devon Rose* is anchored at Dover. I'm just back from a run to Calais."

When she joined him downstairs she was already booted and carried a heavy riding cloak over her arm. "Let me see the orders. What do they say?"

"The orders are secret and sealed, Sabre, but she said it was imperative he receive them immediately. She sent sealed orders off to Drake and Vice-Admiral Borough as well."

Sabre casually slid her thumbnail beneath the wax seal and opened the parchment.

"God's death, Sabre, you cannot break the queen's seal!" he protested.

"Why not? I'm his wife," she asserted.

"That's not the point. These are secret war orders!"

"God in Heaven," she exclaimed, "he won't be pleased with these. Bess has withdrawn her permission for them to sail. She forbids them to enter a Spanish port because it will be considered an act of war."

"Well, at least we have a legitimate reason for going after him. The orders she sent to Drake and Borough are probably identical."

She ran to Shane's desk and resealed the parchment with a blob of melted wax. "Take my saddlebags, Matthew. Let's hurry! We have to reach Plymouth before the other couriers."

The *Devon Rose* sailed past all the ports it had when he had first brought Sabre to London, only this time he was not dawdling to kill time as they sped past Hastings, Eastbourne, and the Isle of Wight. At St. Alban's Head he stopped following the coastline and cut out into the Channel to round the southern tip of Devon, called Bolt Head, and then into Plymouth's harbor.

There were over thirty ships riding at anchor, crowding one upon another. Drake's flagship, the *Elizabeth Bonaventure,* was five hundred tons, bristling with ship-smashing guns, as were the vice-admiral's *Golden Lion* and Devonport's *Defiant.* There were at least ten men-of-war, each over two hundred tons, and a dozen frigates and pinnaces weighing one hundred tons, all equipped with brass cannons that would rain death upon the decks of the enemy.

Matthew decided the best way to get Shane's attention without causing suspicion was to signal the *Defiant.* The messages that went back and forth between the *Devon Rose* and the *Defiant* were so obscure that Shane lost his patience and rowed across to speak with his brother. He

suspected a ruse to enable Matthew to sail with him to
Cádiz, a thing he would permit under no circumstances.
Not only did he not want to put the *Devon Rose* at risk,
but he was under no illusions about the danger of the
mission. Many lives could be lost and he was going to
make sure one of those lives was not Matthew
Hawkhurst's.

When Shane entered the captain's cabin to find Sabre
there with Matthew, his face almost distorted with black
anger. He turned upon Matthew savagely. "Get her back
to London immediately!"

"Shane," she implored, holding out the sealed parchment, "we have orders from the queen!"

He snatched them up and tore them open savagely, the
black anger not abating for one moment. He read them
twice because he couldn't believe the stupidity of them. A
filthy oath fell from his lips and his fist smashed the table.
"Why in hell did you bring me these?" he demanded of
Matthew.

Sabre cut in quickly. "Because she's sent the same orders to Drake and Borough. The couriers are probably
riding to Plymouth and I wanted you to get them first."

A little of the angry mist cleared from his brain as he
realized what she was proposing. He grinned at her as she
said, "Matthew will tell her we were too late; you'd already sailed."

He crushed her to him against the rough leather jerkin
he wore, unmindful of the weapons in his belt. Then he
turned her about and gave her behind a hell of a whack.
"Go home, mistress. Now!"

He said to Matthew, "Drake will be no problem, nothing on earth will keep him from Cádiz, but the vice-
admiral and all the other senior officers in the navy will

obey these orders to the letter, if they receive them. It's my intention to see they don't receive them!" He was gone as quickly as he had arrived.

Matthew eyed Sabre with admiration. "He knew you'd read the orders."

"Aye, he knew and was damned grateful that I acted upon them quickly."

"All those tears begging me to take you to him because you might never see him again were false. You knew he'd disobey the orders, didn't you?"

She stood on tiptoe to kiss him. "Of course," she said matter-of-factly. "Let's go up on deck and see what happens."

Within the hour the *Elizabeth Bonaventure* and the *Defiant* weighed anchor and sailed majestically from Plymouth Harbor out into the North Atlantic Ocean. A dozen small ships played follow-the-leader, and after a lengthy hesitation the vice-admiral aboard the *Golden Lion* had no alternative but to give orders to his captains of the navy vessels to weigh anchor and sail for Spain.

Matthew and Sabre stood for over two hours at the rail until the harbor emptied. They looked at each other forlornly. It was a heavy feeling of deprivation to be left behind. He noticed the familiar light of speculation steal into her eyes and he held his breath. Finally he let it out with a great rush and shouted, "Why the hell not?"

They danced a little jig and fell into each other's arms, laughing like lunatics.

Chapter 18

Matthew was too busy giving orders for setting the sails so that they should keep well behind the fleet of ships sailing the Atlantic, to worry about the consequences. When his conscience nagged him, he pushed away the thoughts. He was tired of his brother always taking the lion's share and he was resentful that Hawk hadn't asked his help on this great adventure. It was the opportunity of a lifetime, and, he reasoned, before the mission was completed Hawk might be damned thankful for his help.

The main fleet of thirty vessels was prepared for the long voyage and well victualed, but not so the *Devon Rose,* which had embarked on the spur of the moment. Matthew had to stop at Brest on the tip of France to take on fresh water and supplies. His hopes for a romantic interlude were rudely dashed, for from the moment the ship entered the Bay of Biscay, Sabre had *mal de mer.* She vomited and retched the five days it took to cross, until finally she had had enough and begged him to turn back.

He laughed at her, told her she was only seasick and her stomach would right itself the moment they sighted Spain. Her queasiness abated slightly, but she couldn't believe the stifling heat of the small cabin as she huddled miserably, clad only in a thin shift. She had brought only warm woolens and velvets, not realizing then that they would be going on a voyage to Spain.

By the time they reached Lisbon, she could stand it no longer and demanded that Matthew put into port so she could buy some cool cotton dresses and a couple of protective sun hats so she could stay up on deck to catch any breeze that fluttered their way.

When Matthew entered the Gulf of Cádiz he cautiously weighed anchor at Faro, which belonged to Portugal rather than Spain. They were well out of sight of the Invincible Spanish Fleet but easily within earshot of the boom of cannons, and he waited tensely for this signal before sailing into the action.

The English fleet stood out to sea off the port of Cádiz. Drake and Devonport knew their only hope in hell was a surprise attack. Drake had a lighter, faster pinnace among the fleet of ships, and he and Devonport decided to board her and go scouting straight into Cádiz harbor.

What they found amazed them. More than thirty galleons and merchant ships sat almost unguarded at Cádiz. Only sleepy skeleton crews moved about in desultory fashion in the heat of the afternoon. They cudgeled their brains to try to remember if this was some sort of religious day or Spanish holiday, for it was certain the port town of Cádiz was totally off guard.

Hundreds of casks made from seasoned wood with sound hoops to hold the seams against wet and vermin were stacked, ready to be taken aboard ship once they had been filled with water, wine, flour, salted beef, sugar, spices, fish, hard biscuit, and dried fruit. It appeared to their trained eyes that most of the ammunition and powder had already been taken aboard the ships, and a few sailors were even now loading such a cargo onto a ship called the *Argosy*. Their small pinnace, carrying no flag, hadn't even been challenged by a port authority. Drake gave the signal to take them back to the *Elizabeth Bonaventure*.

"Even if Vice-Admiral Borough is reluctant to take action the two of us could take Cádiz," Drake said.

Hawk agreed. "If we strike today while they are sitting ducks."

"I am willing to shoulder the responsibility of acting in England's best interests," Drake said. "You heard Borough's jackass suggestion yesterday that we send a message to the governor of Cádiz to parley?"

Devonport grinned. "You intend to plunge in without meetings or even the opinion of the vice-admiral?"

"I do," confirmed Drake.

"I'm with you all the way, Francis. They have two choices. They can either weigh anchor and follow us or turn tail and run."

"I'll go in with the *Elizabeth Bonaventure,* with your *Defiant* at my heels. We'll pick out one ship and destroy it totally and see what happens."

"Let's fire on the *Argosy.* She's loaded with ammunition and gunpowder."

"Then we are agreed," said Drake calmly.

"Matthew, we've sat here in the sun for three days! We can't see anything, we can't hear anything, we can't even smell anything but stinking fish." She wrinkled her nose and cooled herself with a straw fan. "Perhaps they've all been captured," she said, letting her imagination run riot.

"Without a shot being fired?" he scoffed.

"How do we know we could hear anything from here?" she countered. "Let's get closer!"

He had just about decided to sail on to Cádiz when she had challenged him. "You have no idea what a sea battle is like, Sabre. The explosions of the long guns and cannon can make your ears bleed. Ships' guns can be packed with red-hot iron balls, nails, any iron missile that's razor-edged. At any moment the rails or the planking of the deck çan be smashed out from under you. It's like a rain of death to be fired upon. Your fate is even worse if your vessel is boarded by the enemy. A clean gutting from a sword is the best you can hope for. Other tortures aren't so pretty!"

"You are just trying to frighten me!" shouted Sabre, her heart hammering wildly at the ghastly pictures he had drawn. "Don't worry about me, for if I stay here I shall die of boredom and you can feed me to the fish."

He turned from her to shout an order, then said over his shoulder, "You'd best go below."

She set her teeth and shouted, "Not bloody likely! Give me a spyglass so I don't miss anything."

Vice-Admiral Borough was absolutely incensed as he saw the *Elizabeth Bonaventure* hoist her flag and sail past him into Cádiz Harbor. His frantic signals were ignored by the *Defiant* also as it passed, close on the heels of the *Bonaventure.* His unbelieving eyes swept the English fleet and watched the *Golden Hind* follow suit.

Both Drake and Hawkhurst positioned their ships on the port side of the *Argosy,* and as they sailed brazenly into Cádiz Harbor, flying English flags, they caused no small commotion. Panic had set in among the Spanish sailors that they had been caught so unbelievably unprepared.

Hawkhurst's long legs were braced against the roll of the ship. He was stripped to the waist with one arm raised as he issued commands to his gun captains. His arm fell and suddenly the *Defiant'*s double decks of starboard gun batteries erupted with fire. The ship lurched violently with the recoil as his crew hauled the bronze muzzle-loading cannons inboard to reload. The air was filled with black smoke and the reek of gunpowder. The well-trained crew reamed out snouts, put the powder cartridges in place, rammed iron balls into the muzzles, packed and primed the guns, all within a minute, and turned their sweaty, smoke-streaked faces to Hawkhurst, shouting, "Clear!" and watched for his arm to descend again.

Cannon fire filled the air, whether from Drake's ships or from the enemy Hawkhurst could not be sure, but suddenly the air was rent with the unmistakable explosion of powder kegs going up, and the rigging and masts on the *Argosy* were blown to smithereens. The *Argosy* keeled to one side and the sea poured into the open gunports. Most of her crew were trapped under the antiboarding netting that was laced across her decks. The screams of the trapped and drowning could be heard on the shore and on every ship at Cádiz.

The *Argosy* sank in less than two minutes. Then a most astounding thing happened. As Vice-Admiral Borough and his fleet sailed reluctantly into Cádiz, they witnessed the Spanish surrender. Only one ship sunk and they gave up in total defeat!

It was then that the work began. All the English suddenly started pulling together, their differences set aside for the moment. The true leader of this expedition had emerged as Drake and the sailors, to a man, followed his lead. They allowed the skeleton crews to leave their ships unharmed, then systematically they unloaded the Spanish ships of their cargoes and loaded them onto the English galleons.

Hawk was startled to see Matthew board the *Defiant*.

He grinned his congratulations to his brother as Hawk shouted, "What the hell are you doing here? Never mind —we're stripping these ships of their cargoes. Take anything that isn't nailed down—ammunition, food, clothing, saddles, horse armor, tents, wine. The trick is to get the hell out fast before reinforcements come flocking from Seville."

As each ship was loaded it left Cádiz Harbor and set course for England. Then Drake and Hawkhurst set fire to the empty hulls and set them loose on the flood tide. In all they had destroyed a total of thirty-three Spanish ships.

Sabre stood at the rail of the *Devon Rose,* mesmerized at the sight of the burning Spanish galleons that lit up the darkening sky and turned it the color of flame. The horror of the sinking of the *Argosy* would stay with her forever, yet the other things she had witnessed that day had held her spellbound at the railing for hours. Her face was blackened from the smoke of gunpowder and streaked with the tears she had shed. She ached from standing and finally pushed herself from the rail to go below. Hawk caught a glimpse of her as she moved from the rail, and though the *Defiant* was a good two hundred yards from the *Devon Rose,* he could never mistake the sight of her. Grim-faced, he lowered a small boat and rowed himself over to his brother's ship. He came over the side like an avenging angel, blackened with sweat and grime. He did not trust himself to speak. Instead, he strode up to his brother and laid him out flat with one blow—all six feet of him. The crew gaped. Though they were loyal to their captain and would have knifed any other man who came aboard and assaulted him, they stayed out of this one. It was between Hawkhursts.

Almost without breaking stride Hawk strode down to the cabin and flung open the door. Sabre had just washed her face and stood in white pantaloons with a tiny white cotton busk covering her breasts. His face was terrible to behold, and fear gripped her and rippled along her veins. Without a word he picked her up, tossed her over his shoulder like a sailor's canvas bag, and strode up on deck. She pummeled his back and kicked her heels, but unheeding, he went over the side and dumped her unceremoniously into the bottom of the rowboat.

She was so afraid of him at this moment that she did not dare open her mouth to speak. The veneer over the brute male, always so very thin where Shane Hawkhurst O'Neill was concerned, had disappeared completely. He had turned into a savage beast. The small boat banged into the side of the *Defiant,* throwing her backward with her legs in the air. He again slung her over his shoulder and began ascending the rope ladder. Suddenly grinning, cheering sailors were reaching down to haul her aboard, and when they let her go she fell to the deck, mortified to be so roughly handled, her white drawers streaked with the grime from Shane's body. One look from their captain ended the capering, jibing laughter of the crew, and again he hauled her over his shoulder, this time managing to knock the breath from her solar plexus. He opened his cabin door and threw her onto the berth. He rummaged in an oaken sea chest and took out a small, heavy whip. Without taking his eyes from her face he slapped the weapon into the palm of his other hand and repeated the threatening motion half a dozen times.

She whispered, "You wouldn't dare."

"I'm going to give you a good thrashing! You are the

most willful woman I've ever encountered. You have every undesirable Irish trait in the book!"

"And you don't?" she demanded.

He was incredulous. "Still you defy me, after I've warned you time and time again. You've been asking for a lesson—begging for a bloody lesson, and I think it's time I gave you one."

"You are a brute and a bully . . . don't brandish that whip at me," she spat.

"You had better pray I keep brandishing it, because when I stop, I'm going to use it!"

She narrowed her eyes like a cat. "I swear, if you use that thing on me, Shane Hawkhurst O'Neill, I'll take a terrible vengeance . . . one day I will hold the whip hand!"

He lashed out, striking the locker beside the berth. It cracked like lightning, and the tip touched her bare thigh with a sting. Then in a black rage he snapped the whip in half and flung it from him in disgust. He departed before he lost total control, locking the door behind him. Sabre was so frightened and humiliated, she burst into tears. She drew her knees up under her chin, crying and rocking herself. The day had simply been too much for her and she needed the release the good cry gave her. She fell asleep exhausted, without even washing herself.

Early the next morning she awoke with a start and it took her a few moments to orient herself. As memory of Shane's treatment came flooding back to her, her heart sank with a feeling that was very close to fear. He had been so angry and still would be angry, if she knew anything about him. Any moment he would come, and when he did he would punish her. He would probably give her a beating. Perhaps he would even tell her he was finished with her and tell her to pack her things when they got back to Thames View. She was in total misery. No one even had brought her breakfast or inquired if she needed anything.

She opened the two portholes in the cabin and took a deep breath of the sea air. It was not in the least cool or refreshing, and this brought home to her the fact that soon they would again have to cross the Bay of Biscay and the return of her seasickness was inevitable. She felt so sorry for herself that the tears began to slip down her cheeks again.

It was some time before she saw herself in the mirror, but when she did she was so shocked by her appearance that she was suddenly galvanized into action. She stripped off the grimy white pantaloons and busk and poured water to bathe herself all over. She searched through Shane's wardrobe of clothing, looking for an item of apparel that she could borrow. The only things cool enough that would give her a measure of cover were his shirts. She chose a frilled white lawn and rolled up the sleeves to her elbows. Then she opened his drawers until she located a brush and comb and set to work on the disheveled mass of copper tangles.

When no one came to the cabin door by midday, a little of her apprehension started to evaporate, and after two more hours elapsed she was annoyed, then angered. She was highly indignant to be ignored in such a fashion. Rather she would welcome an angry confrontation in which she ducked his blows and he ducked objects she threw at his head. She knew captain and crew would be celebrating the great victory of destroying the Spanish fleet right on its own doorstep, but surely to God someone aboard could spare her a moment's thought.

It was late afternoon before a young cabin boy knocked on the door with a cool lime drink for her. "Thank you," she said diffidently. "Does the captain intend to ignore me and keep me locked up until we reach England?" she demanded.

The boy looked shamefaced. "He's powerful angry, ma'am. If I was you, I'd be glad he was keepin' 'is distance! 'Twer the baron sent this drink, an' he wrote cook a note orderin' a tray fer yer supper an' some wine." The boy touched his forelock and was about to depart when Sabre grabbed his arm. "Wait!" she cried, incensed that Shane didn't intend to come. She'd do something about that or her name wasn't Lady Devonport! She grabbed the white pantaloons and shoved them into the startled boy's hand. "Here! Hoist these up the flagpole. He may have defeated the Spanish, but he hasn't defeated me! If you haven't the guts, tell the baron to do it for me."

The boy grinned and flushed. "I'll do it when nobody's lookin'," he promised.

Hawk wondered what was amusing the men so much. They'd tried to hide their laughter behind their hands, but every time one of them looked his way, the hard-bitten sailors were grinning from ear to ear. Finally he caught one of them pointing and a couple more splitting their sides at his expense. His gaze traveled upward and he could hardly believe what he saw flying at half-mast. They looked suspiciously like Sabre's begrimed drawers, offering him her challenge.

He stared in disbelief for a minute, then he found himself grinning. Finally his roar of laughter could be heard all over the ship. Once he had his mirth under control, he ran down to the cabin and threw open the door. She'd heard his booted step approaching and stood with hands on hips, not knowing what to expect, but more than ready for anything.

Formally he asked, "Are you flying the white flag of surrender, madam?"

"Surrender?" she cried angrily. "Never! Your ship is named *Defiant* . . . you must have named her after me, sir!" She sat in his own captain's chair and as he watched she deliberately lifted one bare leg and hooked it over the arm. She wore nothing beneath the fine lawn shirt and he caught a glimpse of tight coppery curls each time she nonchalantly swung her leg.

He laughed with pure joy. "Sabre Wilde, you're one hell of a woman!" He took only one great step to close the distance between them, and she stopped him with an imperious hand held high and green fire in her eyes.

"Don't think to vanquish me, sir, as easily as you did Cádiz. Don't think you can toss me about like a sack of grain, ignore me and starve me, then stride in here and make love to me!"

He knew he could breach her walls by force, but she deserved better. He would use subtler means, knowing his reward would be the sweeter for it. He bowed to her gallantly; the mocking light was gone from his eyes. He said very formally, "Sabre, would you do me the honor of dining with me? I intend to celebrate our victory and I would like to celebrate it with you."

With equal formality she inclined her head and said, "I should like that above all things, Lord Devonport. I only wish I had something to wear."

He strode over to a trunk in the corner of the cabin and lifted the lid. "There is material in here. I am sorry I have no gown for you, Sabre." He took fresh clothing for

himself from his wardrobe and departed with it over his
arm. "Dinner will be served at six bells."

She discovered the bottom of the sea chest to be
layered with the most exquisite, fragile material of so
many hues, she was torn which to select. Finally she
chose cloth that was almost transparent with silken ribbons of turquoise and golden thread running through it
to make stripes. She cut a piece about a yard square,
wrapped it about her, and knotted it on one shoulder.
When she viewed herself from the right she was completely covered; when she viewed herself from the left the
gown was open from her shoulder to her ankle and displayed her nakedness.

A knock upon the door revealed the baron, who silently and efficiently set an elegant table. He spread a
white damask cloth and napkins along with Italian silver
forks and matching knives. The plates were of heavy
gold, each stamped with a dragon at its center, and the
wine and water goblets were Venetian crystal bowls set on
stems of carved gold and jade. The baron always treated
her with respect, but his looks seemed to have a special
reverence this evening, and she wondered if perhaps
Georgiana had told him that she was Lady Devonport.
She had no time to discover the truth, for as six bells
were struck, Shane formally presented himself at the
doorway. He knocked politely and waited for her to invite him in. He wore tropical cream linen, which emphasized the dark mahogany of his deep tan. He took her
hand and drew it to his lips, then allowed his intense blue
eyes to lick over her like a candle flame. As a slow smile
of appreciation transformed his mouth, the white teeth
flashed in startling contrast to his dark skin.

Sabre's heart turned over in her breast at the handsome figure he presented. His lion's mane of hair fell to his shoulders, its tips bleached golden red from the sun. His masculinity stunned her and her knees were like water for a moment as his presence in the small cabin overwhelmed her.

The baron returned with hot covered dishes and with a large epergne filled with fruit, some of which were unknown to Sabre. When the baron departed and left them to be private, Shane held her chair and murmured, "You are the loveliest woman who ever graced my table." Sabre sat down gracefully and draped her gown modestly to conceal rather than reveal her nakedness. "Something smells delicious, though I cannot name it," she said with relish.

"We have the Spaniards to thank for our supper tonight." He lifted the heavy silver cover from the tureen. "This is paella, a famous specialty of Spain. It is made with chicken and shelled shrimp and spiced with garlic and Spanish saffron. It is served upon a bed of rice and hot peppers." He poured a pale chablis into the goblets and served her a heaping plate of the fragrant paella.

"Whatever are these?" she asked curiously.

"Artichokes with ripe olives at their heart. You break off a leaf and dip it into the melted butter, like this," he instructed. He smiled as she enthusiastically tried each new dish. "An acquired taste, like most foreign dishes. I find the English too ready to turn their noses up at anything different, but I believe in the adage that variety is the spice of life."

"Indeed, my lord?" she challenged with sparkling eyes, wondering if he were using a double entendre.

"However, there are some things that, once tasted, are never forgotten," he added, desire roughening his voice.

She blushed and her lashes fluttered to her cheeks. "What are these fruits?" she asked rather breathlessly, trying to dispel the ardor that was burning deeply in his eyes.

Shane sighed. "Well, I think you know oranges and lemons. These green fruit are limes, and these are grapes and melons. The brown things are dates, very sticky and sweet, and these are figs, delicious but filled with seeds."

She placed a delicate finger on the hard shell of a strange red fruit and raised her eyebrows.

"Pomegranates, an ancient symbol of fertility. The baron, ever perceptive, laid the pomegranates upon a palm leaf. These are phallic symbols; pomegranate female, the palm male."

The corners of her mouth went up mischievously. "I would have to ask, wouldn't I?"

"Sabre, I want to make love to you."

Their eyes met, and in that moment she knew she had accomplished everything she had set out to do. She had bound him to her so that she was a madness in his blood. He wanted her, needed her, and to survive he must have her. She could get away with anything and he would still love her. He was a man of extraordinary strength and she was his one weakness. She had enslaved him.

She moved from the table, carrying the delicate goblet with her. Implicit in their tryst was the understanding that he would not fall upon her, but would await her permission. She sipped her wine, tantalizing him with the slowness of her invitation. Finally, when she had made him wait beyond his endurance, she undid the knot on her shoulder to let the sheath slip from her body, then with a wickedly suggestive finger she dipped into the Chablis and wet each nipple with the tempting wine.

With a growl of triumph he snatched her up and tasted each nipple. His strong hands held her high against his chest and then slowly he slid her naked body down his. The cream linen was rough-textured against her satin smoothness and she gasped with sudden desire as her thighs, belly, and breasts rubbed against his hardness. He kissed the corners of her mouth, her eyelids, the tip of her nose, and, finally, the tempting little beauty spot. Her head fell back sensually as tremors began to shoot through her body and his lips devoured her throat.

Her scented mane of hair intoxicated his senses, making his pulse race. She reached down with avid fingers to delicately trace his thick shaft, then her hand closed over it possessively, making him quiver with anticipation.

She cried softly, "Please, Shane!"

He looked deeply into her eyes. "Please what, Sabre?"

"Please," she begged.

"Tell me, darling . . . say the words."

"I want you now . . . if you don't take me, I'll die," she sobbed.

He filled her deeply, his own excitement spurred on by her wild and frenzied gyrations to take more and more of him deeper inside her. She bit into his shoulder, where she knew the dragon breathed his fire, and tasted the delicious salt tang of his bronzed flesh.

He used her furiously, pushing his great shaft upward, drawing it all the way out, then thrusting the full length in again. She clawed at him, drawing blood, then licked and sucked the tiny crescent-shaped wounds her nails left behind. He was so hungered he feared he might tear her asunder, but she drew him farther inside, then held him viselike while she pulsated and throbbed until their cries of pleasure could be heard up on deck.

They made love in every way it was possible for a man and woman to mate. He took her against the wall, across a low table, upon the floor, then cradled her in the bunk, holding her fast between his legs until she slept, totally exhausted from his pleasuring. She did not awake when he left her to go up on deck to see to his ship.

Three hours later, when he returned to their bed, they could not speak for the first few minutes. They were overwhelmed by the great passion they had shared and relived it in their minds. He touched her cheek with wonder until she came out of her love trance and propped herself against him to talk.

"I would like to throw a masquerade ball at Thames View to celebrate. I shall make it bigger and better than any the queen has ever given."

He kissed the top of her head. "We may get thrown in the Tower for what we did back there. First we ignored her orders to abort the mission, then Drake plunged in without consulting with the vice-admiral. I backed him all the way and will have to take the consequences of my actions. Make no mistake about it, the Navy will make a formal protest and bring charges against Drake and me."

"Pugh!" said Sabre, doing a fair imitation of the queen. "You can charm Bessie Tudor, for you are far handsomer than fat old Borough."

"Poor Bess," he lamented, "she's losing all her favorites. I'm in love with you and now Essex has lost his heart to Frances."

"To say nothing of his fortune," she said, giggling.

He was still for a minute. "Don't you think Frances loves him?"

"Mmmm . . . let's say she loves him with her head, but I don't think her heart is much involved. Anyway, they shall come to the party and you can see for yourself. And I shall invite your friend Charles Blount and Penelope. . . ."

"Next you'll be telling me Penelope doesn't love Charles," he teased.

"Oh, of course she does. She makes herself ridiculous over the damned fellow. I think she's actually going to leave her husband and children to go and live with him."

He wanted to ask her if she loved him, but afraid of the answer, he kissed her hair again and said tenderly, "I love you, Sabre."

She turned her green gaze upon him and said softly, "I know you do."

He was to prove his words over and over in the next few days as they entered the infamous Bay of Biscay. Sabre lifted her head from his arm and moaned pitifully.

"My love, what is it?" he asked anxiously.

"Ooh, I'm soo ill," she whispered.

He was on his feet in an instant, cradling her in his arms. "Whatever is amiss? Was it the food we had last night?"

At the word *food* her gorge rose uncontrollably and she was indelicately sick. "Ooh, I'm seasick," she moaned, "please don't look at me."

"Were you like this before?" he demanded.

She nodded mutely, totally embarrassed by the awful miasma that arose from her. "Please leave me," she begged.

"Of course I won't leave you. You think I can't cope with seasickness?" he scoffed. He tore the soiled sheets from the berth and made up the bunk afresh. Then, as gently as he would help a child, he washed her all over

and put one of his clean shirts on her, then lifted her into
the clean bed. He brought her watered wine and dry biscuit and urged her to put something in her stomach.

A sip and a nibble brought on another attack of violent
vomiting, and patiently he began his chores all over
again. He did everything in his power to make her more
comfortable. He found a fresh-smelling eau de cologne to
bathe her forehead and sprinkled a few drops upon her
pillows. He massaged her knotted stomach and held her
in strong, gentle arms while she retched anew. He tended
her as if she were a baby, feeding, washing, changing, and
when she quieted he held her hand and hummed a lullaby
until she slept.

When she protested at her own nastiness he calmly
replied, "Didn't you nurse me in my need?" He must
have left the ship in the baron's capable hands, because as
far as she knew he never left their cabin for three days.
On the fourth, when she was slightly recovered, yet still
pale and shaky, he carried her on deck for some fresh air,
and while she was up there he had the cabin stripped and
scrubbed to erase the lingering smell of vomit. His un-
ending kindness had a peculiar effect upon her. She began
to brood because she didn't want to be his mistress any
longer, she wanted to be his wife.

Sabre was much relieved when they sighted England
and at last she was able to shake off the queer mood that
had settled over her. She preferred him in the guise of
sinner rather than saint. After all, how could she avenge
herself upon a saint?

Chapter 19

The queen and all England were jubilant at the sea victory of Cádiz. This was a time for heroes, a time when the queen and her council had needed a great show of strength against the enemies who threatened from every direction.

Elizabeth was far too shrewd not to make the most of the fortunate turn of events, and she conveniently forgot she had forbidden them to carry out their mission. The outcry of Vice-Admiral Borough and the Navy were quickly and effectively silenced as she gave England the heroes they craved, to be fêted at every turn.

The tales of entering Cádiz, taking thirty-seven vessels, and setting fire to the Spanish ships, were told, retold, and embellished. England had singed the beard of King Philip of Spain and there was much rejoicing. In her heart of hearts it had always secretly delighted Elizabeth to see her subjects sail impudently into waters Spain had claimed, and now she need keep it secret no longer.

Crowds flocked to the seaports to see England's renowned ships, such as the *Merchant Royal,* the *Rainbow,* and the *Elizabeth Bonaventure,* but the ships that got the most attention and would go down in the history books, when those were written, were the privately owned vessels, such as Drake's *Golden Hind* and Devonport's *Defiant.*

That spring turned out to be the most frantic, gaudy time of Elizabeth's reign. Masques, mummeries, plays, games, entertainments, balls, and banquets filled the days and nights of the courtiers, and court was *the* place to be. The queen kept Devonport at her side, and as always the whims of the queen were law. Court life became one long pageant in which everyone wore costumes, and these became more elaborate with each passing day. Fortunes were spent on clothes and jewels and upon entertainments to outdo those attended the day before.

Sabre visited Walsingham House the day after she returned to court. She was full of her great adventure and bursting to tell Frances, yet her friend seemed preoccupied and had news of her own to impart. "Frances, you haven't heard a word I've said! Something happened while I was gone—tell me."

"Oh, Sabre, so much has happened, but you must swear to keep my secrets," said Frances very seriously.

"I swear! Now, tell me!" urged Sabre.

"The queen was invited to sup at Essex House and at last Robin got her promise that he could present Penelope. I helped her pick out the most exquisite necklace for the queen. Late the next night Robin stormed in here angrier than I've ever seen anyone in my life! The queen had gone back on her word and ordered Penelope to keep to her room. She and Essex had a terrible row where he almost struck her. He swore he would be revenged upon her. Sabre, he wanted to strike out and hurt her . . . so he wed me that night."

"You're the countess of Essex?" cried Sabre happily.

"Hush, Sabre, 'tis a secret," warned Frances.

"Oh, that is the most marvelous piece of news I've ever heard! What a sweet revenge upon the old witch! Oh, I would pay a fortune to see her face when she eventually hears of it!" said Sabre, laughing with joy.

"Mary and Joseph, don't say that," begged Frances, alarmed.

"Why do you look so worried, Frances? Your secret is

safe, and if anyone found out, none would dare to tell the queen."

Frances hesitated. "I think . . . I think . . . I'm with child."

"Oh, Lord, are you sure?" asked Sabre.

"Oh, I've counted and counted until I'm dizzy. I know I've missed one menstrual flow . . . and there are other signs. Don't forget I've already had a child, so I know the signs."

"What signs?" asked Sabre blankly.

"My breasts are sore and—and I'm running to the garderobe to pass water every five minutes."

Sabre was stunned, because she'd been feeling exactly the same lately.

"And of course," Frances added, "I've been vomiting."

"Vomiting?" cried Sabre, alarmed now.

"What is it?" asked Frances breathlessly.

"Oh, your morning sickness reminded me of how seasick I've been."

"Morning sickness is such a misnomer. The nausea comes any time of day when you are carrying a child."

"Does it?" asked Sabre, wanting to know all the morbid details.

When she returned to Greenwich she frantically tried to count the days since her last flow, but for the life of her she could not fix the date in her mind. It certainly seemed a long time since, now that she had begun to really think about it. She deliberately pushed the thought away from her, as her hand caressed one of her breasts, which felt particularly tender. Her imagination was working overtime, she scolded herself, yet the faint apprehension lingered and lingered in the back of her mind.

The queen ordered a new gown for an entertainment at

Burghley's fabulous Theobalds. It was a most regal creation of purple velvet slashed to show amethyst silk encrusted with crystals and pearls. As soon as Sabre saw
the dressmakers giving Elizabeth her final fitting for the
gown, she knew she would have it duplicated for the masquerade ball they were throwing at Thames View. None
had ever dared to chose the costume of a queen, let alone
this queen, but the more Sabre thought about it, the more
taken she was with the unique idea. She knew the queen
had an abundance of amethyst and pearl jewelry to
match the gown, and she had a small crown lined in
purple velvet, encrusted with diamonds, pearls, and ame-
thysts of varying shades of purple which she would un-
doubtedly decide to wear with the gown. Sabre had everything copied, down to the lilac satin shoes and the
lilac fan.

In the beginning she consulted with Shane about the
ball, but since he agreed to indulge her every whim concerning the party, she just went ahead on her own, com-
pleting the arrangements.

She brilliantly decided to hold it the same date as the
Theobald entertainment, knowing all the interesting people would come to hers and all the old dullards would go
to Theobalds. Invitations went out to Essex and Frances,
Anthony and Francis Bacon, both secretaries to Essex,
Penelope Rich and Charles Blount, Dorothy Devereux
and the man with whom she had just eloped, Thomas
Perrot. Sabre even invited Essex's mother, Lettice, although she did not include Leicester on the invitation.
Also invited were the countess of Hardwick, Lady Leighton, Katherine and Philadelphia Carey, Bess Throckmorton and her lover Sir Walter Raleigh, as well as many of
Shane's unmarried friends, such as Lord Mountjoy,

Fulke-Greville, and the banker Sir Thomas Gresham, reported to be the richest man in London, and who had just built the Royal Exchange.

All the queen's maids-of-honor were invited with the understanding that they would be excused if they were coerced into attending the queen at Theobalds at the last moment. Theobalds was indeed a magnificent three-story house, with four square towers and four courtyards. Its hall boasted a fountain that jetted to the ceiling with red or white wine and contained many curious rooms. One was filled with clocks all set to chime at the same precise moment; another was painted to represent the sky, with clouds, planets, and stars in the design of the zodiac. It had a clockwork mechanism in the ceiling that allowed the sun to set, the moon to rise, and the stars to twinkle off and on in the most curious manner. There was a glassed-in gallery that depicted all the rulers of Christendom, along with appropriate costumes and scenes from history. The dreadful drawback of Theobalds was the cramped quarters where the courtiers and ladies were expected to sleep three and four to a bed—with the sexes separated, of course. Another drawback was its distance. They could only go by river as far as Whitehall; then they must travel through the Strand, up Drury Lane into Holborn, along Kingsgate Street, and then on the road now named Theobalds Road. By comparison, how pleasantly simple it was to sail the short distance from Greenwich to Thames View.

Sabre had spared no expense in food, wine, and extra servants. She even had a Hawkhurst vessel bring a whole shipload of early-blooming flowers from France. The freesia, iris, and scented stocks filled the whole house with their fragrance. Sabre spent two days with her hair in curling rags to simulate the tight curls of one of the queen's wigs, and while attending the queen's wardrobe the day of the masquerade, she wore a dainty lace cap to cover her tortured hair.

Sabre helped Kate Ashford lay out the queen's new outfit—into which she would change before leaving for Theobalds—and, with a wicked twinkle in her eye, finally escaped, telling Kate she would see her that evening at Thames View.

Sabre had told Shane that she preferred him as the queen's Sea God for their masquerade, so he simply chose one of his elegant court costumes and was just choosing his rings when Sabre came in from her dressing room.

His mouth fell open at the sight of her. "God's death, I thought it was the queen!" he exclaimed. "Darling, do you think it wise to mock her in this fashion?"

"Wise? When did I ever do anything that was wise?" she asked, laughing. She was delighted by his reaction. "I look just like her when I put on my mask," she said, standing on tiptoe to kiss him.

"What about these?" he asked with a leer, cupping her beautiful breasts.

"I can't do anything about them. I'm a woman, not a little boy."

"You'd better get that wig and crown back early tomorrow before she misses them, young lady," he warned.

"I would have you know, sir, that this is my own hair I've tortured into such an ugly fashion, and the crown is mine—paid for by a certain gentleman admirer."

He groaned aloud at her extravagance and bent to place a kiss upon the delicious swell of her breast. She slapped him with her fan and said in Elizabeth's voice,

"Have done! Have done! Don't defile the queen's most precious person. *Peste!* Those musicians should have been here hours ago. Shane, you don't think Mason will botch up the fireworks display, do you?" she asked worriedly, lapsing into her own voice.

"Stop fussing. A party is supposed to be a treat, not a treatment," he teased. "More planning has gone into this than the Cádiz operation."

"Pugh!" she said, and walked rapidly from the room. After she left he shook his head in wonder at her. She was the sauciest wench on earth, and he wouldn't trade her for all the gold in Christendom.

Every single guest who arrived made a hurried obeisance to her until she whisked off her mask to their astonished relief, and she joined them in peals of laughter. She held herself ramrod straight, spoke, moved, and thought as the queen, and easily succeeded in being the center of attention. When a gentleman would whisper that she had never looked more beautiful she mimicked the queen and replied, "You tell more lies than the pope's epitaph."

When Essex, with the beauteous Frances on his arm, kissed Sabre's fingers, she waggled her rings under his nose. "See, I've mirrors on my rings just like Bess for when we play post and pair later in the card room." He appreciated the humor, for the queen had cheated him out of thousands with her damned mirrored rings.

Kate Ashford wiped tears of mirth from her eyes, as she marveled over each identical detail of Sabre's costume. "They won't look the same tomorrow, Kate," said Sabre outrageously, "for hers will be covered with sweat stains."

Devonport watched Sabre indulgently as the men flirted and danced her off her feet. Each was eager to

dally with "Her Majesty" and try for liberties that she
only ever permitted to Essex, Leicester, and Devonport.
A black-bearded Spaniard turned out to be Matthew. He
kept his distance from Shane, but spent an inordinate
amount of time at Sabre's elbow.

Elizabeth had chosen her courtiers for Theobalds, and
these included Leicester and Drake, Anne Cecil and her
husband Lord Oxford, Sir Christopher Hatton, her lord
chancellor. Since Lord Norris had entertained her at
Rycote and Lord Montagu at Cowdray, she invited them
to escort her to Theobalds by way of returning their hospitality, and saw nothing pecunious in doing so. For ladies she had the duchess of Suffolk, the countess of Warwick, Lady Hastings, Lady Hatton, and Lady Chandos.
For maids she took Elizabeth Southwell and, much to the
girl's disgust, Mary Howard.

The queen's barge had just been refurbished with new
awnings and freshly painted with the Tudor colors and
her pages and maids held up the purple velvet train of her
new gown as she climbed aboard. She graciously greeted
her old bargemaster, George, who had served as the head
rower on the royal barge for many years and knew the
Thames better than any man in London. Everything went
smoothly until there was a sudden holdup and the
queen's barge slowed to almost a stop. Impatiently she
was on her feet in a trice. There, in front of her, blocking
her path, was a most sumptuous barge of scarlet and
gold. She recognized it instantly as belonging to her
hated archrival, Lettice. She swept up to George and
shouted, "Command them to give way in the name of the
queen! Damned impudence," she fumed, angry that Let-

tice's barge was such a showy piece with its scarlet-liveried rowers.

The other barge had no choice but to give way to the queen, but even when they sailed past, Elizabeth's annoyance did not abate. "I thought these awnings were supposed to be new, George."

"Yes, Yer Majesty, brand-new . . . best awningmaker in London."

"What color are they supposed to be, George?" she demanded.

"Why, yer own Tudor colors, Yer Majesty . . . white and Tudor green."

"Tudor green? They never saw Tudor green! Gooseturd green is more like it. Yes, by God . . . goose-turd green!"

"Robert," she said, interrupting Leicester and Hatton's conversation without a thought, "tomorrow I want fresh awnings for this barge. I am the queen of England and will not sail about beneath a goose-turd green canopy. See to it!"

The traffic upon the river was busy, and each time she spotted a private barge she compared it with her own and fumed. When Mary Howard brought her a cup of mulled ale to take the chill off the ride, she snatched it from her ungraciously, ready to find fault with everything. "It seems everyone and his brother are on the river this evening. Where do you suppose they are bound?" Her maids kept silent, inwardly trembling lest she catch wind of the Thames View masquerade. The queen's eyes caught sight of a small luxurious barge in cream and royal purple moored just past Kew water steps. "God's death! There's another puts this tub to shame!" She strode along the deck to the rowers. "George, whom does that barge belong to?" she demanded.

He grinned. "That belongs to the Sea God's mistress, Yer Majesty."

She froze. Had she heard the damned fellow correctly? Her mouth set in a grim line. She was sick and tired of the gossip and innuendo that clung to her favorites. She would see for herself. "George, turn my barge about. We will make a short stop at Thames View."

The river was clogged with boats and barges as they drew closer to Thames View. The gardens were filled with noisy merrymakers, and lively music filtered down to the river from the big house. Four pages, with their small gold trumpets slung about their necks, were scrambling from the barge, and up the water steps when Elizabeth's imperious voice halted them. "Have done! Have done! I'll have no trumpeting pages announcing my arrival. They say I am tricksy as Puck, so we shall launch a surprise attack, like Cádiz!"

Like quicksilver she was off the barge and up the grassy bank to Thames View. Her attendant women trailed behind with heavy feet, knowing that the fat was in the fire and an explosion was inevitable. Robert Dudley, now quite portly in his older years, made no effort to follow her, but Sir Christopher Hatton gallantly hurried to catch up with her. She swept past her subjects, who fell to their knees upon recognizing her. She pushed aside the Thames View servants and strode into the glittering ballroom. Her sharp black eyes swept the room, until with unerring accuracy they found their target. For a moment she thought her heart had stopped. There in the center of the room stood a replica of herself. A very beautiful replica. It was that Wilde woman! Their eyes met and instinctively she recognized the woman as the Sea God's mistress. A dreadful hush fell on the room and Shane Hawkhurst stepped protectively to Sabre's side. The queen's black eyes glittered with anger as she raised an imperious forefinger to point at her imitator. "Mistress Wilde, you are nothing but a notorious trollop. You are banished from my court forever!" She did not trust herself to say more, but turned swiftly upon her heels and retraced her steps to the river. Her eyes had missed nothing. She had seen and marked well everyone who had been in that ballroom.

Hawkhurst was after her in a flash. He pushed aside Hatton and said, "Bess, the girl has done nothing."

Her cold eyes swept him up and down that he had the temerity to speak to her. "You will address me as Your Majesty. The whore mocks and mimicks me!"

"She is no whore!" he defended hotly.

"Do you deny that you are bedding her?" she demanded.

"That is none of your business," he shouted.

"Silence!" she ordered. "You, sirrah, will present yourself tomorrow morning."

The queen went straight back to Greenwich; Theobalds was forgotten. She locked herself up in her bedchamber for the night, pacing the floor and plotting her revenge.

Most of the female guests at Thames View were in panic. They knew the queen's beady eyes had seen them in what was now probably the enemy camp and they knew they would not escape her wrath.

Sabre was livid to have been so singled out and humiliated in front of a hundred guests. She was in a high rage and wanted to smash everything she could lay her hands upon. The moment she withdrew upstairs, the guests departed. Essex and Frances had vanished the moment the royal barge drew up to the water stairs. By the time Shane returned to the house, it had emptied except for the servants and the musicians. He braved the stairs, not knowing what to expect. Sabre needed to vent her temper, and naturally he was her only outlet.

The moment he came through the bedchamber door he caught a shoe, which she'd thrown viciously. "How dare she insult and humiliate me in my own home?" she demanded.

He said matter-of-factly, "Sabre, you knew you were playing with fire when you ordered that outfit."

"So! You have taken sides with her against me, you damned knave!" she cried.

"I defended you hotly, Sabre. You know she is furious with me, and I'm the one who will pay," he countered.

"My reputation lies in ruins! She has called me a trollop before all London and banished me!" She tore off the hated purple velvet gown and trampled it furiously beneath her feet. 'Tis all your fault, you damned rogue. You made me become your mistress!" She flung herself facedown upon the bed and began to sob.

Feeling wretched at her distress, he sat down on the bed and reached out a hand to comfort her. "Sweetheart, don't cry. . . .I can't bear it when you cry."

She recoiled from his touch, her anger still full blown. "Well, sir, it is over. I'll be mistress no more. I'll be a respectable wife or know the reason why!"

"Sabre, you know I love you," he soothed.

"Love me? Love me?" she gasped. "You love me as your mistress, but I'm not good enough to be your wife!"

"Sabre, you know I'm married," he said patiently.

"Then you can get unmarried!" she cried.

"You mean divorce?" he said quietly.

"Of course I mean divorce, do you think I suggest murder, you damned rogue? Since King Henry made it so fashionable, 'tis only a small legal formality. Sir Edward Coke, the attorney general, is a friend of yours, isn't he?"

He looked at her with astonishment. Apparently she'd given it a great deal of thought, and he wondered why the idea had never occurred to him. He could divorce Sara Bishop and marry Sabre. She burst into tears again. "Darling," he said, taking her into his arms and cradling her, "if it's possible, I will get a divorce—I promise you, my little love."

His doublet was soaked as she sobbed out her heart. Her anger reared its head again. "Imagine! Her calling me a notorious trollop! The bloody Virgin Queen! She forgets I'm the one who cleans the stains from her gowns, and many's the time they are covered with *semen* stains!" She looked at him angrily as a suspicion dawned on her. "Have you bedded her?"

He knew at this moment it was an admission she would never forgive. "Sabre, I've never been unfaithful to you; I've never even bedded my wife."

"That just proves what a damned rogue you are! You've treated that woman shamefully and deserve to pay dearly for it."

"But now you expect me to divorce her to marry you."

She stiffened. "I don't expect anything from you, my lord. Matthew would marry me in an instant."

He said angrily, "Matthew always fancies himself in love with my mistresses."

She gasped. It was like a slap in the face to her to be

lumped in with the women he had kept in the past. The
moment he said it, he could have bitten off his tongue.
"Darling, my little love, I didn't mean it. Of course we
shall be married. I'll have the papers drawn up. I'll go to
Blackmoor and settle everything—just as soon as the
bloody queen takes her pound of flesh."

"Don't touch me . . . don't you dare to touch me! I
hope she claps you in the Tower!"

Grimly he stalked from the room. "I'll not stay in this
bloody Bedlam!" he swore. He strode to the stables and
saddled Neptune. He needed the clean wind in his face
and some fresh sea air in his lungs. In that moment he
was seriously tempted to sail the seven seas. He knew a
need to be reckless, as if by risking his life he could purge
himself of the mess in which he was mired. His hand
absently brushed back his long mane of dark hair and his
fingers caught in the strings of the black mask now hanging forgotten about his neck. He glanced down at his
clothes and remembered the outfit he had chosen for the
ball was all black. Instantly he knew where he could go
and what he would do.

Fulke-Greville had taken an Irish fishing vessel off the
Scottish coast as it was buying guns and powder. Its captain and crew now languished in the great Fleet Prison.
At the party tonight he had intended to arrange with
Fulke to pay their fines and secure their release, but now
he decided secrecy was far better. The Black Shadow
would free the Irishmen this night and send them home
to carry on their freedom fighting. He turned the black
stallion toward the city and made his way to the Strand
through lightly traveled streets. At Walsingham House he
quietly stabled Neptune, knowing he could retrieve the
stallion at a later time should it become necessary. On

foot he completed the short journey past the Royal Courts of Justice to the Fleet Prison. It was a grimy, formidable building looking exactly like the stronghold prison it was. London's prisons were run on graft and corruption. A thief or a prostitute could buy a relatively safe night's lodging within its vermin-infested walls.

Hawkhurst, using one of the underworld signals to gain entrance, had no initial trouble. The jailer who admitted him assumed he was a highwayman willing to pay well for a night's refuge. He figured the money was better in his pockets than in those of the magistrate he'd be brought up before if he were arrested.

The stench inside the Fleet almost took Hawkhurst's breath away until he became accustomed to it. The walls were wet with seeping dampness and it was badly lit with primitive lamps that burned acrid animal tallow. He chinked two coins together in his pocket to gain and hold the jailer's attention. Down the first dim passage Hawkhurst had his arm about the man's throat before he knew what hit him, and the man felt something hard under his knee.

"I have found," whispered Hawkhurst, "one of the very best places to cock a gun is behind the knee. When I pull the trigger the bullet goes up along the whole thighbone to shatter it completely, and then if the fellow still defies me, I have the other one to work on."

His arm felt the man swallow with difficulty and he smiled into the darkness, knowing his savagery was about to give him anything he wanted. "Take me to the Irish prisoners who came in last week." Silently, without protest, he was taken where he wished to go. In a trice he had the keys and opened the cell holding the men. All would have gone smooth as clockwork except for the fact

that they were Irishmen and could manage nothing on
earth without inciting a riot. The first man out of the cell,
seeing the jailer incapacitated, looked him up and down
with contempt and spat, "You long streak o' piss . . .
may God rot yer bloody eyes!"

The Irishman behind him wasn't getting out of the cell
fast enough to suit him and shouted, "Bejasus, Sean Mc-
Guire, shut yer bloody mouth and move yer arse."

"Bugger youse," came the belligerent reply.

"Christ, somebody will take youse up on that offer if
we don't get the hell outta here," cried a third man.

The last man out was small and wiry as a terrier. He
had a vicious face. As he came past the jailer, like quicksilver, he kneed him in the balls. The man let out a blood-
thirsty scream that reverberated through the passageways
to alert other guards, who came on the double.

Hawkhurst leveled his gun at the small man and ordered him to move out fast. The wiry man spat on him
and cursed, "May God wither the hand that holds a pistol on me."

Hawkhurst had to fight the desire to render him unconscious with the pistol butt, but forced himself to be
satisfied with a vicious shove in the back to send him on
his way after his countrymen. Then he let the butt fall
heavily on the jailer's temple and stretched the unconscious man on the slimy floor of the dim passageway. He
saw the last man go through the heavy door of the Fleet
before he felt two guards, one on either side, grab him
fast by the shoulders and utter with relish, "We've caught
the bleedin' Black Shadow!"

Chapter 20

Sabre bathed her swollen eyes and tried to think what she
should do. She knew she should leave London in case the
queen decided to punish her further. It soon dawned on
her that she had nowhere to go but Blackmoor. She
started to pack immediately. The first thing she put in her
trunk was the incriminating files from Walsingham. She
would soon have her revenge on Shane Hawkhurst
O'Neill. When he arrived at Blackmoor to serve his wife
with the divorce papers, he would discover he was married to his mistress and the irony would smite him between the eyes. She would be avenged upon him by insist-
ing upon the divorce. If he refused, she had the means at
hand to force him.

A small voice persisted inside her head. What if she
were with child? Wouldn't forcing a divorce between
them be the height of folly under the circumstances? The
answer came back a resounding no. She did not want him
to marry her because of a child. She only wanted to be his
wife if she were the choice of his heart. She would be all
or nothing at all! She needed to be wooed. She needed a
real proposal and she needed to be wed in a church, exchanging vows before God.

She put on a pale aqua velvet traveling gown with a
warm quilted bodice and gathered her hair into a jeweled
net. She chose fur-lined kid boots and took her sable
cloak from the wardrobe. She whirled about with a crystal perfume bottle in her hand as she heard a light tap on
the door. "I'm warning you, Hawkhurst, to keep your
distance!" she called angrily.

Matthew cautiously opened the chamber and stuck in

his head. "Don't throw that, sweeting, you've got the wrong Hawkhurst."

"Oh, Matthew, I thought you'd deserted the ship long ago with the other rats."

"I thought you might need me," he said, surveying the packed trunks. "Where are you going?"

"I'm on my way to Blackmoor."

"That's ridiculous, you can't ride over two hundred miles on your own. Go to Mother at Hawkhurst—it's only forty miles off, but still far enough from the queen's wrath."

"I'm not removing myself from the queen, I'm removing myself from your brother. It's all over, Matthew, he's promised me a divorce."

For a moment his heart soared. He asked, "He knows, then, that you are his wife?"

"No, but he will when he turns up at Blackmoor with the divorce papers for Sara Bishop to sign."

"Sabre, you are deluding yourself if you think he'll divorce you when he finds out you are legally wed."

"I don't think so, Matthew, for I have the means to force his hand."

He scoffed. "He's like a damned dog with a bone—he'll never let you go!"

She tossed her head. "I've Walsingham's secret files on him."

For a moment he looked at her blankly. "Walsingham had secret files on Hawk? For what?"

She looked at him strangely. "You don't know?"

He shook his head, perplexed, then asked incredulously, "You mean he suspected him of piracy? But the queen knew and looked the other way."

Sabre realized she should have said nothing. She veiled

her eyes and changed the subject. "I'm taking the carriage and I'll take a maid and also ask Mr. Mason to
come with me. What about you, Matt, will you come?"

He was sorely tempted, but she had whetted his appe-
tite about his brother. She obviously considered the secret
files damaging enough to use as blackmail and he immediately realized she must be taking the invaluable papers
with her. "Sabre, I can't come tonight, but I will as soon
as I can. You go and tell Mason and the girl to get ready
and I'll have a reliable Hawkhurst man from the stables
drive you to Blackmoor in the carriage. Give me your
trunks and I'll take them down to the stables."

She came forward with gratitude in her eyes and
placed her hand on his arm. "Thank heavens I always
have you to fall back on, Matthew."

He wanted to crush her to him as a wave of desire
swept over him. At this moment he knew she was very
vulnerable, but a warning caution bell was clanging in his
brain. Patience. This woman should have been his
woman, and if he helped along the divorce it was possible
that he would still be able to claim her for his own. He
brushed his lips across her temple and stepped back deliberately, then picked up her luggage and carried it
downstairs. Later, when he stood on the driveway and
waved the traveling coach on its way, the Walsingham
files were safely tucked inside his doublet.

Shane cursed under his breath for not having effectively silenced the guard when he had the chance. There
was no room in the sordid business of espionage for
mercy, and none knew it better than he. In a flash he
undid the fastenings at the front of his doublet and
slipped from the garment like an eel. The two jailers re-

coiled in superstitious horror at the monster painted on
his flesh, but they had not seen his face. Once Shane was
out of their grasp there was no chance this side of hell
that they would recapture him. He was outside the Fleet
in seconds, but the two guards sounded the alarm and,
joined by others, were bent on taking the Black Shadow,
a most prestigious collar.

It was fortunate that Hawkhurst knew London like the
back of his hand or escape would have been an impossibil-
ity. He went neither right nor left, but chose to go up
instead. He climbed to the roof of the massive fortress
because they were close upon his heels and he knew that
though they saw him go up, they were not agile enough
to follow. Moreover, their lanterns were not strong
enough to cast a light past the second story. He surveyed
the streets from his high perch and chose his hiding place
instantly. With silent stealth he descended to the street
and slipped into the churchyard of St. Bride's.

His black doublet had made him invisible, but now
that he was naked to the waist he knew he would be seen
if he made a run for it. He crawled facedown until he had
put many tombstones between himself and Fleet Street.
Suddenly he heard voices much closer than he thought
his pursuers could possibly be. A freshly dug grave
loomed before him and without a moment's hesitation he
jumped down eight feet into the cold, damp shaft. He let
out a breath of relief as he discovered it was the Irishmen's voices he heard. Apparently they were taking
refuge in the cemetery instead of using what little intelligence God had given them. By now they could have been
on a ship bound for home.

Shane stayed silent, for if the noisy bastards didn't

hush their racket they would soon attract their pursuers. The men were having a gentleman's disagreement.

"Youse haven't the brains of a soddin' louse, McGuire. Just for the satisfaction of puttin' yer knee to his cock 'n' balls, youse let them take the poor bastard who risked his life to free us!"

"I don't give a shit. Any bastard stupid enough to risk his life fer others deserves what he gets. Youse two piss-pots shoulda kneed him an' taken his pistol when I created the diversion wi' the guard."

"Yer a vicious swine, McGuire. I never shoulda thrown in my lot wi' youse. We shoulda tried to help the poor bastard, I say."

"Sod 'im . . . and sod youse too!"

Hawkhurst then heard a sound like a shovel being smashed into a man's skull. There was a grunt and then silence. In that moment Shane realized there would never be peace in Ireland, for if the English were driven out and the lords of Ireland ruled their own land, the clans would again turn on each other.

Suddenly the heavens opened and the rain came down in icy sheets. This turn of events, like every other in life, had it advantages and its disadvantages. The men in the graveyard took to their heels and the guards out searching for escaped prisoners would give up and return to the shelter of the Fleet. The disadvantage, however, was that Shane was standing calf-deep in a sea of mud and no matter his agility or strength, he could not climb up the sheer, eight-foot sides of the mud-slimed grave. Each effort brought down more clumps of oozing earth and his feet sank deeper and deeper. Suddenly his feet hit something solid and he realized it was a coffin. The humor of the ridiculous predicament in which he found himself had not escaped him. He banged the coffin lid with his heel and said, "Hello, down there. Sorry to be standing on your head, my friend, but circumstances are beyond my control." He knew one horrific moment as the coffin collapsed and he went through it, then he was out of control. He leaned against the wall of the grave and laughed until the tears rolled down his face. How ignominious to be found down the hole in a quagmire of mud by the gravedigger at first light. Very probably one of the Irishmen lay dead, head bashed in by a shovel, and he would be blamed. No, there was no doubt about it, he could not be found in this predicament. Almost weak from laughter, he used his hands and dagger to cut stepping holes in the grave wall. Though most times the soggy earth collapsed under his weight, occasionally it did not and gradually he raised himself by slow degrees until he was able to haul himself to the mouth of the grave and roll onto the wet grass.

By stealth he made his way back to the Walsingham House stables and was soon on his way home, grateful again to have the great stallion between his thighs. Every once in a while he threw back his head and laughed. Tonight his spirits soared as he returned from the grave. Tomorrow he would willingly spend two hours on his knees begging the queen's forgiveness, but tonight he would make love to Sabre whether she would or not. She was a little wildcat and he was the only man in the world who could subdue her. And he would, he vowed with relish.

Matthew Hawkhurst's mood, on the other hand, was one of seething resentment rather than elation. In his chamber at Greenwich Palace he had pored over the secret files with horror, reading and absorbing it bit by bitter bit. The one galling fact that he could not forgive was that Shane was the O'Neill's bastard and yet he had inherited the Hawkhurst shipping empire along with the title of Lord Devonport. His fist crashed down on the table, sending his goblet of wine spilling across the papers in a blood-red stain. Shane had everything—always had! Georgiana had kept quiet and allowed her bastard to get his, Matthew's, rightful inheritance. They had deceived his father, the poor weak fool, and they had deceived him! In that moment he hated his father, his mother, and his brother with a poisonous venom. The thing that rankled most was that Shane had Sabre. If it was the last thing he did he would take her from his brother! He put the papers away for safekeeping.

By morning the corridors of Greenwich rang with the news that the elusive Black Shadow had been taken in the Fleet, but had managed once again to elude his captors. The man had been masked, but it was now thought that he was in league with the devil, for on his broad back rampaged a hideous monster. The moment Matthew heard the gossip, a picture flashed into his mind of Shane's dragon tattoo and he immediately knew that his brother was also the Black Shadow; it was the one thing missing from Walsingham's secret file.

Matthew, blinded by jealousy and the need for revenge, sought an audience with William Cecil, Lord Burghley, but was better served when Burghley's ambitious son Robert Cecil took time to see him. The queen called Robert Cecil her pygmy fox because of his misshapen back and brilliant mind, and he made the handsome young courtier feel welcome.

Once the greetings were out of the way, Matthew got right to the point. "My lord, the daring escapades of the

Black Shadow are on every tongue to the point where he is being admired rather than reviled. We no sooner put an Irish rebel behind bars than he frees him, with nothing more to aid him than a dark night and a black mask. It has occurred to me that someone in Ireland is calling the shots; someone who holds a high place."

Robert Cecil studied him a moment, wondering what personal ax he had to grind. "Let us get down to brass tacks. I believe you are alluding to O'Neill, and yet he has always been able to disprove accusations of treason and conspiracy leveled against him."

"Nay, my lord, in actuality he has never disproved them, only convinced the queen and council that the accusations were groundless and reassured them that he was protector of the queen's law in the north of Ireland."

Cecil conceded a small bow in Matthew Hawkhurst's direction. He had the mind of a strategist and had always known O'Neill thought himself king of Ireland. Matthew continued. "Set a trap with important Irish hostages, but put them where they will be safe in the Tower of London. It follows as night follows day that the Black Shadow will try to free them."

Cecil finished for him, ". . . and when we have the Black Shadow we will be able to prove him an agent of O'Neill?"

"Precisely!" Matthew nodded, crushing down a growing horror inside himself at what he was doing.

"A little wine? I think you will like this, it is spiced with aromatic myrrh."

Cecil was proved wrong in this, for Matthew found himself vomiting into the first gutter he came upon after he took his leave.

* * *

The queen had paced her chamber most of the night, working herself up to a state of frenzy. Gray dawn had not yet penetrated the corners of her apartment when she began to shout. "Where are my women?"

A few came running.

"I want *all* my women!"

A short time elapsed before all who had been summoned could ready themselves. She was still wearing the purple gown with the bishop sleeves lined with amethyst satin, and her small crown. Most of the assembled women stood before her trembling, though only a few knew of the previous evening's debacle.

In a deceptively sweet voice she asked, "What news of my Sea God?" She stamped her foot at their collective silence and spat, "All deaf and dumb? What news of Hawkhurst?" In her agitation her crown fell askew and she tore it from her head and hurled it across the room, crying, "My crown is a crown of thorns!" Unfortunately her wig came off with the crown and her own graying hair stood up in thin wisps.

"He has taken that sly she-wolf for mistress!"

Mary Howard stood closest to the queen, her lips pressed together in terror.

"You kept it secret from me!" She slapped the girl's face. "And you, and you!" Each serving woman close to her received a stinging blow on the cheek. One of the older women of high rank tried to soothe her. "The temptations are so great, Your Majesty, you cannot blame him."

"Blame him?" flared Elizabeth. "By God's body, I'll blame him. He shall pay for all the pleasure he has had with her. They shall go to the Tower for this!"

Old Blanche Parry, who had been her nurse, pushed through the ranks of women to take charge. "You will make yourself sick over some silly rumor."

"I saw with my own eyes what was going on." Her voice had risen on an hysterical note and Blanche knew she was on the edge of losing control. She said briskly, "It is not as if they were secretly wed, or that she is with child . . . it is only that he is a philanderer, a rake, a deceiver."

The queen heard another of her women say, "Yes, he is the worst of men!"

The queen turned upon her with the light of madness in her eye. "How dare you say so?" she demanded. "You know he is not; it is all her fault!" The queen began to tear at the sleeves of her gown, and the crystal beads scattered everywhere. A quick consultation between the countess of Warwick and the duchess of Suffolk decided that it was a job for Leicester. Only Robert Dudley could handle the queen when she was out of control.

He came hurrying to the queen's apartment clad in a rich velvet bed robe and immediately jumped to the wrong conclusion when he saw her state. She fell into his arms, then pushed him away because he was a man and therefore not to be trusted. He dismissed all her women with an easy command stemming from years of being England's uncrowned king. "Bess, Bess, what can I say? I knew it would come to this when you learned of what he'd done. But, my dearest dear, you have spoiled Robin to the point where he actually believes he can do no wrong. Come, now, my own Bess, be brave. What cannot be cured must be endured," he said heartily.

"Robin?" she whispered.

"You know he's a fickle young devil, and I don't suppose his heart will be involved for five minutes now that he's actually wed her."

"Wed . . . Robin?" she questioned, fear seeping into her pores and creeping along her veins.

"Never let it be said that a little chit like Frances Walsingham can make our Gloriana jealous," he coaxed.

Wildly she clawed the air. Her own darling Essex wed to Frances Walsingham! The corridors of Greenwich were filled with the bloodcurdling scream that tore from her throat before she collapsed. Leicester gathered her up from the floor and carried her to her bed. It took all his strength, and he was quite winded by the time he laid her down and summoned her closest attendants. He was getting too old for all this nonsense.

Hawkhurst, bathed, bejeweled, and arrayed in his finest garments, paced the queen's privy chamber awaiting his chastisement. The small room caged him, imprisoning the essence of him. If anyone had entered the room they would have been able to taste and smell the male recklessness of him. When he had returned to Thames View and found that Sabre had packed and left, he drank himself to insensibility. Now he was in a savage, drink-sodden temper and his three-hour wait for the queen was blackening it minute by minute. A clock ticked on the mantelpiece of the marble fireplace and very deliberately he opened the glass face and plucked off the small pendulum.

One of Elizabeth's favorite tricks to bring a man to heel was to summon him, then keep him waiting for hours. Hawkhurst was in no mood for such games. He debated what he should do. He wavered between summoning her household chancellor or going through the anteroom of the privy chamber, up the short staircase, and straight into her private apartment. Finally he did neither. He muttered, "A pox on her!" turned upon his heel, and quit the palace. For all he cared at this moment, she could add the offense to his other transgressions; he would just as soon be hanged for a sheep as for a lamb!

Back at Thames View the ordered silence of the house inflamed his temper further. "Where the hell is Mason?" he demanded when a housemaid answered his summons. Her eyes widened to saucers at the master's tone, and her voice deserted her altogether. "Don't stand there bobbing up and down like a damned jack-in-the-box, girl."

The poor maid threw her apron over her head and ran to the kitchen sobbing. Within minutes he was confronted by the ample figure of the cook. "If it please your lordship, I'm shorthanded enough with Mason gone and Meg also, for you to render my servants overwrought." She was empress of the kitchen and had been so entrenched for so many years, she dared to speak her mind.

"And just where has Mason gone?" he thundered.

"I'm sure there is no need to take that tone with me, your lordship. They are gone with Mistress Sabre, and I'm sure I don't blame her for going if this is the way she's been spoken to lately."

"If you'd spend less time listening at doors and more time tending your kitchen, this house would be less like Bedlam!"

"I shan't cater to your temper, my lord, because the mistress has up and left you. In my book you pick what you plant, so I'll leave you to your own conscience!"

"By God, woman, next you'll threaten to complain to the baron if I don't watch my tongue!"

"And so I shall, my lord," she said firmly.

Shane threw back his head and roared with laughter. "Go on, Mrs. Creeth, I know when I'm bested."

Shane told the baron of the harrowing night he'd put in at the Fleet and then in the grave at St. Bride's, and they shared the macabre humor of it, but then they talked long of what was on their minds, aye, and what was in their hearts. The truth of it was they almost thought alike. Their hearts were no longer wholly given to Ireland and her eternal call to freedom. They had grown weary of risking life and limb for ignorant ingrates, yet they were cloaked in sadness that there would never be an Irish peace, not while there were at least two clans remaining to murder each other in their beds.

Shane wanted a more settled life, and he wanted to share that life with Sabre. He found himself wandering about the rooms, completely lost without her. His need for her was so acute, he felt mutilated, for she had become a part of him. The house and everything in it reminded him of Sabre. She haunted every room, filling up his senses until he thought he would go mad from loneliness. She'd been gone only days, yet it already seemed forever. One thing was certain; he must get her back and he must bind her to him so that she could never leave him again, ever. He would get Jacob Goldman to draw up the legal papers that would allow him to divorce Sara Bishop.

Even in Goldman's chambers Shane paced the room, revealing his impatience to be done with the whole business.

"Are you sure about this matter of divorce, my lord? Forgive my question, but less than a year ago you were positive you wanted a marriage with Sara Bishop."

"Yes, yes, I'm sure. A year ago it seemed important

that I acquire certain Irish lands, but now I am considering ending my ties with Ireland."

"I see. Have you thought of annulment, my lord? If the
marriage was never consummated, perhaps a legal divorce is not necessary."

"Nay, if I sought an annulment, it would be a religious
matter depending on the whim of the church. They love
nothing better than to drag these things out for years. I
want it quick and I want it legal and binding."

Goldman fixed him with a serious look. "It's a delicate
matter. You must have grounds for divorce and prove
them."

"She has the grounds—adultery. She must divorce
me," Shane insisted.

"My lord, forgive me for being crass, but you are giving her an opportunity to take a considerable chunk of
your wealth."

"I don't give a damn what it costs me, Jacob. I want
that divorce. She deserves to be well compensated for
what I've put her through. In all conscience I must leave
her a wealthy woman to save her face. Draw up the settlement papers and get them to Blackmoor quickly."

"There must be no hint of collusion, my lord. The
settlement must be a private thing between yourself and
Sara, and I cannot involve myself in that process. You
must go yourself and get her signature on whatever settlement you both agree upon. Then we will submit the
divorce to the law courts. Your friend Sir Edward Coke
can expedite things for you, but I cannot."

"Damnation!" said Shane, frustrated by all the red
tape.

Jacob Goldman smiled at his impatience. Shane
Hawkhurst would never have been suited to the law, with

its minutiae of detail that ignored tide and time. "I'll draw up a legal document for you and leave blank what properties you will deed her, what monies and jewels she is to receive, and you can fill them in when you reach an agreement. In return I think you should keep the land in Ireland, since you went to such inordinate lengths to acquire it," said Jacob in an amused tone.

"Ah, Jacob, to be Irish is to know the world will break your heart before you are thirty."

Jacob's lips twitched. "I believe we have a similar saying in Hebrew." They grinned ruefully at each other.

When Shane returned to Thames View, the baron had an urgent message for him from Ireland. The O'Neill had written a curt note of the rumored transfer of hostages from Dublin Castle to the Tower of London. These hostages of the important O'Hara and O'Donnell clans had been in Dublin Castle as insurance against the two great clans joining the rebellion. Shane was aware that O'Hara and O'Donnell were in the thick of it and were O'Neill's staunchest allies, but he resented the curt note ordering him to ferret out when they would be transferred and to free them from the Tower of London. The O'Neill never asked; he took it for granted, as his due.

Shane, his nerve ends rubbed raw by the queen and Sabre and his recent picnic at the Fleet, sat down and sent off an equally curt reply to O'Neill.

Consider it done, but expect nothing
further from this quarter.

S.

Before dispatching the note he showed it to the baron, who nodded his silent agreement. Then he put the matter from his mind and changed the subject. "I'm going to Blackmoor on personal business. I don't know where the hell Sabre has gone, but at least she has a maid with her, and Mason, who is a sensible man. Probably Matthew knows where she is and I suppose I could wring it out of him, but she won't return until I straighten out the mess at Blackmoor. I know her only too well. So, the sooner I leave, the sooner she will be back home where she belongs."

The baron gave him a long look, which he found hard to define. It was a mixture of omniscience, perception, and sympathy, and yet it was a droll look, as if he possessed information Shane did not. He shrugged and packed his saddlebags for the journey to Blackmoor.

Chapter 21

When Sabre's small party arrived at the remote property of Blackmoor, the dogs of the estate, unused to strangers, would not let them past the gates. They were extremely territorial animals who had been allowed to roam freely, so that no human guard was necessary. When Travis, the head groundsman, came to investigate the hullaballoo the dogs were causing, he had to whip them off before the horses and carriage could enter the estate and move up to the house.

Meg was terrified and actually shook in her corner of the carriage. It was not merely the dogs, but the remote wildness of the place. Mason, used to London's sophistications, was determined to take everything in his stride. Whenever he felt apprehensive he looked at Sabre's serenity and was immediately reassured. Blackmoor had no butler but was maintained by a housekeeper-cum-cook who went by the picturesque name of Mrs. Mole. Mason saw that he would have to establish a pecking order immediately, and Meg busied herself unpacking Sabre's trunks, determined not to stray from the safety of the master bedchamber.

Sabre went straight to the kitchens, took a quantity of meat from the pantry, and went in search of the groundsman. "Ah, Travis, there you are. I want you to pen most of these dogs up. They terrify my servants and, I admit, make me a little nervous. I want freedom to roam about without fear of dog fangs sinking into my throat."

"Beg pardon, missus, but they do protect us from danger, an' I don't mean humankind, for we seldom gets strangers lurking about."

"What danger?" asked Sabre uncertainly.

"Over yon' is Exmoor Forest, teeming with beasts. There's wild boars and wild bulls, there's wolves and wildcats too. Some so bold they'd come for our sheep and goats, aye, an' the horses in the stables too."

"I see," said Sabre. "Then pen half the dogs by the sheep and goats and put the others in the stable. They may run freely for an hour each day." She surveyed the pack of dogs that gathered when they smelled the meat she was carrying, and only Travis's whip kept them at bay.

"Those two shaggy gray creatures as big as donkeys . . . are they wolfhounds?"

"Yes, missus, Irish wolfhounds."

"I want to make friends with them. Fasten up all the others and leave those two with me," she directed. She quickly threw the meat to them, It disappeared down their throats instantly. Then she held out a tentative hand and said, "Here, boy, good boy!" They allowed her to pat their matted coats, all the while sniffing loudly about her person to see if she had more meat concealed. Taking all her courage in her hands she turned her back to them and walked slowly toward the house. They followed her instinctively, sensing she was lady bountiful, and as she glanced back quickly, she saw one of the pair actually wagging his tail. Within twenty-four hours the pair of shabby wolfhounds had formed a bond with Sabre and followed her everywhere. When night fell they even lay across the threshold to the bedchamber, and she felt quite secure.

Blackmoor was such a quiet place after London and

the court of Queen Elizabeth, that for once Sabre had lots of time to think. At last she was going to take the revenge she had plotted for so long. She tried not to let her mind go beyond that point. She would tell him who she was and demand her divorce, and there was an end to it! But her treacherous mind kept straying across the boundaries she had set for it. There was *not* an end to it, a small voice kept telling her, for she was carrying his child. The last thing she needed was a divorce. She clung stubbornly to her goal and clamped her mind closed on all thoughts of the future. Sometimes her imagination took flight and she feared that the queen had thrown him in the Tower and he would not come. Other times she feared that he would never divorce Sara Bishop to marry Sabre Wilde; men simply did not marry their mistresses. That night she dreamed of Shane and it was so vivid, she awoke shaking. When he had seen that he had been married to a woman he had taken as a mistress, he recoiled from her in horror. He insisted upon a divorce immediately and returned her to Reverend Bishop, who was determined to spend the rest of his days heaping scorn upon her.

The brilliant sunshine of the May morning dispelled the terrifying dream, and she chose her favorite outfit to lift her spirits higher. It was the fashionable white velvet riding dress with the deeply cut black silk vest. She was just brushing out her burnished copper tresses when the dogs set up such a racket, it sounded as if pandemonium had broken loose. Her two wolfhounds joined the excited chorus of barking and ran through the rooms to the front door of Blackmoor.

She dropped the hairbrush and snatched up the dog whip she carried when she ventured outside, and followed the two great dogs. They were standing on hind

legs clawing the front door and she had to order them
back before she could open it. They sprang through the
entranceway with fangs bared and drooling, and she
thought, God help whatever they are after.

She ran like the wind after the wolfhounds, who
bounded to the gates of Blackmoor. They saw each other
in the same instant. Clad in white velvet, her copper hair
flying madly in disarray, she lifted the dog whip high in
the air.

Hawkhurst, on Neptune, was having a devil of a time
controlling the terrified horse, which reared and
screamed as the two giant dogs flung themselves upon
horse and rider. He stared at her in stunned disbelief,
shouting out over the animals' racket, "Sabre, what the
hell are you doing here?"

Instead of beating off the dogs, she brought her whip
arm down to lash his thighs and legs, and she repeated
the action over and over.

She screamed, "I am here to get my divorce. My name
is Sara Bishop Hawkhurst!"

He was so shocked, he was speechless. He ordered the
wolfhounds to heel, but Sabre urged them on to attack,
and Neptune was lathering in a wild frenzy. With super-
human effort she and the dogs managed to prevent his
access through the gates. He shot her a look that pierced
her soul, then wheeled the black stallion and thundered
off.

She was panting heavily from exertion and from emotion. In a daze she made her way back to the house and
closed the door of her bedchamber to savor her victory.
She knew something important had happened. She could
feel the silk of her undergarments against her body until
she felt she must scream. He was the handsomest man in

the world to her and finally, irrevocably, for the first time she admitted to herself that she loved him. She loved him with all her heart and soul. She ached in her belly for him to lie with her naked all night and make love to her. She knew everything about him, his identities, his treason, his spying, his helping Ireland, and none of it mattered. She had always loved him!

She allowed the deep passion she felt to wash over her. Then she threw the hated whip from her and flung herself down upon the bed to sob out her heart.

Suddenly, the door opened and closed with such a violent crash it almost came off its hinges. She cried out in alarm and arose to face Hawkhurst, angrier than she had ever seen him.

"Explain yourself!" he thundered, taking a menacing step toward her, and she shrank back in fear.

"I am your wife!" she cried out accusingly. "The bride you married by proxy. I was nothing to you . . . less than the dirt beneath your feet! You banished me here, to the back of beyond, while you went off whoremongering with the queen!" The tiny buttons on the black silk vest had burst open and her breasts thrust magnificently from its confines. Her burnished hair swirled about her like a cloak of fire and her temper flamed and crackled, filling the chamber with her injured pride and indignation. "I came to court with one purpose in mind—to get even with you. I was determined to become your mistress— and now I want my divorce!"

"Sabre, you have raised your hand to me, your knife to me, and today your whip to me. Up to now I have exercised great patience with you, but that's it—you've used up every last ounce of patience I ever had. I am going to give you a long-overdue lesson in wifely obedience!"

"I've tasted your brutality before," she flung at him.

"Brutality? I worshiped you! How dared you and Matthew go against my orders and come to court? The court stinks—it is no fit place for a wife of mine!"

"I don't wish to be your wife any longer, I want my divorce!" she hissed.

His angry gaze licked over her and she saw the naked lust in it. "I want my rights," he demanded.

"No!" She gasped. "Don't touch me."

"As my mistress you could refuse me your favors, as my wife you cannot!" He snatched her into his arms and his dark head dipped to burn a fiery trail of kisses across her breasts. His hands tightened on her savagely as he shook her. "All those fights you provoked because I was wed to Sara Bishop. You wicked little bitch, you provoke me more than any woman alive!" He groaned and pulled the velvet riding dress off her shoulders and pushed it down her hips. She kicked free of it and stood resisting him in her silken undergarments.

"How could you deceive me by being two different women?" he accused.

"How can you, of all people, say that? You are at least three different men!"

His mouth came down on hers in a heart-stopping kiss that lingered and lingered. Her defenses were crumbling. As he pulled her to him in an embrace, and as she felt the hard length of his body, she was lost, terribly lost.

"Sabre, I adore you," he whispered, and she melted against him, needing to hear more.

"Shane, please," she murmured.

"Say it again," he demanded hoarsely. "I want to taste my name on your lips."

"Shane, Shane, Shane."

"I really am a bastard, my love. I deprived you of your wedding night. . . .We'll have it now," he promised, quickly removing his clothes.

"But it isn't night . . . it's morning," she protested faintly.

He laughed deep in his throat. "I'll keep you abed until night, never fear."

Then he slowly and leisurely began to pleasure her. The first two hours were well spent in kissing. He kissed her ears, eyelids, her beauty spot, her throat, her temples, her fingertips. There was not one place upon her delectable body that did not receive his worshipful kiss. His hand slid down the warm, smooth curve of her back, pressing her closer, crushing her breasts tightly against him until Shane's thoughts could not move beyond the awareness of her taut little nipples. He tantalizingly caressed her lips with his tongue, while he pressed her hips closer to his, letting her feel the throbbing pressure of his manhood.

They lay on their sides facing each other, their thighs entwined, their breath mingling into one as they exchanged slow, languid kisses. Shane gathered her into the curve of his body and sighed against her lips. "You have bewitched me, Sabre Wilde." He cradled her tenderly in his arms, utterly enjoying the role of husband. "Do you realize how long it has been since we made love?" he whispered. "You add such spice to my life; without you I am like a man starved."

Shane knew well that the torment of delay was a very sweet thing, and the longer the play and more unendurable the waiting, the greater and richer was the final joy of fulfillment. Sabre had been fully aroused for over an hour now, and her desire was so heightened, it threatened

to reach the edges of madness. Her tongue darted out to
lick the corners of his mouth and he lost control. His
open mouth plummeted down in a brutal kiss. His lips
forced hers apart and his tongue thrust through with
overwhelming savagery. His restrained desire broke
through in a rush as he yielded fully to the heat of his
lust.

She could not breathe, she could not form a sane
thought. Her loins throbbed with the scalding heat of his
arousal. She arched against him in surrender as he
plunged into her, and his domination of her gave him
such pleasure that he cried out, "You are my wife and I
will take you whenever I desire, wherever I desire."

Sabre slid her silken sheath from his shaft. "Will you,
my lord?" she said dangerously.

He grabbed her wrists and pinned her to the bed.
"Whenever! Wherever! *My lady!*"

"And I will have my divorce if it's the last thing I do!"
she vowed.

They faced each other naked across the bed, both panting angrily, their blood up.

"I will never divorce you," he said with finality.

"But I have the means to blackmail you. I still have
Walsingham's secret files on you!"

"You false bitch, you told me you burned them."

She tossed back her hair. "What I tell you and what I
do are two different things!"

His eyes burned into hers. "They must be in this room,
close to your treacherous hand." He tore the clothes from
her wardrobe, tore open the drawers and flung their contents to the floor, then moved toward her trunks.

"No, Shane!" she cried out, realizing he would discover them immediately.

He flung up the lids of the trunks and dumped out their contents. "You'll tell me if I have to choke it from you," he threatened.

Sabre went white as her face drained suddenly of blood. The papers were not there! "My God, they're gone! Someone has taken them," she cried.

"What lying jade's trick is this?" he demanded savagely.

"No trick, I swear on my life." She threw open the door. "Meg! Meg, get in here."

The maid came running, and Shane had to snatch up his breeches and struggle into them.

"Where are the papers I put in the very bottom of my trunk?"

The girl was blushing furiously at Sabre's nakedness. "P-papers?" she stuttered. "There were no papers when I unpacked the trunk." Sabre could tell the girl was too afraid to lie.

"Mason," she said aloud. "Let's hope he knows where they are."

Shane looked at her very skeptically as she slipped on her bed gown. When Charles Mason arrived, he kept his face passive, pretending he had not heard the violent shouting match between these two.

"Charles, this is very important. When I packed my trunks at Thames View, I put some papers in the bottom of my trunk and now I can't find them. They've disappeared! Meg says they weren't in the trunk when she unpacked. Do you know anything about them at all?" she begged.

"Madam, I know nothing. I'll go and fetch the driver and ask him."

The Hawkhurst groom who had driven the coach was

duly summoned and looked blank when questioned about missing papers.

Shane's disbelief was growing rapidly. That the file was "missing" he believed a lie. She knew damned well where it was!

The groom turned to Shane and shrugged. "Matthew carried the trunks down to the carriage and they weren't touched again until I carried them up to this room."

"Matthew?" shouted Shane.

"It couldn't have been Matthew," Sabre said faintly.

Shane said curtly to the servants, "Thank you . . . you may leave us alone now."

They filed out and he faced her furiously as he demanded, "Did Matthew know about Walsingham's file?"

"No . . . yes . . . oh, my God, I was so angry with you, I told him I had the means to make you give me a divorce. He looked so blank when I spoke of a file on you that I realized he knew nothing and I changed the subject immediately. He offered to carry my trunks down to the carriage and I let him."

"Do you know what you have done?" demanded Shane. "I've protected him from all knowledge of O'Neill since we were boys. It was all in the file, wasn't it?"

She nodded numbly.

"Was there anything left out of the file?" he demanded.

She whispered, "There was no mention of the Black Shadow."

His lip curled at his own stupidity in exposing himself to this woman. Love had blinded him, aye, and addled his brains in the bargain. He must get to his brother Matthew and try to undo some of the damage done by the revelations of the secret report. "Get dressed. We're going back to London and it's a long ride," he instructed coldly.

"I will stay here," she said.

"Madam, you will do as you are bidden!"

She dare not contradict him again. He looked capable of murder.

The two-hundred-mile ride was fraught with tension. He set a backbreaking pace and through stubborn pride she was determined to keep up with him. A hundred times she wanted to beg him to forgive her for not destroying the Walsingham file as she'd said she had, but she was burdened with guilt and Shane seemed coldly forbidding for the first time since she'd known him.

A hundred times he wanted to take her in his arms and close the chasm that had opened between them, but the suspicion that she had never really loved him and her demand for a divorce kept him coldly aloof.

She had left her servants and baggage to follow at a more sane pace, so as a result she had no change of clothing and few toilet articles to enhance her appearance, yet Shane had never been more aware of her haunting beauty. Sabre felt his eyes upon her again and again, but she kept her eyes averted from what she assumed were his accusing stares.

If he had been alone he would have continued riding, but he saw the fatigue in her face and stopped on the Salisbury Plain to make a little camp for the night and give her a few hours' sleep. He opened his saddlebags and gave her wine, bread, and cheese. He also gave her a solitary blanket and took the horses off to the stream to feed and water them. When he returned, he found her sound asleep, despite the hard ground and the eerie loneliness of the place.

Though she had never spent a night outdoors in the wild before, Sabre was not in the least afraid. She realized beyond a shadow of a doubt that this was due to Shane's presence. He was so sure and strong, he instilled confidence. She knew she was safe if he was beside her. She constantly thought of the child she was carrying and how very differently he would be treating her if he knew of it. She would not tell him, for that would be the coward's way to obtain his forgiveness and a declaration of his love. She longed for his love, but for her own sake, not because of the child she carried.

She arrived at Thames View weary, travel-stained, and hungry, but before she had time to attend to any of her needs he demanded, "Write a note to summon Matthew here."

Without protest she sat down and took up a quill. She addressed the note to Matthew Hawkhurst and said simply:

> Please attend me at Thames View.
>   Sabre

Chapter 22

It had not been a good week for Matthew Hawkhurst. He writhed as if skewered on the point of a sword over his visit with Robert Cecil the week before. He wished with all his heart that he had never suggested the trap, and a hundred times a day prayed that Cecil would not act upon his suggestion.

He was keenly resentful of his brother and still coveted Sabre, yet the thought that he might have betrayed Shane caused him an agony of fear that grew daily. Then it happened! The rumor swept through the court that the Black Shadow had been taken at the Tower of London while trying to free political Irish prisoners. Matthew was stunned. The plan he had suggested had been carried out immediately and the quarry had already been trapped. Upon hearing the news Matthew actually entertained the idea of suicide. Then a clearer head prevailed as he realized he must do everything in his power to try to undo what he had done.

He was enormously relieved to learn that the identity of the Black Shadow was as much a mystery as it had ever been. No one could identify him, so Matt realized it was not Shane who had been taken. The man refused to speak and it was rumored that he was being racked to loosen his tongue.

Matthew was almost euphoric that it was not his brother in the Tower and he was able to sleep for the first time in about ten days. Nevertheless he wanted to confront Shane with the Walsingham files and then burn the papers as fast as he could. He was elated to receive

Sabre's note. She had obviously changed her mind about
Blackmoor and returned to Thames View.

He stabled his horse and went up to the house. "Sabre,
you look so pale. Are you ill?" he asked anxiously.

She searched his face, not wanting to believe that he
had stolen the papers. "I had a tiring journey, Matthew.
You said you would follow me to Blackmoor, but I see
you must have had more pressing business."

"Sweetheart, I'm sorry. I want nothing more than to
spend the rest of my life with you," he avowed.

A dark shadow fell across the entrance to the salon
and Matthew nearly jumped out of his skin as Shane's
tall figure materialized. In a deadly quiet voice Shane
said, "I will say this once. This is my woman—today,
tomorrow, and forevermore. Never try to take what is
mine!"

Matthew was on his feet, spitting venom. "You took
what was mine—my inheritance—my title—you are
nothing but O'Neill's bastard!"

Shane said quietly, "I always did my best to shield you
from the knowledge. We are full brothers, Matthew, both
sprung from the loins of O'Neill."

A look of horror came over Matt's features. Then, as
full realization hit him, he tore the papers from his doublet and flung them down before Shane. "They are burning a hole in my chest. For Christ's sake, destroy them
before they do irreparable harm."

"It is too late," said Shane sadly.

"I beg your forgiveness; I did not know!" Matt swore.

Shane shook his head impatiently. "The man they are
torturing in the Tower is the baron."

Sabre cried out in alarm, "Oh, my God, tell me it isn't
so!"

Matthew went white. "It's my fault! I went to Robert Cecil suggesting they transfer O'Hara and O'Donnell from Dublin to the Tower of London. I told him he'd trap the O'Neill's contact, knowing that it would be you."

Sabre swayed, her lips colorless, her eyelids fluttering like dying butterfly's wings. Shane's strong arm was about her instantly, lifting her to the couch piled with soft, brilliant cushions. He filled a goblet with wine and held it to her lips.

"This is all my fault," she whispered. "Instead of burning the papers I kept them for my own gain, and now I have come between two brothers who once loved each other." Her tears wet her cheeks and she shivered with the horror of it all.

The two men looked at her and said together, "We still love each other." Then Matthew added, "It is my fault. I will go to Cecil and tell him they have the wrong man. I will tell him I am the Black Shadow!"

"You young fool—you will do nothing to connect the prisoner with us. Thank God servants enjoy such anonymity at the queen's court. None recognize the baron. We will devise a plan to rescue him, never fear."

"Shane, this is the Tower of London we are talking about!" Matt pointed out.

"I didn't say it would be child's play," said Shane.

"For Christ's sake, if you have a plan, let's hear it!"

He looked at them both with irony. "You have both betrayed me, yet still expect to be privy to my plans." He picked up the Walsingham files and said, "I'm needed at court. I hear the queen is brokenhearted over Essex. We will leave you to rest, madam." He bowed gravely to Sabre and propelled Matthew toward the front door. He did not need to tell him to keep from Thames View until he was invited.

Shane was absent the rest of the day, yet Sabre knew him too well to suspect him of frittering away precious time kissing Elizabeth's feet. Each minute he spent with the queen was a necessary minute to help him secure the baron's release. She remembered only too well the things Shane had told her in fevered delirium about the baron. She pushed away the unthinkable words of the sentence that would be carried out if they learned he was the condemned Fitzgerald, earl of Desmond. It was barbaric to torture men and almost inconceivable that this still happened in the enlightened year of 1587.

Sabre felt exhausted. She should never have put her unborn baby in jeopardy by riding so hard from Blackmoor. She took a supper tray upstairs and climbed into the large, soft bed to eat. The memories the bed held haunted her. She recalled the first time when they had eaten together in bed and then she remembered vividly his angry ravishment, but then all the happiness and pleasure they had shared since outweighed that one night of horror.

She finished her wine and blew out the candles. She needed to sleep—surely a good rest would restore her spirits. But sleep would not come. She examined Matthew's betrayal and knew his coveting her had a great deal to do with it all. Why had Shane forgiven him? she wondered. Then she knew the answer. It was because Shane was a truly good man . . . a fine man . . . and, oh, God, how glad she was that he was her husband and the father of her unborn child. Even though she had stubbornly demanded a divorce, it was the very last thing she really wanted. She would love to have been wooed and to have received a formal proposal of marriage from him. She would love to have stood beside him and exchanged vows in the church. But what was done was done and she wouldn't exchange husbands with any other woman on earth. She shivered at the thought that it could so easily have been Shane who was now a prisoner in the Tower of London . . . a prisoner who was at this very moment being tortured. *No,* her mind screamed, *do not think of the baron, that way lies madness.* She could see him in her mind's eye when they had stood on either side of this bed and administered to Shane when he lay near death. Death . . . that's where Shane's reckless behavior would lead him if she did not keep him from O'Neill.

The bedchamber clock chimed three, and she caressed her belly, where the child lay secure for the moment. She was determined that this baby would have both mother and father to cushion him against a harsh, cruel world. Suddenly the chamber door opened, and she struggled up onto the pillows as Shane's dark figure advanced into the room.

"I'm sorry to disturb you, Sabre, but I must talk."

"It's all right, Shane. It's impossible for me to sleep. . . . I've been trying for hours."

He lit the candles and sat down close beside her on the edge of the bed. "I've racked my brains over an escape plan for the baron. I've examined every avenue of thought, every idea, and discarded them one after another, for they were all flawed. The only sure way for a prisoner to leave the Tower of London is dead, in a coffin."

She gasped, and sought one of his strong, brown hands.

"I've procured a drug that simulates death. It slows

the heartbeat down so much that not even a pulse can be detected. The only problem is how to get it to the baron. It would be so simple if he were in the Fleet or Newgate. I would hire girls from the brothel to go in and pleasure the guards. They are open to any bribe, but the Tower of London is a different kettle of fish entirely."

She clutched his hand tightly. "Shane, if you go in and try to get the drug to him, you will be implicated, then they will have both of you!"

His rough thumb rubbed the silken skin of her hand as he said tentatively, "It would be impossible for me to go in alone, but . . . we could do it together, Sabre."

"What are you talking about? They would never let me inside," she cried fearfully, shuddering at the mere thought of the Bloody Tower.

He brushed the flaming tendrils back from her temple with his free hand. "Sabre . . . if you dressed as the queen you could go wherever you wished."

She stared at him wild-eyed. "You are mad; I could never get away with impersonating the queen!"

"You've done it successfully before and could again," he urged.

"No! Shane, don't ask it of me!" she begged.

"I do ask it of you, Sabre. It is the only chance the baron has. You go in as the queen and I go in at your side as her Sea God. If we act with confidence and authority and arrogance, none will deny us access to him. I will arrange for a whole retinue of attendants to accompany us, and between us we can pull it off!"

"Shane, it is impossible. I can duplicate the dress and the hair, but my face is nothing like hers. The guards would know immediately that I was an imposter!"

"How often do you think the guards have seen the

queen? Most, probably never, and the ones who have, only from a great distance. You will carry a stick mask to hold in front of your face and protect you from such sordid surroundings; Sabre, it's all in the attitude! I have every confidence in you."

"Shane . . . no!"

"Sabre, if you will do this thing for me . . . I'll give you your damned divorce that you want so badly."

She didn't know whether to laugh or cry. She shivered. "Shane, I'm so very frightened . . . hold me."

He gathered her to him, longing to absorb her body into his, to pull her into the bed and lose himself in her. Yet he felt a crushing guilt at what he was asking her to do. How could he be such a swine as to risk her safety? He loved her with all his heart and she was infinitely precious to him, and yet he was willing to gamble her freedom, perhaps even her life, to help the baron. The inexplicable truth was that he knew together they were invincible. Together they could overcome any danger, any odds, and he loved her best because, like himself, she had the courage, the raw guts, to risk everything and take pleasure from the heady, reckless hazard.

With infinite gentleness his lips began to kiss her. His fingertips feathered her temples and cheekbones, then stroked her hair as he murmured against her mouth and throat all the love words that filled his heart. "Sabre, I love you beyond life. You are a part of me . . . the other half which makes me whole." He cradled her against his heart, which beat madly. "My lovely one, I adore you," he whispered, and a tress of her hair brushed against his face. He stroked her possessively. "You have the most wondrous hair I've ever seen, and all men who lay eyes upon it must ache to caress it and play with it like this.

My love, you enthrall me. Your image is ever before me, night and day. I have an unquenchable thirst for you. When I glimpse you across a room I must draw close, and when I'm close to you I must touch you. Once I've touched you, I have an uncontrollable desire to touch you all over. Your fragrance fills my senses, and I never get enough of smelling you and tasting you. Your voice and your laughter arouse me immediately, no matter who is there to see. Sabre, my darling, you hate me because I didn't come myself to marry you, but, oh, my darling, don't you see I would have wed you and left you and never come to savor and cherish you as I do now? By becoming my mistress you snared and enchanted me for all time. Now we are bonded . . . you must feel it, darling . . . it's so strong, it's so right!"

The rapture of his closeness enveloped her, and she felt precious to him and deeply loved and cherished. In that moment she knew that with his strength beside her she could do anything. Her fear receded and she wanted more than anything in this world for him to come into the bed with her and join his body to hers. They were starving for each other. It was a need so great, it transcended mere hunger and thirst. Their love for each other was so strong, it was a force to be reckoned with.

First light found her torturing her magnificent copper tresses into the ugly simulation of Elizabeth's wig, and she shook out the purple velvet gown and took the small crown from its jewel case. Now that she had committed herself to this insane venture, Sabre decided she would give it everything she had. She knew that in order to carry it off successfully she would have to *become* Elizabeth.

She sat before the pier glass and paid infinite attention

to the details of her makeup. She applied powder to whiten her face, then she was rather liberal with the rouge pot to copy the queen's slightly raddled cheeks. She applied the lip salve in a way that narrowed her lips into a straight, firm line, then turned her head from side to side to gauge the effect.

When Shane came in to see how she was progressing, he gave her such a look of approval and gratitude that her confidence was bolstered considerably. They did not really trust themselves to enter into a conversation, but each supported the other with a quiet air of confidence.

He chose a flamboyant outfit of gray velvet slashed with amethyst satin, then pulled on gray suede thigh-boots. His choice complemented her elaborate purple gown perfectly. They were both costumed for the roles they would play as if they were about to step out onto the stage of the Rose Theater, but the parts they played were a matter of life and death.

They traveled by closed carriage, following the River Thames all the way to the Pool of London, where numerous Hawkhurst vessels were anchored. There, to Sabre's amazement, they transferred to a barge done in the Tudor colors of green and white. It was not the royal barge, but at a glance it could pass for it. Somehow Shane had assembled three ladies-in-waiting, a young page, and two gentlemen attendants for himself. They looked so authentic, they would have fooled Sabre had she not known for certain they were bogus.

It was a drab, pewter-colored day and she shivered with apprehension as the barge made its way to the water gate of the Tower. Shane handed her a golden face mask on a long stick and suddenly her insides were jelly, her mouth was so dry her lips stuck to her teeth, and her eardrums were ready to burst from the thunder of her heartbeat.

Much too quickly the barge drew up and Shane was assisting her to alight, face-to-face with half a dozen yeomen of the guard. Her feet stumbled, Shane placed a firm, steadying hand to the small of her back, and the portcullis was being raised to permit the entry to the first set of heavy, iron-studded doors.

"Open in the name of the queen," piped the page.

"Open in the name of the queen," repeated the yeomen of the guard in their deep, stentorian voices.

Shane handed her the precious vial, and as she tucked it securely between her breasts her mind scattered into millions of fragments and her chest constricted so tightly, she thought she could not breathe. Then, like a miracle from out of her childhood, the words of a novena her father had taught her came to her rescue.

"Oh, holy Saint Jude, apostle and martyr, great in virtue and rich in miracles, near kinsman of Jesus Christ, the faithful intercessor of all who invoke your special patronage in time of need, to you I have recourse from the depths of my heart and humbly beg you, to whom God has given such great power, to come to my assistance. Help me in my present and urgent petition. In return I propose to make your name known and cause your name to be invoked."

Suddenly Sabre realized the Tower guards were much more nervous than she to be so suddenly confronted by the sovereign of the realm, and she sought to put them at their ease.

"Gentlemen, gentlemen, no ceremony, please. I am here on a whim. Rumor that you have the Black Shadow safely behind bars has piqued my curiosity. So I have prevailed upon my beloved Sea God to escort me to see for myself." She swept along the passageways of the lower Tower, raising with imperative gestures each guard who bowed and scraped before her. She had to take a deep, steadying breath when the queen's chief dungeon master was called for to escort her to the prisoner.

He came with alacrity, but was loath to let her see the prisoner, who had been racked in the night. Instead, he invited her to his comfortable office to take refreshment while the governor of the Tower was summoned.

"Sirrah, if I had wanted to take tea I would have gone to a tea party! I forbid you to disturb the governor of the Tower—he is out of favor with me at the moment and I don't wish to be burdened with his postulating!" She lowered her mask and looked directly into the eyes of the aging dungeon master. Then very sharply she demanded, "Were you a guard when I was imprisoned here, sirrah?"

"No, no, Your Majesty." He rushed to assure her that he had had nothing whatsoever to do with that miscarriage of justice.

"And a good thing too!" she rapped out sharply. "Lead on!" she ordered.

The party had to pause outside the cell while keys were produced and the door unlocked.

"I think just Lord Devonport and I will see the infamous prisoner. My attendants don't have the stomach for such." Inside the cell Sabre glanced at Shane and wished she had not. His mouth was set in grim lines and she feared his control would snap at sight of the baron. "This prisoner has been racked!" he ground out.

"Aye, my lord, and still not a word out of him."

Sabre forced herself to look at the baron. He was conscious and she knew he recognized them. "Not a word, you say?" she demanded sharply, to cover her distress.

The dungeon master hauled the prisoner up viciously. "On your knees before your sovereign, you dog!"

' She stepped close and touched his neck, then slipped the vial into his shackled hands. "You fools!" she accused. "This man cannot speak . . . he has had his vocal cords cut! See you these two small knots upon his neck?"

Though there were no real knots, the man nodded as he felt the prisoner's neck.

"Lord Devonport, what do you think?" she demanded.

"You are right, Your Majesty. Torturing this man is a waste of time and energy. He will never speak."

She turned upon her heel and made a rapid retreat and the men followed her instantly. "Do you know what I think, sirrah?" she demanded. "You have been gulled! This is not the Black Shadow. This is some poor scapegoat they sent in here to fall into your clever trap."

"We'll all be a laughingstock," said Devonport with disgust.

Sabre knew a hint when she heard one. "Ah, no, my friend, for my loyal dungeon master and his guards will not breathe a word of our visit. He was chosen for this job because of his discretion." She waved an all-powerful hand. "Discretion deserves reward."

Lord Devonport slipped a heavy pouch into the man's eager hand and they made a rapid exit.

When Shane saw that Sabre would be all right after the ordeal he had put her through, he sent her home and was off to further his mission. Though her part in this was over, his was most certainly not. He was off to bribe the coffin maker who picked up the dead from the Tower of London.

Back at Thames View, Sabre tried to rest, but she was too keyed up to keep still for long. She didn't expect to see Shane again until dawn of the next day, when he would bring the baron home in his coffin. In the afternoon the carriage drove in, bringing back Mason and her young maid Meg. She felt guilty for having dragged them off to the wilds of Devon only to have them turn around and come all the way back again.

"I was a nice change, Lady Devonport, but I must confess I'm glad to be back in London." His use of her title startled her, but then she realized that at times she and Shane did tend to live at the top of their voices, and she flushed at all the other things this man must have heard.

"Charles, for the next few days we don't want any visitors intruding at Thames View. The baron is gravely ill and Shane will be bringing him home tomorrow. Now that you are here to take care of everything, I will leave all in your capable hands. I'm going for a ride. Perhaps if I get some fresh air, I'll be able to sleep tonight."

She did manage to get some rest when she fell into bed exhausted from the day's ordeal, but by three in the morning she was wide awake and filled with apprehensive dread for the baron and for Shane's safety.

When Shane finally arrived driving a rough wagon, she hardly recognized the shabby, nondescript figure. He looked unwashed, unshaven, with lank hair falling into his eyes. He was a frightening sight, but when she saw the width of the shoulders and saw him haul the wooden coffin from the wagon single-handed, she knew it was he. Between them they were becoming masters of disguise.

He carried his friend upstairs and laid him on his bed. Sabre took one look and her heart sank. It was too late; the baron was dead.

Silently, grimly, Shane began to strip him, and Sabre, realizing he intended to cleanse the body, ran for soap, hot water, and towels. The baron's body was badly bruised and the arms and legs were dislocated from their sockets.

Shane glanced up at Sabre. "My love, if this is too much for you, get Mason to come and help me."

"No, the worst is over," she said sadly.

With a quick wrench Shane jerked one of the dislocated arms back into its socket.

"Oh, please, can't you leave him in peace?" she begged.

"Nay, the joints will stiffen and he'll be crippled the rest of his life if we don't act quickly."

"He lives?" she asked incredulously.

"By the bones of Christ he had better live or all our efforts will have been in vain!"

The legs proved more difficult to straighten, and it took all the strength of both to accomplish anything. Finally, with Sabre sitting on the baron's chest to hold him immobile, Shane was able to pull down on each leg hard enough to hear it snap back into its socket. Then they bathed him and rubbed his joints with oil of camphor. Then Shane built up the fire; they covered him warmly and left him to sleep off the effects of the drug and wake from his comalike state.

Through the long night she voiced all her fears to him. "Shane, you realize it would be you they would have taken in the Tower if you had been in London that night? They would have recognized you immediately and found you guilty of treason. You would be dead by now—

hanged, drawn, and quartered!" She shuddered and the tears spilled down her cheeks. "One day it will happen—it is inevitable, unless you sever the ties with O'Neill completely."

He looked at her for long minutes. "I have finished with him. He has my message by now."

She wanted to believe him, but she had the measure of O'Neill and hoped to God he had too. The Irish prisoners from Dublin were still in the Tower and she knew O'Neill would never rest until he'd exacted Shane's promise to get them released.

They nursed the baron for two days and nights, and when he awoke the first word he murmured was "Georgiana."

Shane looked across at Sabre and grinned. "I have an excellent idea. I'll take him to my mother at Hawkhurst for a long convalescence away from London. When I come back we will talk about this divorce you have your heart set upon."

She opened her mouth to protest, but all she managed was a faint "You would really divorce me?"

"Sabre, I couldn't have done this without you. You were magnificent. I will not go back on my word. You deserve anything you desire."

Chapter 23

Mason, with a swollen black eye, faced his master with shame in his heart. "My lord, she's been abducted. I tried to prevent it, but failed miserably. I've been in a frenzy to have you return."

"Matthew!" thundered Shane. "I'll cut out his bloody liver . . . I'll have his balls! By Christ, I've warned the young fool over and over again."

Mason looked doubtful. "My lord, I have grave doubts that it was Matthew's doing. The men who took her were rough . . . Irish. . . ."

"Irish!" echoed Shane, cold fingers of fear gripping his heart. "O'Neill," he whispered, "only he would dare!" O'Neill had clearly seen that Sabre was his one vulnerability. He clenched impotent fists and cursed heaven and hell in that moment. He vowed that if grave harm came to Sabre, he would murder his father and there would be an end to it.

Without wasting further time he went upstairs and packed for a journey. He hoped against hope that it had been Matthew's men who had taken her. He found him at court and knew with his first glance that he was not involved, for Matt was as open and easy to read as a book. When Matt saw the dark anger in his brother's face he feared the worst. "Is the baron dead?" he groaned through bloodless lips.

Shane shook his head in the negative. "Sabre was abducted from Thames View," he said curtly.

"Who? Where?" demanded Matthew.

Shane shrugged to show his ignorance but ground out, "I'm sailing for Ireland on the flood tide."

"O'Neill?" Matt whispered. "I'm sailing with you!"

Shane shook his head, but Matthew insisted. "Both his sons will confront him with this!"

At the Pool of London, Shane chose the first Hawkhurst vessel with a full crew. It was the *Winged Dragon,* set for a voyage to the Canary Islands. Shane spoke with his captain. "We must leave on the next tide, but I won't ask you to go one league out of your way. Take us home to Devonport and from there I'll captain my own ship, the *Defiant.*" The *Defiant'* s crew had been sent home on leave following the victory at Cádiz, and though all the sailors on all their merchant vessels were Hawkhurst men, Shane would feel more secure with his own personal crew aboard the *Defiant* in case it came down to a battle. He would be prepared and ready for any eventuality.

The two men who grabbed Sabre spoke with such thick brogues that she could hardly understand them, yet she knew instantly whose men they were and where they were taking her. They had soon felled poor Mason and carried her to the bottom of the garden and put her aboard a small Irish bark. She grew alarmed as the small fishing vessel left the Thames Estuary and it dawned upon her that this wretched little boat would put out to sea. Her nausea began immediately and she knew that her pregnancy combined with seasickness would soon render her helpless. She had no time to waste, but must bargain now for safe conduct.

"I am Lady Devonport and demand that you show me every respect."

The master of the bark looked sharply at the two men

who had captured her. "He said t'grab his whore, not his wife, boyo!"

"That's the one, no mistakin' the hair. Lass, are ye whore or wife?" he demanded.

"I'm both," she said bluntly. "I'm also daughter-in-law to the earl of Tyrone, who sent you for me, and in about two minutes I'm going to need the help of you gallant gentlemen," she said with irony.

The men looked at each other uncertainly. They hadn't spoken to the O'Neill personally, but had been hired by one of his men to seize the wench and carry her to Dungannon Castle. They dared not take the chance of mistreating her and raising the ire of the O'Neill, so as one man sought a blanket to wrap her against the brisk chill, the other, with gentle but strong hands, held her firmly as she retched over the side of the boat, making sure she did not face windward.

In spite of her present situation and what might lie ahead of her, Sabre felt an inner calm, for she knew beyond a shadow of a doubt that Shane would come for her. No matter the risk to life and limb, Shane would rescue her. She was his woman, and the deep knowledge of it gave her the security of a rock.

What a fool she would be to divorce him just to feed her silly pride. He was everything she had ever wanted and then more; he was everything any woman could want. She shivered as a frightening thought struck her. If she divorced him, some other woman might snatch him for a husband!

The little bark had been fortunate, for the English Channel was unusually calm, and once it had rounded Land's End and entered the Celtic Sea, the small vessel, with the strong winds at its arse, had fairly scooted up the Irish coast, heading toward the Mountains of Mourne.

The sailors had hung a blanket across a small space to allow Sabre a small amount of privacy while attending to her personal needs and they had brought her warm soup three times a day. She accepted it gratefully, knowing it was the same food the men were fed, and marveled at the wiry strength they displayed on the meager fare of cabbage and potato soup. By the time they reached the Mourne Mountains in the Irish Sea, Sabre's seasickness had abated. The magnificent sight took her breath away and as the small bark maneuvered its way into the dark waters of the long, narrow Carlingford Lough she realized that she owned this land she gazed upon. This beautiful passage from the sea up to Newry was why Shane Hawkhurst had married her.

She spoke her thoughts aloud to the men behind her. Her arm swept the vista. "All this is mine! 'Twas why the son of O'Neill married me." They silently thanked the saints that they had not mistreated her, for the simple statements she made rang with the power of truth. She drew strength from the land and somehow felt Shane's presence drawing closer and closer.

The Hawkhurst vessel, as a matter of fact, had made the voyage so swiftly that it was only hours behind the small bark. Sabre was amazed when she neared Dungannon Castle. It was a formidable fortress with a great circular keep, an upper and lower ward enclosed by a vast curtain wall, and a pair of two-story towers of furnished rooms. It was well fortified by what seemed like a whole army, bristling with weapons including cannon.

When O'Neill first glimpsed her he was angered that she had not been bound, but she came forward with such pride blazing from her eyes, he knew instantly that he dealt with no ordinary woman.

"If I am a guest here, perhaps all is not lost, but if I am a prisoner, I fear for you and may God help you!"

The red-haired giant tried to stare her down with an arrogant male pride that matched her own. "Silence, woman!" he commanded when she failed to even blink before his stare.

"Shane never said no to you, but what he gave, he gave freely. He did it for love. Try to coerce him and he will kill you."

O'Neill's mouth set in grim lines and his chin went higher.

Sabre flung her magnificent hair back and stepped one defiant step closer. "I am Lady Devonport! I am your daughter-in-law! I carry your grandchild in my belly! A royal prince of Ireland by blood!"

There was not a murmur in the vast hall as every man strained forward, holding his breath for the next pronouncement.

She lowered her voice and said simply, "You hold me at your peril."

O'Neill raised his voice to the servants of the hall. "Well, don't stand there like bloody stones, prepare a bath . . . food . . . build up the fire. Cannot you see my daughter is exhausted? Plenish the best chamber for my guest!"

He could see that only burning pride kept her on her feet.

A few hours later, after she had been bathed and fed, she lay upon a featherbed beside a blazing fire and drowsily drifted off to slumber. She was aroused by raised voices below in the hall. One voice gladdened her heart, yet she could hardly credit that miraculously he had arrived for her almost upon her heels. A secret smile tugged at the corners of her mouth as she realized the speed at which he must have traveled for her.

The O'Neill and his two natural sons stood face-to-face hurling insults and threats back and forth until the air was blue with Irish curses. They slanged each other with every foul name they had learned from the age of three.

"I wish to Christ I'd never laid eyes on you. If you've harmed one hair on her head, you're dead meat; pickings for the vultures!" threatened Shane.

Sabre realized she had better stop it if she could before there was murder done, or before stiff unbending pride made the men such bitter enemies that only death would put an end to their hatred. She pulled on her warm gown, took up a branch of candles, and descended the tower steps. She paused at the entrance to the great hall and called, "My husband, please believe that I have received much hospitality and every honor from the earl of Tyrone."

"Sabre!" cried Shane with relief, sheathing his weapons. He was at her side with his strong, supporting arm about her in less than a moment, while Matthew stood challenging his father with his weapons still drawn.

"Not one more thing will I ever give you!" vowed Shane. "I could forgive anything but this. Only evil could prompt you to take the one thing I love and hold dearest to use as hostage. Take, take, you only know how to take. Well, you've taken the last thing from me, O'Neill!"

Perversely, the great O'Neill was not shamed to have his sons stand before him and curse his existence. He was bursting with pride that he had bred two such wolves whose ferocity could put the fear of the devil into men.

He had not been unafraid himself when they drew their weapons upon him, even though he was surrounded by an army.

Suddenly he began to laugh, and the sound of it rolled around the great hall. He looked over at Sabre with fiery admiration in his eyes. "By God's cock, I know why you chose her—she's a match for you, but that's only because she's Irish! Take your woman, she's worth an O'Hara and an O'Donnell any day!"

Shane came back to stand beside his brother, but still had a possessive arm about Sabre.

O'Neill said, "Ye say I never give ye anything, so just to make a liar out of ye, I'll give ye a little gem of information. Philip of Spain sails his Armada for England in August."

Shane looked at him through narrowed eyes. He did not doubt for a minute that the O'Neill knew Philip's plans. He was only suspicious as to why he should be sharing his knowledge with sons more loyal to England than Ireland.

"Well, lads, will ye stay and get drunk wi' me tonight?"

Shane declined. Drink-sodden Irish tempers would flare up like flash fires once the sun was down and the smoky Irish whiskey was liberally passed around. "I've better things to do," said Shane bluntly.

O'Neill eyed Sabre with a leer. "Ye've yer work cut out for ye, lad."

Shane saw Sabre favor the old man with a wicked smile and knew they shared some secret.

Sabre's eyes widened when they left the fortress, for outside waited the entire crew of the *Defiant*. Dwarfed between the two tall Hawkhursts she looked up at Shane. "Did you expect to fight a battle?"

"In truth I didn't know what to expect, but I was ready to wage war to get you back."

Matt spoke up. "We had one hell of a time. The *Defiant* couldn't go any farther than the Lough, so we left her anchored at Shane's own town of Newry, piled the crew into the lifeboats, and rowed up the River Bann and the River Blackwater."

"You make me feel like Helen of Troy," said Sabre appreciatively. "Now I suppose you've to do it all again to get back to the ship."

" 'Tis nothing," boasted Matt. "Every man jack of them would have gone twice the distance."

Though the night was black and chill for July, and her feet and skirts were drenched from the rough terrain they walked, she had never felt safer in her whole life. These were *men,* and more, these were *her men!*

Shane bent down to murmur, "I'm sorry to drag you from your warm bed. Let me carry you, love."

It was on the tip of her tongue to refuse, for he must be every bit as weary as she, but she longed for his touch and in a weak moment gave in to the need for him. She stopped in her tracks and reached up loving arms. "Please pick me up?" she whispered, and with a satisfied grunt Shane swept her up against his heart. He was instantly conscious of the blood flowing hot and thick in his veins and of the heavy, sweet ache that flooded his loins. Whatever good intentions he'd had about giving her a divorce vanished the instant he clasped her to his body. Her breast was crushed against his chest, his arms held her slender thighs, and her delicious buttocks brushed the tip of his manhood, ripe and swollen with desire. The exquisite torture drove him forward, dispelling any fatigue he might have felt. If Sabre insisted on keeping a

barrier between them, he decided in that instant, he
would enjoy smashing it.

There was something wickedly exciting about being
carried so close in Shane's arms. It was a singularly erotic
journey for both of them. Never had she been more aware
of his powerfully muscled torso, and as the wind blew
strands of her hair across his cheek, he thought he would
go mad with longing. When they reached the boats, he
did not relinquish her, but sat her between his legs where
she was secure and sheltered and intimately close to him.
Though they were in a crowded boat, for them the world
receded until they were aware only of each other and
their longing. She drew strength from his strength, her
weariness drained away, and she was left with such a
heightened feeling of anticipation for the love he would
make to her when finally they reached his cabin aboard
the *Defiant*. She had somehow fallen madly in love with
her husband and craved the drugging, passionate kisses
only his mouth could give her.

When they reached the ship, he lifted her once more
into his arms and climbed the rope ladder to the deck
with one strong arm. As her arms crept about his neck,
he could not resist the tempting mouth just below his
own, and captured her lips in a searing kiss that left them
both dizzy with hot desire. He swept down to the captain's cabin and laid his precious burden upon the wide
berth. He lit the lamp, then went down on his haunches
before the safe in the corner of the cabin. He held something in his cupped hand as he came back to the bed.

"Sabre," he whispered tenderly, "can we begin again? I
swear to woo you as you deserve. I pledge on my honor
not to rush you. All I ask is a chance to make you fall in
love with me."

She almost told him how madly she loved him already, but liked the notion of being wooed so much, she held her tongue. His arms encircled her in a surprisingly gentle embrace. His lips and tongue slowly explored the warm honey of her mouth. Then he drew back with a deep sigh and lifted one of her hands to his lips. He placed a tender kiss upon her palm, then filled it with a chain of diamonds. "Good night, my beloved," he whispered, and arose reluctantly from the edge of the bed.

"Where are you going?" she asked in alarm.

"I'll never force you to share my bed again, darling. I'll bunk in with Matthew on the voyage home."

She blinked, not believing that he had left her to sleep alone, and had sworn to do so for the rest of the voyage. She looked down at the fortune in diamonds he had poured into her hands and a sob caught in her throat. It wasn't jewels she wanted, it was the hard, muscled length of him. Her body screamed with her need to have him fill her, and now, of all ridiculous things, he had decided to play the gentleman and give her the wooing of which she accused him of cheating her!

Chapter 24

It was a long time before she succumbed to sleep but once she did, the erotic dreams that filled the remaining hours of the night and the early morning made her blush profusely long after she had awakened from them.

Shane and Matt lay in twin berths talking for hours. They spoke of their childhood and of their deep love for Sebastian Hawkhurst. They both agreed they would have preferred him to be their blood father, yet secretly each was proud that the blood of Irish kings ran in their veins.

"Do we believe him about Spain?" asked Matthew.

"We had better believe him. He has worked hand in glove with Philip of Spain to know the exact date the Armada sails against England. That is when he will begin the Irish rebellion, while Bess has her hands full."

Matthew said somberly, "You paint a bleak picture . . . war with Spain, then war with Ireland."

"I'm a realist, Matt. If we meet Spain head on and fight the battles at sea we will snatch victory for England. Then perhaps we can work out a lasting peace. Ireland is different. The battles will be fought on land. It will be a long and bloody business. You know how service with the English army in Ireland is dreaded. No matter how many times England crushes her under its yoke, rebellion will break out again, for the Irish are fanatics, mad buggers. They'd rather fight than eat!"

"Our time is short; will you go to the queen or Burghley with the information?"

"The *Defiant* and I are going home to Devon, for that is where the Armada will land if we allow them to get that far. I'll sail you across to Liverpool and give you messages for the queen and Burghley. I'll alert Drake and the lord high admiral, Howard. The Navy has been preparing for quite a while, for it has been no secret that Philip means to sail against us. I want you to order all Hawkhurst vessels home to Devonport. I'll give you written orders for the captains."

Matthew felt honored to be trusted again with these weighty responsibilities and knew at last that he was forgiven for his treachery. "You'll have little time with Sabre," said Matthew on a personal note.

Shane smiled into the darkness. "Time enough for a wedding. Spain . . . England . . . the whole bloody world will have to wait."

First light saw the *Defiant* weigh anchor and head down the Carlingford Lough to the Irish Sea. Hawkhurst was a man who captained his own ship, and Sabre found him on the quarterdeck.

"Sweetheart!" he welcomed. "This glorious land belongs to you." He took her small, cold hand and warmed it with his own. She gazed upward at the mountains shrouded in mist. "Perhaps we should let O'Neill have it," she said softly.

"Sabre, take a lesson from me—hold what is yours!"

Her eyes flew from the mountains to his face, lingering on the hard, chiseled mouth and strong, arrogant jaw. His prominent cheekbones reinforced the impression of power and ruthless vitality. His dark, harshly handsome features brought a rush of love, and she whispered, "I will . . . I will hold what is mine."

"We're about to cross the Irish Sea to Liverpool. If the weather holds, we'll be there before dark. Will you give me the pleasure of your company and dine with me tonight?"

"It will be a great honor to dine with the captain of the *Defiant,*" she said with a provocative sideways glance.

God's breath, he thought, *does she know what her smile has just done to me? Of course she knows,* he thought, *Sabre is all woman.*

"I had better go below, for once we are in the Irish Sea I shall disgrace myself."

He lifted her hand to his cheek in a quick caress and said with concern, "Love, are you still seasick? I cannot fathom it, you should have had your sea legs long ago. Rest while you can and I'll come to check on you in an hour."

"Try not to rock the boat," she said, laughing as she disappeared belowdecks. Sabre experienced only nausea with no retching or vomiting, and once the ship docked at Liverpool even the nausea disappeared.

Shane and his brother were closeted together over two hours before Matthew departed the ship with letters for the queen and written orders for the Hawkhurst captains.

Shane and Sabre sat down to a delicious seafood dinner catered by a famous master chef of Liverpool—steaming silver tureens filled with chowder bisque, scallops, shrimp, crab, and lobster. There was everything from delicately baked whitefish to succulent, almost decadent golden fried oysters.

Sabre was most reluctant to try the oysters, but Shane tempted her over and over by extolling their virtues and begging, "Trust me, darling, they are delicious." Gingerly she bit into one and to her surprise she loved it. "Mmm," she teased, "more delicious than making love!"

He scooped her into his lap and fed her half a dozen more. She shivered as his strong brown fingers brushed her lips. "You are cold, love," he exclaimed, misreading her shiver. "I swear Liverpool is the dampest city on earth." He opened the door on the small brazier and fed it with coal, then poured them each a goblet of Chablis and pushed a large, sprawling chair before the stove. He pulled her down onto his knee again and she laid her head against his wide chest, hearing nothing but the heavy hammer of his heart. They sat quietly in a close, warm silence, and he knew by the way her body had relaxed against his, there was no barrier between them in this moment.

"You do not fear Philip's Invincible Armada, do you?" she asked in wonder.

"Nay. Though Spain may have the finest ships in the world, battles are won not by ships, but by the men who sail them. England outclasses Spain by courage and genius of seamanship. They don't stand a chance."

Confidence, that is the secret of his success. He never doubts himself, she thought silently, *and by association he has given me confidence in myself. What a priceless gift,* she reflected.

His eyes moved down the length of her body, watching the play of the fire's light over the silk of her gown where it clung to her curves, leaving little to his heated imagination. He wondered how long he would be able to remain in this position before his aroused condition became obvious. "Sabre," he began tentatively, "you told me at Blackmoor that you wanted me to woo you, to propose marriage to you, and to exchange wedding vows in church with you, and believe me, darling, when I tell you that I want those things even more than you do . . . but . . . sweetest . . . we don't need to divorce . . . we can do these things without going through a divorce."

"Can we, my lord?" she asked solemnly, with wide-eyed innocence.

"Sabre, will you marry me? I want to take you home to Devonport; we can be wed in the church there."

She wanted to tease him, to leave him in an agony of uncertainty while she pretended to ponder upon his proposal, but she loved him too fiercely to make him wait one moment longer. "I love you with all my heart. Of course I will marry you again."

Suddenly he felt almost shy with her. If he fumbled now, he would look like an untried boy attempting to mount his first conquest. He stood up with her in his arms and carried her to the berth. Gently he kissed her eyelids and the tiny black beauty mark on the tip of her cheekbone that he adored so much. "Good night, my dearest, darling Sabre."

Suddenly she knew he would not touch her before their wedding night. She closed her eyes to dispel the sharp disappointment that washed over her. Pray God they reached Devonport soon or there would be two people dying of starvation.

As soon as the *Defiant* rounded Lizard Point at the tip of Cornwall, Hawkhurst unfurled the sail with the magnificent dragon symbol to announce the arrival of the Sea God to his people of Devonport. Beside him Sabre could not believe the throngs of cheering townspeople who crowded the stone-walled wharves waiting to receive their legend. Horrified, she cried, "How can I face them in this gown I've had to wear for over a week?"

"Your beauty will blind them, as it did me," he promised.

It was noon and the bright sun blazed across the dazzling harbor, making everything seem so warm and welcoming. Sabre gazed at the big house atop the cliffs and it was love at first sight. Flowers grew everywhere in profusion, all down the cliffside and along every pathway. The whole town, it seemed, loved him, and the way they smiled at her, they were prepared to love her too. He took her hand and carefully guided her down the gangplank to the wharf, where he mounted some stone steps and held his arms up for silence.

"I have urgent news for you. Within the month Philip of Spain sails his Armada against us." The vast crowd were silent as they hung on every word. "Devonport has the finest seamen in England. We will sail out from our home port and destroy the enemy!"

The cheer that rose up deafened them. "Soon our port will be overflowing with vessels from the navy and with Drake's ships. Our streets will serve as home base for such famous men as Hawkins, Frobisher, Howard, and Raleigh. Let's show them our hospitality and open our hearts and our homes to them!"

Again the voices swelled in a cheer to show their generosity. He held his hands up for silence. "The most important news I've saved for last . . . we are going to have a wedding! You are all invited!"

The crowd went mad. It surged forward and lifted the happy couple to its shoulders and carried them all the way up the cliff to the doors of Devonport House. The servants had been preparing food since the dragon sail had been sighted two hours past. They always cooked enough to feed the whole crew of their master's ship when it sailed into home port, but news of a wedding to which the whole town was to be invited sent them scrambling to triple their preparations.

"I have nothing to wear," wailed Sabre with chagrin.

At Thames View she had enough gowns and jewels literally to sink a ship, but here she had only what she stood up in. He swept an arm about her to lead her up the main staircase. He opened the door to his mother's bedchamber and threw open her wardrobes.

"Georgiana is every bit as vain and extravagant as you are where fashion is concerned. Among all this I am certain even you, my darling, will be able to find something that strikes your fancy. I must go and open the wine cellars for the upcoming celebration and write a note for the chaplain to expect us at the church shortly." He kissed her tenderly. "I'll order you a bath brought up."

"Shane"—she put a tentative hand out—"my lord . . . are you sure . . . you wish to marry your mistress?" she asked in a small voice.

"Oh, my darling, my little love, I will accord you every honor. I will always call you my lady."

Her voice trembled with her great love for him. "I promise to always call you my lord."

The church was such a simple little whitewashed building, Sabre feared she was overdressed to exchange their holy vows, but Lord Devonport was resplendent in black and gold. The silver tissue gown Sabre had chosen had stood out from the others in the wardrobe as most suitable for a wedding. She wore her long copper tresses brushed out, and in place of a headress wore the simple chain of diamonds he had given her. She carried white roses hurriedly cut from the garden by the admiring servants.

The church was crowded and the doors were left open so that some of the people gathered outside could hear the exchanged vows.

Ignoring custom, Shane took both her hands into his and looked deeply into her eyes during the entire ceremony. He was determined to show her that this time he took his vows most seriously, and Sabre paid rapt attention to each word, each detail, so that she would remember it forever.

In an amazingly short time it was over, except for the celebrations, which would go on all night. They were showered with rice and flower petals as they made a slow progress back to Devonport House. Then the doors were thrown open and the people of the town took turns to come in for refreshment and drink a toast to the newlyweds.

The gardens were filled with dancing and musicians playing on their homemade instruments. Shane took Sabre out into the gardens, where they danced with as many of their people as their feet would allow. As the sun set over the sea, turning everything to crimson and then sudden blackness, the tension between the lovers grew in intensity. Finally he took her firmly by the waist and made his need known to her.

"Sabre, I can wait for you no longer." She stood on tiptoe, slipping her hands behind his neck to tangle in his lion's mane of dark curls, and reached up her soft mouth to him. A great cheer broke out among the revelers, which rose to fever pitch as he swung his bride up into his arms and carried her to his own private wing of the house.

His own bedchamber had been prepared for them and there was a light supper with wine laid out for them. A cozy fire had been lit and the room was filled with fresh flowers. He let her feet touch the carpet, but kept his arms about her possessively. "Are you happy?" he murmured against her lips.

"Oh, yes," she breathed, "so happy, I'm afraid."

He slanted a brow at her.

"Afraid we'll never be this happy again."

"It will get better and better, I promise," he said.

"This is a beautiful room. It's your chamber, isn't it?"

He nodded. "My private sanctuary." Reluctantly he released her so she could explore her surroundings. She looked through the tall windows, far out to sea. She ran a caressing hand over the luxurious furs on the bed and opened the massive wardrobe that stood in the corner.

Suddenly she stiffened and a gasp escaped her lips. Her hand shot inside the wardrobe and pulled out a handful of transparent, erotically explicit garments. "Private sanctuary? You lecher! You whoremonger! If you think I'm going to sleep in the same bed as you've—"

"*My lord* lecher, *my lord* whoremonger, Sabre. Remember your promise to always call me your lord." The sheen of desire glittered in his eyes.

"You will not touch me!" she spat.

He grinned with genuine amusement at her protests and pulled her sharply against him. His mouth plunged down on hers and took liberties that reminded her vividly of the night she had lost her virginity to him. He crushed her body to him so she could feel the desire that drove him. He held her firmly, enjoying the twisting and turning of her soft body as she tried to escape him.

"You will not!" she cried fiercely.

"Oh, but I will, Sabre, I will," he insisted as he deliberately unfastened her gown with sure fingers and pushed it from her shoulders. His lips seared a path down her throat and his tongue shot out to lick the high crown of her breast where it stood out impudently. His impatient hands pulled the remaining clothes from her body, but his mouth never left hers. He kissed her so hungrily, so demandingly, that a wave of pleasurable desire swept through her body, draining away her urge to escape. Suddenly her mouth softened and eagerly accepted the invasion of his probing tongue. She was lost, lost. The taste of him sent a wildness singing through her veins so that she flung back her head and screamed with the excitement he aroused in her.

He undressed slowly and when he bared the dragon her eyes dilated with pure sensual joy. He groaned. "My God, it seems I've waited a lifetime for this night."

"And I," she breathed, as her tongue shot out to taste the copper-colored nipples on his deeply tanned chest. He lifted her high and demanded hoarsely, "Open your legs to me, love." She wrapped her slender limbs about his back as he lowered her onto the tip of his swollen shaft. He tightened his hold on her, going up inside her tight silken sheath inch by inch, and at the same time his tongue slowly filled her mouth until she thought she would die from the twin sensations.

His strong hands lifted and lowered her buttocks in an exquisite rhythm that turned her to fire. Her fingers threaded through his long dark hair and she pulled his head closer to hers, for she could not get enough of him. Suddenly she went taut, then melted into him, tearing her mouth from his so she could cry out her pleasure.

He kept himself firmly inside her and carried her to the bed. She longed for the great muscled length of him, the heavy weight of him atop her woman's softness. A dark magic flared between them that they longed to continue forever. The feel of his hair-roughened chest against her rosy nipples caused such a heightened sensation, she knew she must scream again.

He looked down at her eyes, drowsy with desire, her mouth so soft and ready to do his bidding, and was filled with such reckless male power that he thrust hungrily into her, holding her prisoner as he drove deeply into her hot, silken softness.

With sensual abandon she arched to meet his every thrust so that he went deeper and deeper inside her. They both silently prayed that it would go on for long minutes more before they reached a climactic explosion, and miraculously it did, but then inevitably she felt her body contract from too much pleasure.

Shane's whole body ached with the need to release the pent-up desire that surged through him, and when he felt her body shudder with spasms, he could hold back no longer. His movements and his mouth became violent as he, too, at last knew fulfillment and his hot seed flooded into her.

The rest of the night they lay clinging to each other, kissing, caressing, touching, tasting, whispering, then finally sleeping. Sabre awoke with such a lovely languor spreading through her body and into her breasts that she knew even in sleep his hands had stayed possessively on her body.

Suddenly she was wide awake. "Shane, Shane, I forgot to tell you." She shook him gently. "I'm with child."

He blinked, only half awake. "So soon?" he puzzled.

"No, Shane, it happened long ago."

He was awake now as he demanded, "When? How long have you known? Were you with child when you demanded a divorce?"

"Yes, but, I didn't really want—"

"God's death, were you with child when you went into the Tower for the baron?" He snatched her by the shoulders and pinned her to the bed. "Damn, I can't even beat you. You reckless little witch!"

"My lady witch," she corrected him, tossing her copper hair over her naked shoulders.

He grinned widely, feeling himself to be the luckiest man on earth, then he reached out strong hands until she lay tucked in the curve of her husband's body. He nuzzled her and sighed contentedly. "There's no escape for you now, my darling, for we are truly one."

She mocked him lovingly. "What? No more dropping me from your arms to go running off on your adventures?"

He shook his head. "You will stay beside me always, where you belong, close to my heart."

In October Dell introduces a writer of exceptional talent, Elaine Coffman, and a book that will capture your heart, *My Enemy, My Love*. Enjoy the following excerpt.

April 1860
Memphis, Tennessee

"This *is* the Ragsdale Plantation?" the dark-haired stranger asked.

"Yes," she answered.

"Do you live here?"

"Yes."

"Where's your master?"

She blinked at him. "My master?"

"Your master, my sweet simpleton, would be the person who owns this plantation and pays your salary."

She blinked again in confusion. "My salary?" Had the blow she'd dealt to his head addled his wits?

"Hellfire! This conversation is going nowhere fast. One round of questions with you goes in more damn circles than a spinning top." He scowled at her, his head still feeling as if it were making a few revolutions. "You do know what a top is, don't you—that cute conical device that spins on a steel-shod point?"

He was staring at her with an intensity that made her feel a few points below stupid. She hesitated, then her irritation, as it usually did, got the best of common sense. "I am familiar with the *toy* you speak of. Have you lost yours?"

She had an inkling that restraint did not come easy to this man, for his entire body screamed irritation; his hands clenching in a manner suggestive of a powerful desire to be placed around her neck. Having acquired a pretty fair grasp of the somewhat monstrous, if not twisted, complexity of his mind, she decided to jump before she was pushed. "I don't work here," she said, her throat closing with the involuntary gulp that comes after being force-fed castor oil.

She wasn't convinced he wasn't a thief, but she knew one thing—he unequivocally was a breed of man she was unaccustomed to. There was no decorous behavior, no soft and lilting speech, no glorious and dignified respect for her gender. Not one drop of the milk of human kindness flowed through his veins. He was everything a well-bred man was not: a resolute barbarian, wholly uncivilized, offensive, and basely crude. His language was atrocious and unfit for a lady's ears, his manners despicable—belonging in a barnyard—and his bearing bordered on debauchery. Any woman would be a fool to give him a second glance. She looked at him again.

His eyes traveled across her face, not with cold indifference, but lingering on each detail with the heated devotion of a man with an appreciative eye for feminine flesh. The hot weight of his eyes on her mouth . . . *Lord! Is this what it's like to be kissed? Only better?* She watched him across the short space that separated them, feeling her senses peppered by diversions, as if she could still feel the gentle caress of his breath stirring more than the soft blond curls that had fallen on her face. It was frightening, this new realm of perception, these new emotions not guided by reason. The onslaught left her uncertain and beguiled, unable to respond normally.

"You may not work here, but it's apparent you're not the lady of the house. Who are you?" he said. "Some poor orphaned relative?"

"Poor orphaned relative?" she repeated, her brow creasing in puzzlement.

"Damn! My brains have been addled by a half-wit! I'll see if I can phrase it simply enough for even your inadequate mind. If you don't work here . . . and it's obvious you aren't the lady of the house . . . what the hell are you doing patrolling the premises like some three-headed dragon?" Immediately his face illuminated with understanding. "Of course," he said with new insight, "you're here for the amusement and companionship of one Francis Ragsdale. You're his mistress, is that it?"

It was the last straw, an insult past tolerating. He had thrown her to the hay, crushed the life out of her, cursed like a field hand, and now had the unmitigated gall to call her a mistress. Eyes shimmering with tears, she stammered, "What kind of monster are you to even suggest such a thing? I would never . . ."

He saw the horrified expression in her green eyes and interpreted it correctly. "Spare me your incessant chatter expounding your virtue," he said. She started to speak, but he cut her off. "I know, I know, I've shredded your reputation and defiled your honorable name. Tell me, angel, have you ever bedded a man?"

She spoke with that puzzled softness compounded of confusion and distraction. "Not by myself, but I helped my aunt once."

"Hellfire and damnation . . . I didn't know it could be a family undertaking." He smiled then, looking at her with an expression that wavered between tolerance and disbelief. "I have a very lurid imagination, but the vast possibilities of what you've just suggested escapes even my creative powers." He considered her a moment, humor playing about the corners of his mouth. "So . . . you helped your aunt bed a man, did you?" He gave her a lazy smile of admiration—considerably warmer than its predecessor. "Tell me, sweet . . . how, exactly, did you manage to do that?"

She looked at him as if she were convinced fools grew without watering. "It was quite simple," she said in that breathless little way she had, thinking surely no one could be this dense. "My aunt's cousin, who happens to be a man, was kicked by a horse and I helped her put him to bed."

His entire body relaxed and one corner of his mouth tilted up in a rather charming, lopsided manner. Then a smile that would've knocked the most celebrated beauty in Memphis flat on her bustle split his face. "You," he said honestly, "are either functioning with half a brain or you're undeniably innocent. Tell me, angel, which is it?" Seeing her blank face, he added, "What I want to know is . . . have you ever done anything with a man that could make you pregnant? You do know where babies come from, don't you?"

She felt sick. Her usual headlong lack of caution had once again put her in a vulnerable position. "I didn't just get off the boat," she said, glaring at him. *Please, dear God, don't let him ask me that again.*

"Well? Have you ever been on a belly ride?"

She tried her best to form a mental picture of that, her eyes almost crossing from the effort. But it was no use. Mental pictures didn't seem to be forming. She directed an angry glare toward heaven. *Thanks,* she mumbled under her breath. *What fool said, if God doesn't give what we want He gives what we need? I need this?* For the first time in her eighteen years she questioned the workings of divinity.

"Don't answer," he said. "I have other ways of finding out."

They say the heart's letter is read in the eyes . . . and he was sending her a billet-doux that would scorch the paper it was written on. She was green as gourds, as far as men were concerned, but a plastered wall could read the intent in those hot eyes.

"You have the morals of a jar of slop," she said. "I'd rather die than have you touch me." She rose to her knees, forgetting his threat, the consequences if she moved.

It happened so fast, she had no time to react. A hand shot out, clamping around her wrist, yanking her around and jerking her into his arms. It was at this point that she realized, for the second time that day, that a body was pressing her back against the hay.

Feeling the sting of tears, she moved her hands to push against his chest. Beneath her fingers she could feel the restraining wall of muscle that surrounded a heart beating with irritation.

"Dammit! Hold still!"

Scorched but not defeated, she was gaining momentum like a rolling snowball. What had transpired between them, instead of making her submit, made her more stalwart in revolt. Every intolerable insult she had suffered made her anger more instant and furious. Like her prideful South, convinced she was right, she was determined to the last drop of her blood to defend her honorable person, despite the opposition. She was one angry, defiant woman.

She bucked again, hoping she jarred his arrogant brains. She did, and the face before her loomed, ominous and dark. "I'm warning you . . ."

Apparently unaware a woman and glass are ever in danger, she replied, "What else can you do besides curse and make threats? You better guess again if you think your words are going to frighten me." Spitefully, she wiggled again.

He contemplated showing her just what other things he could do. His head pounding, his patience tried, he looked down for a moment at the snarled ball of yellow fluff with the sizzling green eyes that were shooting daggers through him. For some perverse reason he found what he saw enchanting, and that irritated him. Then he made another startling discovery: The man who desires a woman that irritates the living hell out of him is supremely frustrated. And that made him speak with more anger than he actually felt. "For your benefit," he said succinctly, "I will repeat myself once, and only once." He paused, and then phrased the words with great care. "Keep . . . your . . . lily . . . white . . . ass . . . still!"

Her mouth dropped faster than ripened fruit. They eyed each other, each one looking for a place to drive the fatal shot. His head was splitting and he wanted answers to some questions. Her nerves were frazzled and she wished she'd hit him harder. They were like two cats thrown over a fence with their tails tied together. Every time one moved it caused the other discomfort. Lamentable though it was, she was too angry to see the flash of compassionate admiration in his eyes for what it was. Honest.

A disturbing smile curled across his lips. "What's the matter, sweetheart? You afraid I'm going to toss your skirts?"

The heart that had been pounding furiously crashed to her feet. She was too nervous, too frightened, and too inexperienced to artfully evade the bluntness of this brute with any finesse. "Toss my skirts?" she repeated, thinking surely he didn't mean it literally.

"Rape," he said, feeling as deranged as she was from the thrill he received in scaring the overstarched drawers off her.

She gave him a sour look. "It crossed my mind."

"A short trip, obviously."

Her flayed skin burned under the prick of his amusement, while her bewildered constitution considered another alternative. Feeling the stinging swell of tears behind her eyes, she discovered what a hopelessly embarrassing situation it is to be bested by a man.

The stranger studied the delicate heart-shaped face, the tightly held mouth that tried in vain to quell its own trembling. The thought that he could have pushed her too far lingered like the after-burn of a slap. Intuition told him that overriding her fear was a spirit that would push her to fight to the finish. Any other time he would've given her a run for her money, but right now his head was hurting like a son of a bitch. "Don't worry," he said, "I'm not going to rape you . . . at least I don't think I am."

The darkening shadows within the barn lent sharp outline to the beauty of her face, but it was her hair that held his attention. He had never seen hair that fair, nor that curly. This woman's hair had not been crimped; it crinkled and curled as tight as the wool on a newborn lamb, and of its own accord. He lifted his hand to rub the back of his knuckles across the fresh texture of her cheek. Her eyes, as they watched him, held the soft impatience of a little creature nuzzling for its milk. *Little mouse, if that look was meant to distract me, it's doing the trick, but I'm not too sure you want my thoughts headed in the direction they seem to be taking.* He closed his eyes, sorry that he was putting her through this cat-and-mouse routine— ready to wring her neck one minute, wanting to feel her body respond with passion the next. He opened his eyes slowly, making no attempt to hide the sleepy, heavy-lidded look. "No," he said, his words gently spoken against fragrant curls, "I'm not going to rape you. . . . Perhaps I'd settle for a kiss."

"Either way I lose."

His face darkened with annoyance, but his voice still maintained that tone of mocking sarcasm that made her want to slap his arrogant face. "You sound like a woman lacking experience in either."

The look she gave him declared her innocence, but she was too beautiful to be that. "Innocence or guile?" he said, then paused. "I wonder if it's possible?" He closed his eyes, unable to distinguish if it was because of the dull throb in his head or his overriding impulses. When he opened them, he focused on her face, as if considering something for a moment, then he answered his own question. "No," he said, "not innocence. Not with a face like that." A tapered finger trailed from the point of her temple to follow the curve of her lips. "Poor buttercup. It doesn't matter anyway." He laughed a low, husky chuckle. "No, don't look like a skinned rabbit. You're safe for now. Thanks to this rumbling in my head."

The heat of his body was burning a hole through her and she squirmed beneath him. A blue flame flared in his eyes. "Have a care, girl, I'm no eunuch."

She endured his dissecting gaze because she was afraid if she said anything he would put her in a more uncomfortable position than the one she was already in—an absurd idea, really, for as far as uncomfortable positions went, this one was in a league all by itself.

She cast an eye up at him, and what she saw made her draw in a sharp breath. A fool could see what he was thinking, what he intended to do. He was going to kiss her!

It wasn't the idea of a kiss that worried her. She had been kissed before—sloppy youthful pecks on the mouth, chaste kisses on her cheek, even a fairly long, inexperienced kiss from a childhood beau who pressed his tight dry lips against hers until they both collapsed with laughter. But this was no laughing matter. This was no callow youth experimenting behind the smokehouse. This was Adam *after* the apple, all full of knowledge and information. And that frightened her. *Apples . . . temptation . . . sin . . .* She knew what happened to Eve, skipping around Eden buck naked.

"You don't have to look like a scalded cat. It's been years since I throttled my last woman," he said with a deepening smile.

"Why are you doing this?" The words croaked from her dry throat as she pushed against unsympathetic chest muscles. What little energy she possessed was spent on that tiny protest. Not a thimbleful of resistance remained. "I'm sorry I hit you. It was an honest mistake. If you had any feelings at all you'd let me up."

"Oh, I have feelings," he said, his gaze following the velvet line of throat to the rise and fall of generous breasts, "and they are functioning perfectly."

He did something quite delicious with his hips as he spoke and that was the spark that revived her. Suddenly finding the spunk she was famous for, she said hotly, "If you value that homespun hide of yours, you'll let me up."

Showing no surprise, he said, "My, my, now we're cutting our teeth on threats. Should I consider that an advancement in stupidity, or a retreat in logic?" He had planned to say more, but the tempting little filly beneath him bucked like her first saddling, sending fragmented shards of glassy pain shooting through the top of his skull. "Damn your eyes! Be still!"

She stared up at him, wide-eyed. His furious grimace struck fearful defiance to her very soul. He spoke under his breath, saying what he'd like to do to her. Thankfully she was unable to understand that indistinct garble of words. He cursed again, and roughly jerked both of her hands above her head, locking them in one clenched fist as he clamped his other hand upon her overproductive mouth. It tasted like sweat, leather, and horse. She squirmed and mumbled against his hand, trying to expel it along with a few salty words.

The flecked green eyes glaring at him were dilated with anger. "Hellfire, you stupid woman. Don't you know what I could do to you?"

It really mattered little if she knew or not. What mattered here was whether *he* knew. The immediate press of her panic button came from lying prostrate beneath a body that not only knew, but knew plenty. That made her squirm again and repeat salty, muffled words against his hand.

"Holding you," he said, shifting his weight to immobilize her, "is about as easy as tying a bell around a wildcat's neck. Don't you have any fear? I'm going to move my hand, but you open that mouth of yours again and so help me God, I'll clamp it shut . . . permanently." He read defiance in her eyes as he lifted his hand. "Don't you dare say another word. You're in no position to argue."

"That's pretty obvious," she said. "Naturally, you're the strongest."

He gave her a look that could boil water with the leftover heat. "I also happen," he said softly, "to be on top." The slow movement of hipbone against hipbone, although commonly flagrant, was a pretty lame trick. But quite effective.

She felt the first stirrings of a sweet response that she was unprepared for—a slow awakening of sleepy innocence, a naked awareness of intimacy that beckoned like curled fingers calling her to follow—then leaving her trembling at the precipice of a whole new world that yawned before her like a smoldering abyss. Out of the blur a face took form above her. She had been right to think him the old serpent, the tempter; for surely he dangled before her like Eve's apple. One bite . . . just one succulent bite. *No! No!* . . . her mind was screaming, fearing the loss of Eden, the regions of sorrow and torture without end. She was frightened, bold, shy, reckless —afraid of him now for softer reasons—and that made her harsh. "Get off me, you oaf! Why don't you go blow up a train or something?"

He had the audacity to look amused. "Tough little baggage . . . I'll hand you that. Are you always this entertaining?"

"Do you always take this kind of pleasure with helpless women?"

A smile seemed to loiter about his erotic mouth. "I take extreme pleasure," he said, lowering his head and brushing his lips across hers, "with helpless women. I also give it."

Another surge of breathless desire ran through her with such suddenness she accepted, as the absolute gospel, every word he spoke.

Unable to think of anything clever to say, and some primeval female instinct telling her that resistance would only serve to . . . She snapped her eyes together, but it was no use. Even with her eyes closed, her cheeks continued to burn beneath the gentle pressure of his kiss.

Warm and dry, his hands moved across the wisps of hair along her nape to rest on each side of her face. Talented fingers traced the outline of her ear, stroking the sensitive lobe, and then slipping around to the back of her head while his thumbs stroked the pulsing softness of her throat.

She gave a tiny, strangled whimper, and he kissed her forehead reassuringly. "Don't be afraid, little buttercup," he whispered, then lowered his mouth to press against the black silk of her lashes. "I won't hurt you." His tone was strangely gentle, soothing. He was beginning to draw her into his powerful control with the innocent reassurance of his kiss and the gentle stroke of warm, strong hands.

By kissing her, he had taken the upper hand, dissolving her defiant anger. Suddenly she was in way over her head.

This man had outgeneraled and outfought her at every turn. And now they were on his home ground, grappling in an area in which he possessed an inordinate amount of experience—and, she'd be willing to bet, even more creative inventiveness. Muscle, maleness, and magnetism shrieked his expertise with a thousand tongues. Every movement of his lithe-limbed body declared promise, delight, and delivery. As that distressing fact glared like a red flag, her body weakened. It collapsed completely when she saw through a tear-shimmering blur that the monster was laughing. Laughing! He obviously knew the knowledge she possessed about sensual pleasure could be expressed in one word: *nothing*.

Shaking, she was filled with remorse. Nothing in her gentle southern breeding or education had prepared her for this. It was humiliating enough to find herself two blinks away from crying, and now her self-reproach was sharpened by one glaring fact: She was at his mercy and she knew it. To make matters worse, he knew it.

She listened to the soft tapping of rain on the roof; the sound of a bird nesting in the rafters making her wish she could sprout wings and fly away. It just wasn't her day. Everything from hairdo to resolve was collapsing around her. With a sickening sense of dread, she dared wonder what was next.

She didn't have to wait long. Once again his mouth came hungering, but instead of a deep, satisfying kiss, he brushed his lips across hers: once, twice. Three times he faintly touched his warm mouth to hers, saturating her with unfulfilled promise. Something about this was immensely frustrating. If she had possessed any strength at all she would have pushed him away. As it was, every ounce of strength was used to clamp her mouth shut while something deep within her said *don't*.

He lifted his dark head, the gray eyes giving her a puzzled look. As if finding what he sought, he lowered his mouth to hers once more. The man-smell of him was terrifying, yet his touch carried reassurance. His lips were warm, dry, and smooth—pressed against hers softly, as if giving her time to adjust to the strange feeling, like a new colt being broke to bridle. Her fear receded and the pressure increased, bringing with it the subtle touch of his tongue.

Without breaking the kiss he brought his practiced fingers to her lips and with subdued pressure parted them. His hands moved across her, one following the line of her throat, the other nestled in the downy soft hair just below her ear. She never thought a kiss between a man and a woman would be like this. It was addictive, carrying both promise and fulfillment, settling around her like a sweet, drugging cloud of opium smoke.

A head swimming with emotion is mindless with lack of control. Thoughts, as soon as they entered her head, rolled right out her mouth, with no regard for consequence. Confusion permeated every limb, leaving her weak-kneed and out of focus. It was the effect of this dreamlike state that prompted her to whisper, her mouth moving against his, like a seduction. "I feel as limp as a dishrag . . . a scarecrow with no stuffings."

He laughed, of half a mind to tell her she didn't have a thing to be concerned about. The soft feminine swell of flesh beneath him said she was stuffed with something that felt mighty damn good. He smiled down at the angelic honesty lying prone beneath him. "I'd be happy to fill you," he said in husky tones, "but not with straw."

His mouth came seeking, driving all thought of meaning from her mind, while his was filled with images of what it would be like to bury himself within this whimsical creature with the apple-green eyes.

He raised his head. "I haven't had a kiss like that since I learned to dress myself," he said. A smile spread in teasing mockery. "That was a kiss, wasn't it?"

Her eyes flashed. "You tell me. You're the one with all the experience. What would you call it?"

He raised a brow, a wicked smile curved his mouth. "Well, if I was blindfolded, my first guess would be I'd had too much to drink and woke up with my tongue stuck to the pillow."

What kind of satyr was she up against? The man had a face that belonged on a gold coin, the body of a Roman gladiator, the discernment of a wizard and the disposition of a jackass. Blushing violently, she said, "Do you know what you are? Disgusting." She had a few more choice selections to deliver to him but he placed two fingers over her lips to silence her.

"That," he said gently, "is one of your problems, angel. You talk too much. Now be quiet, and let's try again."

"Again? Why I'd sooner—"

Rude though it was, he had a way of interrupting that was really quite pleasant. It was a few minutes before she found the necessary air to say, "Instead of ravishing me, why don't you just steal what you came for and leave?"

He studied her, allowing his curiosity to move over her exquisite face. "I hate to disappoint you, buttercup, but this is *not* ravishment, and I didn't come here to steal anything. This will probably chaff you all the way down to those little pink toes, but I'm an invited guest."

The perfectly shaped mouth he had been admiring dropped open like a dew-filled tulip. "Oh." She looked at him with disbelief. Then her eyes narrowed suspiciously. "I've never seen you around here before."

"I have the perfect explanation for that," he said. "I've never been here before." Then, with a soft muttered oath, he released her wrists and sat up, propping himself against the wall. Gingerly, he touched the back of his head with a handkerchief removed from his pocket.

She scrambled to a sitting position, rubbing her wrists as she watched him dip the bloody handkerchief in a water bucket. "You're bleeding," she said.

He cocked a brow at her. "That's what generally follows a head-cleaving. Don't tell me drawing blood wasn't your idea. It sure as hell wasn't mine."

With a groan he closed his eyes and dropped his head, his wrists resting over his knees, which were bent before him. She glanced in the direction of the barn door, rattling gently against the force of wind-driven rain.

"Don't even think about it," he said. "Do you think you could outrun me? I wouldn't advise you to try. Even with my head busted, it would be a miserable match. You'd never make it."

Her frustrated gaze flicked back to his face. There wasn't a sliver of emotion in those cool eyes regarding her. He settled himself more comfortably against the stall, lanky legs crossed, his arms folded across his chest.

"Where is everyone?" he asked.

"They've gone to a Church Basket Meeting . . . a picnic," she answered, and then thought that wasn't too clever of her to reveal that. "But they're due back soon . . . any minute now . . . before dark."

Gray eyes glanced toward the barn door, passing over long shadows of late evening creeping across the floor. "They better get a move on. It's almost dark," he observed. "Is it their habit to take everyone with them and leave you here alone . . . *unprotected?*"

That last word went across her like a rasp. "I'm not completely helpless."

Touching his head, he curved his mouth into a smile that left her a witless lump, boneless as a jellyfish.

"No, you're not helpless. I've proof of that," he said rather good-humoredly.

Fighting back a smile she said, "We've had an outbreak of fever in the slave quarters so the household help is down there. Today was my day to oversee. That's why I'm not at the picnic. I was just coming back to the house for more quinine when I saw you."

"So . . . we're all alone?"

The humor drained, like blood, from her face. She shifted, feeling the strain all of this was placing on her nerves. She said in a desperate voice, "I've already told you they will be returning shortly."

Amused, he watched her. "Smooth recovery. You know, you're a very clever girl. Beautiful. Intelligent. Clever. You even cover your mistakes with finesse. I like that. You don't often see that quality in a girl as young as you."

"I'm not that young," she said with irritation. "You make me sound like a . . . ." She immediately conjured up all kinds of fun he could have with the rest of that and snapped her mouth shut.

"Child . . . innocent child . . . inexperienced child," he offered before another one of those gut-twisting smiles spread across his face. Then he said, "No," and giving her the once-over, added, "you're no child, innocent or otherwise."

The rain passed, leaving as quickly as it had come, taking with it the welcome chill. The air was heavy now, saturated with moisture, the stillness interrupted by the steady drip of rain off the eaves and the croaking chords of bullfrogs in the distance. Everything was so still—she could almost hear the evening mist as it rolled up from the river.

"How old are you?" he asked.

The sound of his voice after a moment's lapse startled her, and her voice was like a bark. "Eighteen." Then speaking more softly, she said, "How old are you?"

"Twenty-eight."

So many conflicting emotions were doing flip-flops within her, she was beginning to feel deranged. Her insides were playing leapfrog, jumping from fear to anger. Next came anxiety, and embarrassment followed by humor, and now she was on the verge of liking the man.

He was still watching her silently. She looked at him, met his stare, and looked quickly away, as though he might be able to learn something about her, some secret she was hiding. She was an interesting combination, mouse and tiger. Two opposites he would have never expected to see living in harmony within a body that should, by all rights, be captured on canvas and hung over a gentlemen's bar. There was a tenseness in her tightly drawn mouth with its perfect shape and rose-petal blush.

"Who are you?" he asked.

"No one you'd be interested in knowing."

Oh, but he would, he would. It was unlike him, but he checked himself, keeping his badgering thoughts to himself. "Do you know Mourning Howard?"

She looked at him as if he had insulted her. "I might. Why?" She made a move to get up, but discovered her skirts were pinned beneath the sharp points of the rowels on his spurs.

"Would you move your feet? My skirts are caught." She tugged at the fabric, but he made no move to lift his feet. He was certainly different from the men she was accustomed to. He did not treat a lady like a lady. Of course, she didn't exactly look like a lady; wearing her oldest dress, her skirts rumpled, her hair going in more directions than a road map.

"I asked if you knew Mourning Howard. Do you want to answer my question, or does this stubborn streak mean you'd rather kiss?"

If the devil can't come, he will send someone, and she was convinced this man was the replacement. "I *know* Mourning Howard but I don't know you or why you want her."

"Just tell me where I can find her."

"Not until I know why."

"You're a daring little saucebox, aren't you?" His look was direct. "It's perfectly honorable, I assure you. She's the reason I'm here."

Her head flew up, her eyes widened. Her heart threatened to fly right out of her chest. Panic. Alarm. A swiftly spreading sense of dread. Emotions crowded along nerve passages all at once, not one of them getting through, leaving her blank. "What—" It came out as a croak. She tried again. "What are you going to do with her?"

Amusement glittered in his eyes. "Do? Why, nothing. Not in the sense you mean, anyway." She was even more alluring when she blushed. "Her mother is married to my father. I've come to take her back to Texas with me."

All the color he had admired in her lovely face vanished. Instantly. *"You've* come?" she managed to squeak. "You've come to take her with *you?"* It was obvious he wasn't going to help her make a fool of herself, merely giving her a look that said she was giving a gilt-edged exhibition all by herself.

The grooves on either side of his mouth deepened. "As an escort, nothing more. I've just come from St. Louis, so it wasn't out of my way to stop here in Memphis." Seeing the shocked look on her face, he added, "At her mother's request."

She was deathly pale. "You can't be," she said. "There must be some mistake. All the way to Texas with you? But you're . . ."

As if reading her thoughts, he said, "Listen, my little paragon, I don't seduce family members, if that's what you're thinking. Even I had a mother. And, believe it or not, unlike you, I have a name."

"I know who you are, Clint Kincaid."

He stared at her with an expression that was startled, but difficult to read. "Who the hell are you?" he asked.

"Mourning Howard."

"Oh, shit."

It was her turn to smile. He eyed her with amused astonishment and then threw back his head in laughter, but only momentarily. As soon as the skull-splitting pain ricocheted from temple to temple, Clint groaned. "I guess I deserved that," he said.

"Yes . . . you did." The look he was giving her made her uneasy. Mourning bristled, then changed the subject. "You're early. We didn't expect you until next week."

"Finished my business in St. Louis a little ahead of schedule," he said. Eyes gray as goosedown considered her. So this was Caroline's daughter. Too bad. She was a real eyeful, but she was family. That made a difference. A *big* difference.

"Why in God's name didn't you tell me who you were?"

"I just did."

"I mean earlier."

"You didn't ask."

"Christ! Now we've regressed to platitudes. I don't think I deserve that," he said flatly.

Mourning smiled, thinking he deserved anything she

decided to throw at him, including the cast-iron skillet and the rolling pin.

Clint's face darkened. "Are you packed and ready to go?"

A flash of irritation came and went. "I'm packed and ready . . . but I'm not sure I want to go . . . at least not all the way to Texas with you."

"Why is that?" he asked in a blandly curious tone.

"Because I have decided I don't like you."

"Don't tempt me," he said, "or I might take the time to find out just how true that statement is."

"You lay one hand on my person again and I'll . . ." Mourning couldn't think of a warning foul enough to threaten him with. Any fool knew the devil wasn't afraid of anything—except God—and He had been avoiding her a lot lately. She looked around for something to throw.

Clint laughed.

And that made Mourning furious. She jerked her skirt, which gave with a loud rip, and scrambled to her feet.

For an injured man he moved surprisingly fast as he grabbed her wrist. "Don't be in such a hurry," he said softly. I know you hate to leave such a romantic setting, but do you suppose you could see to my head? I think I'm in need of a stitch or two."

"Come into the kitchen," she said sharply, then yanked her arm free. She turned and hurried from the barn. She stepped lightly across the barnyard to avoid soaking her slippers in the mud. She did not wait for him, the *ching, ching, ching* of his spurs telling her that Clint Kincaid was following close behind.

Experience the Passion and the Ecstasy

A magnificent array of
tempestuous, passionate
historical romances—from
the pageantry of Renaissance
England and Venice to the harsh
beauty of the Texas frontier.

☐ **THE RAVEN AND THE ROSE**
by Virginia Henley   17161-X $3.95

☐ **TO LOVE AN EAGLE**
by Joanne Redd   18982-9 $3.95

☐ **DESIRE'S MASQUERADE**
by Kathryn Kramer   11876-X $3.95